Hearthstones:
Keep The Home Fires Burning

By MaryLee Marilee
and
Sheryl Drake Lawrence

Paper Bridges
Books

Hearthstones: *Keep the Home Fires Burning*
A Paper Bridges book/November 2010
Published by Paper Bridges
www.hearthstones.net

ISBN 978-0-9831765-1-0
(Print Version)

Scripture references taken from
King James Version of the Holy Bible.

Paper Bridges
Linking Author
To Reader
P.O. Box 142
Loudonville, OH 44842
email: Publisher@paper-bridges.com

DEDICATION

To our mentor, Dr. Richard A. Snyder:

There was this guy, see, who taught at this college, see, although he didn't know if writing could really be taught. And day after day, year after year, all these other guys and these chickybabes would show up to rattle their white bones of hate, telling him that it was a dual portrayal of a wedding and a funeral, pushing him closer to a fated streak across the quad.

Their cuteness and sentimentality had necessitated his checking his sugar level twice a week. And the shaky, paper bridges had collapsed under him so many times, that he dieted continually. He had taken to wearing reading glasses in case the failure of recognition should be on his part — the faces in the line-up blurry.

Some of his students felt hugely and tended to write hugely. Some felt not at all and wrote less. The ghosts were most consistent in never saying what goes without saying and rarely said it. Anyone at risk of having an E^2 greater than the E^1 was issued Dramamine® at the door, although if it didn't work for the writer, the readers' request for second crack would most surely be honored.

The teacher, a Chinese Druid given to quoting proverbs near the end of the grading period, begged for more showing and less telling but was destined to be forever ruffled as the proposal to hire two part-time un-rufflers for the English department had never gone through.

To his students, he simply said, he said simply, "Aren't you glad that you came to a liberal arts college?"

Some were overwhelmed, some were under-whelmed, and some weren't whelmed at all or even whelmable.

A few said, "Yes. Thank You Dr. Arles."

THANKS

MaryLee Marilee: Without my best friend/co-author, partner-in-crime Sheryl, this book would never have come to fruition. Sheryl's the catalyst that lights my creative spark, the sounding board that keeps me on track, the therapist who helps maintain my sanity. I need also thank my entire family, who've not only given life, but an abundance of grist to grind in the creative mill of imagination.

Sheryl Drake Lawrence: I just want to thank my best friend and writing partner, MaryLee Marilee, who never doubted that we would write and publish books together.

Map of Homesteads

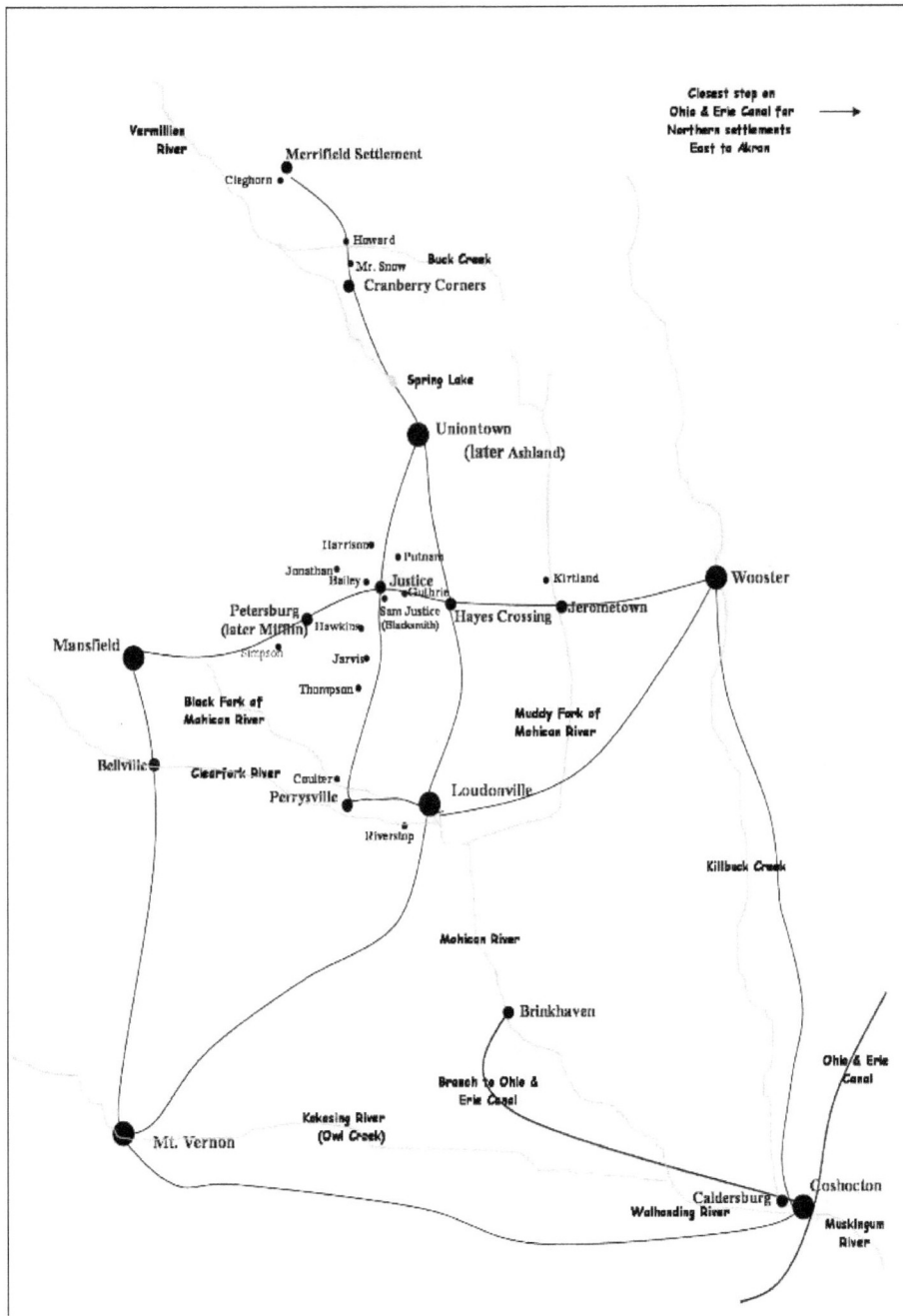

Chapter 1

Birthin'
December 1815,
Vermillion Township

"She's been laboring fifteen hours already, Ma. When's this baby going to get here?" Jeremy paced as he spoke to "Ma" Hawkins, a squat woman whose weathered look made her appear close to sixty. In actuality she'd seen just forty-five winters.

"Now don't you go gettin' your cock feathers in a ruff. These things take time—'specially a first birth." With familiar ease, Edith lifted an iron pot off the trammel, put on a soup kettle, then swung it back over the open fire. "Why don't you go put those hands to useful work, like mendin' harness or splittin' wood or some such."

Jeremy hesitated, then donned his coat and hat. "You'll call if anything happens?"

"Course I will. Now scoot." Edith turned back to the fire, muttering under her breath. "No place for a man at a time like this."

Jeremy stopped at the door. "Did you say something?"

"No. Just get yourself out from under foot, now. This here is woman's work."

"I'm goin', I'm goin'." Jeremy thumped the door shut. "Woman's work—Ha! I've done woman's work for years. Now's a fine time to get kicked out of my own house," he grumbled as he walked to the woodpile behind the barn. He already had enough wood split and stacked to last a good five months. But he picked up the splitting maul and went to work on some more. "Women have babies all the time, 'Yust like an olt zow poppin' out pigs,'" he mimicked his father's declaration, accenting every other word with a strike of the maul. But he couldn't forget. No matter how hard he swung, he couldn't pound the image of his own mother's agony out of his head. He could still hear her muffled cries as she delivered her thirteenth child—her only daughter.

Jeremiah, the second-oldest of Peter Harrison's nine sons, drifted back to his sixteenth year in Fayette County, Pennsylvania, where his mother had struggled to keep up with all her work during the last few months of her thirteenth pregnancy. "I'm so tired, Jeremy," she'd tell him. But she never said a word to Father, only dragged herself through each day, keeping all the little boys fed and busy, while the older ones helped with the farming.

Since the rest of Father's family still lived back in Germany, and Ma's people had settled down south, there were no relatives nearby to help her. For suggesting the idea that his mother needed help, Father made Jeremy her "kitchen boy," and eight-year-old Ezra took Jeremy's place in the fields.

Jeremy propped the splitting maul against the wood-pile and peeled off his wool coat. According to the neighbors, early winter had been fairly mild so far, temperatures hovering around freezing. But no one could convince Amanda Jane the season felt pleasant. This transplanted southerner started shivering at the first sighting of a snowflake and hadn't stopped piling on shawls ever since.

"Mandy," he sighed. "Will you ever get used to all this, my little yellow bird? Will you ever get used to me?"

He grabbed the maul and returned his attention to the woodpile. As each log took the brunt of his blow, he imagined splitting the head of the man who'd caused his wife all this pain. Another swing brought two halves of wood neatly to his feet.

"If anyone deserves a split head, it's Mandy's mother," he breathed between clenched teeth. "That sanctimonious, self-righteous, social climbing shrew!" his maul punctuating each word. She paid him to bring her daughter here—to get her "out of the way." That's how Jeremy sized up the situation.

Yet in spite of the way he had acquired his wife, he truly had come to love Amanda Jane. Jeremy never dreamed he'd have any wife, let alone such a beautiful one. Now, at twenty-nine, standing five-foot-ten with a stout, muscular build, he looked gigantic beside Amanda's tiny, four-foot-eight-inch frame. Even now, ready to give birth, she couldn't weigh more than 95 pounds soaking wet.

She looked so delicate and fragile—not at all the kind of woman the trials of this wilderness called for. He wanted to protect her from its harsh reality.

Although fourteen years her senior, Jeremy felt much more than fatherly protectiveness toward his tiny wife, as the familiar ache and swelling in his britches kept reminding him. He stood stock still for a moment, breathing deeply, taking in the view.

His land. His own land. It gave him a heady feeling. Until six months ago, he'd given up the hope of ever having his own place, had resigned himself to working in his father's kitchen for the rest of his days. Yet here he stood, with a 160-acre quarter-section in exchange for making Mandy his wife—a double gift in his eyes.

He so wanted to make her happy. She deserved the life of comfort and luxury she'd been born to, not this Spartan existence of a settler's wife here in the Ohio Country.

"I wish I could make it all up to you, Mandy," he thought out loud. "Somehow, some way, I'm going to make you happy." He leaned the maul against the woodpile, picked up his coat, and headed back toward the cabin. "I don't care what that Hawkins woman says, Mandy needs to know someone cares what happens to her." He stomped around the barn back to the house.

Jeremy pushed open the door.

"What are you doin' back in here already?"

"Before you hustle me out, I've got to tell you I aim to stay with Mandy till this thing is all over."

"Birthin's no place for a man–"

"I'm staying. So that's that." He hung his coat and hat back on the peg behind the door with an air of finality.

Confounded by this turn of events, Edith Hawkins gave a grunt and glared at him. "Well then, you better wash up good and clean."

He took the bar of lye soap and worked up a thick lather. "How's she doing?"

"Resting right now, so keep your voice down."

"Are the pains any closer yet?"

"Nope."

"Still around ten minutes apart?"

"Near as I can tell."

"Look, Ma. I know you're not happy about having me in here, but I can help."

"Never saw a man yet who was any real help to a woman. Just makes more work and causes a whole lot of grief."

"Think what you like, but I intend to be at Mandy's side when this baby comes."

"You ever help at a birthin' before?"

"No. But I do know about taking care of babies."

"How do you know anything about babies?"

"I raised my own little sister from the time she was born." Jeremy rinsed his long arms and sloshed water on his face.

"That so?" With new interest, she handed the drying cloth.

"There were nine of us boys all together, not counting the ones Ma lost. She all but gave up on having a girl. But number thirteen turned out to be little Sadie. She was my shadow for a lot of years."

"Bet your ma was glad for some help after all those boys."

"She never had the chance to know Sadie. My mother died giving birth to her only daughter."

4

Edith stood in silence.

"Father put me in charge of the house and all the 'woman's work' as you call it. I raised Sadie from the time she was just a squirming little pup."

"Well then," she paused, considering. "I reckon you can stay." Edith turned to the fire and gave the soup a stir, and the rich aroma of venison and vegetables filled the cabin. "Want some soup? It's ready."

"Sure do. It smells real good. Maybe Mandy'd take a little bit. She hasn't eaten a thing since last evening."

"We'll see." Edith ladled up a bowl full. "Not always a good idea to give a laborin' woman anything solid. Just some tea, or a little broth, maybe."

Jeremy blew across a spoonful of the steaming soup, then put it back in the bowl. "Won't you sit and eat? I'd be honored to share my table with you."

Edith Hawkins reached for the other bowl and filled it for herself. "Thank you kindly." She sat across from Jeremy and started to eat.

"Do you mind if I ask a blessing?"

"Go right ahead, if you've a mind to. But I don't take much to all that God talkin'. I say them that's strong and able don't need a God. Them that ain't, don't belong out here."

"I'm not asking you to pray. I'd like to give thanks, is all."

"Well, it's your roof we're under." Edith Hawkins stiffened and grimaced, as if anticipating a bitter tonic.

Jeremy bowed his head. "Father in Heaven, thank You for this food and this day. I'm mighty glad you sent Ma Hawkins, here, to look after Mandy. I don't mind telling you, I'm worried. She's so little and helpless. Please give her strength to get through this—and if you see fit—to bless her with a healthy baby. Thank you, Father. Amen."

Edith took up her spoon and began to eat in silence, studying on the tiny woman-child huddled in bed beyond the fireplace—a petite little southern belle thrust into the role of a settler's wife here in this Ohio country.

She knew establishing a home in the wilderness took strong, determined women. Hardship usually weeded out the faint-hearted or the foolhardy. Only the most courageous, like Edith Hawkins, managed to stick out those early, difficult years before Ohio gained her statehood. When Edith came here from Pennsylvania, her nearest neighbor lived more than 30 miles away, and the closest midwife nearly double that distance.

Edith blew on a spoonful of the hot soup and recalled the first time she had given birth, unattended in a dirt-floored cabin. She lost that baby. She also lost the next four babies that followed in quick succession. But she learned. *"I swear I'll never sit by an' watch another woman go through that kind of sorrow, if there's ary a thing I can do to help."*

That's how Edith Hawkins—now one of the oldest women in Vermillion Township—came to be a midwife. Eventually, folks simply took to calling her "Ma." As new settlers continued to pour into Ohio, and the canopy of virgin forest gave way to patches of cleared farmland, she took the newcomers' womenfolk under her wing. Whatever reasons brought them to this place, they all had one thing in common—survival.

Ma came across as gruff and short-tempered with the men, yet she displayed unquestioned patience when it came to help-ing the women who needed her most. Amanda Jane fell into that category. This tiny woman-child intrigued Edith Hawkins.

"Mighty good soup, Ma." Jeremy soon emptied his bowl. "Mind if I have some more?" Just as Ma Hawkins pushed her chair away from the table, Jeremy jumped up. "Don't disturb yourself, I can get it. You sit and eat."

Jeremy went over to the fireplace in the center of the cabin, pulled the trammel away from the fire, and dipped out another bowlful of soup.

Ma watched with an unbelieving stare as he sauntered back to the table. A man who didn't expect to be waited on. "Now I've seen it all," she muttered between bites.

6

From the bed behind the fireplace, Mandy roused when another spasm of pain gripped her.

"Oh, help me. I can't do this. I can't—"

"Mandy? You all right?" Jeremy jumped up from the table, knocking over his chair. He hurried around to the bed. She grabbed his hand and squeezed, as her contraction tightened. When it finally began to subside, she loosened her grip, but she wouldn't let go of his hand.

"Jeremiah?"

"Don't talk, Mandy. Save your strength." He took a damp cloth and wiped her forehead. "Take it easy, my little yellow bird. It'll be over with real soon."

"I don't know if I can do this," she whispered.

"You're doing fine. Try and relax between the pains if you can." He cradled her hand until she closed her eyes, but as he placed it back under the cover she stirred.

"I'm thirsty." He rose to fetch her a drink, but before he could take a step, she caught his arm. "Jeremiah! Don't leave me. Please don't leave me!"

"I'm right here." He knelt back down so he could look into her eyes. "I won't leave, Mandy. I promise. I'll just go fetch you a drink. Would you like a little soup broth maybe?"

"No. Just water."

Ma Hawkins rounded the fireplace at the very instant Jeremy turned, almost spilling the cup of water she carried.

"Sorry, Ma. Didn't mean to get in your way."

Ma grumbled, "Men are always in the way."

* * * * *

After twenty-four hours, Amanda's pains still came at ten-minute intervals. Jeremy and Ma Hawkins had taken turns sitting up with Amanda through the night, but the longer her labor continued, the weaker she became. By morning she began to babble, apparently reliving a part of her life back in Charleston, South Carolina.

"Papa? Where are you Papa? Down by the ships? I want to see the ships... such pretty sails. No! Go away, you. Get away from me! Don't touch me! Don't do that!"

Amanda heaved and gasped, and Jeremy held her hand tighter.

"Take it easy, Mandy. You'll be fine." But Jeremy didn't believe his own words of encouragement any more. He turned to Edith. "How much longer can she take this?"

"Couldn't rightly say for sure. Ain't easy for the small ones."

Once again aware of her surroundings, Amanda whispered, "Jeremiah, if I die in this promise me–"

"You're not going to die, Mandy," he cut her off. "I won't let you die!" Jeremy held her hand tighter. "Isn't there something we can do, Ma?"

"Well, there is one old trick we could try to get the pains movin' along. You got a feather handy?"

"A feather? What good's a feather?"

"Never mind what for, it's too hard to explain. If you want to help, just get one."

Jeremy eased Amanda's hand under the cover. "Try to rest a few minutes, Mandy. I'll be right back." He hurried around to the door and disappeared outside.

Ma Hawkins dipped a cloth in cold water, then squeezed out the excess moisture. As she wiped the beads of perspiration from the tiny forehead, Amanda caught her wrist. "I don't know if... if I can keep on–"

"Now shush. You're doin' just fine. You're not the first woman to go through this, you know." Her gnarled fingers wrung the cloth again, and she continued to wipe down Amanda's neck and arms. "It'll be over with soon, you'll see. If you can work with the pains instead of fightin' agi'n 'em, it'll go a mite easier for you."

Jeremy rushed back into the cabin, slamming the door. He bounded around the fireplace to Amanda's bedside. "Here's the feather you wanted, Ma. Don't know how it's gonna help, but here it is." He thrust the feather to her.

"Where'd you get this?"

"In the barnyard—tail feather from Ol' Jake."

"Then you better go wash yourself up again. And wash that feather good, too."

He walked back to the wash basin. Once he'd scrubbed himself and the feather, a considerable amount of time had passed. "I'm clean... again. So's the feather." He handed her the dripping plume.

"That thing's awful wet."

"Well, o'course it's wet. I just dipped it into hot water."

"Can't use it wet. Got to be dry to do what we need."

Jeremy grabbed the feather and headed back around to the fireplace, mumbling. "Wash the feather, dry the feather. Horse-feathers! She's just using this blasted thing to keep me out of the way." He waved the feather over the fire until it dried.

"Here's the clean, dry feather, Ma."

"All right, you hold Amanda's head up." She handed Jeremy a small bowl. "And keep this bowl close by. She'll need it."

Ma placed her hand gently on Amanda's forehead. "Amanda, honey, we're gonna try and get things movin' along, if we can. Set her up a little more there, Jeremy. Good. Now, I've got this here feather. I'm gonna tickle the back our your throat with it and see what happens. Open your mouth up now."

Amanda shook her head and made a face. Jeremy looked quizzically at Ma. She gave him a stern stare, as if to say, 'don't you dare question me.'

"Come on, open up, Mandy," he coaxed. "Ma wants to help.

Amanda opened her mouth. After the feather did its work, she gagged, and Jeremy held the bowl as she retched into it. Immediately another pain struck with increased force. She grabbed his arm and strained. "Pull on me, Mandy. Pull!"

That pain had barely eased when another one began to tighten its grip. The intensity pushed Amanda back... back...to the edge of delirium...

"Papa... Papaaa! Help me!" Amanda screamed. "Let go... let go of my dress... don't tear... party dress... let me go... let go! Don't! Papaaaaa!" She shrieked, and a strong pain tightened, yet again.

With a great heave, a gush of water spewed forth. "Things are gonna happen quick, now," Ma said. "Push, girl. Push hard!"

A tiny head began to emerge.

"Bear down. That's it."

"Can't... do... it..."

"Come on, Mandy, you can do it. Push," Jeremy coached.

Amanda gathered everything she had left, and as she gave one final push, she passed out.

With practiced skill, Ma worked her fingers around the exposed head until she got a good hold on a tiny, slippery shoulder. Then she tightened her grip and pulled.

Silence.

The tiny boy, blue and full of mucus, didn't move. Ma worked over him, holding him upside down to clear his air passage. "Come on, little fella. Take a breath."

Jeremy concentrated on Amanda, unconscious, but still breathing.

Ma covered the tiny nose and mouth with her own mouth and blew. She waited a few seconds, then blew again. The little chest moved, and a pathetic cry broke through the tension. As the baby gasped for breath, his cry became louder.

"He's alive!"

"Here," Ma handed the baby to Jeremy. "Wrap him up in those blankets while I tend to your wife."

"Is she gonna be all right?"

"Got to get this bleeding stopped." Ma kneaded Amanda's mushy stomach, waiting for the afterbirth. "I reckon she'll make it. All tuckered, though. She's been through a lot, bringin' this little tyke into the world."

"She's been through more than you'll ever know." Jeremy turned his attention to the baby resting in his arms, all red and squirming now, searching for his mama's breast. "Sure hope Mandy takes to this little guy," he muttered. But he had his doubts.

* * * * *

"You got quite a job ahead o' you," Ma Hawkins told him. Amanda and the baby both slept. "She lost an awful lot of blood. With her bein' so small, it might take a goodly spell till she gets her strength back." Ma dried the last of the supper dishes and handed them to Jeremy.

"Don't you worry. I'll take good care of her—and her baby." Jeremy said.

Ma gave him a curious look. "Her baby?"

"I mean our baby, of course."

"I, ah…" Ma shifted her weight from one foot to the other. "Well, I hate to admit it, but for a man, you did a fine job." Jeremy caught the hint of a smile as she reached for her shawl. "I'll stop by to check on her in the mornin'. If I come by way of my sister's place, I'll see if Ellie Mae can come to help out some." Ma hesitated, then turned back to face Jeremy. "I know it's none o' my business, but what's a frail little thing like her doin' out here? She belongs back East in a mansion house with servants to wait on her and lots of fancy clothes to wear."

Jeremy shook his head. "It's a long story, Ma. Maybe someday, I'll tell you.

Chapter 2

Jonquils
Spring 1816

"Jeremiah!"

"Coming, Mandy." He swung the barn door shut and headed for the cabin, carrying a frothy bucketful of milk.

"Jeremiah, hurry!" At Amanda's panicky shout, he ran, milk sloshing as he went.

"Oh, Jeremiah, I thought you'd never get back in here," Amanda paced back and forth, bouncing the red-faced, bawling infant, then she burst into tears herself. "He keeps crying and crying. I already fed him, but he won't stop. What do I do with him?" She thrust the squalling bundle into Jeremy's arms.

"Take it easy now," he laid the baby over his shoulder and patted his back. A few taps brought a loud burp, and the baby settled right down. "He had a little gas, that's all." Jeremy continued to pat and walk Little Ben. "He's settled. You can take him."

As soon as Amanda cradled the baby back in her arms, he resumed his crying with added force.

"What am I doing wrong?"

"Try putting him up over your shoulder, Mandy, like this." Jeremy helped Amanda prop up Little Ben. His head began to bob around, and he quieted. "He wants to look around and see what's goin' on, that's all."

"I'll never get used to all this," Amanda muttered. She patted the baby, and he spit a wet burp down her back. "Oh, now look what he did. All I ever smell like any more is sour milk." She bent to reach for a rag to wipe her shoulder, and as she did, the baby pitched backward. Jeremy scrambled to catch mother and child. He was left holding Ben while Amanda fled to the bedroom—crying again.

Cocking Ben in one arm, he knelt to stir the fire and add more wood. Even though Amanda had trouble learning to care for this baby, she did insist on keeping the cabin extra warm for Little Ben.

It took Amanda nearly four weeks to regain much of her strength, after her traumatic, birthing. She'd been so weak those first few days, Jeremy worried that she wouldn't have milk enough to feed the baby. They did have a freshened cow, so that eased his mind some.

Ben's fussing brought Jeremy back to the moment. He gave the fire a final stir, pulled up a chair, then sat down and laid the baby across his knees. Rocking his legs back and forth, he patted Ben's back with one hand and rubbed his tummy with the other, a trick he'd learned while caring for sister Sadie. Content, the baby soon slept, but Jeremy continued the rhythm until he felt certain Ben slept soundly.

Little Ben. Jeremy liked the name. Bently Harrison. Simple, straightforward, unpretentious. Once Amanda had regained full consciousness after his birth, Jeremy asked her what she wanted to call the baby.

"I haven't even thought about a name," she said. "You name him, Jeremiah." But when he suggested two or three names, she'd disliked them all.

"Why don't we name him for your father, Mandy. Would you like that?" Tears welled, and he feared he'd triggered the wrong memories again. But she nodded her head in agreement. "What's his full name?"

She swallowed and took a deep breath. "Joseph Alexander Bently the Third."

"That's a mighty big moniker for such a little guy. What if we called him Bently? Ben for short."

Her silence hung between them. After a few moments, she said, "Bently Harrison. I like it."

Jeremy breathed a sigh of relief. He'd solved one problem, anyway.

"Jeremiah?"

"What is it, Mandy."

"Thank you… for giving the baby a name."

"Bently? Why that's your father's–"

"No," she cut him off. "I mean your name—Harrison. Thank you for giving us both your name."

Her gratitude touched him. For the first time she'd opened her heart a crack. Just maybe, she might come to love him in the way that he hoped.

The baby stirred, and Jeremy noticed that he'd stopped patting Ben. He resumed the rhythm and studied the little bundle on his lap. Babies sure had funny bodies, all heads and bellies and wrinkled knees that hugged at their chests like frogs. But such delicate toes and fingers. Ben was perfectly formed and beginning to get chubby, now.

After a slow start, much to Amanda's frustration, they had finally mastered the knack of nursing. Jeremy assumed that sort of thing came naturally for a mother and baby.

He remembered his own mother with a baby at her breast much of the time. He'd often seen her holding a nursing baby on one arm while stirring a pot with the other.

After twelve babies, she'd become an expert. But little Sadie, number thirteen, never had the chance to nurse. Jeremy learned how to make a passable substitute for mother's milk by adding a bit of molasses to cow's milk to nourish his baby sister.

Amanda had so much trouble trying to nurse Ben at first, Jeremy didn't know how to help her. Ben would suckle with such gusto that Mandy cried at the pain. And since it took a few days for her milk to come in, the baby would work a few minutes in frustration, then he'd cry, too. Jeremy encouraged her to eat and drink as much as she could and to be patient with the whole process. But it seemed he spent as much time soothing the mother as he did quieting the baby.

Ben slept soundly now, and Jeremy carried him to the cradle near the big bed and laid him on his stomach. He tucked in the little comforter Ellie Mae Thompson had brought over, then turned and sat on the edge of the big bed beside Mandy. She lay so quietly, he thought she'd fallen asleep. But every now and then an involuntary sob would shake the bed. Jeremy kicked off his boots, eased beside her, and folded her into his arms.

For the first time, she did not pull away.

He whispered in her ear, "It's gonna be all right, Mandy. I promise." He began to stroke her hair with one hand and pull her closer with the other.

She stiffened at first, then let him hold her tighter. He wiped a tear from her cheek and kissed where it had been. "Let me kiss all your tears away, Mandy," he whispered.

The months of anxiety and disappointment, frustration and hurt all boiled out in a fresh gush of tears. Clinging to Jeremy, Amanda sobbed as she never had before. He waited till the tears were spent, then he began to stroke her hair, her cheek, her shoulder, her arm. She snuggled closer, and he kissed her.

He could hardly contain himself. She had never let him touch her this way before. All these months through her pregnancy and after, they'd lived together as husband and wife in name only.

He swelled in anticipation.

She felt the strange bulge between his legs as he drew her closer, and she started to pull away.

"It's all right, Mandy. It is," he said, trying to reassure her. "This is just the way of things with a man." He continued to stroke her, to soothe her, to try and quiet her fear. "I won't hurt you, my precious little yellow bird. You should know that by now." She let him continue to stroke her arm, and he drew her closer, once again. "I'm not the one who hurt you, Mandy. I don't ever want to hurt you. I want to love you."

He kissed her, and this time, she kissed him back.

* * * * *

Sunshine. It felt so good to soak up its warmth. After coming to this bone-chilling climate, Amanda thought she could never get warm again. But this sunny April day brought a glimmer of hope. The air still felt chilly, but this morning Jeremy told her he smelled spring in the air.

She moved Ben's cradle into the pool of light under the south window and stood watching him wave his tiny fists at sunbeams. Her mothering instincts may have unfolded slowly, but now she felt much more at ease with Ben. She discovered he wouldn't break like a china doll, and that a good cry once in a while didn't hurt him at all—"strengthens his lungs," Jeremiah told her.

"Jeremiah," she half whispered. He saw to it that she always drank plenty of fresh milk to "fatten up that little fella'." She still hardly believed a man could show so much interest in a baby not even his own. But from the start Jeremiah told her, "Mandy, it'll be our baby you're havin'. A new start, a new home, and our new baby."

At first, she thought he simply patronized her to get his own place, but she now realized he really did love Little Ben. She'd even begun to let herself believe that someday, perhaps, Jeremiah would come to love her, too. Why, he'd taken care of everything during her confinement, hadn't he? Even now, he brought Bently to her for those late-night feedings.

She watched her baby in the cradle. He kicked so much, she could hardly keep him wrapped in his blanket anymore. He stayed awake longer now, too, content to lie there and survey his new world. When she moved over by the window, Ben focused on her face and smiled.

Amanda scooped him up and hugged him so closely, he gasped. "How could I ever have hated you, my precious, sweet little bundle," she said, covering him in kisses. She placed Ben back in the cradle and tucked the blanket tightly around his wiggling body. "Little Ben, you've melted my heart—you and this gorgeous sunshine."

A sudden knock at the door made her jump with fright. It couldn't be Ma Hawkins. She'd gone to Mt. Vernon with Harmon on his last mail run and wouldn't return for two more days. Jeremiah certainly wouldn't knock. Who else could it be?

The knock came again, and she froze.

"Hello? Helloo-oo! Mrs. Harrison?" a woman's lilting voice called. "Are you in there, Mrs. Harrison?"

It took a moment for Amanda to realize that she was Mrs. Harrison, having heard herself called by that name so seldom.

"Who is it?" She forced the words out in a squeak.

"It's me, Jeannette Bailey. I've come to pay a call. May I come in?"

Amanda went to the door and opened it a crack. "I'm sorry. You startled me, is all," she said in her soft, southern drawl. "Please, come in." A fleshy, young woman in a yellow, calico dress bounded into the room, squeezing a bouquet of yellow jonquils in one hand and throwing off her bonnet with the other. She thrust the flowers at Amanda and bounced over to the cradle.

Amanda stood paralyzed.

"I just had to come see this new little neighbor of ours," she said, reaching for the baby. Amanda wanted to snatch Ben up, but before she could move, Jeannette Bailey cuddled him in her arms.

"Oh, I just love babies, don't you? I've been dying to come over here to visit ever since you got here to Justice, but Luther said I had to wait till the weather straightened out some. Said I could go along to town with him the first nice sunny day we had. But I told him, 'Luther, we just have to stop and see that little one over at the Harrison's.' So he said we could stop, but only for a bit." She snatched a breath and continued without missing a beat.

"We're on our way to Uniontown to sell the last of Luther's wolf pelts, and he says he can get four dollars for the full-growed ones. Can you imagine? Four dollars each! He has four of 'em to sell, and he said maybe I can get some store-bought goods for sewing with some of the money. Can you imagine? Store bought! Well I–"

"Excuse me," Amanda interrupted, "but where did you say you're going?"

"Uniontown. It's a settlement about six miles north. Luther says they're paying out the wolf bounties there. That's so much closer than traveling all the way to Mansfield or Wooster settlements. Besides, when Luther goes that far, he won't ever take me along. Says I slow him down too much when he needs to make good time. But today he said I could come along. And since your place was right on the way, why I told Luther–"

"Excuse me again, but what did you say your name was?"

"Oh, how stupid of me. I'm Netta. Netta Bailey. Jeannette's my given name, but everyone calls me Netta. Luther says it fits. I don't know why he says that, though. We live about a mile south of here. Ellie Mae told me—that's Ma Hawkins' sister, you know. Ellie Mae, she told me you had quite a time bringing this little bundle into the world. Is that true? Oh, I can't wait to have my own little one. I haven't told a soul the good news, yet, 'cept Luther o' course. But he said I shouldn't go out 'till I felt up to it. He didn't want me losin' this one like I lost the first one. But I feel so good this time, I don't see how anything could go wrong."

"You're in... the... family way?" Amanda asked.

"Yes, isn't it wonderful? I'm so excited, I hardly can stand it. That's why I just had to stop and meet you and your little sweetheart. I couldn't wait to tell another woman my happy news. I couldn't come to your cabin raising to meet you last fall, 'cause I was feeling so poorly then. I was four months along, and just feeling so sick that whole time? But I lost that baby, and I can tell you, I thought the world was gonna end. But Ma Hawkins, God bless her heart, Ma told me the ones you lose before their time's up, well they wasn't right to start with. So it's best to let nature take her course.

"I didn't believe her at first, but she told me she lost five babies before she had Harmon—that's her oldest boy, you know. Well, anyway, she said I was young and healthy, and there wasn't any reason why I couldn't have lots more babies. And wouldn't you know it, here I am, another one on the way! Can you imagine? I'm feelin' so good this time. It's different from the last time. I feel all full of energy. I just know this one's gonna be all right. So I had to come and see you when Luther said I could go to town with him. He doesn't let me come along very often—even when I am feelin' fine." Netta cuddled Ben for a few seconds as she caught her breath. "What's his name?"

"Bently. Ben for short."

"What a perfect name. He's beautiful, just beautiful. Oh, my goodness, I didn't even ask you whether you minded if I held him. But of course, you don't, now, do you."

Netta finally shifted her gaze to Amanda. "Oh, I hope you like jonquils. I do so love to see spring flowers lift their lovely heads after a long, ugly winter. My Grandma Rosanna sent five bulbs along when Luther brought me out here. She said they wouldn't bloom the first year I planted them, but you know a wondrous thing? This spring they had two flowers each. Two! Can you imagine? Two flowers! Well, I didn't think you would have any flowers yet, being so new out here and all, so I told myself, 'Netta, since you got double blooms, why don't you just brighten up Mrs. Harrison's day and take some over to her.' By the way, what is your given name?"

"Amanda Jane."

"Amanda Jane. That's pretty. I have a cousin back East named Amanda. We all call her Mandy. It's all right if I call you Mandy, isn't it? Well–"

"I do prefer Amanda, if you please."

Little Ben began to fuss. "Oh, my, I believe this boy's hungry." He began to search at Netta's breast. "I'm afraid I won't be much help at all for another four or five months, little fella. Here's what you want." She handed Ben over to Amanda and took back the bouquet of flowers.

Amanda hugged her baby, relieved to have him back in her arms. "I have to nurse him now. Do you mind if–"

"Oh, no, no, no. Go right ahead," Netta cut in before Amanda could politely excuse herself to the other room. "I don't mind you feeding him at all."

Since Netta had already started babbling again, Amanda felt obliged to stay, rather than retire to the bedroom for what she considered to be a very private function between mother and child. So Amanda covered her shoulder with a small blanket, discretely unfastened her bodice and put Little Ben to her breast, while Netta puttered about filling a crock with water, chattering away as she did so.

Amanda tried to pay attention to the one-sided conversation, but her focus kept returning to the flowers waving in Netta's hand. How could something so pretty come from something so ugly? She looked at Ben. Blooming Sunshine. That's what you are my little one, she thought—my own, blooming sunshine.

Amanda forced her attention back to Netta.

"…it's just so exciting, can you imagine? Store-bought goods to sew up baby things!"

"Jeannette," Amanda jumped in when Netta took a breath, "could I trade you something for one or two of those jonquil bulbs?"

"Why of course you can. There ought to be at least ten of them by now. Bulbs, I mean. They multiply you know. But I daren't dig 'em up till fall. Why, by that time I should have my very own baby! Can you imagine? Maybe you could come to call and pay me a visit then, and I can see to it you get some bulbs to take home and plant. It's just so nice to see 'em pop up and bloom after a long, cold winter."

Netta continued her babble, but Amanda's mind drifted back to another field of jonquils far away—only Grandmother used to call them daffodils—blooming sunshine.

Greetings to the Howard Family,

I am so glad we got a chance to help you folks out with your cabin raising last week. Always good to see new people move here to this Hio country. You sure do have a nice homestead staked out there.

Our trip up your way looking for a breeding buck found us a right smart deal on a little feller. Made a down payment on a young Merino ram from a Mr. Snow close by to youens. And besides even that we got to meet you good folks and lend a hand with your cabin. I expect that was more so we could join in the feed for Harvey's part. In truth he ain't so helpful as much as he hates food packed for travel. Good food is way up on his list of wants. Hot and in aplenty.

I believe my Harvey did friendly up to your husband Zack. Even told me on the way home he wished youens lived closer so's we could nabor back an forth. We helped with a cabin raising down our way last September for a young couple who just moved here. The Harrisons. Wife is a young thing from down south. Seems nice enough. But she is mighty young. It felt real good to meet a woman of my own years in you. So nice and so easy to talk to. We do have many good women down here. I even have some of my own people right near. But I shore would like it if you and me could grow to be friends.

I do confess, we have one nabor woman here in the Justice settlement I can hardly abide. Mind, there is not a drop of harm in her. So it is pissy of me to say. But Harvey calls it true when he says that Netta Bailey's mouth runs like the flapper on the backend of a duck. He and I do not agree on many a thing. But there it is. He also says that Luther Bailey keeps him a Indian squaw somewheres out in the endless forest who never speaks a word. When he cannot stand to hear any more of Netta's brainless chatter he disappears into the woods for a few days. I knowed that Luther lit out at times. But about that other I cannot rightly say.

I will get my nephew Harmon Hawkins to tote this letter for me next time he heads up north of Uniontown. He can bring it to youens up in those Fire Lands. Harmon is my sister Edie's boy. He carries a heap more reasonable than sending post by regular mails as the US Post Office charges 6 cents for one page local delivery! If it comes 30 miles or more they charge 10 whole cents! And only cash money. Will not take trade goods like most folks here abouts.

You will soon see how scarce hard money can be out here if you do not know it yet. Got to save all we can to make land payments and to pay the taxes. Govermint will not take trade neither.

But Harmon ain't so choosy. He carries all our letters round these parts. Course to get anything from back east we still have to depend on regular US mails. At 25 cents a page! Downright robbery! But me and Harmon got us a good swap going. I bake him a pie every week and he totes letters for me. No matter how many pages long. That is if I can get the paper. Says he likes to visit round anyhow. So taking along a couple letters is no bother to him. You ask me, I think Harmon has got him some few sweet hearts roundabouts. Keeps him on the move to see them all.

Hope youens get all settled in. It is a good time of year for moving and settling. Still plenty of time to get some clearing and a little gardening done. Before it is time to gather stores in for the cold months. Winters in this territory can come on mighty hard. I been in the Hio for over ten years now. Here with Harvey for the last three winters. I always been mighty glad to have lots of wood and food laid by.

Guess I should finish this letter up and get it sealed before Harmon comes a-tootin on that horn of his. That is how we know it is mail time. When we hear Harmon blow that loud horn. Please write back and tell me how you are taking to country life after living in the big city so long. How do your youengs fare in their new environs?

I hope we can meet up again real soon. With the roads improving maybe we can work at getting our husbands to bring us together now and again. Least ways we got to come back up your way to fetch that young ram when he grows to a serviceable age.

Please write me back.

Your new friend,

Ellie Mae Thompson (Johansen that was)

P.S.

Thought you might like a receipt I got from my sister Edie. She is the midwife in these parts. Says she makes it for Harmon and her other two boys still at home. Tom and Willie that would be. They take it on the road when they travel to market and such. Makes them something quick and hot to eat along with jerney cakes.

Pocket Soup

Leg of veal. Bone in. Take off skin and fat.

2 dozen chicken feet—clean.

3 gallon water.

Let it bubble slow in a covered pot till like jelly.

Strain through sivve. Take off all scum and fat.

Fill tin cups with jelly and set in pan of boiling water to simmer till it gets thick as glue.

Cool. Then turn out on a flannel till dry enough to carry in a pocket.

To eat, take a piece the bigness of a walnut and put in pint of boiling water.

Makes a nice broth.

July 12, 1816
Fire Lands, Ohio

Dear Mrs. Thompson,

Thank you for your kind letter which was my first post in this territory. We are "beholden" to you and your husband for helping with our cabin raising, and to all the generous people we have met since our arrival. I did so appreciate that you also helped me with even the few possessions which endured our journey. I did keep a proper house back east, though you would not think it by the evidence of what arrived here.

It was hard to leave everything familiar, but once I turned my back, it went easier. Mama's mantel clock made, by Mr. Eli Terry, and the Sheffield plate did not make it over the mountains of Pennsylvania. My pewter, all but three spoons of it, is in the Monongahela, which we took as far as Pittsburgh to the Ohio River.

Each thing that was lost past the border of our own Connecticutt, I said to myself, "At least it was a some-thing and not a some-one." Having made it with all seven children alive and well, I know we fared better than many.

I was especially grateful for all your good suggestions on that day when I felt rather overcome with it all. You seem such a confident woman, and that I admire. Perhaps you would not mind if I turn to you from time to time for advice, all this wilderness living being so new to me.

You warned of harsh winters to come, but it seems this year of 18 and 16 has been unnaturally cold everywhere. Why, I had clothes freeze on the line just last week! Who would believe such a thing in July? I will heed your warning to put in stores.

The children have adapted to this new country easily and thoroughly and love to explore. They don't seem bothered by the isolation or frightened by the dangers as am I. I try not to infect them with my fears and have learned to let them out of hailing distance of necessity.

Nathaniel, our oldest (though not the first born as my Lucy died in the cradle), goes hunting with his Father and is making us proud. Simeon, our second son, plans to trap in our creek for pelts to barter this fall.

I have been making the black salts for trade as you "schooled" me to do. Nate made the wooden cradle needed for making the lye. He shovels ashes into it, then Simeon pours water over all to leech out the resulting caustic. I am making use of the wild mustard, and have also tried the bark of the spice bush for making my tea as you suggested.

The girls, Lizzie and Leesha, are out looking for berries. They hunger for fruit. I warned them not to eat anything before they bring it back for our inspection, but their father told them to watch and see if the birds are eating the berries. That will insure their being non-poisonous. They wanted to take Elijah with them, but I do not think that a toddler has any business away from his mother's side.

I worry about the middle boy, Christian. He's moody and wanders off alone too often. The move has seemed hardest on him. He talks of running away and returning to Connecticutt. I fear he might try it and face alone the perils we barely survived together.

Levi, the twelve-year-old, met with an accident our first night in the new cabin. You must remember him—he is twin to Lizzie, and the one who shinnied so high up that huge tree despite my pleas to come down, going out onto that thin, top branch.

Well, after all you good citizens had gone, the children went down to the creek, and the next thing Lizzie came running and screaming (and Lizzie does not of usual scream) toward the new cabin. Her twin had somehow been sliced open across the ankle by a sharp rock, cutting a blood vessel. I saw him coming behind, hopping along very fast on one foot.

Even at a distance, I could see his life's blood flowing from the wound. I closed the space and grabbed his leg, tipping him over. I held it up, pressing the wound with all my strength, which slowed but did not stop the loss. When my husband Zachary arrived gesturing for me to give over Levi's foot, it was a hard thing to cause my hands to release it, knowing that my boy's life would flow the faster from him. But Zach grabbed it from me. His hands have always amazed me, those huge paws that can swallow up objects whole. As soon as he wrapped them around Levi's ankle, the bleeding stopped.

Father stitched up Son's wound, and all treated the whole incident as a small matter.

But that night, I could not keep the picture from my mind— Levi with that pale color to his skin turning dizzy and sick at his stomach. Between Levi's accident and hearing the men's talk that day (of how fierce were the wolves this year, and of the bear that made off with Asa Wheeler's hog, and the first death in the township of the boy who died of snakebite), I have to tell you, I had myself in quite a state—so affright that my only wish was to turn around and go right back home to Connecticutt.

Danger, it seemed, lurked all around us. But my dear husband reminded me that this is our home now, and he used those big hands of his to wipe away my tears.

I saw how it weighed on him, the responsibility of bringing us here, keeping us alive and well, knowing that whatever happens rests on his head. So I am trying to be stronger, for his sake and that of the children.

I was so delighted with the apple seeds you sent along with your letter, mine having been washed out of our flat-bottomed boat in the Wolf Rapids, that being where we took the wrong fork and were stranded until some friendly Indians helped set us right. If we had not lost so many of our supplies at the rapids, I could have done so much more—but no, this is not a land for maybes and would-have-beens. That much I have already discovered.

As my husband has seen fit to remind me from time to time, we must look only forward to insure our survival in this wilderness. So, instead of seeds, I was spared this writing paper (excuse the watermarks), a parting gift from my sister who promised to keep up a correspondence. And here I am, already using it to write the new friend I have made on this adventure.

So, Mrs. Thompson, how does your family fare? I am glad that your Harvey took a liking to my Zach, as that will assure our meeting again, I think.

Thank you for the "receipt for Pocket Soup." We have no chickens as of yet, but I will surely try it when we do get some. Here is one of my favorite concoctions, although I rather doubt I shall be able to obtain its ingredients way out here:

Cologne Water
3 quarts spirits of wine
7 drachms oil of lavendar
1 drachm oil of rosemary
4 drachms essence of lemon
8 drops oil of cinnamon

I approve the idea of our becoming better acquainted through these mailings. I am without the companionship of another woman nearby. I will be eagerly awaiting your reply.

Your new friend, Libby Howard

P.S. I was born Olivia Lane McNally, but am now Olivia Howard. Please call me Libby.

Chapter 3

Yellow Dress
Summer 1816

Amanda listened to raindrops pattering against the shake roof, the soft, splash as they dripped off the eaves. She took up her quill and began the letter she'd put off writing for so long…

4 July, 18 and 16

Dear Grandmother Bently,

I find it difficult putting words to paper to tell you of all that has transpired since June last, when I had to leave Charleston. Life here is so different from anything I ever dreamed possible.

I know Mother would disapprove of any contact with me, but I have felt a great need to write to you, Grandmother. I wanted to let you know I have a son, born the second of December, 18 and 15. His name is Bently. I think Father would be pleased.

Jeremiah Harrison and I married in a short ceremony on July fourth, 18 and 15, near his home in Uniontown, Pennsylvania. His sister Sadie stood up for me, and his brother Michael stood up with him. No others attended our simple nuptials. I wore the beautiful, yellow, silk dress you made. I wish I could put into words how much the love you put into that dress means to me, Grandmother.

The yellow, silk dress. Grandmother designed that gown to steal the show at Charleston's final ball of "The Season" last year. Yet fate decreed it become her wedding gown instead. Under the circumstances, the high-waisted style turned out to be a blessing, and she never ceased to thank God (and Grandmother Bently) for that.

Amanda put aside her quill, pushed back the stool, and tiptoed into the bedroom. A rope bed stood in one corner; in the other sat a trunk which safeguarded the few keepsakes Amanda retained from her life in South Carolina. Mounted on the wall above the trunk, a small shelf held her hatbox.

Since Ben already outgrew his cradle, Jeremy had mounted a small bunk with high, railed sides to the wall behind the fireplace. Amanda peered into the crib where Little Ben still slept. Ever so softly, she tiptoed to the trunk and gently lifted its lid without a squeak, carefully setting the latch so it wouldn't slam shut.

On top, a layer of plain, muslin fabric kept everything beneath it clean. She folded the muslin and put it aside on the bed, then lifted out a pale yellow, watered-silk dress. It had a low-cut bodice decorated with amber, tatted lace. Yellow satin ribbon, trimmed the dress's short, puffy sleeves, woven skillfully throughout the lace. A sash of the same bright yellow encircled the bodice just below the garment's high waistline.

The skirt itself fell in simple, straight lines gathered slightly in back. Hemmed at ankle length, ten rows of amber, tatted lace trimmed the skirt's bottom.

Amanda hugged the dress. "I wonder if it still fits?" Casting a quick glance back at the sleeping baby, she laid the dress across the bed and started unfastening her house dress. In an instant she stood stripped to her chemise and under drawers. Tenderly, she slipped the dress over her head.

She had a bit of difficulty fastening the bodice down the back. Since Little Ben still nursed, her bust line had grown considerably larger than it had been at this time last year. She fumbled with the last hook, then caught her breath in surprise when she felt a rough hand assisting her own.

"Looks as beautiful now as it did our wedding day."

"Oh, Jeremiah, don't do that to me! You liked to scare me right out of ten years growth!" she scolded. Little Ben stirred in his sleep. "Shhh! We'll wake the baby. He needs a longer sleep."

Jeremy took her by the hand and pulled her into the main room of the cabin. He put both hands on her shoulders and slowly turned her around, then stepped back to take in the whole picture. "Don't stop. Keep turning," he directed. "Do you know how beautiful you are?"

"I feel so foolish. I didn't even hear you come in, with it storming out there so. You caught me acting like a school girl playing dress-up."

"You're young enough to be a school girl, you know. What's wrong with that?"

"But I'm a mother, now. I shouldn't indulge in such silly distractions."

"Maybe you should take time to play more often, Mandy. Do you know, this is the first time I've ever seen you smile like that? It lights up your whole face."

Amanda blushed and lowered her head.

"It's all right," Jeremy stepped forward, cupping her chin in his hand and lifting her face up to his. "I've been waiting a long time to see you happy. Sure wish I could see you this way more often." He gave her a light kiss on the cheek. "Happy anniversary, my little yellow bird."

Her eyes sparkled. She turned and dashed back into the bedroom, reemerging seconds later with a bundle under her arm, a parasol handle over her wrist, and the hatbox in her hand.

"Would you hold this for me, Jeremiah?" she asked, handing him the hatbox. "I may as well put on the whole thing, now that I've gone this far."

She took the bundle from under her arm, propped the amber, lace-decorated parasol against the wall and unfolded the Spencer: a short jacket made of heavy, amber silk that matched the tatted lace trim of her dress and parasol. Long sleeves, puffed at the shoulder, tapered to a tight fit below the elbow and extended to a point well below her wrist. She slipped it on with ease, but had some difficulty fastening the front hook.

"Looks like motherhood's changed the fit some," Jeremy said, with an ornery grin.

Amanda blushed again as she took the hatbox from Jeremiah. She opened the lid and lifted out a buckram bonnet covered with white and yellow daisies and festooned with amber lace and yellow bows. She stepped over to the mirror above the wash basin, standing on her tiptoes in order to see. (Since their heights differed so, Jeremy had positioned the mirror high enough for him to see into when he stooped, and low enough for her when she stretched.) She gingerly adjusted the hat, then with a flourish tied its amber ribbon around her chin, which pulled the bonnet's brim tight around her cheeks.

She reached into the bottom of the hatbox and pulled out a small, black, oval case. Gazing at the case, Amanda's light-hearted mood vanished. Inside, a large, ivory brooch, set in gold, rested upon a bed of Spanish moss. The brooch, itself was attached to a string of amber beads. As she lifted the precious jewelry from its little nest, she couldn't help but think of Grandmother Bently the last time she'd seen her, standing by the dock when Amanda left Charleston.

Snuffling back a tear, she tried to fasten the clasp behind her neck with shaky hands.

"Here, let me do that." Jeremy took the necklace and fastened it in place around her throat, kissing the back of her neck as he did so. She gave a slight shiver, then reached for her parasol. As she turned to face him. Jeremy took in the whole of her—so tiny and delicate, so vulnerable and helpless. He couldn't help but think how out-of-place she looked in this rustic, hand-hewn cabin.

"Oh, Mandy, I still can't believe you're really mine. What a prize you are, my little yellow bird! Do I really get to keep you?" He looked around the cabin. "I know this is no planter's mansion," he said with a sweep of his arm, indicating the coarse furniture, the rough, puncheon floor, and the smudged hearth, "and it's a mighty long way from fancy, Charleston ballrooms. But, may I have the pleasure of this dance, my lady?" he asked, making a deep, exaggerated bow. With a pseudo-somber expression, he offered his arm.

Amanda slipped her tiny feet into the amber, silk slippers, opened her parasol, and gently placed her hand on Jeremy's firm, hairy arm. She stepped forward beside him, and together they made a ceremonial promenade around the cramped room.

Amanda started to giggle, "Jeremiah," she drawled, "You should inform the orchestra master that a waltz simply won't do as proper music for a cake walk." Jeremy let out a big, bellowing guffaw, then they both started laughing so hard, Jeremy collapsed into a chair by the fireplace, pulling Amanda down onto his lap as he did so.

"Oh you gorgeous, gorgeous woman, you," he said, enveloping her in a crushing bear hug. He covered her mouth in a long, passionate kiss.

"Mandy?" he asked in a rough voice when he finally came up for air. He hesitated a moment. "Why don't you let me help you out of that dress? With all this rain, there's no more field work for me today."

Amanda rose slowly from his lap, lowered her eyes, and inched the parasol shut. Jeremy stood, lifted her chin, untied the bonnet's ribbons, and carefully removed her hat. He put it into the hatbox, then took the parasol and propped it over against the wall. He turned to face Amanda. She blushed as she fumbled with the hooks of the Spencer.

"Here," he whispered. "Let me do that." His hands were big, but not clumsy. He unfastened the hooks one by one, then held the jacket for her while she slipped it off.

Amanda stood stock still, holding her breath, as Jeremy laid the Spencer across the back of a chair. Taking her by the shoulders, he slowly turned her around and unfastened the necklace. The weight of the brooch made it slip down into the front of her dress. She reached to retrieve it, but he stopped her hand in mid-air. "Let me do that, too."

He slid his hand between her breasts, lifted out the necklace, then kissed softly where it had rested. After he placed the jewelry back in its case, he began to unfasten her dress, one hook at a time. He kissed her back each time he moved lower.

When the top of the dress lay open, he pulled off the sleeves and lifted it up, over Amanda's head, so it wouldn't get dirty brushing against the ash-covered floor by the hearth. He'd never forget how much this last, tangible reminder of Charleston meant to her.

She stood trembling in her chemise—in anticipation, he assumed. "I love you, my little yellow bird," he whispered into her ear.

Amanda shuddered again, but not a quiver born of desire. Even though Jeremy treated her most gently these past few months, that first, violent opening still haunted her; the horrifying memory prevented her from finding any pleasure in their marriage bed. She shivered again.

"You're cold, Mandy?"

Jeremy engulfed her in a hug and swept her off her feet, cradling her in his arms. "Then let's get you under warm covers, young lady. The plans I have for you do not include your nightgown."

* * * * *

5 July , 18 and 16

Grandmother Bently,

I will endeavor to finish this letter today. It started raining yesterday, so Jeremiah spent the remainder of the afternoon inside with me. He has been good to me, Grandmother. He treats Little Ben like his own child. In a manner of speaking, I suppose he really is.

Ben gets so excited when Jeremiah comes in from outdoors, he waves his little arms and kicks his legs just to see him. Sometimes Jeremiah laughs so hard at Bently's antics, tears stream down his cheeks.

Jeremiah loves Bently. I believe he also cares for me, which is more than I dared to hope. Life is

not easy for us, but I am trying very hard to be a
good wife. It is so different here, and I still have so
much to learn. I wish I had paid closer attention
when we visited at your orchard, Grandmother.

Amanda let her mind wander back to her Grandmother's
peach orchard in the spring, where she remembered clouds of
pink flowers a-buzz with honeybees. By late July, branches
would be hanging heavy with peaches.

"I'm so hungry for a sweet, juicy peach," Amanda whispered
to herself. Grandmother hand-delivered the first peaches of the
season to the Bently kitchen. She never allowed servants to do
for her what she could do for herself. In a time and place that
accepted slave labor as the norm, Lillian Bently did the unheard
of—she hired her workers.

"No human able to get out of bed and do a decent day's
work has the right to expect someone else to do it for him," she
always said. When Amanda and her sisters asked why she didn't
own slaves like everyone else, Grandmother would point her
finger at their noses and say, "The only person you can own is
yourself. Don't ever forget that."

"I wish I'd have paid closer attention to you, Grandmother,"
Amanda thought. She continued with her letter…

You know so many of the things I need to know
out here. But Jeremiah is teaching me. And I am
trying hard to learn. He's been so patient with my
efforts at learning to cook. Sometimes I wonder how
he can stand to eat one more griddle cake. But he
simply smiles and tells me that I make the best
flapjacks in all of Ohio.

Jeremiah is kind to me. Will you tell Father that?
Tell him I am trying to be happy here. But it's so
difficult. I miss home. I miss warm weather. I miss
your peaches, Grandmother. But most of all, I miss
you.

Dear Mrs. Howard,

I hope this finds you folks getting settled in all comfortable like. I have been keeping a ear out for Harmon to come tooting on his horn with a letter from you. Though I have not had any word yet, I aim to start another letter to let you know how life goes for us down here in Vermillion Township.

This past week has been unbearable hot. After all them cold spells so late this crazy year a hot spell feels ungodly. The apple crop does not look to ripen proper with all these wide swings. We was hoping to have fruit for all the nabors this year as we have the only apple trees old enough to bear in these parts. Maybe as fall comes on this weather will sort itself out.

Our biggest excitement of late has been the critter what come to visit here last evening. Long about sundown a skunk walked right into the cabin big as you please to say howdy-do. We got no proper door you see. Harvey never seems to get round to hanging one. Always something else needs done first. Ever since I been here we have got by with heavy quilts hangin cross the doorway. That is for 3 winters now. It is not bad in summer. But in winter we get right cold with even 3 quilts up and a big fire built.

Well this skunk walked in right under the quilt. I need not tell you what happened next. The old boy let loose. And we all made a hasty exit out-a-doors. I grabbed the bedding before I ran. Hoping to save it from too big a dose of pole-cat perfume. I have not gone back indoors in 2 days except to hold my breath and run in for a few necessaries for cooking. Might take a spell to air out the cabin enough till it is fit to live in again.

Meantimes we have set up keeping house out here under the elm tree. I had forgot how much more work it is to do everything the hard way. It is 10 years since I come to this part of the country and had to live this way before our cabin got built. Seems different now that we do not have to live like this anymore.

I got right used to having a soft bed and a proper hearth to cook on. Now my eyes are permanent red from the smoke of the camp fire. Why last year Harvey even built me a clay oven right next to the fireplace so I can bake a real loaf a bread now. Seems somehow funny he could find time to make a clay oven but not a front door! His stomach always did rule his head. Maybe this smelly business will provoke him to build a proper door at last.

August 5, 1816

What a wonderful day! Two great things happened. First off I got your lovely letter. Second thing is we got to move back inside after our skunk visitor. The cabin is not so sweet smelling. But it is a far sight better than it was 5 nights ago.

I about give up on hearing from you. Thought maybe homestead life got too much and youens headed back east. I am so glad to hear that you are still in these environs and all is going well. Except for Levi's mishap. I am glad he is young. He will heal fast. It was good to get the names of all your youngens. I could not rightly say who was who with so many running round. But I sure do recollect that boy up a atop that tree. I am glad your brood is settling in. By now maybe Christian has took to the new place.

Talk round here is for starting up a school. I hope township officials do more than talk. Get down to books and a teacher. Our youngest boy Theodore needs more schooling than I can fit betwixt all my chores and helping out my sister tend to birthings and such.

Netta Bailey will be the next to pop here abouts. Leads me to wonder if Luther gets her to shut her mouth at tender moments. Or maybe he just puts a pillow over her face. Or she might prattle through the whole dern thing!

I got to admit I do enjoy having a baby around some again. It has been so long since mine was little. Having grandbabies is much more fun. When they get to be a bother you can give them right back to their folks. My little grandbaby is a real joy to me. Josephine is her name. We call her Josie for short. My son

Jason is her father. He and his wife Mary Sue homestead about a 1 day ride from here. Nice visiting distance when the weather is fair. In fact they are farming my old place.

All my girls are getting to marrying age. Flora Jean is the oldest at 17. She is keeping school at a settlement south of us called Perrysville. Lives with the Coulters. They give her room and board and cloth goods in trade. Gets home to visit one Saturday and Sunday a month.

Always the book smart one of the bunch was Flora. My own ma taught her to read and write back in Penna when she was but 4 years of age. The girl thought she knew more than me from then on and was not shy to let folks know it, neither. A lot like my mother herself truth be told.

Flora Jean cried at leaving Penna most of the whole trip long. But she took to life here in the wilds of Ohio well enough. That did surprise me some. When she fixed her mind on going back east to finish her schooling I did not think to see her ever again. But sure enough she come back. Heart set on teaching school.

Rode home with Brother Jonathan after one of his market trips to Penna. Quite a different girl by then. To my thinking she come here by choice that time. Wanted to bring her learning to this wilderness and pass it on. I got to say I felt like we was real mother and daughter for the first time when she come back. And her already grown. I hoped to have her with me for a time. But she stayed a few weeks then went off Perrysville way to teach. She figgered children round abouts would not listen to a home girl. It was a wise call I think.

So we still do not have a school round here. And Theodore drives me plum crazy. He spends some time out in the fields with Harvey. But not enough to suit me.

The other two girls Johannah and Katrina are my twins at 15. Irish twins I tell folks. Though I have nary a drop of Irish blood in me. They are the same age by 11 months. Johanna thinks she is ready to find herself a husband and settle down to raising a family. Would take over the run of this place if I let her.

But my Katrina is a different kind of bird. Happy-go-lucky is that girl. How many times I have come upon her out in the hen house singing to the chickens. Just like her Uncle Jonathan always did.

But Theodore is not my own flesh and blood. This is a second marriage for Harvey and me. His first wife died of the consumption when Theodore was 9. And my first man took off on a trip downriver to market and never did come back. The word husband used for Tobias does stretch it a mite.

Some say Injuns got Tobias. Others say river rats.

It was the year of the troubles in 18 and 12. You may not know about them as you are new to these parts. But that river-running scallywag Old Zeke told me straight out that he spied my man down in New Orleens with a copper-headed floozy. Saw them in the Basin Street district.

I only know I was better off without that one. Though it is not wise to tell most folks such a thing. Truth be told, I always did the biggest part of homestead chores anyways. With Jason to help.

After Harvey lost his missus some folks from Perrysville introduced him and me. The Coulters in fact. I could see right off he had more than he could handle alone. We cast our lots together as they say.

But putting two families together can get testy at best. Fur has got ruffled round here more than once. Harvey is even more hard headed than me if you can credit that. So far we manage to smooth out the rough spots and keep moving ahead.

I cannot say what it would be like to live with just Harvey alone. With all these children in the mix we had to jump right into the harness and start pulling together to keep both these families moving forward. Easier to keep moving on together than struggle alone, they say. Lord knows it is hard enough with a good man.

But one thing keeps pecking away at my brain. I see how one horse can move along better all by its lonesome instead of in a pair if that other horse keeps pulling it off track to some wheres else. Or even stopping dead in its tracks. And if I was none too clear I have said more than once that Harvey is a horse's patoot. But I am not ready to give up on him yet, no matter what my sister Edie says.

I am sure glad that Harvey and your Zach hit it off. Maybe we could get our men to plan a fall hunt for storing up winter chuck. Would be a good excuse for us to meet up again. We can both work on planting that idea.

Glad to hear the seeds found a happy home with you. Harvey had two trees full growed and bearing when I moved in. Thanks to a man name of John Chapman who travels these parts planting apple trees. Some say he is tetched. But it is nice to have fruit for eating and putting by. I sure hope it ripens this strange year.

Till the berries come again next year one thing you might try feeding your family is rose hips. They are ready to gather in early fall and keep well all winter. They are a bit tart but seem to perk a body up when it lacks the nutriment of fresh fruit.

Youngens might complain of stomach cramps if they eat too many at once. So eat them in small amounts. Most pleasant way I have found is to make a rose-hip tea. Use a handful of hips the bigness of a small egg to one large pot of hot water. Let it steep a goodly time. Then sweeten with honey if you have some. That tea helps keep away winter sniffles and is mighty tasty, too.

Another thing I did discover to use out here. Acorns for buttons. Take the little cap off the nut and cover it with a scrap of cloth to match a shirt or dress. Or just use it as it comes. Course you need to find good stout ones that will not crush if you punch holes in them to sew em on. Works fine for lack of real buttons. Got to make do a lot out here.

I hope you do not find my writing too unsmooth. I hid out in the barn when I shouldda been at lessons. I could hear my mother calling for me. Eloise Maevis! I confess to you that is my proper name. Thank the Lord and my sister for not saddling me with it for life. Edie took to calling me Ellie Mae for short. Our mother hated that. But I reckon Edie and I did not turn out the city-fied kind of girls she wished for. We left that to sister Tabitha.

You wrote such a pretty letter. I hope you will write again. Maybe we will even meet again before the snow flies. We can only hope.

Meantimes I better stop boring you with this long book and save some for another day. Maybe you will tell me a little about your family back in Connettycutt and how you ended up in those Fire Lands.

Your friend, Ellie Mae for short

Dear Ellie Mae,

You mayn't even have gotten my first letter, but here I am writing another. It is Monday, washday. Do you think Chinese women do their washing on Monday? I think that God does his washing on Monday. I took the small children and went to the creek right after breakfast. When my hands go numb from the cold water, the children grab them and rub them back to life. That is their washday job. If it hurts too badly, they stick my hands in their shirts and squeal and dance from the shock of it.

I am down to wearing one petticoat of necessity and threatening to make use of Zach's spare trousers. He says if I do, he will make me a corncob pipe. I think there is still too much city in me for that, so I am holding off.

Zach says he will dig a well next year so we shan't have to carry water from the creek. We have plenty of flow this year, but he has heard that it dries up in a hot summer. We have drunk from wagon ruts and mud puddles on our journey, though it was not pleasant, and I would just as lief not have do so again.

He and the older boys have cleared half an acre, girdling the larger trees. In the spring, he will plant corn between the stumps. Zach says we will buy a milk cow. The baby, Elijah, has been sickly and needs milk. He has heard of one for sale, and an Indian has offered to guide him to it for one dollar. It seems a steep price, but do we need it. Zach will be gone a few days.

August 2, 1816

Today Christian discharged his firearm in the cabin. It was an accident, but now a hole in the roof of our new cabin! Right before winter! And after everyone worked so hard. I'm afraid that I lost my temper. We had words, and he's gone. I started after him but Elijah clung to my skirts and wailed, he not being well, so I had to let Christian go. This would happen with Zach away! When Nate and Simeon came back from fishing, I told

41

them what had transpired. Nate set out to find his brother. If he does not overtake him in the first overland stage of the journey, he will return alone.

August 3

No one returns. I try to stay busy. How clean can you sweep a dirt floor?

August 4

No one. No one. Elijah worsens. Listless, he doesn't cry. I would pinch him just to hear him wail. Simeon tried to be the man of the house but could not bear the burden of my constant looking to him, so now he goes fishing from dawn to dusk. Leesha and the twins keep the fire tended and run to the creek for cool water for the baby's head.

This land will take my sons. I know that now. Why did we come here? Had we sons to spare? A mother holds all her children in her heart, yet she holds them in different places, recognizing what each brings to her: the child of pride, the child of pain, the child of comfort, the child of a special night of love. It is this last who is beside me now, burning with fever. He dreams a restless dream, eyes flickering back and forth beneath lids. What does he see, this dark-eyed baby of Zach's and my love?

I no longer need worry about that extra petticoat, as I have torn it into strips to soak him with cool water. And here is Lizzie, my child of comfort, with a fresh bucket and a pat and a kiss for mama. She is a wise one, my Lizzie. She tells me that she had a dream and all will be well. But for my own sense of impending doom, I would believe. I can't afford to dream or to sleep. Were I to sleep... but I am writing to you, my new friend. I will watch over my chicks. I will keep them with me. I will, I will.

August 5

He lives, Ellie Mae. Though I slept, the miracle happened. His fever broke, and I woke to his wail—of hunger! And before I cleared the sleep and tears from my eyes, I heard the voice of my beloved call out for anyone who might be wanting fresh milk still warming in the vessel, and next came the mooing of a cow, and not only a cow, but one freshened and in want of immediate milking.

We all started to talk at once. It seems that the Indian who led him to the cow demanded another dollar to get him back through the Black Swamp, but that wouldn't have left enough to buy the beast. So Zach made his way home alone. As the swamp is too large to cross in a single day, he had to climb up in a tree to sleep. There was some encounter with wolves, as evidenced by the flank of the bovine beast, but Zach insisted there was no risk to him in it. He was not about to let "the damned hounds get my boy's damned animal in that damned swamp."

He's back, my man, in all his cursing splendor.

And by midday, the boys were back, dragging an eight-point buck ("in the velvet," they said, which is something about the antlers) and with no word of what had transpired previously, but for a sheepish grin from Christian and a peck on the cheek. Life goes on, theirs, and so mine.

September 1, 1816

Today I received your nice, long letter all full of news. What an adventure you had. I have not met a "pole cat" and am just as glad not to have had that pleasure. I am sure that you will get that door now. But how lucky you are to have a real oven! I mentioned this to my husband in hopes of getting one for myself but was reminded of all he must do before the snow sets in. I think that a proper floor would be even higher on my own list of priorities, but it is nice to dream.

I hope the matter of the school is progressing. I'm sure the subject will not even be raised up here for a few more years, until there is more of a population to educate. I appreciate how hard it is to find the time, and were we but closer, you could throw your Theodore in with all mine. I have enough to fill a school room as it is. Perhaps you could send Theodore to the Coulter's to be taught by his sister. But no, he'd hardly take that any better than from his mother. No doubt he would end up disrupting her new class.

It sounds like happy coincidence that you get the opportunity to enjoy your grandbaby so much. It must be a comfort to have Jason settled, and so close by, too. With all those daughters ripening on the vine, you will no doubt be in for quite a harvest.

Elijah is recovered and has regained in only two weeks' time the weight that was lost during his illness. I might have lifted a feather, he was so light (and so hot and so dry, but no, that is done and all is well, so look ahead—but it was a near thing, Ellie Mae, you know it was).

So you have your Irish twins, Jo and Rini, or what do you call them for short? I'll bet that does make people sit up and take notice. I did not realize that they were not all yours, but this is surely common with life being so uncertain. You and Harvey may have had a lot of troubles in your pasts, but I'm glad that you're making your way in this life together now. I do hope that you have not been left with an aversion to women of auburn locks. Your other man must have been a rapscallion. No doubt you are well shed of him.

As to your inquiry of our relations and how we came to be here, this piece of Ohio Fire Lands was deeded to us through Zach's family, as his parents' land was destroyed during the troubles with the English. That day of destruction, on July 14 of 17 and 78, saw both Zach's birth and his mother Elizabeth's death, for whom my own Lizzie is named.

All those years as others awaited their recompense from that war, Zach's father, Eli, remained steadfast in asserting that not a thing on this earth could serve as payment for the loss of his dear Elizabeth, for nothing here was half equal to her value. Two years ago, he joined her, never having taken another wife, as he was certain she would "take it out of my hide" when next they did meet.

The deed to this parcel came to Zach shortly after his father passed, he being the only issue of that union. He thinks of this as his parents' land, though neither one saw it. He is sure they are watching us now and offering encouragement. The only person he really has any ties to back east is his Uncle Law. Uncle Lawrence Howard is a barrister by profession, though I am not sure whether this resulted in the name or was preceded by it, as no one calls him Lawrence but merely "Law." The day Uncle Law brought the Fire Lands deed to Zach, that was the day my world turned upside down.

Myself, I am one of five daughters to Shaun and Vera McNally. My mother had no sons and saw to our education herself. She deserved a better husband than she got, he of the footloose and fancy-free variety, but made the best of what she had.

We sisters are as follows in age: Abigail (called Abby), Olivia (your own Libby), Rosalinda (Rose), Henrietta (Hattie), and the baby, Suzannah. These dears are the ones I have found hard to leave.

Abby is our old maid schoolmarm. She is so like Mama, strong and sure. She still bosses us, and we let her. I am glad, with us grown and gone, to think she still has her chicks, a schoolroom full. Rose and I are like your Irish twins. For two months of the year, we are the same age (some years Papa was home more than others). What's more, family lore has it that until we were five, we thought we were one child named Olivia Rose. For that was the way Mama always said it. "Olivia Rose, come and show me your sums." "Olivia Rose, it's dinnertime."

Papa was the one who called me Lib. Always looking for the pot of gold at the end of the rainbow, he. Going off to seek his fortune like a man young and single when he was neither. A dreamer, Mama called him. It was seven years from Rose to Hattie for that was his next stop home after his long explore into the wilds of Canada, a cold and barren land. Yet he spoke of mountains and lakes and woods that go on for a million years, all things of amazing beauty.

He was of the Irish, my Da, but Mama did not let us take on that word nor any that were his. She held herself as being much above him and his. It is told that at the birth of each babe, he would beg her to "name me wee bairn Caitlin for the poor, dear sister o' mine what met her fate too soon." To this she replied that he had done his part in the matter and should now leave her to do hers.

Being witness to this exchange at the birth of Hattie, I can't call a lie to it. In fact, our mother did name that child after her own brother Henry, a tax collector who was known to spit on the Irish should he meet them, his brother-in-law being no exception. And, though I can't credit this, the truth is that Hattie was never in league with us, but kept herself apart and spied and tattled whenever she could.

She lives in Massachusetts and is married to a large land owner (I mean by this that the man and his holdings are both very ample). We seldom hear from her, as she seems to hold herself above us still, though how she can after marrying a fat, bald-headed man named Rupert, I cannot say. In truth, we used to devil her to no end—all ally against her and call her Etta. This drove her to black rages. "Etta," we would call, "Et a what?" So she never lacked for things to tattle of.

And dear Rose, my other self. If I started a sentence, she finished it. We lived on the same street for years. After Abby moved to be nearer her school, Rose and her family moved into Mama's house. Her husband, Garth, kept accounts for the mill where Zach ran the lumbering operation. Rose is still teaching drawing room arts to young ladies above the school-room age, as we both did. It worked so well, my teaching them French and needlepoint, while Rose taught them music and sketching.

We even had our babies in the same years, though she gave up the contest after three, as her constitution was not as strong as mine. She always said that she would have kept up if Garth had his way, but she had begun with the using of "C" names and could think of no more than the three that she fancied.

And Zannah, she was the reason Rose moved into Mama's house. Zannah was only three when Mama died, same age as Rose's little Caitlin. So it seemed to suit. But Caitlin grew up and Zannah did not. I guess that last drop of the old man was too pure, because the child who was a large part of him is the only part of our Zannah. Such beauty I have never seen always with that sweet, angelic expression of hers, while Caitlin would grow petulant and jealous of the new babies as they came along, Caleb, and in his turn Cole.

So we lived and had our babies and taught our young ladies and fed our men and feathered our nests and loved our men and had more babies.

So it was until the deed came.

Father Eli had gone and baby Elijah had come (I knew he would be my last before the doctor said it). Fourteen years I spent in that house, in that kitchen, in that bed. And here stood Uncle Law with a piece of paper in his hand and Zach with a look in his eye that resembled too much of Shaun McNally before a goodbye. I heard my husband say, "stifled" and "hemmed in" and "new territory" and "adventure." His final words—"for the good of all."

Well you know the rest. That is the story of my people and how I came to these environs, as you inquired.

Now I must go. The sun is setting, and the children are quarrelsome because I have sat here all afternoon scribbling.

I have shown Zach your letter, and he approves the idea of a hunt in the fall. He does not yet commit to my coming along, but we can continue to hope! I look forward to seeing you in the near future.

Your friend, Libby

Chapter 4

The Surround Hunt
October 1816
Vermillion Township, Ohio

"Godalmighty, I can't believe the size of that varmint," said Sam Justice, the township's only blacksmith, and one of the first settlers in these parts—not to mention the man from whom the settlement of Justice derived its name.

"I thought I was a goner," Jeremy said, wiping at his head with a bloody handkerchief. "If Jonathan had missed that shot, you'd be digging my grave for sure." Jeremy propped his gun beside a feed barrel sitting in the corner of Luther Bailey's barn and sank onto its top to steady his legs. The township men slowly straggled back to Luther's after the day's big surround hunt to rid the farming community of crop-destroying varmints.

"Lucky I had a clear shot," piped up Jonathan Johansen.

"Lucky, my ass. That was crack shootin', if you ask me. And you didn't ask me, but I'm a-tellin' you just the same," said Anson Guthrie, taking a long swig from the jug of corn liquor the men had started to pass around. "I never seen such a long shot take down a bear that size in all my born days," he said, wiping the lip of the jug before passing it on to Jonathan, who took a deep pull, then handed it to Frank Putnam.

"I can't reckon why I missed that first shot," Frank hollered into Sam Justice's good ear, after he sampled the brew. "Had me a clean shot, too. Can't figger it at-all."

"Could be your good eye don't see so straight no more, Frank," said Sam. "Here, hand me that jug. I gotta see how this batch of Luther's stacks up ag'in mine," he said, reaching for the jug. Sam wiped its lip with his palm, took a long swallow, and then wiped his mouth clean with the back of his hand. "Not bad, Luther. Not bad." He nodded to Luther Bailey, who'd started to clean his rifle along with a group of men gathered near the base of the hayloft ladder.

"Here, Jeremy," said Sam. "I think you need a slug o' this stump juice worse than any of these no-accounts." He handed the jug of whiskey to Jeremy, whose hand shook as he accepted it. "I know you seldom tipple like the rest of us reprobates, but it looks like you could use good slug. If I was you, I believe I'd put a little of that juice on my face, too," said Sam, nodding toward Jeremy's oozing wounds.

Jeremy tried to pour a splash of liquor onto his handkerchief, but his hand shook so, he succeeded only in spilling it on his pants.

"Let me do that," said Zach Howard, taking the jug from Jeremiah and swiftly soaking the cloth. With a gentle touch Zach's big hand eased the saturated cloth against Jeremy's shredded cheek. He jumped at the alcohol's sudden bite. "A little sting now'll keep it from festering later," Zach said, sopping more of the elixir onto his own handkerchief and placing that one on the side of Jeremy's bleeding neck. "You're gonna have yourself quite the battle scar, friend."

"I can just hear Mandy when she sees me," Jeremy said, holding the cloths against his skin. "If she swoons at a little bitty cut, what'll she do when she sees this?"

Zach took a drink from the jug, then sent it along the line of men until it made its way back to Luther Bailey. Luther shook it sideways, then took the last swig. "I'll break out another 'un." He headed to a trap door in the far corner of the barn floor and disappeared below. By the time he brought up a second, dust-covered jug, a few more hunters had straggled into the barn. With joking and back slapping, the men greeted one another after a long day of tromping through the wooded thickets of Vermillion Township.

"How'd you all do at your end?" asked Tom Hawkins. "We got us a pile of critters out east of Justice. Coon, deer, catamounts, bear."

"Bet you ain't got no bear to equal the one Jonathan took down," Anson Guthrie piped up. Anson made sure he also sampled from the second jug Luther started around. "Got him the granddaddy of all bears hereabouts, he did," said Anson. "You didn't ask me, but I'm a-tellin' you just the same."

"We got two bruin sows and a couple of last spring's cubs," said Tom. "Nothin' worth makin' much over."

Anson handed the jug to Tom, and he drank liberally before handing it to his younger, red-haired brother, Willie Hawkins, who'd entered the barn behind Tom. Willie took a small sip, then glanced over and saw Jeremiah sitting on a barrel in the corner, holding a bloody handkerchief to his neck, and looking peak-ed.

"What happened to you?" Willie hurried over and squeezed Jeremy's shoulder.

"Had a little run-in with a charging bear," Jeremy answered, taking the handkerchief away for a moment. Flaps of skin hung loose where bear claws had swiped against Jeremy's head.

"That looks bad. I better go get Ma to sew you up right away," Willie said.

"Aw, he don't need no stitchin'," sneered Harvey Thompson, giving Jeremiah a slap on the back, after walking into the barn. Harvey stood a head taller than Jeremy and outweighed him by at least eighty pounds. "I had scratches lots worse 'an that. Healed up with no fancy sewin', neither," he said, showing off the ugly scar over his eyebrow. "Hell, just give him a few more swigs from this jug and he'll be fine." Harvey took a pull himself, then handed the jug over to his 13-year-old son, Theodore.

"Ain't he a bit young for tippling?" asked Sam, watching the boy take a slug.

"He can shoot a buck deer at over two hundred yards. That makes him good as any man here," answered Harvey in an ugly tone. "Has to learn to hold his liquor sometime, don't he?"

Theodore glared at Sam and took another long drink. Then he passed the jug to Levi, the youngest of Zach Howard's four sons here this day. Levi accepted the jug eagerly, but before he had a chance to tip it up, Zach cuffed his ear and grabbed the jug away. "What do you think you're doin' with that?"

"Theodore's pa let him have a drink. How come I can't?"

"First you got to prove you're man enough to handle it, son," Zach answered.

"That face really don't look too good, if you ask me," said Anson Guthrie, pointing to Jeremy. "You didn't ask, but I'm a-tellin' you just the same." He paused. "Zach, hand that jug back here, will you?"

"Ma's gonna get awful riled when she finds out Jeremy needs sewed up and nobody sent to get her," Willie pushed.

"Guess it would be a shame to let such a purty face heal up all lumpy now," Harvey laughed, giving Jeremy a playful poke to the shoulder.

"No doubt some stitchin'd help heal it up better," offered Jonathan. "Likely go down a mite easier for your little misses, when she sees you, too."

"I'll go get Ma." Willie starting toward the barn door.

"Don't bother your ma," said Zack Howard. "If you find me some stout thread and a needle, I can sew him up. That way we won't have to bother any of the women folk. You don't want to go stirring 'em all up this late in the day, now, do you?"

"You can do that?" Willie asked. "Sew up a person?"

"Sure he can," piped up Levi, who at 13 stood almost eye to eye with his father. "See, he sewed up my foot. You can hardly even tell it." Levi pulled off his boot and showed his foot all around. "I almost cut my foot clean off, too!"

"What do you think?" Jonathan asked the friend whose life he'd saved that day.

"I think I'd rather not trouble the women, if I don't have to," said Jeremy. "You're right, it probably would go easier on Mandy if my face didn't look so terrible when she sees me. Sure you're up to it, Zach?"

"Question is, are you?"

"Let's get to it while this corn liquor's working on me."

"Luther, you got any sinew?" asked Zach. "That's the best. But thread'll work fine if you don't."

Luther ducked out the barn door and headed for his cabin.

"Better give Jeremy a few more pulls on that jug," said Harvey, giving Zach a playful poke. "He's sure gonna need it, now."

When Luther opened the cabin door, he found his ample wife, Netta, sorting through a crate of dirt, taking out lumps from time to time as she babbled away to the petite Amanda Harrison, who sat near the table holding Luther and Netta's newborn daughter. Amanda's own Little Ben slept contentedly on a mat by the hearth.

"I feel so wonderful after Rosanna's birth, I can hardly believe it," said Netta. She tossed another brown lump into a second crate sitting beside the dirt-filled one. "Ma Hawkins said I was a natural-born mother if ever she saw one. Now wasn't that nice of her? Told me she never did see any woman give birth so quick and easy as I did. I know it's 'cause Luther left his pants hanging over the end of the bed every night that last month or so. They always say if a man leaves his pants hanging over the end of the bed, it'll make for an easy birth. And sure enough, Ma told me I had an easy one. It's a fact." Netta grabbed a quick breath and continued. "But Amanda, I've got to tell you, for a spell there, I thought I was gonna turn inside out for sure. I know I don't need to tell you about the hurtin' part. You know well as I do, a woman can't be a mother without bearin' the pain. No way round it."

"Netta." Luther announced himself abruptly. "I need a needle and stout thread."

"Luther!" Netta jumped in surprise. "Oh, my lands, I can never hear you come up to the door in those old moccasins you insist on wearin'! You liked to scare the wits right out of me!"

"Too late for that."

"Are all you men back from the hunt so soon?" She paused long enough to grab a breath and glance out the window. "My goodness, the sun is settling low already. I better get supper on. Do you know what, Luther? Amanda and me dug up jonquil bulbs this afternoon. And can you believe it? We lost all track of the time befo–"

"Needle and thread?" Luther reminded.

"What on earth do you want with sewing things? Just let me go look," she struggled to rise from where she squatted on the floor. "My sewing basket's over on the bureau. But I need to wash this dirt off my hands first, before I can get–"

"Don't stir yourself. I'll get it." Luther walked to the tall bureau, took her sewing basket down, and headed back toward the door.

"Are you taking the whole thing?"

"Yup."

"Don't you dare lose my silver thimble out of that basket, you hear? My Grandma Rosanna gave me that thimble, and I'd be awful upset if anything happened to it. Luther… Luther!"

The door slammed shut before Netta could finish. "Now what in blue blazes do you suppose that was all about?" Netta asked. "I will never understand that man, long as I live. Yesterday it was a piece of cloth and string he wanted. Something to do with straining another batch of corn juice for his still. Said he needed a new cloth to tie over a keg when he poured off the vat. But a needle and thread? Now tell me, what can a man want with needle and thread?"

"Maybe the cloth tore and he needs to fix it?" Amanda offered.

"With Luther you just never know. But why on earth would he be straining mountain dew now? 'Course, after a whole day of hunting I reckon all those fellas worked up a powerful thirst," Netta said. "Did you ever notice how much more they drink when they all get together? Luther nips some on his own, and sometimes he does take more than a sip or two. But when three or four of these bucks get together, they sure do seem to put away a lot more than any one of them would drink all by his self—all added up together, I mean."

Amanda gave her a quizzical look, trying to comprehend what Netta had just said. "Jeremiah seldom touches spirits, himself," she responded in her soft drawl, patting Rosanna lightly against her shoulder. "He keeps a jug for medicinal purposes, of course, but I haven't known him to take a single swallow since we arrived last year."

"Not too many like that 'round here," said Netta with a shake of her head. "Why, every time we have a frolic in the township, Luther takes at least two jugs along. And Sam Justice—you met Sam. Luther says he makes the best corn liquor in the whole township, even if he is deaf as a post. Well Sam always brings at least three of his jugs. Then after all the work gets done, Anson Guthrie breaks out his fiddle, and we all get to dancing. Why, you should hear Anson play! You know, I think the more that man drinks, the better he can play that ol' fiddle! Can you imagine? And you should see his nose! I swear every time he takes one more swallow, it turns a brighter shade of red! Oh, I can't wait till our next frolic. I just know you're gonna love it. Then you can meet every one else round about here, too." Netta brushed her hands, knocking off the loose dirt after sorting out all the jonquil bulbs.

"I'd best be getting some food ready for Luther. He works up a powerful hunger when he hunts." Netta rose and went to clean up at the wash stand over by the door. "Why don't you and Jeremy stay to supper, Amanda? Won't be any more trouble fixin' for four than it is for two. Luther told me not to fuss for all the hunters today. Said everyone would have to head home for chorin' time anyhow. But you and Jeremy don't have so far to go. Your chores could wait a little while longer, couldn't they? Then you could stay on to eat with us. Oh, please say you'll stay. I so seldom get company, I really hate to see you go."

"I don't know, Jeannette. I'd need to ask Jeremiah before I can say yes or no."

"He's out to the barn with all those hunters. Why don't you go ask him?"

"Oh, I couldn't do that! Go out there, among all those men… and… and guns?"

"Why not? They're just a bunch of overgrown boys," Netta teased.

"It's not just that, exactly." Amanda hesitated. "It's… well, it's—"

"It's seeing all those dead animals, isn't it. The first time I saw the kill after one of their surround hunts, I almost swooned myself. But you'll get used to so much blood out here. After a while, it gets pretty usual," Netta answered. "Want me to ask?"

"Oh, if you would I'd be ever so grateful. I'll stay here and keep an eye on the babies."

Netta took her shawl off the hook and headed for the door, wrapping it around her shoulders as she went. "He better not lose that thimble, that's all I got to say," she mumbled on her way outside. "My Grandma Rosanna gave me that thimble. Been in the family for generations. Told me so herself."

Long before Netta reached the barn, men's hearty laughter drifted out into the late afternoon shadows, conveying their jovial mood. Acrid odors of corn liquor, spent gun powder, congealed blood, and sweaty hunters greeted her as she pulled open the barn door to enter the dusky interior.

"Luther, are you done with my sewing basket yet?" She marched into the barn, letting the big door slam behind her. Immediately the men's conversation ceased. "My thimble better still be in that basket, or I'm gonna be awful upset with—"

Netta stopped dead in her tracks when she saw Zach standing over Jeremy, pulling a needle and thread back from his cheek to tie off a stitch. She looked over and noticed the huge Harvey Thompson sitting on the floor with his head propped between his knees, looking a decided shade of pasty gray. She glanced back at Jeremiah. "Oh, my Lord, Jeremy! What happened to your face? Someone better go fetch Ma Hawkins quick. You're bleeding all over the place! I'll go get bandages, and hot water, and a poultice an–"

She didn't get a chance to finish the sentence before Luther grabbed her and clapped his hand over her mouth. "Hold your tongue, woman" he said. She nodded yes, so he let her go.

"Luther, what's wrong? How did Jeremy get hurt? What's Amanda gonna–"

Luther clapped his hand over her mouth again, this time holding it there as she stood bug-eyed, watching Zach sew up Jeremiah's face. When Zach finished the last stitch, Luther let Netta loose again. She stood silent for a full minute before attempting to speak.

"Luther?" she asked hesitantly. He made a move to muzzle her again, but Jeremy raised his hand.

"It's all right," he said. Jeremy dipped his handkerchief into the bucket of water that sat on the barrel beside his seat. He wrung it out and mopped up the blood that had trickled down his neck. "Netta, you think you can get Mandy fixed to see me like this without getting her all upset? Can you do that?"

Netta opened her mouth to speak, but at a stern look from Luther, she simply nodded yes.

"Tell her I had a little run-in with a bear, and that Zach stitched me up just fine. Can you tell her that without getting her stirred up?" Jeremy asked.

"I'll do my best." She swallowed, shot a quick glance at Luther, then took a big breath. "But what am I gonna tell her about dinner? I mean... well, I came out here to ask if youens could stay to eat. I reckon you better stay now. You need to get some nutriment in that stomach of yours, build up a little strength before you head for home in that condition."

Netta paused, looking nervously from Jeremiah to Luther. "I'll go back and tell her you're staying to supper." She turned and made a beeline for the barn door. "But God better help me think of something to say about that face of yours awful quick," Netta babbled her way out of the barn. "What a fine bucket of mash this day has turned into," she mumbled, heading toward the house. "Still don't have my thimble, neither. He best not lose Grandma Rosanna's thimble."

After the barn door banged shut behind her, the buzz of men's conversation resumed.

"Don't know how I could o' missed that shot," Frank said to Harvey Thompson, whose color began returning to normal. "Just can't figger it at-tall."

"Reckon that ain't all you can't hit, Frank," Harvey said with a leer and a wink to Luther. "We all believe you're still childless for want of good aim." He made an obscene gesture, then took the jug from Frank and had another long pull. "'Sides, with that fleshy woman of yours, you probably can't find the right place to plant your pecker no how. What do you do, Frank, punch a different fold every night?"

Men laughed all around.

"I bet I have it a sight more pleasur'ble than you, pokin' away at that scrawny Ellie Mae. She's nothin' but a skinny pile o' bones."

"I like the small ones, Frank. Always did."

The men returned to cleaning guns and tormenting one another, while Netta trudged back to the cabin with a slow, steady pace instead of her usual bubbly bounce. By the time she took off her shawl and hung it on the peg behind the door, she still hadn't thought of a way to break the unsettling news about Jeremy's brush with death.

"You're awfully quiet, Jeannette. Is something wrong?" Amanda asked.

Netta moved over to where Amanda sat near the fire and took Rosanna from her, hugging the baby tightly to her breast. "It's just that... well... you see, I'm not exactly sure how to tell you." She paused and took a deep breath, then plunged ahead. "There's been an accident, and Jeremy got himself hurt, but–"

"Oh, my God! He's dead!" Amanda's hand flew to her throat and she turned a deathly shade of white.

"No! No, it's not that at all!"

"Jeremiah!" she screamed hysterically. "Jeremiahhhh!"

"No, no! He's not dead! Amanda. Do you hear me? He's fine!" Netta hollered to try and make herself heard above Amanda's shrieks. But her shouts managed only to awaken Little Ben, who raised his head from where he still lay on the blanket by the fire, adding his own wail to the sound of his mother's scream. Not to be outdone—and frightened in her own right by the commotion—baby Rosanna joined in, too.

"No, Amanda," Netta hollered again. "Get hold of yourself!" She grabbed Amanda's shoulder and gave a stern shake. "Jeremy's fine. He's not dead. Jeremy's alive!"

Amanda stopped in mid-scream, when she finally heard Netta's voice rise louder than her own. "He's not dead?"

"He's quite alive," Netta said. "He only got mauled by a bear, is all."

"Thank God he's alive!" Amanda breathed a sigh of relief. "A bear? A *bear*? Did you say a BEAR?" The word turned into another, protracted scream.

"He just got his face scraped up some. But Zach Howard sewed him all up. He's gonna be fine!"

All that screaming had finally cut through the din of men's voices out in the barn, and at the sound, Jeremy took a deep breath, then rose from his seat on the barrel. He headed for the cabin on wobbly legs to calm his wife and son. By the time he opened the door, Netta stood over Amanda waving a dish towel in her face, and the babies lay side-by-side on the hearth blanket, in a wailing contest of their own.

"Jeremiah! You're not dead!" Amanda gushed with tears when she saw him wobble through the door.

Luther came into the cabin close on Jeremy's heels, ready to lend a hand with the women, or to catch Jeremy if he should keel over.

"It's all right, Mandy." Jeremy's head spun from all the "medicinal" whiskey he'd downed to help numb the pain. He sank to his knees beside Amanda's chair, kneeling with the injured side of his head facing away from her. He took her in his arms and patted her as he would Little Ben. "I'm fine," he breathed, with the distinct odor of whiskey on his breath, "really, I am."

Netta retrieved baby Rosanna, but both babies still cried full force, seeing, perhaps, which could hold out longer before giving in to silence. Netta handed Rosanna to Luther, then she picked up Little Ben and began to jiggle him to quiet his wails.

Jeremiah reached into his pocket for a handkerchief, then realized his own bloodied one would never do to dry his wife's tears "You got a clean hankie, Netta?"

"Oh, my, yes," she said, balancing Little Ben on her hip with one arm and reaching into the pocket of her apron to retrieve her hankie. "I got it out clean this morning," she said, handing it over to Jeremy. At the sound of his daddy's voice, Little Ben finally began to quiet down, and in Luther's arms, baby Rosanna quieted, too.

"Here, blow." Jeremiah held the hankie up to Amanda's nose, and she blew.

She studied Jeremy. "Are you really all right?"

He tried to nod, but the movement triggered pain that made him stop in mid-nod. Instead he breathed, "I'm fine, Mandy. Just caught a bear paw with my face, is all."

"Let me see."

"It's not too pretty. You sure?"

She put one hand on each of his shoulders and eased him around so she could get a good look at the bad side of his face. The tails of the stitches stuck out in four, long lines down Jeremy's cheek and neck. They did look gruesome. Even so, Jeremy presented a much better picture than he had an hour earlier. "Does it hurt?" she asked, touching his cheek ever so slightly.

He winced, but said, "Not too bad. I got enough whiskey in me right now to deaden it some. Reckon I'll feel it tomorrow."

Amanda took a deep breath, put on a brave face, and rose to her feet. "Jeannette, I don't believe we'll stay to supper. I should take Jeremiah home and put him right to bed." She took Little Ben back from Netta and began to gather her things. "Luther? Would you mind hitching Patsy up to the cart for us?"

"You up to drivin'?" Luther asked Jeremiah.

Jeremy rose from where he still knelt, and immediately a wave of dizziness hit him. He sank onto the chair.

"He won't need to drive the cart," Amanda said. "I can do it. It's not that far."

"I'll hitch my pony on behind and drive it for you," offered Luther, "give a hand with your ev'nin' chores." He handed baby Rosanna to Netta and headed out the door.

"Oh, I do wish you could stay and eat something first," Netta insisted. "It won't take but a minute to heat up the stew and make some good, strong coffee. That's what you need, Jeremy. Hot coffee to steady you, some. I can make it up real quick—"

"Mandy's right. We better be going. Soon as I can get these wobbly legs of mine to work."

Luther got the Harrison's horse and cart hitched up in short order. By then, most of the hunters had already dispersed, heading to respective homes, suppers, and chores of their own.

Jeremy stood again, this time a bit more slowly, and he took Amanda's arm as they walked into the evening twilight. It wasn't clear who steadied whom.

Luther helped Amanda into the cart, handed the baby up to her, and then gave Jeremiah a boost, after the smaller man wavered a bit trying to climb aboard. Luther stepped up last, picked up the reins, and gave them a brisk smack to get Pasty moving.

"Oh, Luther, wait!" Netta hollered. "Amanda's jonquils! We can't forget the jonquils!" She disappeared back inside and came out a moment later with the crate of spring bulbs in one arm, and baby Rosanna balanced in the crook of the other. She heaved the crate into the cart and waved Luther on. "Bye, bye, Amanda! Don't forget to plant those bulbs soon as you can. Come back to visit us real soon!" She stood waving. "And I hope your face gets better right quick, Jeremy," she hollered louder as the cart pulled farther away. "I'll have supper all ready for you when you get back, Luther!"

Netta's voice faded into the distance as the cart headed toward the Harrisons.

October 31, 1816
Justice Settlement
Vermillion Township, Ohio

Dear Libby,

I am mighty sorry you could not come down from them Fire
Lands with your men folk. But Zach carrying that nice letter you
wrote was darn near just as good. We was a might too hopeful
with our schemes, you and me. We should have knowed better
than to think your mister would drag the whole fam damily
down here for a hunt. I did like reading the account of each
one of your boys. I saw the proof of your words with my own
eyes. I am guessing that after a day of tramping tall grass for
the men, they are all sound asleep out in the barn.

Ellie Mae Thompson unfolded the letter Zach Howard had
hand-delivered two days earlier, when he and his boys arrived
for the big, Vermillion Surround Hunt at her Harvey's special
invitation. Reading Libby's letter once more took the edge off
the disappointment of not being able to see her new friend in the
flesh...

October 20, 18 and 16
The Fire Lands, Ohio

Dear Ellie Mae,

I am so dismayed I was not able to come down with Zach,
but he is right in saying that a hunt is not an occasion for
women and babies. It is the time of year when weather can
quickly turn wet and cold, so I shan't take my little Elijah out in
it, after his recent infirmity. Zach and the older boys will leave
for your place at first light. I will give him this letter to carry to
you in my stead. No doubt you will be busy with so many
mouths to feed, but perhaps you might find time to pen a
few lines in reply, so that I mayn't find the whole thing such
a terrible disappointment.

Mayhap I should tell you a bit more about our children,
since you will be spending time with some of them. Our oldest
living is Nate, who has his father's love of wood and hunting

and the outdoors itself. His nature is quite sunny. Strangers always mean new friends to him.

Next comes Simeon, who has been from birth a water baby, always most happy in his bath. He loves the summer, with its swimming and fishing. He enlisted the other children to dig out a swimming hole in our little creek and rigged a rope swing where they spent much of the warm weather swinging and dropping into the water. Now that fall is here, he works on his trap line.

Christian is a wanderer, like his granddad, worrying me to distraction with his absences and coming back with stories and all manner of interesting things, such as bird eggs and arrow tips. He has a moodiness and temper which from time to time cause me dismay.

And how to describe Levi? An accident waiting to happen would be apt enough. A whirling dervish would also suffice. He began running at eight months and hasn't slowed down since. I must warn you, he will bear special watching, Ellie Mae.

Levi's twin, my Lizzie, blossoms before my eyes. She has a humor and a practicality which make her an ideal companion. She is a hard worker, so I not only enjoy having her at my side but appreciate that she keeps up her end of the chores. I know not what I would ever do without her.

And Leesha, at almost ten, is the sweetest and most loving child of all. Though understanding the realities that necessitate our killing for food, she sheds a tear for each ill-fated animal. I thought she would be my last, for the doctor had warned me, first after the birth of the twins and then more strongly after Leesha came, that I would not be able to carry and deliver another child without risk of my life. I made no mention of such talk to my beloved, but was careful to recuperate for a long while after the difficult birth of the twins and was careful for quite some time after that.

With Lucy (who died in cradle) coming in '98, Nate in '99, Simeon in 1800, Christian in '01, and then the twins being so difficult in '03, it did seem prudent to recoup.

After the birth of Leesha in '07, the doctor saw fit to talk to Zach himself.

Never have I seen that man of mine in such a state, so very angry with me. He will usually give in to my whims with a laugh and a well-placed swat, but on that day, I saw fury in his eyes, and to me he would not speak, that day or the next.

Finally I could bear his shunning no longer, and when I heard him from the other room asking Sister Rose how I and the new babe faired, I rose from my bed and stepped haltingly into his view, the babe in my upraised arms, asking did he not love the beautiful new daughter I had given him, and falling into a fit of weeping. There was a wetness on my limbs, and Rose grabbed the baby as my head began to swim.

I remember babbling as Zach swept me up and carried me back to the bed about how sorry I was not to have been honest with him and swearing that I would never keep the most incon-sequential thing from him again in this life, if he would but for-give me and love me again, because if I had lost his love, I could not bear it. He barked to Rose to send for the doctor and spoke to me then, tenderly and in my ear, telling me how I could never lose his love no matter what foolishness I might get up to, unless, of course, I managed to kill myself, for on that point he remained adamant that he would never forgive me.

Well, enough about me. Obviously, I recovered. Another time I will tell you how Elijah came to be.

Thank you for the sample of rose hip you sent in your last post. The twins, once they knew what to look for, came back with a bucket full. You give me such useful information. Acorns for buttons! I never would have thought. You have twice my imagination, Ellie Mae. I long to see you again, but for now this post and the presence of my boys with you will have to suffice.

Look after them for me, friend.

Yours, Libby

P.S. Did the apples ever ripen? I dreamed of apples last night: pies and tarts and all manner of pastries. Twilight descends, and I lose the light. Goodbye for now.

Ellie Mae refolded her friend's letter and placed it carefully in the bottom of her hatbox. Then she took up her quill to continue on with her own missive, in order to have it finished before Zack left at first light to return home the following morning…

Your Nate has made lots of new friends here. Especially my nephew Willie of a like age. Willie is much shorter than Nate. And with a mop of red curls. Makes quite a site when he stands by that 6-foot towhead of yours. Willie is a prankster, he is. And Nate did seem to take to his jokes more than we all do.

Why that nephew of mine once whitewashed my man Harvey's black horse, if you can credit that. I do not think Willie ever knew how close he come to getting the tar beat out of him that time. Harvey does have a temper. Only thing I could think to do was strike a bargain of my own with the old devil on what it would take for him to forget the whole thing. Like I did not know what that might be. Men! They ain't hard to figure. Whole thing was worth it just to see the look on Harvey's face when he laid eyes on that white horse out in Blackie's stall. I do believe he first thought it was a ghostie standing there. His mouth dropped open and he got right pale.

Men and their ways. They do try a woman sorely. Course your Zach looks to be a different kind of character all together. Never met his like in these parts. I can tell you that plain. Such manners! He made me feel like the queen of Sheba at my own table with all his praise over my stew. I reckon he was powerful hungry after all day hunts. But he did not have to take on so in front of Harvey. I know I ain't heard the end of it yet.

You are right about that Levi of yours. He will do anything. I saw him set a bucket on his head while Harvey's Theodore stood a short piece away holding up a gun. Theodore was looking over his shoulder shifty like. So I hustled over to see what mischief they was up to. Sure enough, Theodore was just raising up the gun. Seems they had a dare going. Theodore aimed to shoot the bucket off Levi's head.

I did not waste time talking to that Theodore. Instead I hollered—Levi Howard, get that bucket off your head this instant or I will have your pa box your ears! At that second I wished I knew your boy's middle name to make sure he took me serious.

Well the bucket hit the ground and all I saw of that boy was a streak heading to the barn. Theodore acted all casual like and spit over his shoulder. I swear, sometimes I want to back hand that boy. I found our men folk and told my tale. Much good as I figured it to do. About what I thought. Harvey looked all casual like and said something about boys being boys. Then spit over his shoulder. Zach went off looking for his son. He did appear like a man about to box some ears.

Theodore. What went wrong with that boy, I can not rightly say. But mothering him is a trial. He just turned 13 and looks big for his age. But his daddy treats him like a man already growed. Though most times he still acts like a child. The moods you note of your Christian can be nothing more than a hard age for him. With Theodore, I have seen it over all my time here at Harvey's. More worrisome to me is seeing how that boy would rather break something down than build it up. Even the dogs keep out of his path. But there is no talking to that father of his about any misdeeds nor sneaking or thieving done by his one and only son. Harvey will not hear of it. Theodore tells his pa that I made it all up to get him into trouble. Then Harvey will give me the devil, if you can credit that.

You may not take to this, but I will tell you who your boy Nate looks a pair with, and that is my Johannah. She is a big girl. Used to hard work and rough ways. The right stuff for a farm wife. And at 15, she is itching to get a start on life. When she looked at Nate, she got these big cow eyes. He did not seem at all taken with her. But I better leave one eye and one ear open tonight, or I fear she will be slipping out our new door.

Yes, I did get one at last.

Now that Simeon of yours is a real looker. I think he had a hankering for my Katrina, as she did for him. He is so dark and acts so much like his pa, don't he? He and Katrina kept giving each other the eye, but nary a word passed betwixt them two.

To speak the truth I did not hardly see a thing of that Christian. He barely come inside long enough to eat.

I guess the men done right well with their hunting. They harvested a pile of critters. We quartered the deers and bears. Will render the bear grease tomorrow. We just kept the hind quarters and the backstraps of the venison and will feed the rest to the dogs and pigs. Harvey says the big cats ain't worth fooling with. We have a heap of hides to flesh out and salt down now.

Do not know if I am up to the task of curing them. It is a most odorous chore. A Indian woman south of here does curing for folks. She sends back the softest buckskins in these parts. Dry deerskin is worth 12 and a half cents a pound for barter goods. But cured buckskin goes for twice that much. And it will bring real cash money!

Harvey wears buckskin britches most days for work. They hold up like iron in these environs which is a blessing. Only trouble is they get over-warm in hot weather. I tried making a skirt from buckskin once. Ended up being so heavy I could hardly move let alone work in it. Gave up that idea right quick. Now I know why them Injun women wear skimpy dresses. Too heavy to carry round a proper one.

The apples did finally come on. Even with this strange year of so much cold. I swear we had a frost every month of summer. Who could believe such a thing? Seems we ended up with nigh on to the only fruit in these parts. We waited a powerful long time to pick them, too. Got 10 bushels off one tree and 8 bushels off the other. We shared some with my sister Edie and her boys. You recall as I mentioned she is midwife in these parts.

We shared apples with my little brother Jonathan, and with my boy Jason and his wife Mary Sue. Got to watch out for that little grandbaby of mine. Miss Josie. See she gets plenty of hearty nutriment.

Also gave half a bushel of apples each to our nearest nabors round about Justice when I done some other swapping with my sorghum brooms. Just made me up a new batch of them brooms.

First off that would be the Baileys as I have mentioned before. Luther and Netta. Did I tell that Netta had her a little girl? Name of Rosanna. Cute little thing, too. I did not go to the Baileys myself but sent over my trade goods with Lucy Jarvis. She and Henry live close by the Baileys. So Lucy give me some of Netta's bees wax candles what they already swapped for and took one of my brooms for her. That is cuz I do not have a half a day to waste on Netta's prattle.

I got some of Lucy's soap in trade, too. She makes the best in these parts. I think Lucy will be the next to pop. Mark my words. Though there has been no mention of any baby yet.

There is also Frank and Emma Putnam. Emma has a loom and does weaving for folks. Whenever I get enough yarn ready for a sizable piece of cloth she weaves it up for me. In trade I give her some wool to keep for her own. She is childless and near to my own age. Her husband Frank has but one good eye.

Then there is the Guthries with their daughter Clara. She is sweet on my nephew Tom. But he is one who needs to be told what he thinks. And Clara has yet to tell him. Traded for some of Winnie Guthrie's cup cheese.

The last family was the Harrisons with their little Ben. Now Jeremy Harrison was mixed up in the trouble that I have yet to speak of. As was my brother Jonathan.

Guess I am dancing round it cause I do not want you to get all scared and pack up to go back East. But I know your boys will be full of the story. So let me just say that bears most always run away from people. Not at them. Except for Frank Putnam with the one good eye wounded this one.

To make a long story short the varmint charged Jeremy Harrison and my brother Jonathan shot it dead. But not before it took a swipe at Jeremy's face. Your Zach stitched him up good as new.

I was glad to see that bear took down. He is the one with that chewed off ear. The one what killed my good buck sheep last spring. They say that if you keep pigs handy the bears will leave sheep alone. They hanker after the taste of pork over mutton. But this particular bruin seemed over fond of my sheep. I got a good look at him back then. Only wished I had me a gun handy to shoot him when I had the chance. Then Jeremy would not be hurting like he is today.

To top the whole thing off, I have no way to get my ewes bred this fall. Leastwise not till that lamb grows up to breedin age. The young one what Harvey paid down on, up there in them Fire Lands this past spring.

I am so wore out after this long day that my eyes are starting to cross on me. This candle has burned clean down to a nub. I got to get up before dawn to get all these men fed. So yours can get on the road back to you. I will keep thinking on ways that you and me can meet up again, Libby. Mean times let us keep on writing. Please write back soon as you can. Before winter sets in dead wicked and closes down the roads betwixt us.

The dark days are not my favorite time. But I do get a rest from all the garden chores then. Just sit and spin till my hands get sore and I have to stop. This winter I can write to you. If I can find anything more to write on. I have wrote this letter down on the last paper out of my hat box. The paper round it is worth more to me than the fool hat. The only thing my ma sent to me out here from Penna. If I had my druthers I would ruther have the good money she paid for the sorry thing. I could go out into the woods and gather up feathers and nuts and a bird's nest. Surely make up something more sightly for free of charge. Compliments of Mother Nature. But they say it is the thought that counts. And Harvey says that I would gripe if I was hanged with a new rope. Well I sure enough would if that blasted hat was on my head at the time.

There, my prattle has run dry. I hope to hear from you real soon.

Your friend, Ellie Mae Thompson

P.S. I will send what apples as your men can carry. Give the children a hearty boost going into winter.

P.S. Again. I sure hope you will continue on with that story you promised to finish on Elijah. I got right taken up with your tale and could not believe what you picked for a stopping point.

Chapter 5

After The Hunt
October 1816

"Hello the house!" Willie called, riding up to the Harrison's cabin early the next morning. "Anybody alive in there?"

Amanda stuck her head out the door. "Willie, is that you?" The door fell shut behind her when she stepped outside. "Am I ever glad to see you."

Willie dismounted and tied his horse to the porch rail. "How's Jeremy doin' this mornin'?"

"His face is all puffed up. I know it must hurt him awfully bad, Willie, but he won't let on. I don't know what to do to ease his pain. I can't doctor the way your mama does."

"She figured as much. That's why she sent me over with this powder. Told me how to mix it up for Jeremy's face," he said, holding out a small, buckskin bag. "All I need is some hot water and a cup."

"I have water heating for tea. Come on in. Jeremiah will be glad you came." She stepped back inside. Willie followed close behind.

"Who's here?" Jeremy asked, from the bedroom behind the fireplace. He sat on the edge of the bed pulling on his socks, trying to see through eyes puffed nearly shut. "That you, Willie?"

"Sure enough. Ma sent me over with this miracle-cure powder to get that face of yours healed up so you'll look real pretty again," he said, setting the bag on the small trunk beside the bed. He took off his wool jacket, hung it on a peg, and headed for the wash stand between the two rooms.

"She told me, 'You be sure and wash up proper, 'fore you go messin' with this medicine, you hear me, Willie?' Ma never did think I could do anything to suit her," he said, working up a good lather in the basin. "She couldn't come herself, 'cause she had to go off to help birth another baby down south of here. Reckon she'll be gone two or three days."

"Who's having a baby?" Amanda asked.

"New folks settled down near the river. Name's Yeats, I think. The Coulters sent for Ma late last night. Said this new lady needed help, so Ma high-tailed it to Perrysville right after dark. Gave me strict orders to get this powder over here at first light. She said you needed to put some on your face right away to keep that wound from turning septic."

"I hope it can take the swelling down some. Awful hard to see with both eyes puffed up like this," Jeremy said. He tried to stand, but he sank back down quickly when a wave of pain and light-headedness hit as he changed altitude.

In front of the fireplace in the cabin's main room, Mandy pulled the kettle off the coals and carried it to the table. She poured a big mug clear full. "Here's hot water, Willie," she said, taking it around into the bedroom. "What else can I do to help?"

"Would it be asking too much to cook me up some breakfast? I headed out first thing after chores. Didn't take time to eat."

"Of course I'll feed you," she said.

He picked up the pouch and poured a small portion of its contents into the mug of water. "You got a spoon I can stir this up with?" he called. "I need a clean cloth, too—for dipping in this potion."

Amanda brought him a spoon, then went to the other trunk sitting at the end of the bed to take out a clean handkerchief. "Will this do?"

"Perfect," said Willie. "Now I have to dip it in this juice, squeeze it out tight, and lay it across your face, Jeremy. Might feel kind of hot, but Ma said to put it on as hot as you can stand it. Something about drawing out the puss so's it won't fester so bad." Jeremy winced when Willie laid the cloth across his face. "Too hot?"

"No, it'll be fine. Kind of a shock, is all," Jeremy answered. "I think I better lay back for a spell, though," he said, swinging his feet on top of the feather tick.

"When that cools off, I need to dip it and make it hot all over again," Willie said. "Ma said to keep doing that till this stuff cools down. Then you're supposed to drink up what's left."

Jeremy tried to nod, but the pain of moving his head stopped him. He raised his hand instead, to acknowledge Willie's directions.

"I'm supposed to leave the rest of this pouch so's you can mix up more juice and put it on his face at least three times today, Amanda. Ma said by tonight, the swelling ought to be down considerable. His face shouldn't hurt so bad, if you do what she says."

"I'm grateful for your help, Willie." Amanda smiled, then she left the bedroom to work on his breakfast.

"Ma's coming over to check that face herself, once she gets back from Perrysville. She don't trust no one to doctor right, you know," Willie said, shaking his head. "You should of heard her when she found out Zach sewed you up. Wouldn't believe any man could sew a body up as good as she can."

"He did a fine job," said Jeremy. "Guess we'll see how fine after it's all healed."

"Ma wants to take the stitches out next week and judge for herself," Willie said, taking the cloth off Jeremy's face and dipping it into the hot liquid once again.

Amanda moved to the bedroom doorway and called, "I'll have breakfast ready real quick, Willie. I hope you like flapjacks." She moved back around the fireplace to stir up the bowlful of batter and drop cakes on the griddle. "Jeremiah says I do make good flapjacks," she called.

"Best in the whole township," Jeremy piped up from the bed. He tried to sit up again, but quickly returned to his prone position. "Reckon I better wait to do my chores till after I get some food in my belly. I feel kind of woozy."

"Don't you fuss about chorin'. I aim to do your milkin' before I head back home," Willie said. "Orders from Ma. 'Sides, somebody else's work is always more in-ter-es-tin' than your own."

Amanda busied herself by the fire, dipping batter, then flipping the cakes when bubbles began to show through. Before long, the aroma of flapjacks filled the cabin, and Mandy had a hot stack all ready to eat.

Willie replaced the hot cloth on Jeremy's face two more times while Amanda prepared breakfast, and now the medicinal infusion had cooled sufficiently to drink.

"Think you can sit back up now?" Willie asked.

Jeremy eased his way into a sitting position and swung his legs off the bed. "I think that stuff made a difference already," he said, gingerly touching the good side of his face, which was almost as puffy as the injured side.

Willie handed him the mug, and Jeremy drank down what was left of the lukewarm potion.

"Wheeew! I'd make a face after drinking that, if my face was working right," he said with a chuckle. "You know, I do feel some steadier. Maybe with a little food in my belly, I'll be able to do my own chores after all."

"Better not. Ma'll have my hide, if she finds out I didn't do what she sent me to," Willie grinned. "'Sides, I'm in no hurry to go home. Nothing there but more work."

Amanda placed the plateful of hot cakes on the table and called the men to come and eat. Jeremy and Willie came around from the bedroom just as Little Ben began to stir on the blanket where he lay by the fire. Amanda picked up the baby, raising him over her shoulder. He wiggled so, she could hardly hold on to him.

"Y'all go ahead and eat while I tend to Little Ben. He's soaked clear through," she said, taking him into the bedroom where she kept the clean baby clothes.

Jeremy and Willie pulled chairs up to the table and dug into the plate of hot cakes. By the time they'd finished eating, Jeremy's color had improved considerably. He pushed back from the table and proceeded to pull on his boots.

"What do you think you're doing?" Willie asked.

"I'm going out to the barn and tend to Bertha," Jeremy answered. "Don't bother arguing, 'cause it won't do a bit of good. Fresh air's just what I need right now."

"Suit yourself, but you got no business climbing the mow to throw down hay," Willie answered. "Why, you're just plain lucky to be alive today."

"Shhhhh!" He stopped to listen intently. In a raspy whisper he said, "She doesn't know exactly what happened out there, and I don't aim to tell her, either."

From behind the fireplace divide they heard the sound of a soft lullaby, accompanied by the babble of a baby's gentle giggles.

My Dear Ellie Mae,

The apples were a wonderful gift! And thank you so for the hospitality to which you treated my family. I am grateful that you took special care of Levi, keeping him out of harm's way. He does require extra guidance. The boys made much ado over the bear incident, but Zach assures me they dramatize. I am glad that I did not see the creature nor the wounds inflicted myself, as I much prefer Zach's version and yours.

Nate was full of talk about his new friend Willie, but made no mention of any cow-eyed looks from any female, not that I expect he would tell his mother such a thing. I would not discourage Nate from such a direction, but neither would I offer encouragement too soon, as I intend to grow old day by day, not have it thrust upon me in the form of grandparent-hood tomorrow. (I am hoping that your new door creeks outrageously so that you would have been roused by any clandestine activities between the house and barn.)

You are right about Simeon, though. He seemed overly quiet amid all the chatter of their homecoming, then suddenly blurted out that Katrina's laugh is like a bubbling brook. He turned quite red at what he had said, his brothers having a great laugh at his expense. On occasion they look at him and let out what they feel is a young girl's laughter reminiscent of a bubbling brook. In truth they sound like braying jackasses and raving lunatics.

Young love! It takes me back these many years. When I was that age, a young man by the name of Royce, the son of an old friend of Mother's, was calling on me. Zach always seemed to be passing by whenever we sat on the porch swing and would shout out to Royce to thank him for taking such good care of me, referring to me as his intended.

Since Zach had barely spoken to me, I found this behavior quite vexing. The longer he carried on with it, the more egotistical I regarded him.

When he asked Royce one autumn day to stand up with him at our nuptials, why I saw a patch of dark red in front of my eyes, and before I knew that I had opened my mouth, I heard my own voice screaming at him to never speak to me again with his ridicule and bad jokes. He looked very solemn then and walked away, so I thought that would be the end of it.

Within a month, Royce sent me a note saying that he could no longer see me, as he and Zach had engaged in a contest for my hand and Royce had lost. He did not mention what the contest entailed, but I sent a note back saying that if he were thick-skulled enough to have engaged in such a thing without thought to consult me about my sentiments in the matter, it was probably for the best, because I might slap his face if again we did meet. I learned later that the dolts had jumped into the icy river in December, and that Zach had stayed in the longer, making him the "winner."

I now realized Zach was in earnest in his attentions, but by this time I was so annoyed over being treated as barter goods that I refused to see or speak to him. This went on for some months until the summer's charity auction.

I prepared a picnic basket (which included some of my prize-winning quince jelly, by the by), as did all the young ladies, including my sister, Rose. The bachelors assembled on the day of the auction to begin the bidding. There were a few lively bidding contests, though it was all in fun and for charity, of course. But generally it was already known who would end up picnicking with whom that afternoon.

When Rose's basket came up, can you imagine my consternation when Zach Howard began bidding on it? I gave my sister a hard look, but she seemed as surprised as I. I looked daggers at him, but his smile looked as egotistical as ever it did. My basket was won by Garth Tallmadge, and Garth suggested that we make it a foursome. So that is how the four of us came to travel together to a meadow with a few big shade trees. (It is the prettiest place—stream running through with sycamores lining its banks.)

Now, as you may have guessed, Ellie Mae, those two young men had plotted together, but all my jealousy allowed me to see was that Zach and Rose sat closer than I thought seemly and spoke in a tone just low enough that I could not make out what they said, as we all rode together to the meadow. Garth did irritate me by making conversation that served only to impede my eavesdropping for most of the trip.

As we lay out the cloth and table service, my sister told me that Zach wanted to spend the afternoon with me, so that I might get to know him better to correct the false impression I seemed to have of him, but he was afraid if he forced me into his company by bidding on my basket, that I would be resentful and all would come to naught.

She also saw fit to point out that, although he was right on that score, I was now angry with him for not bidding on it. She added that she should probably tell the poor fool that he could not win me no matter what he might do and so should move on to some more tractable female.

Her words did sting me with their truth, so I made an effort to be somewhat polite throughout our meal, and what I saw surprised me. Zach seemed in earnest and somewhat shy. Our party did have a very enjoyable afternoon, which was the first of many, I might add. During the next winter, we ice skated and went on sleigh rides, taking off our gloves and holding hands under the warm blankets.

On the first nice day of the following spring, we all revisited our picnic spot, though the ground was still too damp with rain for sitting. It was alive with color, dogwoods in bloom. Zach took me on a walk apart from Rose and Garth to a certain spot beside the stream where the water was shallow and rippled noisily over the rocks (later he told me that this was so no one would hear if he stammered and stuttered, as he was that nervous).

There he asked me to be his wife, kneeling on the wet earth. I don't have to tell you what answer I gave. I still associate the smell of damp earth after a rain with that first kiss, and truth be known, I go outside and breath it in deeply to this day, getting that quivery feeling in the bottom of my stomach and a weakness through my limbs.

We arrived back at the buggy arm-in-arm to find Rose and Garth in an embrace. Upon seeing us, Rose ran up, grabbing my hands and asking if it was to be a double ceremony. We hurried home to tell Mother. We were wed in the garden that July by Reverend Posey. (I know that this was not the story promised, but this one had to come first for the other to be understood, so I hope you are not too perturbed with me.)

I had thought that Rose and I would always live on the same street, we with our babies born in the same years (her Caitlin was born the same year as our Lucy, with Nate and her Caleb being of an age, as are Simeon and her Cole). She has written me that her boys want to know if their cousins have shot a bear, but that I, under no circumstances, am to say yes and thus encourage them.

Rose says that she has not yet decided whether she will ever forgive Zach for bringing us to these Fire Lands. Her daughter Caitlin helps teach our young-lady students in my absence, her French being almost as fluent as mine. But Cait has never been able to do more than prick herself with a needle.

And then there is my baby sister Suzannah, innocent and sweet no matter what her age, embroidering a riot of blossoms on every linen in the house. Zan looks for me to show me her work, Rose says, so she plays the piano to soothe Zan at those times. It broke my heart to hear that. Had I not so many small ones of my own, I might have brought Zannah with us, but she does dote on Caitlin so.

I just hope that Rose meant Zannah looks from room to room for me, not at the house down the street nor in the city. We lost that poor lamb once when naughty Cait let her out of the garden gate. They were both seven then (as would have been my Lucy had she lived—Rose and I and Mother all having given birth that same year). Zach and Garth searched for hours in the rain. Thank goodness my niece had sense enough to find shelter for them in a stable until the storm had past. Then niece came leading her simple auntie home by the hand, recalcitrant (stubborn as ever and not one whit sorry).

What haunts my thoughts is that the girls are of an age, eighteen, and beauties both, one dark and one fair. I fear that the world Zan needs guarding against now is the world of men —those who would not understand her condition of mind and those who would not care. I pray that Caitlin does not still leave open the garden gate.

Zach and the boys have been splitting more logs into planks and tinkering with a design for stacked beds to give us additional space in this small cabin for the winter. My Zach talks of wood in his sleep. After working so many years in the lumbering mill back East, he cannot bear to burn all these board feet of hard woods as he clears the land. Some of it is a necessity, and he doesn't mind burning the worthless wood that gives us the black salts for gunpowder and lye for trade. But as it burns he talks of hard woods and soft woods and tries to tell me what purpose each kind of log would best suit. What he can't bring himself to burn, he is drying. I know not what we will ever do with it all, but he and the boys have split many logs for faster drying and are waiting for colder weather to split it into planks for flooring (something about frosty weather making it easier to split, I believe).

He and the boys "threw up a shed." Their latest project is cloaked in secrecy, as they work out behind that shed while Levi keeps watch for any nosy girls who might come around. Zach will not tell me what they are up to, but he says quietly in my ear that it will make a new woman of me. I ask him, "what, begging your pardon, is wrong with the old woman?" to which I get a laugh and a swat in passing.

Well, my friend, it is getting late and needs must I bring this epistle to a close. Stay warm, and write me when you can. I fear the winter may be a long one with little news to break the monotony.

Your faithful friend,

Libby

Chapter 6

Fire
November 1816

"What am I supposed to do with this lard now, Jeremiah," Amanda called out the door.

"Hold on, Mandy. I'll be right there," Jeremy hollered back, as he cleaned butchering tools out behind the shed.

"Is this stuff supposed to smoke so much?"

"Holy Moses, Mandy, don't let it burn!" He dropped the hog scraper and ran for the house. Mandy held the door open as he rounded the corner and made a bee-line for the fireplace. He grabbed a cloth to shield his hand from the hot bail and swung the pot away from the fire in one, smooth move.

Mandy stood aside, ringing her hands. "I ruined it, I just know I did."

"It's all right," he said, giving the lard a stir. "I don't think it's ruined. The cracklings just stuck to the bottom. We caught it in the nick of time."

"I can't do anything right." She sank to a chair by the fire.

"But it'll be fine, Mandy. You didn't ruin this batch of lard. It'll make great pies after it hardens."

"I ruin pie crust, too."

Jeremy pulled Amanda up from the chair and gave her a big bear-hug. "Mandy, my little yellow bird, when are you ever gonna believe you're doing a good job? You've learned so much already. I'm proud of you, you know."

"Really? You're proud of me?"

He leaned down and gave her a big, sloppy kiss. "Yes. I'm very proud of you."

"But I've foozled so many things. My soap won't harden the way it's supposed to. I can't get butter to turn out right, and I can never–"

"I've gotten kind of fond of that soft soap of yours. It's real nice. The trick to butter's all in the temp'ature, though. You'll catch on soon enough."

"What about that chicken? You can't tell me I didn't botch that up royally."

"I have to admit, no one could have eaten that chicken. But it was the first one you ever cleaned and cooked. How were you supposed to know you had to gut her after you plucked her clean, if no one ever showed you how?"

"I tried so hard, Jeremiah. I wanted to surprise you with roast chicken when you got back from hunting. I really did try."

"You surprised me, all right. But don't you see, Mandy, that's why I'm so proud of you. Because you are trying to learn all these things. You're doing lots of them already, too. Why, I'd put your flapjacks up against anyone's in this county."

"They don't turn out too badly, do they."

"I'd say you've got flapjacks mastered."

"You must get awful tired of griddle cakes."

"Have you heard me complain? You keep my stomach full, don't you? You've worked hard to learn to cook. "

"I'm not very good at it."

"Well the least I can do is eat whatever you put in front of me. Besides, I like your flapjacks… even if we do have 'em every day."

"Almost every day," she said, stroking his scarred cheek softly.

Muffled cries came from the bedroom, and Amanda started around the partition.

"Let me get him up," Jeremy said. "With all this butchering the last two days, I haven't seen much of the little fella." Jeremy strode past Amanda into the bedroom, where he found Little Ben standing at one corner of his bunk-crib, shaking the sides with all his might. When he saw Jeremy, his face broke into a big smile.

"Well, hello there, Little Ben." Ben got so excited at seeing his papa, he let go of the sides and plopped down backward onto his chubby bottom. He wasn't very steady on his feet yet; at eleven months, he'd just learned to stand alone. Ben let out a big squeal, and he giggled when Jeremy scooped him up and swung him above his head. "Aren't you full of vinegar this afternoon!" Jeremy cocked Ben on his hip and carried him back around to the main room.

"Look at this bright-eyed rascal, Mandy. He sure is glad to see his papa today." Jeremy tickled Ben under the chin, and the baby gave out another squealing giggle. "I'll bet this little guy's hungry, aren't you, Ben? Want a nice pig's foot to gnaw on?"

"Oh, Jeremiah, give me that boy! Pig's foot, indeed!" Amanda reached up for Ben, but he clung to Jeremy's arm when she tried to get a hold on him.

"Guess he missed me. Boy, you sure got some grip, there, son. Won't be long till you're big enough to help your papa with butchering."

"Pa-Pa," Ben mimicked.

Jeremy sat down by the fireplace and put Ben on his knee; Little Ben giggled when Jeremy bounced him up and down. "Look, Mandy. He's a born horseman, if I ever saw one."

Amanda opened the door to the porch, leaned out to snatch up that morning's pail of milk, and quickly slammed the door shut behind her. "I don't know how anyone can like this kind of weather. It's cold enough to freeze your breath out there. Look. This milk's frozen all around the edges!"

"It's not winter yet and already you're complaining about the cold. What are you gonna do when it really turns bitter?"

"I'll never get used to this climate," she muttered, pouring a little of the milk into a small pan. She began to warm it, and herself, by the fire. After a few minutes she stuck her little finger in the milk to test its temperature. "Just about right." She poured the warm milk into a little wooden mug with handles on either side that Jeremy had made for Ben after Amanda's milk dried up.

"Here you are, sweetheart. Papa will help you take a drink, won't you, Jeremiah." Amanda handed the mug toward Jeremy, but Ben managed to grab one handle and pull, spilling most of the milk all over himself. He coughed and sputtered in surprise, as Jeremy rescued the cup. "Oh, just look at what you did now, you little imp," Amanda scolded. "You're wet all through. Now I'll have to change your clothes all over again."

"Might as well let him drink the rest of it first," Jeremy said, handing the cup back to Ben. At that moment Lucky ambled through the bedroom door and began to lap spilled milk from the floor. "Looks like the Lucky cat's taking care of that mess."

With smacking and sucking noises, Ben finished the last of the milk in his cup. Then Amanda lifted Ben from Jeremy's lap and held him at arm's length to avoid getting herself milk-soaked. She carried him back into the bed-room, sat him on the big bed, and began to change his clothes.

"You think you can finish the lard up by yourself, Mandy?" Jeremy hollered from the other room. "I want to take some of this fresh pork over to the Hawkins' place before it gets dark."

"Go ahead. I'll tend to the lard after I change Ben."

"You'll be sure to get it dipped into the crocks before it thickens, won't you?"

"Go on, Jeremiah. I'll do just fine. Give Mrs. Hawkins my best, won't you?"

"Don't worry about milking Bertha. I'll be home by chore time." Jeremy took his coat down from the door peg and stepped out into the brisk air.

Back in the bedroom, Ben lay trying to chew on his toes while Amanda struggled to dress him. "You are the squirmin'est li'l thing. How am I supposed to get these leggin's on if you keep putting your feet in your mouth, you little dickens?" She leaned over to tickle his tummy, and he grabbed for the braid twisted on top of her head, pulling it loose. "Now look what you did." Amanda pushed the hair back as best she could while she finished dressing him.

After warming some more milk and fixing a little cornmeal pap, Amanda fed Ben, then put him back in his crib. "You sit in here and play nice, now, while I go finish up that lard." She handed Ben a little stuffed rabbit she'd made from fabric scraps, and it went straight to his mouth.

On her way out of the bedroom, she paused in front of the mirror to fix her hair. Lingering a few minutes on tip-toe, she stared at her slightly distorted image. "If only Grandmother Bently could see me now," she whispered to herself. "She'd be so proud."

Amanda drifted back to another day, and another life…

Late June, 1815
Charleston, South Carolina

She stood on the dock, waiting to board the north-bound ship for Philadelphia, Pennsylvania. "Amanda Jane, I want you to have this," Great Grandmother Bently said in her no-non-sense manner, thrusting a small, oval box into Amanda's gloved hand. "Lord knows I don't put much stock in showy things, but He's the only One knows if we'll ever see you again." She gave Amanda's hand a squeeze. "I want you to have this brooch. It belonged to my mother, and to her mother before her." Grand-mother gave her a crushing hug. "Be sure to keep it safe." She turned and stomped away, completely ignoring her grandson, Amanda's father, who stood shoulder to shoulder with the captain of the ship, busily counting gold coins into the man's outstretched hand.

Amanda swallowed the lump in her throat and willed away the threatening tears. Before she tucked the little, black box into her reticule, she cracked the lid to take a quick peek inside.

A large, ivory brooch, set in gold with a large, drop pearl at its base, rested upon a bed of Spanish moss, attached to a string of amber beads. She snapped the box closed, dropped it into her handbag, and drew the drawstrings tight.

Without a backward glance, she hurried up the gangway and disappeared onto the crowded deck…

…Amanda's hand flew to her throat, reaching for the heirloom reminder of the life she'd left behind. But the spot where her brooch normally perched remained empty this day. With such messy butchering goings on, she'd left it snug in its tiny box, on the shelf above the bedstead. She tucked the wisps of auburn hair back into her twisted braid, re-securing it on top of her head. Gazing more closely into the wavy reflection, she suddenly caught a hint of her mother's smile. Abruptly she turned away and headed around to the fireplace.

Amanda had taken so much time feeding and playing with Little Ben, that the lard had already begun to thicken. "I'll just have to warm it back up, so I can dip it out," she said aloud. She eased the kettle back over the fireplace and poked at the dying embers, trying to coax a little more heat from them. "This will never do. I need more wood."

Amanda wrapped her shawl around her shoulders and hurried outside, but she didn't linger outdoors any longer than absolutely necessary. Grabbing an armload of wood, she scurried back into the cabin, letting the heavy, wooden door slam shut behind her. "I'll never get used to this climate," she said through chattering teeth.

As she walked over to the fireplace, she stepped on something soft. Startled, she hopped backward. "Oh, Lucky, why do you always do that?" The proud, calico cat stood at her feet, guarding a dead mouse, waiting for a pat of approval and a word of praise. Amanda backed away from the mouse and dropped her load of wood near the fire. Although the sight of a mouse no longer sent her into one of her cleaning frenzies, she still couldn't bring herself to touch one—not even a dead one.

"That's a good kitty, Lucky." Amanda hurried to the door and opened it a crack. "Now get that thing out of here." By now, the cat knew this procedure quite well. Lucky picked up her prize and trotted out the door.

Amanda shivered again, slamming the door tight. Then she poked up the fire and added all the wood she'd brought inside. In a matter of minutes she had a roaring blaze under the kettle of lard. She stood rubbing her hands, trying to absorb the heat.

Since the Harrison's fireplace stood in the center of their cabin, it made a divider of sorts. Most settlers normally laid up a chimney on the north or west side of a cabin. But Amanda had begged Jeremy to put theirs in the center, so the small structure would seem a little more like two rooms. Since she'd come from a twenty-room townhouse in the heart of Charleston, he granted her wish to try and make this cabin more bearable.

The loft above had plank flooring over half the cabin's area, which made for a low-ceilinged, storage space above the bedroom, leaving the beams above the living area open to the roof. From those beams hung strings of beans, onions, apple rings, and other foodstuffs drying for use over the winter. Jeremy had closed off the east wall next to the fireplace below, further separating the bedroom into a private space of its own.

Leaning against the fireplace at that divider stood a ladder leading to the storage loft. Amanda climbed up to retrieve the crocks stored there among the bags of potatoes and seed corn, the piles of pumpkins and squash. She shuffled things around and finally located the crocks, sitting inside Ben's outgrown cradle.

Below, the fire burned so hot that the lard began to spatter onto the flames every now and again. It continued to boil harder, causing the fire to blaze up ever higher. Amanda panicked when she looked down and saw flames jump out toward the hearth rug. In her hurry to get down the ladder, she knocked two crocks off the edge of the loft and sent them crashing to the floor below. A wave of nausea seized her when the acrid odor of burning fat reached her nose; she stood a moment, holding tight to the ladder until the queasiness passed, trying to regain her equilibrium.

"Oh no," she gasped, looking down at the shattered crockery. "Jeremiah's going to skin me alive when he finds out I broke his mama's crocks." She glanced at the lard bubbling over the edge of the pot and hurried down the ladder.

Scurrying to the fireplace, she grabbed the pot's bail without thinking about how hot it had become. As soon as she touched it, she jerked her hand away, setting the pot to swinging.

The instant it swung forward, hot lard sloshed out and caught fire before it even hit the floor. She tried to pull the pot away from the fire, but burning lard flowed across the floor, catching the hem of her skirt on fire, too.

She slapped and stomped, trying to put out the flames with her hands. Then she saw Ben's milk-soaked gown hanging over the chair, and she grabbed it to slap at the flames around her feet. This time, she managed to extinguish the smoldering fabric. After she had her skirt under control, she looked up to see that the lard had already run across the puncheon floor to the bedroom doorway. The curtains hanging there to act as a room divider were completely engulfed in flames.

"Ben!" Amanda tried to run through the flaming doorway to reach her baby on the other side, but before she could get through, the curtains fell, causing a swoosh of sparks as a wall of fire rose up in front of her. By that time, the clothes hanging on pegs around the bedroom wall had burst into flame, and they, in turn, ignited pitch in the loft planking above. She heard Little Ben crying in terror.

"I'm coming, Ben!" she screamed.

She looked around for something to throw over herself in order to break through the wall of flames. All she could find was her shawl. She grabbed it, dunked it in the water bucket sitting beside the door, and wrapped it around her head and shoulders. As Amanda tried to push through the flames now engulfing the whole fireplace wall, her skirts caught again. She slapped at the flames with her wet shawl, and the loft floor began to groan.

Little Ben let out a piercing scream.

"My baby! I'm coming!" Again she tried to break through the flames, but the loft floor let out a loud crack, forcing her to back away. It came crashing down.

"Noooo! Little Ben!"

Amanda ran outside to the cistern pump, which stood be-tween the house and barn. She worked the handle with all her might, trying to fill the bucket underneath the spout. She pumped and pumped, but the bucket sat there, bone dry.

In her terror and haste, Amanda forgot to prime the pump.

* * * * *

Jeremy had just reached the Hawkins' place when he saw an unusual amount of smoke rising from the direction of his own farm. He turned, spurring his horse into a gallop, and arrived back home just in time to see the roof of his cabin cave into the ball of flames.

He found Amanda with hands blistered, still standing at the cistern, pumping into an empty bucket.

Chapter 7

After the Fire

One hand badly burned and bandaged, Amanda huddled in the corner wrapped in a blanket. She picked at it with the fingers of her unbandaged hand, never noticing Netta and the other women bustling around the roomy Bailey cabin, as they chattered about the past week's news and prepared a dinner for the work crew of men.

Every time the fire cracked or popped, Amanda jumped, but she never uttered a word to anyone; she simply sat and stared into the fire with an empty gaze.

"Do you think she'll snap out of it pretty soon?" Netta asked. "Lord knows I've tried everything I can think of to get her to talk to me."

"Hard to tell," said Ma Hawkins while she kneaded bread dough.

"She's been like that ever since–" Netta caught herself and stopped short. "She's been like that for days now. I tried talking to her. My goodness, I tried. But it's like talking to Luther sometimes, only worse, if you know what I mean. Why, that man can sit stock still, staring at the fire like that for hours at a time, not even hearing what I say to him. Can you imagine?" Netta stopped long enough to snatch a breath. "But it's been five days since... since the, ah... accident. You'd think she'd snap out of it pretty soon, now, wouldn't you? Why in the world she was ever rendering lard indoors is way beyond me. Jeremy ought to know better. How could he let her tend to such a smelly business indoors? I ask you, how could he?"

But Netta didn't give anyone a chance to answer. "She's just got to get on with living, forheavensakes. There's work to be done, and she does have a husband to take care of, after all."

Ma Hawkins interrupted before Netta had a chance to catch another breath and rattle on. "Far's I can see, that's one man don't need takin' care of." Always one to express herself in a short, no nonsense manner, Ma attacked the bread dough with a vengeance, almost punching it instead of kneading.

"That Jeremy is quite a man, don't you think Lucy?" Emma Putnam, up to her chubby elbows in flour, stood at the sideboard shaping pie dough. Emma may have been a trifle slow catching on to most things, but once she mastered a task, she put her entire being into its completion. Lucy Jarvis sat nearby peeling apples for the pies. She giggled and turned a bright shade of crimson. Though no one could call Lucy a pretty woman, the big-boned girl with large hands and feet, wide ears and a toothy smile had been told she was the kind of hard-working wife material any settler would welcome.

"He is a married man, Missus Putnam. Just remember that," scolded Ma.

"Oh, forheavensakes, Edie, don't be such a stick-in-the-mud. The only in-ter-estin' thing we got to talk about is men. You sure can't blame a girl for eyein' a handsome one when she sees him, now, can you?" said Ellie Mae, standing next to the fireplace adding potatoes to the stew pot.

"Course you can't. It's just human nature to look now and again." Netta jumped back into the conversation, as she stood at the table chopping turnips. "Too bad his face got all tore up like it did. It's healing up nice, though. If you look at him from his good side, you can hardly tell he ever had a run-in with a bear. He is still a mighty good-looking man."

Lucy giggled again. Her ungainly appearance didn't quite match the quick, easy blushes and giggles that escaped her. Yet people felt drawn to Lucy as soon as they made her acquaintance. She had a way of disarming folks and putting them at ease.

"Lucy, you take care you don't peel away too much of them apples," directed Ma. "They's mighty dear rations this season, what with this crazy weather we've had all year long, killin' so many crops."

"I can't see why Ellie even brought fruit to waste on a bunch of thankless men, if you ask me," grumped Winifred Guthrie, helping to peel the last of the precious apples. "You didn't ask me, but I'm-a-telling you just the same." Winifred had a way of spreading a wet blanket of doom-and-gloom wherever she went. "Oughtta keep 'em all hid away clean till spring, when children need a good dose of fruit to perk 'em up from winter doldrums. That's what I say."

Edith Hawkins slammed down the bread dough, as if in finalé. "There, that can rest a bit before makin' up loaves." She covered the flat lump with a piece of cotton ticking Netta used for a towel.

"Jeannette, you got any pun'kins I can put on to stew? Those men are gonna be awful hungry when they come back over here. This stew don't look like nearly enough to feed all them mouths."

"Oh, my, yes. We have loads of pun'kins this year. Why, my Luther says I grew the biggest pun'kin he ever did see. Can you imagine? I think he's proud of me. Says whenever he sees it, it reminds him of me. Isn't that sweet? And people say Luther's not romantic. I can't imagine why they say that, can you? Oh, I know he's awful quiet most times, and he can get real gruff after he's been gone for weeks at a stretch, but anybody would get grumpy after being alone out there in them woods for so long, now, don't you think?" She paused to breathe.

"The pun'kins?" Ma pointed to the door. "The men'll want to eat tonight?"

"I'm going, I'm going." Netta bounced her ample self toward the door, started out, then grabbed her shawl before hurrying into the brisk, November day. The sun peeked through snow clouds, lumbering by on a north-west wind. When Netta pushed open the door an icy gust blew into the cabin.

Amanda jumped at the blast of cold air, pulling the blanket more tightly around her tiny frame, shrinking further into the corner. She stared at the fireplace with a panic-stricken look. It had been five days since the fire, and she still hadn't uttered a word to a soul.

"Here they are." Netta blew back into the room, carrying two large pumpkins. One bounced on either hip as she kicked the door shut again. "Looks like it might snow, if it gets any colder." She handed one pumpkin to Ma and plopped the other on the floor beside the table sitting in the middle of the room. "These are just the little ones. Aren't they something, now?"

"What time do you suppose the men will be back?"

"Wouldn't you know, Lucy's the one asking about the men," Emma teased, pinching the edge of a pie crust. Lucy blushed again. "Here, these pies are ready," said Emma. "You want to put 'em in that fancy reflector thing of yours, Netta? I ain't sure I remember how you work that contraption."

"You can do it, Emma. It's not that hard. I need to tend to my Little Muffin."

"Do I just set 'em inside there, or what?"

"Scrape some coals out onto the hearthstone first. Then set the pies right on top of 'em and push that reflector up behind, close as you can get it. Oh, my, I can tell it's way past time for Rosanna to eat. Just look at the front of me!" Wet patches showed through the bodice of Netta's dress where milk had leaked from her ample bosom. "I do hate waking her up when she's asleep so sound. But I can't stand to wait another minute. My goodness, I believe I'd have enough milk to feed triplets. Can you imagine? Having triplets, now!"

Netta chattered away as she bounced to the other side of the room and leaned over the cradle. "Is my little sweetie-pie awake yet? Wake up, you little muffin... come on... wake up. It's time for you to eat, my little rosebud. Come to Mama. Let's fill up that little tummy of yours!"

Netta lifted the chubby bundle, slowly squirming awake. "There you are. Can you smile for all these nice ladies who came to help out today?" The baby let out a howl. "Well, is that any way to greet our neighbors?" The baby, crying louder and louder, finally worked her way up to a hearty wail.

"Oh, my, my, my, my, my! Hush sweetheart. It's all right. Mama's got just what you want." Netta jiggled the baby while she quickly unfastened the top buttons of her bodice, then plopped a breast into the baby's searching mouth. "There, that's better." The baby coughed and sputtered, as it seemed the abundant milk gush would nearly drown her. Finally, she settled down to a loud suckling, pacified for the time being.

"Isn't she just something?" Netta sat in a rocking chair near the cradle, rocking and jiggling as the baby smacked away. "I love this little rosebud to pieces. She's such a doll baby. We named her Rosanna after my grandmother, you know. But Luther just calls her Bubbles. He says the only things she's any good at is crying and eating and making bubbles. Isn't that cute? Bubbles! Your daddy adores his little Bubbles."

Netta tweaked the baby's cheek, and Bubbles let out a loud howl. "All right, all right. I'll leave you alone so you can eat." Netta's chatter obviously bothered the nursing baby, but it taxed Netta considerably to remain silent for very long. "Isn't she just something?" Netta stopped talking and rocked, trying to concentrate on Rosanna's dimpled face.

Emma Putnam didn't have any children, nor Lucy Jarvis, as of yet. Winifred Guthrie had only Clara living, nearly a woman now herself, and Ellie Mae's children were mostly grown, too—which is why these women came to help out on this particular day. At a normal cabin raising the whole community would turn out to work, children and all. Everyone would enjoy a big frolic upon its completion.

But this wasn't a typical cabin raising, by any stretch of the imagination. Under the tragic circumstances, Ma Hawkins thought it best to keep the environs as peaceful as possible around Amanda. So all the families with boisterous children had agreed to stay at home.

This smaller group of capable women now chatted amiably while they continued dinner preparations for the working men. As Netta sat nursing her Rosanna, no one noticed Amanda rise from her spot in the corner. She dropped the blanket and inched her way over to the rocking chair where Netta sat. When the group saw the injured woman standing over her, stock still, all chatter immediately ceased.

Amanda sank to her knees beside Netta and held out her hands in silent supplication. Without a word, Netta handed over the baby and watched, spellbound, as Amanda rocked back and forth on her knees, gently patting the baby over her shoulder. Rosanna let out a loud burp. Netta smiled and opened her mouth to say something, when she caught Ma Hawkins' stern gesture to "hush and stay still."

Amanda settled down onto the floor, and with her unbandaged hand she unfastened her bodice, put Rosanna to her breast and quietly began nursing the baby.

Everyone remained silent, not knowing what to do or to say.

Ma hurried across the room and motioned for Netta to get out of the rocking chair. Then Ma put her hands under Amanda's elbows, coaxed her to her feet, and guided her into the rocker. Amanda began to rock back and forth, while the baby, already full, suckled at the empty breast and began to fall asleep.

Ma took Netta by the hand and pulled her back across the room with the others.

Lucy stood with tears streaming down her face, watching the scene unfold before her. She picked up her knife and tried to resume cutting apples, wiping away tears with the back of her hand every now and again as she did so.

Soon, a rich contralto voice began to hum a soft lullaby. Ma nodded her head when Amanda began the old Welsh lullaby; she smiled, mildly surprised at the large voice coming from a tiny package…

> *"Sleep my child and peace attend thee,*
> *All through the night.*
> *Guardian angels God will send thee,*
> *all through the night…"*

Amanda stroked Rosanna's silky hair and traced the outline of a tiny ear with her finger, not once moving her eyes from the tiny face. She continued to rock and sing.

"Netta," Ma whispered, "get busy and fix a cup of tea. I think she's finally comin' around."

Netta took the water kettle from its place on a tall, iron trivet in the coals and filled her company teapot with boiling water. She measured out a thimbleful of black tea from the tea tin she kept on the highest shelf of the pantry cupboard, then she added a generous handful of the chamomile flowers she'd dried this past summer.

While Netta puttered around making tea, she resumed a babble of empty words to fill up the silence. Soon Emma, Lucy, Winifred, and Ellie Mae were engrossed in new gossip about the traveling preacher, Reverend Harold P. Longbottom, who was due to come through these parts in another two or three weeks.

"Seems the Justice of the Peace near Mt. Vernon ran into him when he was crossing Owl Creek. And he says the preacher was carrying a deck of cards and a bottle of corn liquor. Can you imagine? A man of the cloth drinking and card playing? I mean, really now, it's only gossip, but there has to be some reason for saying such a thing in the first place. Why would an upstanding man like a Justice of the Peace spread something like that, if it wasn't true?"

"It sounds like a lot of empty talk, if you ask me," said Emma, cleaning up the flour mess from making pie crust.

"But I heard it from someone who ought to know such things. Mrs. Crittenden herself talked to the Justice's wife, Opal Ann. And Opal Ann said it's the God's honest truth. She saw the cards and the bottle herself. She said that Rev. Longbottom claimed he was holding them for a fella who just went across the river. Had to take off in a big hurry when he saw the Justice coming. Something about refusing to pay an outstanding fine he didn't agree with and not fancying bein' toted off to the whooscow, or some such-of-a-thing," said Netta.

"Sounds like a pretty lame excuse to me," said Winifred, washing up the dishes from the pie-making. "Far as I'm concerned, you can't trust a one of 'em any farther than you can throw a dead cat, that's what I think."

"Trust who?" asked Emma.

"Men, that's who."

"Oh. I thought you meant preachers."

"Can't trust them, neither," said Ma, keeping a close eye on Amanda.

"You know, maybe that preacher had a good reason for saying what he did, Edie," Ellie Mae chided her favorite, older sister, as she added the last of the vegetables to the stew pot. Ellie stood a good six inches taller than Edith. But Ellie still had some bounce left in her step in spite of the trials she'd already lived through. She certainly had a more positive outlook. Edie called her younger sister the "infernal optimist."

"Do you always give people the benefit of the doubt?" Lucy asked Ellie Mae.

While the other girls talked, Netta had pulled a stool over to reach the shelf above the window. She climbed up and took down her best, china tea-cups. "Would you girls like to take a little tea break now, too? I don't often get the chance to use my good china cups, so they're a bit dusty," she said, wiping the inside of each cup with a corner of her apron. "They belonged to my grandmother, you know... the one we named little Rosanna after? She gave them to me just before Luther and me left Virginia to come out here.

"She told me, 'Jeannette,' she always called me Jeannette. She said, 'Jeannette, you're going to the end of the world out in that wilderness. I want you to have something pretty to remember me by.' So she gave me these tea cups and saucers. Aren't they beautiful?" She held them up to the light so the girls could admire the flowered pattern. "See? Roses. Isn't that nice? Roses to remember my Grandma Rosanna. And now I have my own little Rosanna." She glanced across the room and gave Amanda an uncertain look.

"The tea. I better get the tea," Netta continued to babble. "It's probably steeped long enough by now." Netta assembled all the cups on the table and poured each one full of the steaming, aromatic brew. "Sit down for a bit," she motioned to the other women. "I'm afraid I don't have any real sugar to offer you girls, only honey. We really should have a cone of real, white sugar to go with these fancy tea cups, but we'll just have to make do with honey.

"Did I tell you Luther found us a honey tree just last week? I do like honey. It tastes so much milder than blackstrap, you know. The taste of molasses is just so bitter. I don't like it much, do you?" Netta didn't give anyone a chance to answer. "The honey tree was a really big one. My goodness, Luther brought home a whole bucketful. And he said there's at least four more bucketsful left in that tree! Can you imagine? So much honey in one place! He wouldn't tell me where it was, though. Said I'd prob'ly blab it all over the township, then he wouldn't have any left for trade. I guess he's right. I suppose I do talk a mite too much every now and again."

"Humph," Ma Hawkins chuckled under her breath, but loud enough for all to hear. "Jeannette, bring a cup of that tea over here to Amanda." She bent down to face Amanda. "Amanda Jane, would you like a nice hot drink? Jeannette has a cup of tea for you." She eased her hands under the baby to lift her away from Amanda. "Rosanna's asleep, now. It's time to put her back in the cradle for a spell."

Ma tried to take the baby, but Amanda shrunk away from her, holding the baby even closer. She didn't seem to hear Ma talking at all. She put the sleeping babe over her shoulder and gently patted, waiting for another burp. Rosanna began to fuss at being disturbed. "There, there, Little Ben," Amanda said. "We'll get that nasty ol' burp out, then you'll feel all better, won't you."

Ma stood rooted in front of the rocker, staring at Amanda in alarm. She'd handled a lot of tough situations out here, but this new turn of events unnerved her.

Rosanna let out a loud burp.

"Doesn't that feel better now, Ben?" Amanda cradled the baby back in her arm and rocked. Rosanna resumed suckling at the empty breast, falling asleep once more.

Ma shuffled back to the table and sank heavily into an empty chair by the girls. Reaching for a cup of the tea, she took a long swallow, then heaved a worried sigh, shaking her head. "How much more can this poor child take?" she muttered under her breath. "Ain't this little thing suffered enough already?"

"She almost died having Little Ben, didn't she, Edie?" Ellie asked.

"I never lost a mother yet, but this poor gal come awful close," Edie said, taking another swallow of tea. "I ain't managed to pry the whole story out of Jeremy yet, but I do know that girl had a mighty hard time takin' to motherhood." Ma drained the dregs from her teacup. "On top of everything else, now she's got to abide empty arms."

The Bailey's dog started to carry on outside, signaling an approaching rider. The women heard a horse trot up to the porch and come to a stop outside the cabin. Immediately the dog ceased his barking.

"Must be someone Rufus knows." Netta stood and walked to the door. She pulled it wide open and saw Jeremy Harrison swing down from his horse and tie it to the hitching post out front. "Oh, am I ever glad to see you! Are you boys finished with that roof already?"

"Nope. Others took a break when this freezing rain started in. Don't want anyone sliding off a slippery roof. This little shower ought to pass soon. So, I thought while I had the chance, I'd come check on Mandy. Has there been any change yet?"

"Why..., yes... but I, ah..., " Netta stood stammering for a moment longer.

"What's the matter, Netta? The cat never gets your tongue. Can I come in?" Jeremy walked past her into the cabin, shook off his wet coat and hung it on the peg next to the door. "Ah ha! Caught you girls sitting down on the job!" He took in the somber faces of the group, then saw Amanda in the rocker nursing Netta's baby.

"Mandy? You doing better?" He strode over to Amanda and took her hand. "Mandy, look at me. It's, Jeremiah."

She raised her head and stared with glassy eyes at the man who stood before her.

"What's happened, Ma? Why is she trying to feed Netta's baby? Mandy lost her milk three months ago."

"She thinks Rosanna's her own Little Ben. I don't know what to do with her," Ma told him. "This is way beyond my kind of doctorin'. I can deliver babies, and set bones. I can treat the ague and swamp fever. But I sure don't know what to do for a addled mind," Edith said.

"Losing Ben's a shock. It's too much right now. But she'll come out of it," said Jeremy. "I know she will. She has to."

"I heard tell of a woman losing her mind down Zanesville way, five, maybe six years ago," said Winifred, sipping on her tea. "All her children drowned when their flatboat hit a big patch of rocks and broke all to pieces below the falls. Been tetched in the head ever since, she has."

"You hush that kind of talk," Ma scolded. "She hears every word we say, even if she don't let on." Ma turned to Jeremy. "Amanda's young and strong, don't you forget that. A young sapling might bend in a wind storm, but it always bounces back. You wait and see if she don't bounce back, too."

Jeremy knelt by the rocker and put both hands on Amanda's shoulders. "Mandy, look at me. I love you. But Ben's gone. It's nobody's fault. Do you hear me? It's not your fault. He's gone and we can't get him back. We have to go on without him, Mandy. We have to move on."

"Jeremiah?"

"It'll be all right, my little yellow bird. I promise it will."

"It was so cold."

"I know. But it's over."

"The fire… I just wanted to warm up–"

"Mandy, we need to give Rosanna back to Netta. She's sound asleep. This is Netta's baby. Not Ben." Jeremy eased the baby out of Amanda's arms and handed her back to Netta, then he motioned for Ma to bring over a cup of tea. As she crossed the room with the tea, Jeremy tenderly rebuttoned Amanda's bodice. He took the cup from Ma and placed it in Amanda's unbandaged hand, wrapping her fingers around it, and, still holding her tiny hand in both of his own, raised the cup to her lips. "Drink, Mandy. This will warm you up."

She took a small sip of the hot liquid.

"Isn't that better?"

"Uhhmm hmmm."

"Drink some more. Come on, that's my girl." He lowered the cup into her lap.

"Jeremiah, I'm so tired..."

"We'll put you to bed for a nice rest. You'll feel better when you wake up." He turned to Netta. "Is it all right if she can lie down for a while?"

"Of course it is. Put her right up on my bed." She opened the stairway door that led to the large loft. "Oh, wait, I have to put the comforter back up there. I'll get–"

Before she could fetch the blanket off the floor, where Amanda had sat all afternoon near the hearthstone, Ellie Mae swooped it up, over her shoulder and carried it up the stairs.

Jeremy handed the tea cup back to Netta, lifted Amanda into his arms, and carried her up the steep, narrow steps to the second-floor bedroom. Lowering her onto the feather tick, he tucked her beneath the comforter Ellie Mae laid across the bed.

Mandy looked so tiny under that thick coverlet. "Jeremiah," she said, touching his scarred cheek.

"What is it, Mandy?"

"I'm going to have a baby, Jeremiah. I'm three months along."

December 5, 18 and 16
Vermillion Twp.

Dear Libby,

All hell has broke loose round here. Guess I will tell it in the order I got it. Seems my father, Lars Johansen, had a mishap moving a load of mash for his latest batch of corn likker. My Pa is an old hermit living down in the Hio hills. I can call him that and get away with it. But no one else had ortta try it.

He and Mother had a parting of the ways when she got tired of farming life and wanted to go back to the city. So she headed for her folks place in Philadelfia, while Pa headed deeper into the hills. He has a still set up and puts out some of the best double-back corn liquor in those parts. Jonathan travels that-a-way once in a blue moon and brings back a jug of Pa's finest for Harvey. Brother Jonathan found Pa after he laid under his wagon for two days. Lucky thing he happened down south in them hills by Athens to see Pa after the surround hunt or no doubt we would be waiting on two funerals.

Do not rightly know what went wrong, but Pa ended up under most of a ton of mash. No one else dared to say but I xpect he was sampling his last batch a mite heavy before he tried to move that wagon. Jonathan sent a runner back to fetch us and a good wagon to move Pa in since his wagon got all tore up. Took more than two weeks till we got down and back.

We kept Pa likkered up most all the trip home so he did not feel much pain. Good thing he makes such strong corn juice. The way of it is, Pa has a broke hip and cannot do for himself fixed that-a-way. So he is living with us till he mends. God help him. I hope he mends fast. Not to say I mind caring for Pa. Not at all. But he is the most contrary old coot I know. Keeps trying to get out of bed and hobble round on a old crutch-stick he talked Harvey into making for him. Sister Edie could not do much to set the bone proper after such a goodly time passing. But she did tell him he better keep off that leg if he ever hopes to walk close to straight again.

Jonathan lit out to Penna straight away to go tell Brother Jason about the mishap. Do not know as I have mentioned Jason before. He is the next in line after Edie. My son Jason is named for him. Brother Jason lives with his wife and about 8 children by now, I think, back in Penna. On Mother and Pa's old farm place just east of Philadelfia. Brother Jason looks in on Mother when he makes trips into the city. No doubt he will tell her about Pa. I sure hope she does not get to feeling too morose over being away from Pa when he is ailing. Take her a notion to come out here. If God is listening maybe He would keep them two apart till the old coot has healed up enough to live back on his own.

My Ma and Pa have not slept under the same roof since I was but a 5 year tot. I do not recollect much. Being as I was so young. But I do remember the day Pa moved to the barn. Edie must have been 15. She is 10 years older than me. She moved out to the barn and set up housekeeping for Pa. I wanted to bunk out there with them. But Mother would not hear of it at what she called my tender age. I did manage to spend most all my waking hours out there with Edie. I was her shadow back then. Sure did admire her. Still do.

Now I am not saying that Pa never went in to visit Mother. Jonathan did come along some years after. But by then I had moved myself out to the barn too. Mother kept Sister Tabitha and Jason indoors with her along with baby Jonathan. Seemed to be all she needed. Tabby fell between Jason and me. She was the quick one of us girls. Always out shining me at lessons and such. And here I am telling you this, Lib, when you know your own tongue and French to boot. I got enough trouble to speak just one!

So far having Pa here is not as bad as I thought. Pa never did have a gift for getting on with folks. But he took a shine to Theodore. Been teaching him to whittle. Keeps them both busy and out of my hair a good bit of the time. Credit it or not, I been able to get more done with Pa here keeping Theodore busy than I could without him. Hard to figure, ain't it? I decided it was best to keep Pa over here at our place with Edie so busy looking in on that Harrison gal every day.

Which brings me to the real tragedy what struck in these parts. Fire at the Harrison place. It happened while we was on the road back home with Pa. The Harrisons lost their baby in a fire that pretty near destroyed their cabin. I spoke of that little southern girl before, you may recall. Can you believe she was rendering lard inside? Jeremy seems such a practical sort. I would not reckon him for giving in to Amanda on such a daft idea. Cold outside or not.

Amanda got her some bad burns, but my sister says what hurts most is where it does not show. In her mind. She acts touched in the head after losing her baby that awful way. I got back from fetching Pa in time to help feed the work party of men who went to build the Harrison cabin back up. So I saw with my own eyes how she did not speak or even seem to see any of us till Netta nursed her own Rosanna. When I heard Amanda call Netta's baby Little Ben like she did, goose flesh raised up all over me. I try not to think of the way that little tyke met his fate. Losing a little one is hard enough without thinking of them last few minutes of his short life.

December 10, 18 and 16

Lib,

I have not got back to this letter until now. Harvey kept me busy getting vittles ready for him to travel. That man can not take a trip no where but what he has to carry along a whole sideboard worth of food. He left this forenoon on his last supply run down Mount Vernon way before winter sets in dead wicked. Took along those wolf scalps to sell and some of the bear meat to trade. Also took a few jugs of Pa's last batch of corn juice and a half-bushel of apples.

Turns out we was some of the lucky few to have apples set this year. Our piece of land sets up so nice and high, the late frosts did not touch it. Harvey figgered apples might turn out the best trade goods he could take. Pa kept saying he wanted to squeeze some for apple jack, but I put my foot down firm about that. No hard cider when children need nutriment.

Harvey should be back seven days from now. If all goes smooth for him. That will give me time to sew him up a shirt for Christmas before he gets home. I just got back a nice piece of cloth goods wove up by Emma. Took down another batch of wool yarn for her to weave me up some more.

We do not fuss much the way some do for Christmas. But I try to make something special for Harvey. The children each get a little sweet or whatever Harvey can trade for. I also knitted them each a pair of slipper socks after they bedded down nights. Got them hid in my bed pillow so they do not find them. It is getting right lumpy by now.

Better bring this letter to a close. Pa is hollering for his crutch stick. I keep hiding it to make him stay off that blasted hip. I have a soup cooking on the fire. Need to make up some corn cakes to go with it. Pa sure is no bother to feed. Eats anything I put in front of him. Guess he got awful tired of his own cooking. Course I expect he always drank a lot more meals than he ever ate.

Hope you and yours fare better in those Fire Lands than we do down in these parts of late. Good luck on your first winter out here.

Your friend as usual.

Ellie Mae

Chapter 8

Funeral
December 1816

Amanda and Jeremy spoke very little to one another after the fire. Since their total existence had come to revolve around an eleven-month-old baby, without him they felt awkward in one another's presence. Winter nights dragged by in virtual silence, with Jeremy spending more and more time outside the cabin. A constant ache gnawed at his gut that no amount of wood-chopping could pound away. The rebuilt shed overflowed with a new supply of firewood, yet he continued to chop and split more, in an effort to deaden the hurt.

Thanks to the community's help, the Harrisons had a new roof perched atop the charred, base logs of their cabin, and a brand new fireplace and chimney stood on the north wall. The cabin felt bigger now—more spacious and uncluttered—with one, large room rather than the two small ones. Jeremy also put together a table and chairs from rough-cut wood and built a platform of planks to serve as a bedstead in the corner.

All the neighbors chipped in what food, clothing, and utensils they could spare to help Jeremy and Amanda replace what the fire had destroyed. Lucy Jarvis and Netta Bailey gave Amanda a new sewing basket, along with enough cloth goods to make up the necessary layette for the baby she said she expected "sometime in the spring."

Though claiming to be nearly four months along, she still hadn't felt a quickening; neither did her waist appear much thicker. Yet night after night, she'd sit stitching baby linens— each jab of the needle bringing her one stitch closer to filling empty arms.

After a few weeks, Jeremy became so concerned about Amanda's "condition" that he decided to have a talk with Ma Hawkins.

"I don't like it. Shouldn't she be plumping up some by now?"

"Maybe so. Maybe not. Every baby's different, even for the same woman. Could be she'll go along and then just pop all-of-a-sudden like. Some do that a-way."

"But could she be... well, do you think Mandy might be grasping at straws here?"

"Cook this whole thing up in her head, you mean?"

"She misses Little Ben so much. It's not as bad as it was right after the fire... once she snapped out of that funny spell. But, now... well it's almost like she's got her mind dead set on trying to fill the empty spot Ben left by dreaming up another baby."

"I've knowed it to happen to a woman. False pregnancy, they call it. Happens to dogs sometimes, too. Want youngens so much they fool their whole self into believin' it's true. I hear tell sometimes a dog can even get to makin' milk. Can't say as I ever heard of any woman goin' quite that far, though."

"What can I do to snap her out of this?"

"Nothin' much you can do, 'cept wait for nature to run her course. Sooner or later the body puts itself to rights. Give her time."

So Jeremy kept chopping and splitting wood, and Amanda kept stitching flowers on baby coverlets, while time continued to apply its healing balm.

Another two weeks slipped by when Henry Jarvis sent word that the traveling Methodist Preacher would come through on Saturday next. He asked whether the Harrisons would like Reverend Longbottom to conduct a belated funeral service for Little Ben.

Jeremiah hadn't taken time for any kind of service when he buried the little tyke. With bad weather already upon them, the need to rebuild forced him to push ahead quickly. The fact that Amanda had spent those first two weeks in a state of shock, or a "mite touched in the head," as the neighbors whispered among themselves, her condition made it difficult even to consider a proper funeral at the time he'd laid Little Ben to rest beside the sapling apple tree.

"Maybe a good service is just what we need to put this all behind us," Jeremy told Amanda that night at supper, relieved that she'd at least listened to his proposition about a funeral without getting all upset.

Amanda wiped the two plates from Ellie Mae and stretched to put them beside the cups from Lucy on the shelf above the cabin's one window. Jeremy had fashioned a make-shift window for her out of oiled cloth. You couldn't see much looking out, but at least it allowed a little sunlight to enter the cabin.

Amanda shuffled across the room and laid her towel over the back of a chair beside the fireplace. She stood, smoothing at it, oblivious to her actions. "Could we have a nice song, do you think?" she asked Jeremy, sitting in the other chair.

"I don't see why not. I'll talk to the preacher and tell him we'd like some singing."

"No morbid Bible readings, though. I don't want any of those dust-to-dust passages they always insist upon using."

"If that's what you want, Mandy, that's what we'll have. I'll see the preacher gives a proper, uplifting service for Little Ben." Jeremy watched Amanda closely for a reaction. She stood fairly relaxed, and for the first time, she didn't wince at the mention of the baby's name. He rose from his chair, stood behind her, and slipped his arms around her waist. "We're going to be all right, Mandy," he said in an effort to reassure himself as much as her. "We'll start all over again, just you and me."

"You and I and this new baby, Jeremiah."

"Mandy, honey, are you sure? Really sure? I mean, you're still so tiny and all. I have trouble believing—"

"Don't you want a new baby?"

"More than anything in the world." He gently turned her around to face him. "I want us to have a baby. Our child this time. Yours and mine. But Mandy, you've been so upset. I'm afraid... I mean... well, sometimes the mind can play awful tricks on a person."

"I haven't lost my mind, if that's what you're thinking. I admit, I did get a bit addled, right at first. I simply was not myself for a while, that's all. But I'm past all that, Jeremiah. Really, I am."

"I want to believe it... that we're gonna have a new baby to love. I do."

"Well it's true. We are."

Jeremy gave her a big, bear hug and lifted her off the floor. "My little yellow bird, how I do love you."

* * * * *

"In the book of John, chapter 11 and verses 25 and 26, Jesus said, 'I am the resurrection and the life; He that believeth in me, though he were dead, yet shall he live,'" intoned the smooth voice of Reverend Harold P. Longbottom. "'And whosoever liveth and believeth in me shall never die'." His voice rose and fell with large, hollow, vowel-sounds, as he gestured with one hand and waved his Bible with the other.

Amanda stood beside the tiny grave next to the newly planted orchard and clutched Jeremy's hand. All the friends and neighbors from nearby homesteads stood around them in a tight circle. Lucy Jarvis dabbed at her nose with a hankie, while her husband Henry clapped a firm hand on Jeremy's shoulder. A gust of wind caught Amanda's skirt and whipped it around her legs. She shivered and pulled her shawl tighter around her shoulders. Jeremy stepped closer to shield his tiny wife from the wind.

"Jesus also said, 'Suffer the little children to come unto me and forbid them not: for of such is the kingdom of God.'"

Amanda squeezed Jeremy's hand. Feeling her begin to shake, he dropped her hand and folded his arm around her tiny frame.

"Let us bow our heads in prayer." The Reverend closed his eyes, and holding his Bible between clasped hands, raised his head high. "Oh Lord, we come before you this day, humbly beseeching that you bestow upon us Your Glorious Presence, as we dedicate the life of this little one, Bently Harrison, into Your everlasting care." The words slipped off his tongue like a wagon load of apples rolling downhill. "I never knew this little tyke. He was plucked away before he had the chance to live but a few, brief, months on this terrestrial sphere. But we know that during his short time among us, he brought unmeasured brightness into the lives of his parents, Amanda and Jeremiah Harrison."

Jeremy tightened his arm around Amanda. *"Funny,"* he thought, *"I never did know who Little Ben's real father was. Somehow, it just never seemed all that important. Whoever he was, he sure missed out on knowing one of the best little fellas this world has ever seen."* Jeremy wiped the back of his hand across his eyes, thankful he'd gotten to be the one Little Ben called "Pa Pa." He brought his attention back to the prayer when he felt Amanda stiffen at his side.

"...and we ask Your eternal blessing upon this tiny one, cut down in the bud of his life... pushed beyond this vale of tears into everlasting eternity to sit at the feet of our Lord Himself... "

Amanda started to cry, and Jeremy pulled out his hand-kerchief, putting it into her shaking hand.

"...we ask that You keep him enfolded in the bosom of Your protective wing, foreverandever. In the name of the One Who gives us all eternal life, AMEN."

The neighbors stood quietly, shuffling from one foot to the other, mumbling quietly among themselves as the Reverend paged through his Bible.

Frank Putnam whispered to Luther Bailey: "Cain't rightly say I understood all them fancy words that Reverend throwed around, did you?"

"Nope," said Luther. "Liked the singin' tho'."

Ma Hawkins, standing nearby, overheard. "'T'warn't worth frettin' your measly head over, Frank," she mumbled loud enough for those around her to hear.

The Reverend cleared his throat. "The honorable Jeremiah Harrison will now share a reading with the company assembled here today. Mr. Harrison, if you please," the Reverend said, gesturing to the spot beside himself and turning aside as Jeremy stepped to the head of the grave.

Frank started to say something else, but Ma Hawkins poked him in the ribs with her elbow. "Shhhhht! Maybe that Reverend don't have much worth listenin' to," she hissed, "but this here's one man 'at does. Hush up, now, both of you."

"Friends, neighbors. If you folks don't mind, I'd like to read one of my favorite Psalms. Psalm number 30:

> *'Sing unto the Lord, O ye saints of His,*
> *and give thanks at the remembrance of His holiness.*
>
> *For His anger endureth but a moment; in His favor is*
> *life.*
>
> *Weeping may endure for a night, but joy cometh in the*
> *morning...*
>
> *Thou hast turned for me my mourning into dancing;*
>
> *Thou hast put off my sackcloth, and girded me with*
> *gladness; to the end that my glory may sing praise*
> *to Thee and not be silent.*
>
> *O Lord my God, I will give thanks unto thee forever.'"*

Jeremiah tucked his small, worn Bible into his shirt. "You folks have all done so much for Mandy and me. We'd have nothing, if it weren't for your generous hearts. We thank you from the bottom of ours. And thanks for coming out on such a cold day to pay your respects to our Little Ben." He turned to Rev. Longbottom. "Reverend, would you ask a blessing on us, so these folks can get out of the cold and go inside where the ladies have a feed all set up?" Jeremy stepped back beside Amanda and held her close.

The Reverend cleared his throat with a loud rumble. "In the book of John, Chapter fourteen, Jesus said, 'Peace I leave with you; My peace I give unto you, not as the world giveth, give I unto you; Let not your heart be troubled, neither let it be afraid.'" He paused, then in loud tones of finalé he boomed, "'In the world ye shall have tribulation, but be of good cheer; I have overcome the world!' May the Lord add His blessing on each and every one of us gathered here today, and may He see us all safely to our respective homes without harmful incident, either natural or man made, and keep us safe until again we all shall meet. Amen and AMEN."

* * * * *

"I want to thank you, Reverend, for giving Little Ben such a fine service." Jeremy stood outside the cabin door talking with the Reverend Longbottom after all the women and children had gone inside to spread out dinner.

"Think nothing of it, friend. All part of the calling. I've been told I do conduct a good funeral, ifIdosaysomyself."

"It was mighty kind of you to let me say my piece to all our neighbors. Mandy and me'd sure be in a tight spot without their help."

"That's what the brotherhood of man is all about, my friend."

"I don't know how I can ever repay all the kindness done for us, but I aim to help out wherever I can," Jeremy said, pausing a moment. "Speaking of which, I don't have any hard cash money right now to pay you for that funeral service, Reverend. But if you'll accept our hospitality, you're welcome to stay on with us for as long as you're leading meetings here in the township."

"Why, thank you. I appreciate that kind offer. And I accept."

"I reckon the ladies ought to have dinner 'bout ready. I better go out to the barn and get the fellas moving this way. Might take some doing if they broke open any corn juice already."

"Jeremiah, my friend, would you be so kind as to allow me the privilege of announcing dinner to the masculine assemblage? That way you can go look after that pretty little wife of yours. By the by, since I'll be staying on for a few days, I believe we can dispense with all this 'Reverend' business, don't you? Please, feel free to call me Hal."

"Don't know as I'd feel quite right doing that, Reverend."

"There's no sin in using one's Christian name, you know."

"Seems a mite improper, somehow."

"Well then, could you bring yourself to call me Pastor Hal?"

"I think that'd go down better."

"All right. Then Pastor Hal, it shall be. Now, if you would kindly point me in the direction of the byre, I shall fetch the men to the awaiting repast. I might even partake in a bit of an appetizer myself."

Jeremy, though no teetotaler, showed honest shock at the Reverend's disclosure.

"Now, friend, surely you know even Christ Himself was known to provide alcoholic refreshment at social gatherings, though the most quoted example happened at a wedding rather than a funeral. While I do consider it my duty to point out the dangers of dissipation and to revile excessive indulgence of the devil's brew, I also consider it my clerical duty to emulate to the utmost of my ability, One so esteemed as our risen Lord, Who in His infinite wisdom and compassion, provided us with the warmth and gratification of such liquid comfort."

Jeremy nodded in seeming agreement, chuckling to himself while the Reverend made a beeline for the barn.

Inside the cabin to one side, the ladies had two tables loaded down with food. Jeremy had rigged the temporary tables and benches from puncheons left over after replacing the scorched, cabin floor. Although a bit rough, they did serve the purpose.

As usual, Ma Hawkins took charge of dinner preparations. She had older children arranging benches around empty tables, sitting in the center of the cabin. Little boys kept crawling underneath or scooting back and forth on the benches, daring one another to see if they could slide without getting splinters in their hind quarters. Young girls quieted babies and kept toddlers away from the hearth, while the women uncovered dishes of potatoes, squash, pumpkin, roast venison, baked turkey and stewed rabbit.

Ma had the older girls busy cutting pies and put Netta Bailey in charge of keeping the kettles boiling to have hot tea at the ready. Netta rattled away to Amanda, who sat in a chair by the fire, rocking and patting baby Rosanna.

Most folks knew to bring their own plates and utensils to a gathering, since no one had much in the way of extras. Lucy usually brought one along for the minister, too. "Do you think we'll have enough food for everyone?" Lucy asked Emma, who dabbed a bit of butter atop a dish of baked hominy.

"We always do, don't we?"

"'Except when there's a travelin' preacher to eat," Ma Hawkins piped in. "You girls be sure and see everyone gets a first helpin' before you let that Reverend come round and sweet-talk you out of seconds, you hear?"

Just then Jeremy walked through the cabin door and dodged his way around children, as he crossed to the fireplace where Amanda sat.

"You all right, Mandy?"

"I'm doing fine." She held Rosanna over her shoulder, gently patting her little bottom. "I got nice and warmed up here by the fire. Netta asked me to look after Rosanna while she tends to the beverages and keeps the kettle boiling."

"Would you like some hot tea, Jeremy?" Netta asked, offering him a steaming cup. "I was just telling Amanda how much I like the way you got your cabin laid out now," Netta rattled. "Seems so much bigger this way. Why, I do believe it's almost as big as ours. 'Course Luther put a whole second story on top, instead of a low roof like youens have. But down here, there's almost enough room to hold a dance, don't you think?"

She didn't give him enough time to answer. "'Course we won't be doing any dancing tonight. But maybe at some gathering more fittin', we could get Anson Guthrie to fiddle and Harmon Hawkins to call. Then we could have us a grand ol' time, warming your rebuilt cabin up proper."

Jeremy rescued the cup of tea Netta had been swinging back and forth while she talked nineteen to the dozen. "That sounds real nice," he said, turning to Amanda. "Mandy, honey, I asked the Reverend to stay on with us while he's holding meetings here in the township... be a way to repay him for Ben's service and all. I hope that's all right with you." He took a long drink of the tea.

Netta jumped in again before Amanda could answer. "That Reverend Longbottom sure seems like a nice fella, don't you think? After all the gossip we heard about him, I wasn't sure what to expect. Opal Ann, that's the Justice's wife, you know, well, Opal Ann didn't have much good to say about the Reverend. Course, she don't have much good to say about many folks, come to think of it. Do you know, she says he carries a deck of cards with him? Can you imagine that? Not that I see anything wrong with a little card playin' now and again. Don't get me wrong. But for a man of the cloth to lower himself to such worldly ways, well, it just surprises me, is all. And him being a Methodist, to boot. After meeting him, I got to say, he sure does give a nice service, though, don't he? Such a strong voice, too. Just booms right out." She stopped to snatch a breath.

Jeremy took advantage of the pause. "I'd better go check on our Reverend and the rest of those fellas. See what's holdin them up. Never knew any one of those boys to be late for a feed, once it's ready." He handed Netta the empty cup, then patted Amanda on the shoulder. "Be back in the twitch of a donkey's tail." He headed for the door.

"Jeremy?" Ma Hawkins called to him as he crossed the room. "What's keepin' them men critters? You go tell 'em to get their beehinds in here before this food gets cold."

"On my way, Ma," he said, pulling the door shut. The sound of men's laughter greeted him as he neared the barn door; he heard one voice raised above the rest:

> *"When the Methodist Preachers come down,*
> *A-Preachin' that drinkin' is sinful,*
> *I'll wager the rascals a crown,*
> *They always preach best with a skinfull."*

The voice let out a loud guffaw, amid laughs and snorts from the rest of the men.

"Like that one, Reverend?"

"Too much, my friend, too much. I do believe you've given me pause to question the veracity of my ways. But perhaps with just a small sip more, I'll be better able to contemplate the comportment of my present circumstance."

"Does he want another drink?" Frank asked.

"Reckon so," said Luther.

"Pass him the jug, then," said Sam Justice. Sam supplemented his income as blacksmith by operating the biggest still in the township, and he turned out some of the best corn-liquor around.

"Seems a shame to waste all that good corn on nothin' but preachin', don't it Sam?" commented Anson Guthrie.

"Speak up, man. You got marbles in your mouth?" Sam had been left quite hard of hearing since a shooting incident years before.

"I said," Anson began to shout, "It's a shame to waste good liquor on preachin'."

"Not if it's good preachin', it ain't."

"Hell, you can't tell the difference between good preachin' or bad preachin, if you can't hear neither one."

"You bunch of mangy roosters slaked your thirst yet?" Jeremy made his presence known from the back of the crowd. "Ma sent me out here to fetch you in to eat, before she decides to dump your share of vittles to the hogs and say the devil with men for today."

"She says the devil with men every other day, don't she?" Anson Guthrie added with a smirk.

"Guess we better cork the jug and snap to it, boys. The almighty Ma has spoke," pronounced Harvey Thompson with a snicker. "No sense seein' good food wasted on a bunch a smelly ol' hogs! If we go riling up the women, they may take a notion never to feed us again," he snorted, taking one last pull on the jug. "Here ya go, Rever'nd. Have one more slug to get your stomach juices workin' real good."

"Better not breathe too close to any of the women," said Sam. "Don't know as they'd take kindly to a man of the cloth tipplin' out here with the rest of us degenerates."

"Not to worry, my friend. Not to worry." Longbottom reached into his vest pocket and pulled out a few dried mint leaves, which he popped into his mouth. "I always keep my freshener handy, gents. Never know when one might be called upon to minister in the close proximity of a distressed female in need of clerical reassurance and comfort."

"What'd he say?" asked Sam.

"Never mind," said Anson Guthrie. Just git a move on."

* * * * *

"Magnificent provender for the sustenance of one so fortuneate as I to partake in this delectable repast," oozed the Reverend. "May I be so bold as to inquire which luscious morsel your lively fingers have contributed to the festal board?"

Confused, chubby Emma leaned toward Lucy and whispered, "What did he say?"

"He wants to know which pie you made."

Emma Putnam turned back to the Reverend. "I made this pumpkin pie. Want some more?"

"My dear lady, I thought you'd never ask," he said, watching her serve up a generous slice. "And might I have a taste of that luscious-looking apple pie, as well?"

Emma would have given him the whole pie, if Ma Hawkins hadn't caught her eye from across the room. She gave her a stern look. The Reverend went back to the center table, sat down beside the prettiest girl he could find and devoured his dessert.

"That's the third time he's been back for pie, Emma," Netta whispered in her ear. "While you were out back, he talked that Guthrie girl, Clara, into giving him seconds."

"Well, I feel sorry for the Reverend," Emma said. "I bet he don't get a good meal in him more'n once a week, traveling all the time like he does."

"And him with nothing but corn dodgers and dried meat in his saddlebags," added Lucy. "No wonder he's so skinny."

"How do you know what's in his saddlebags?" Netta asked Lucy.

"He told me... when I gave him his plate to eat on... before he asked the blessing!" she said, getting louder at each statement and turning her usual shade of beet red.

"It's all right, you don't have to get all flusterbated," Netta consoled her big-boned friend.

"You know, now that I study on it, I bet he gets a big feed like this at least once a week, maybe more," said Lucy.

"Really? You think so?" Emma asked with her usual baffled expression.

"Think about it. He holds services every three or four days in a different place. An' most folks carry in a dinner when they haven't heard good preaching in a month or better. So what do you think?"

"He does preach nice, don't he," said Emma.

"As preaching goes, he's not too bad," Netta offered.

"Got to agree with you," answered Lucy. "But he can't carry a tune in a bucket."

* * * * *

Jeremy saw the last of his neighbors safely into their wagons and on their way home before sundown; most would have time to spare before evening chores. The women had cleared up inside, so he left Amanda resting while he drew a bucket of water and headed to the barn to get an early start on his own chores. As he opened the barn door, he was startled to hear someone call his name.

"Reverend. I forgot you were still here."

"I thought we had dispensed with this 'Reverend' business."

"I'm sorry. You're right. It's Pastor Hal. Guess my mind got to wandering. I'm not used to having anyone talk to me when I do chores."

"Quite all right, my friend. I was just seeing to the comfort of my horse."

"I'll throw some hay down, soon as I'm done milking Bertha, here," Jeremy said, giving the cow a loving pat and scratching her between the ears. "She always likes a little attention before we get down to business."

"Most females do, I've found."

"You married, Pastor?"

"No. The kind of itinerant life I lead is not conducive to the comforts of a hearth and home."

"Bet you get awful lonely."

"On occasion. But work keeps me quite busy, and I meet so many generous people in my travels that the twinges of lone-liness are not overly burdensome. I've learned to adapt." He walked over and gave Bertha a pat on the side. "Besides, as long as you're getting free milk, my friend, why buy the cow?"

* * * * *

"Wonderful breakfast, Mrs. Harrison." Reverend Long-bottom pushed himself away from the table and used his handkerchief to brush the crumbs from his trousers. "Absolutely marvelous."

"Mandy always makes good flapjacks, Pastor. Why, I'd put 'em up against anyone's in the township. She'd win the prize, for sure." Jeremy rose from the table and stretched. Then he step-ped over to the door and donned his coat and hat. "I better tend to my chores before it gets any later. Bertha's gonna wonder what's kept me so long this morning." He ducked out, pulling the door shut behind himself.

Amanda shivered. "I was hoping you didn't mind griddle cakes again, Reverend," Amanda apologized in her soft drawl. "They're the only thing I'm really any good at."

"Well, I must say, your cooking these past few days has most definitely put mine to shame, Madam. But please, call me Hal. Reverend sounds so formal."

"Oh, I couldn't. I mean, it's just not done."

"I insist. I'd feel much better if we could have a more... congenial understanding."

"But Hal? It's too... well, I mean, it feels much too familiar."

"Then why not call me Harold. Would that be more acceptable?"

"Perhaps 'Pastor Harold' would do. But only if you cease to call me Mrs. Harrison."

"That's a fair request. I noticed your husband calls you Mandy. May I address you by that name?"

"No. Please, I really prefer Amanda. It's Amanda Jane, actually... my proper, Christian name. Back home everyone used the entire thing, but around here, the neighbors just call me Amanda."

"Amanda Jane. I like it. That's what I shall call you then. Amanda Jane." He rose from his chair, pushed it back under the table, and began to clear away his dishes.

"You don't have to do that, Rev... I mean Pastor Harold," she blushed.

"On the contrary. I insist. After providing me with such gustatory delight, helping with a few dishes is the least I can do to repay your most gracious hospitality."

Amanda lifted the kettle from the coals, walked over to the wash stand and poured hot water into the basin. "Since you put it that way, I suppose it'd be all right."

Harold Longbottom put the dishes in the basin, then rolled up his sleeves. "And where, may I be so bold as to inquire, is 'back home,' for you, Amanda Jane?" he asked, sloshing dishes in the water. "With that lovely accent, I deduce you must be from somewhere in the southern reaches of this great land."

"Charleston. Charleston, South Carolina." She stood, wiping a plate over and over.

"The way that drips off your tongue, you make it sound like the most charming place on earth."

"Oh, it is, it really is! It's simply wonderful! Seeing ships anchored in the harbor... walking along The Battery... and in spring, when the wisteria blooms, why the scent nearly makes a body swoon! During the holidays, everyone decks their town-houses with evergreens. I imagine the servants are busy hanging the greens right now! Grandmother always sends pine boughs to town the week before Christmas."

The more she talked, the more animated she became. "There's just no place like Charleston during the 'Season.' It starts right after the holidays, with everyone giving parties and receptions and balls. The very best one comes last... the St. Cecilia Ball? It's the highlight of the whole Season." The exuberant outburst colored her cheeks, and she turned away as she struggled to regain some semblance of control.

After a long pause, Pastor Harold said, "You must have left a great deal behind in Charleston, Amanda Jane."

More composed, she turned back to face him, showing little of the previous moment's emotion. "That was another life," she said, in a formal, lifeless tone. He watched closely when she reached to put the plates on the shelf above the window, noticing the slight bulge at her middle. "That life is very far away from here, Reverend," she said, reverting to the formal.

"Would you like to tell me about it, my dear?" He spoke in a soothing, liquid tone. "I think you have a great need to release all the anguish you have hidden deep inside," he said, gently touching her shoulder.

"I... I can't." She twisted the towel in her hand and began to shake. "I just can't!"

He took her by the elbows and eased her into the nearby chair. "It's all right, my dear. That is precisely what I am here for... to help soothe those festering injuries of the soul." He leaned over the chair and patted her shoulder. "I surmise you're in great need of my comfort, Amanda Jane." Slowly, he knelt beside her and took her hand. She began to weep. With a practiced flourish, he drew a kerchief from his vest pocket. "Let all those tears loose, my dear. Go right ahead. Have a good, long cry. You certainly deserve one."

At that moment, Jeremy opened the door and walked inside with a frothy bucket of fresh milk. "What's wrong? Mandy?"

Longbottom rose and walked over to Jeremy. "She has a great need to unburden her soul, my friend. I sense she has trouble relating certain, ah... facts, about her previous life in Charleston."

"She's never told me much about any of that, Pastor. Is there anything I can do?"

"At the moment, my friend, no." He leaned closer, and in a conspiratorial whisper said, "Perhaps it might be best if you were to remain outside the cabin for a time."

"Whatever you think is best."

"If I can but unearth the roots of her distress, I believe she will be better able to deal with her coming tribulation."

"Her what?"

"She is in the family way, is she not?"

Jeremy showed honest surprise at Pastor Hal's perception.

"You didn't know?"

"It's not that I didn't know... exactly. It's just that, well, Pastor, she had such a hard time losing Little Ben. Was even 'unbalanced' there at first, you might say. Some of us thought maybe she'd cooked the whole thing up in her head... wanting a child so bad and all. Know what I mean?"

"Hysterical pregnancy? Quite a common phenomenon, I've been told."

Jeremy looked more closely at the small bulge in Amanda's middle. "Guess I should apologize for ever doubting her."

"That can wait for another, more appropriate moment, my friend. At present, we have her current anguish to remedy."

"I'll be out in the barn, if you need me." Jeremy headed back outside, setting the bucket of milk near the door as he left.

The Reverend strode back across the room to Amanda and pulled the other chair close to hers. When he sat down and put his arm around her shoulder, a fresh round of tears burst forth. In a few moments, her sobbing eased, and she blew her nose.

"I'm so sorry, Reverend. I didn't mean to break down."

"It's Harold, remember? And what do a few tears matter when one is obviously as distraught as you. Now tell me, Mandy," he said, cleverly slipping in her familiar name. "What has really brought on all these tears? What have you left behind in Charleston that causes you such distress?

"It happened so fast... my leaving home and getting married and coming here." She sat in silence a few moments.

He waited patiently, patting her hand.

"It was all Mother's doing... sending me away." Her voice sounded full of anger. "I didn't want to get married! I didn't even know who they'd picked out for me... a second cousin of Mother's, or something." Her little frame shook with a fresh round of tears.

"Why did I have to go away? I loved it so in Charleston. I loved going to the parties, and to the races, and watching the ships sail into the harbor. Going to visit Grandmother at her peach orchard... that was the best part of all. Why wouldn't they let me stay with Grandmother?

"Why did they have to send me so far... into this... this... wilderness? I had no choice. It all happened so fast..."

Late May, 1815
Charleston

The doctor closed the door to the third-floor bedroom and met Amanda's mother in the hall.

"Will she be all right, Dr. Ballard?"

He took Evangeline Louise Bently's arm and guided her onto the upper piazza. With such balmy weather, the fragrant wisteria vine clinging to the balustrade hummed with the constant buzz of honey bees. "Mrs. Bently, I'm not sure how to broach this," the doctor began. "I suppose it's best to come right out with it." He sighed and took a deep breath. "Your daughter is pregnant. I calculate she's nearly three months along."

Mrs. Bently paled as she stood at the railing.

"Maybe you'd better sit down." He assisted her to a large porch chair, then took a small vial from his bag and held it up to her nose. "Take a few deep breaths, Miss Evangeline." She did as she was told. "There. That's good. Are you all right?"

She smoothed her skirt, then pulled a lace hankie from the wrist of her day coat. "This is a bit of a shock," she said, dabbing at her forehead with the hankie. "I'll be fine." She brought her tiny hands to rest primly in her lap. "I suppose the real problem now is what to do about this... ah... distressing turn of events."

"Amanda Jane will recover... in time. But I'd advise you to send her out of town as quickly as possible... to Miss Lillian's orchard, perhaps? It will be easier to avoid unnecessary gossip if she's out of the main social stream."

"I feared it might come to this," said Mrs. Bently. "I don't believe Amanda Jane suspects a thing, however. She believes her discomfort has arisen from a stomach complaint brought on by her... ah... her ordeal." Evangeline sat quite still for a few minutes, apparently lost in thought. "How much did you tell her, Doctor?"

"I haven't told her anything, yet. As far as she knows, she's had a thorough examination to rule out any permanent damage from that unfortunate encounter."

"How is her health? Other than for this complication."

"Physically she's quite fit. But I'm afraid that brutal violation has left grievous scars on her mind, Miss Evangeline."

Mrs. Bently sat contemplating the situation. A short, buxom woman in her mid-forties, Evangeline Louise held a place of prestige within the circles of Charleston's gentry. Her mother's family, the Tedrows, had been charter members of the St. Cecilia Society at its creation in 1762. After Evangeline wed shipping magnate Joseph Alexander Bently III, she assumed her own place among the hierarchy of Charleston's social order.

Yet, in spite of her impressive connections, Evangeline Louise Tedrow Bently felt so unsure of her position in that most elite of societies, that her fear of scandal and social expulsion drove what little motherly affection she may have felt far into the background.

"What about extended travel? Would she be fit enough to withstand a longer trip?"

"What are you thinking?"

"I have distant relatives up north who might be able to help us with this... delicate situation. I'd have to talk with Joseph about it, of course. Do you think travel to Pennsylvania is out of the question?"

"Physically she can stand quite a lot," he said, pulling at his beard. "She's young and in good health, in spite of the pregnancy. A longer trip is not likely to hurt the baby, if that's what you want to know. But I would advise any extensive travel be undertaken before she is six months along. After that, it's definitely out of the question."

Mrs. Bently arose from her chair. "Thank you, Dr. Ballard." She strode to the doorway leading to the third-floor hall. "I will see you out, if you wish."

"That won't be necessary," the doctor said, rising and donning his hat. "I'll see myself out. If I can be of further assistance, or if you'd like me to speak to Joseph, please, don't hesitate to send word. I plan to hold hours at my office the rest of the day."

"Thank you. We can manage." She dismissed him with a nod and a brusque wave. As he turned to go downstairs, Evangeline marched down the hall to Amanda's bedroom. She gave a curt knock on the door. "Amanda Jane, I need to talk to you."

"Mother?" Amanda squeaked out the word from where she lay ensconced in the huge, four-poster bed.

"How much did Doctor Ballard tell you?" Evangeline asked, pushing the door open as she entered the room.

"He said in a few months, I'd be good as new."

"In six months, to be exact. That means we must work quickly to make the necessary arrangements."

"Arrangements? What do you mean, arrangements?"

"You must leave Charleston right away, Amanda Jane. You're pregnant. You're going to have a baby."

"But I thought... isn't it just... stomach trouble? Oh dear God, No!" She threw herself face down on the pillows and began to sob hysterically.

Never one to tolerate emotional outbursts of any kind, Evangeline turned on her heel and left the room, slamming the door behind herself, leaving the servants to deal with Amanda Jane's hysterics.

Later that evening, Joseph Bently tapped on his daughter's bedroom door. "Mandy?"

"Papa, is that you?"

He eased the door open a crack. "May I come in, daughter?"

"Of course," Amanda said. He stepped into the room and she wailed, "Oh, Pappaaaa!" A flood of tears erupted before he could reach her bedside.

He sat his bulk down on the edge of the bed and gathered her into his arms. "Don't cry, my Mandy."

"My life is ruined, Papa. Ruined!" She convulsed into a fresh round of sobs.

"Shhhhh, everything is going to be all right. Your life will not come to an end over this. I promise." He held her close until her tears were spent. "Here, now. Blow." He handed her a handkerchief, and she blew. "Wipe your eyes, my dear. We have some important matters we need to discuss."

Amanda did as she was told, rearranging herself and straightening her brocade bed jacket. She avoided looking directly at her father while she smoothed at the coverlet.

"I know about the baby. Your mother told me." He waited a moment. She avoided his eyes. "Look at me, Amanda Jane," he said. "This is not the end of the world. Why, you are about to embark upon one of life's greatest adventures!"

"But Papa, what am I going to do? I'm not married. I'm not even betrothed!"

"Your mother has taken it upon herself to find a... ah... suitable husband for you among some of her distant relatives in Pennsylvania. No, now, don't protest before you hear me out." He took a deep breath and forged ahead. "You have a baby to consider now. That life you carry is far more important than feeling sorry for yourself and crying over romantic notions that can never come to pass."

He paused, knowing she was thinking of all the parties and balls she'd miss, the thrill of a proper engagement and a large, lavish wedding. "A marriage contract has nothing whatsoever to do with love. Your baby needs a responsible father. And you, my Mandy, need a dependable husband to look out for you. Someone to care for you and your baby." Amanda sat in silence, staring at the covers.

"I know it's a bit much to swallow all at once. You'll just have to grow up faster than any of us had anticipated, my dear." He patted her shoulder. "Your mother is arranging to send you to her cousin, Camellia Harrison, near Uniontown, Pennsylvania. Several of her boys must be in their twenties by now, I'd imagine. I intend to send a letter of explanation along to Camellia, so she and her husband, Peter, can decide which of their sons is best suited to the task of looking after you."

Amanda tried to object.

"Now, let me finish, please. Then you can say what you will. I plan to see that you and your new husband have a sizable piece of land on which to make a good start. I hear that the land in the Ohio country is worth more than gold."

"Ohio?" she squeaked.

"No one will know you way out there, Mandy. It'll be much easier for you to make a fresh start... a clean break. As far as anyone need know, you'll be a brand new family settling in a brand new land."

"Oh, Papa, I'm so scared! Must I go so far away?"

"This is the best choice, Mandy. It really is."

"Why can't I go live with Grandmother out at the orchard?"

"The farther away you can get from this cesspool of 'Charleston Society', the happier you'll be. Believe me, I know whereof I speak." He paused, then he shifted his massive weight and rose from the bed. "I realize I ask a great deal of you in this. But I have faith that you can do it, my dear. You are tougher than you realize. Don't forget, you have Grandmother Bently's blood coursing through your veins."

"How soon do I have to leave?"

"Your mother has booked transport on next week's ship. She said Dr. Ballard advised you should complete any travel before you're much further along... less danger for you or for the baby that way, I'm told."

"Oh." She gazed out the window a few moments. "Then I suppose I'd better pack."

"Amanda Jane, you will live through this."

"I'll never see you again, will I Papa."

"I'll be home tomorrow evening, Mandy—"

"After I leave for Ohio. I won't ever see you again."

Joseph Bently squared his shoulders and took a deep breath. "It's not likely."

"I love you, Papa..."

...Amanda wiped her eyes. "I miss Father so much," she said, snuffling back tears.

"Have you written to tell him that?" Reverend Longbottom asked her. "To let him know you've managed to make a good life in this wilderness?"

"I wrote, months ago. But I haven't heard a word back from anyone," Amanda said, heaving a sigh. "Not that I ever really expected to."

"I realize what you have here may pale in comparison to the opulence of a Charleston Townhouse," Longbottom said, sweeping his hands around the rustic cabin, "but as wilderness homes go, you are quite well off, you know… in spite of your most recent... ah… setback."

Amanda looked around, seeing her refurbished cabin as if for the first time. The fire had wiped out all trace of her previous life, and the newly built furniture gave it a clean, sturdy, simple appearance. "It is a good, solid house, isn't it."

"And a good, solid man lives in it with you."

"Jeremiah has been so good to me. I really am lucky to have him. I know that."

"Maybe you should let Jeremiah know of your gratitude, too, my dear."

"I will." She sat in silence for a moment. "I do understand now. Papa was right in sending me out here."

Harold Longbottom rose from his chair, picked it up, and put it back by the table sitting under the south-facing, oil-clothed window.

"Thank you, Rev—"

"It's Harold, remember?"

"Thank you."

"For what? For allowing me to alleviate your distress by lending a sympathetic ear? All in the fulfillment of my sacred calling. Or, as some more aptly phrase it, all in the line of duty, my dear. All in the line of duty."

He crossed back to the fire where she still sat and leaned in closely over her shoulder. "Don't forget, Mandy dear, I will return on this circuit approximately eight weeks hence, and I shall be most eager to talk with you again. In much greater depth, if you desire." He touched her arm in a most intimate manner.

She looked deeply into his eyes and blushed in sudden confusion. He abruptly straightened and smacked his sides. "Well, needs must I be on my way. I have untold miles to travel before I find repose on the morrow. Another group of malfeasant transgressors awaits the enlightenment of my inspirational exhortations."

"What did you say?"

"Twenty-five miles to the next stop on my circuit."

* * * * *

"I believe you will find your wife considerably more composed than when you saw her last," Reverend Longbottom said as he packed his horse.

"You got her to talk?"

"Of course, my friend. All in my ordained capacity as clerical confidant." He tied the saddle bag tight. "I simply applied a little artful manipulation, and her numerous heartbreaks began to flow."

"What did she tell you?"

"There's too much to relate in detail, but I did gather that her home life was a bit... how should I put it... lacking in the basics of human compassion?"

"Her mother's a cold-hearted female, that's certain sure."

"Misguided, perhaps. I know her sort. But it would seem that you are the one who has reaped the most benefit from Amanda Jane's unfortunate circumstance, would it not?"

"That's the God's honest truth, Pastor Hal. I gained more by this union than Mandy could ever hope to. And I don't mean just the farm here, either. She's told me that I saved her life by taking her as my wife. But the fact is, she's the one who saved mine."

"Really? How so?"

"It's a long story. Would bend your ear more than you got time for today. Let's just say that by choosing her to be my wife, it made a whole new man out of me."

"I am a trifle confused here," said the Reverend, removing his black, broad-brimmed hat and scratching his head. "She told me that her father composed a letter for your mother, who was to choose Amanda's husband from among her sons. So how did you, a son, come to do the choosing?"

"My ma died in childbirth fourteen years ago, Pastor. Mandy's mother never knew that. When Mandy arrived, all tiny and scared, holdin' on to that letter like it was her last handle to life itself, well, my heart went out to her, right then and there. 'Course Father took the letter. But since I was the one filling in for Ma all those years... doing the cooking and cleaning and such... well, he told me, 'dis Voman trrrouble, you take care of,'" Jeremy mimicked his father's thick, German accent as he leaned against Rev. Longbottom's horse.

"My oldest brother, Paul, already had a girl. Was just waitin' for the right time to pop the question. I'd wager he hasn't found the right time to pop it yet. And I'd be surprised if Homer or Brandon or Ezra will ever get married. They're all married to Father's farm. No room for women in their lives.

"Father apprenticed the twins out to the blacksmith and the miller in town, and they still have at least two more years of training before they'll be free to work on their own. So that just left Michael, at seventeen... not much older than Mandy... and John, at only fourteen. From my way of lookin' at things, with Mandy headed for the frontier, she needed someone who could teach her country ways, seeing she had the city upbringing she did. And there I was, still doing woman's work all those years after Ma died. I sure did fit the bill. Just made good sense for me to be the one marryin' her. I was older. I could take care of her better than any of the others. I knew how to look after babies, after raising sister Sadie the way I had to. And if that wasn't enough, I fell head over heels in love with Mandy the first time I laid eyes on that little yellow bird, standing there tiny and scared in her pale, golden dress."

"Not to mention that you acquired a farm, free and clear in the bargain."

"That's a fact. It truly is. I knew there'd be no other way on this earth I'd ever see a place of my own. Figured I'd be stuck taking care of Father's kitchen for the rest of my born days."

"Tell me, how did you take to the child?"

"Right from the start I thought of that child as my own. I truly did. I think for a while right after Little Ben arrived, Mandy had a harder time taking to him than I did. But we both got real attached to the little guy. He was mighty special."

"So I gathered."

"It was as hard on me as it was on Mandy, losin' him the way we did."

"She did not divulge her feelings about the child to me. I rather suspect her torment about the tyke is still too acute to discuss openly, as of yet."

"It hurts. That's a fact. I'm the one had to pull what was left of him out of the ashes. Wrap that charred, little bundle for buryin'." Jeremy's voice cracked. He wiped the back of his hand across his nose. "I want to thank you again for doing such a nice service for him, Pastor. It meant a lot."

"All in the line of clerical responsibility, my friend. I'm glad I could be of assistance." Longbottom tightened the last bundle onto his saddle, gave the cinch a sharp pull, then led his horse to the barn door. "And now, once again, must I embark upon the trail of Divine Missions."

"I'll get the barn door." Jeremy moved forward and opened the door, as Reverend Longbottom led his mount outside.

"Take good care of that marvelous lady of yours. She will be in great need of your assistance during her coming confinement," he said prophetically. "I shall return to this vicinity eight weeks hence." He swung up into the saddle and started out at an easy trot. "Godspeed, my friend, until again we shall meet."

* * * * *

Coming back from his errand to find Christmas greens a few days later, Jeremy poked his head in the cabin door. "Mandy?"

"Jeremiah!" She jumped in fright. "You liked to scare the wits right out of me!" she scolded.

"Sorry. I didn't think about startling you. Close your eyes, I got a surprise."

"A surprise! What kind of surprise?"

"Close your eyes, and you'll find out soon enough." He ducked back outside for a few minutes, then he stuck his head in through the door. "Still got 'em closed?"

"They're closed," she said, wiping her hands on her apron and holding them over her face. She heard him wrestling something in the door. "What are you doing, Jeremiah?"

"No peekin'. You'll see soon enough." He jostled something across the floor to the far corner of the cabin. "All right, you can look now."

She took her hands away from her eyes. "What in the world?" She stood looking at the huge, green, pine branch he balanced in the corner.

"Well, what do you think?"

"You've lost your mind, that's what I think." She took in the spectacle of a grown man holding part of a pine tree inside.

"You asked for some greens. This is green."

"Normally people decorate with a few small boughs draped over the doors and windows. They do not bring whole trees into the house."

"It's just one big branch. I thought that's what you wanted," he said, looking a bit confused. "Took me all morning to find it. Not too many pines in these parts, you know."

"Well," she stood pondering, "then it'll have to do. But take that thing right back outdoors and cut it up into suitable pieces."

"You know, Father told us that back in the Old Country, folks would sometimes bring a whole tree inside and dress it up fancy with baubles and candles and such," he said, moving his branch around so it would balance by itself in the corner. "'Course, he never let us fuss much at home for Christmas." He turned the branch again, first one way, then another.

Amanda studied his actions. "Would you like to decorate your, ah... tree?"

"I think I could rig up some kind of base, so's it won't fall down." He flashed her the smile of an excited, little boy, then hurried out to the barn to construct a stand for his tree. Meanwhile, Amanda busied herself looking for things around the cabin to use for decorations. She took a handful of acorns from a bag among their replenished provisions and tied a thread onto the cap of each one in order to hang it on the tree.

When Jeremy brought his stand in the house and anchored the branch firmly, he proudly stood it in the corner, then went back out to the barn to put away his tools. Before he returned, Amanda wound a string of dried, green beans around the branch, making it swag here and there for effect, then she carefully hung each acorn on "Jeremy's tree."

She stood back to take a look. "Hmmmm, needs something more, I think." She rummaged around in her sewing basket. "This might work." She held up a sizable scrap of yellow calico that Netta had included in the basket. Amanda tore the fabric into strips.

"What're you up to, Mandy?" Jeremy asked as he reentered the cabin.

"You'll see." She took each, yellow strip of fabric and tied it into a festive bow. Then attaching a thread to each one, she hung bows all over the tree branch. "There. What do you think?" She stood back to take in the full effect of her creation.

He came to her side and put his arm around her. "I think it's the prettiest Weinachtsbaum I ever did see."

"What's a vinacckks... what you said?"

"In German it means Christmas tree. That's what Father called it."

"I thought you said he never let you have one."

"He didn't."

"Then how can it be the prettiest one, if you never saw one before?" she teased.

"Well it is the prettiest, and that's a fact." He lifted her off her feet and gave her a big, bear hug.

"Oophhh! Be careful, you'll squash the baby!"

"Plumb forgot about that," he said, easing her back onto her feet.

"Oh my! Jeremiah, I felt something! I really felt something!" She flushed with excitement while she cradled her stomach with both hands. "It moved! It finally moved!"

Timidly, Jeremy put his hand over her stomach, too. "You sure?"

She took his hand in hers and eased it over to one side. "There... did you feel that?" She waited a moment. "There it goes again."

A big grin spread across Jeremy's face as he felt a faint flutter beneath his fingers. "What a wonderful Christmas present," he said, moving his hands to her shoulders and pulling her into his arms. They stood for a time in the easy embrace. "Mandy... I'm sorry I didn't believe you right away... about the baby, I mean."

She remained silent for a moment. "I know it seemed kind of strange... me staying so tiny and all. I'm sure I felt life long before this with Little Ben." She turned to face him. "To be honest, Jeremiah, I was beginning to question it all, too. I know I haven't been, quite... myself, lately."

Jeremy raised her chin slightly to gaze into her eyes. "Mandy, my little yellow bird. Do you have any idea how precious you are to me? I would do anything in this world to make you happy. And if believing in a baby was gonna make you happy, then I was all set to believe in that baby, too." He touched her cheek, then timidly touched her stomach once more. "But by gum, there really is gonna be a baby! We'll just have to fatten you up, girl, that's all there is to it."

"I have another present for you, Jeremiah. It's not much, but I did make it myself." She hurried to the bed in the corner and pulled a small package from beneath her pillow. "Here." She blushed as she handed him the package. "Merry Christmas."

"For me? You made something for me? I thought all you been making lately was baby duds."

"Only when you were indoors watching me," she said. "Whenever you went outside I worked on that," she said, nodding at the package. "Ellie Mae gave me the yarn, so I had to make something special for you with it," she said, getting impatient as he looked over the package. "Well, what are you waiting for? Aren't you going to open it?"

He untied the string and pulled back the piece of buckskin folded around the gift.

"Hold it up. I want to see if it's big enough," Amanda urged, exasperated at Jeremiah's slow, deliberate progress.

He held up a deep-gray, cardigan sweater, knit in an intricate, cross-hatched pattern. "It's beautiful! Way too good for the likes of this farmer to wear."

"Put it on. I want to see if it fits."

He pulled the sweater around his shoulders, pushing his arms into the sleeves. Only his fingertips peeked out from the bottom of each sleeve. "I think it's big enough."

"Oh, no! I was afraid they'd end up too short, so I kept adding and adding. I guess I added too much!"

"Well, my hands won't get cold his way." He enveloped her in a big, fuzzy hug. "Thank you, so much. It's the best sweater anyone ever made me."

"You're just saying that to make me feel better. I know you are," she pouted.

"No I'm not. Fact is, no one ever knit a sweater just for me before. Growing up, I only ever wore hand-me-downs. That makes this one mighty special." He released her, then folded the sleeves up to make a cuff. "Now, I have a gift for you, too. I didn't make it... exactly. Just fixed it up some. It's too hard to explain. You'll just have to see it." He started outside, then stopped. "Don't go away, I'll be right back!"

While he was gone, Mandy bent over the fireplace and brushed the coals off the lid of the spider. Luckily, her original, iron pots survived the fire. When she lifted the lid the aroma of rabbit stew wafted up at her. She gave it a stir, took a taste from the spoon, then added a pinch more salt and a little water from the kettle on the hearth. Rabbit wasn't the usual fare for Christmas dinner back home, but here, it seemed appropriate.

Jeremy strode back inside, closing the door with a thud. "Here, Mandy. Merry Christmas," he said, handing her a small, wooden box. He took a breath and forged ahead. "I know it can't make up for losing your pretty, yellow, weddin' dress in the fire, but I thought you might want... well, I figured maybe..., oh, just open it."

Amanda took the smooth, walnut box from his hand, feeling its silky texture against her skin. "This box is magnificent, Jeremiah. Did you make it?"

"I did. But that's not the whole gift. Open it. Then you'll understand."

She eased open the lid as if something would jump out at her. When she had the top off, she lifted the small, leather patch that covered the contents. "My brooch! From Grandmother Bently! Oh, Jeremiah, you saved my brooch!" she squealed.

"I found it, cleanin' up after the fire. That pretty box you had it in was all black and crumbly, and the beads all melted. But that pin there was still in one piece... a little black and tarnished. I put it in my pocket and decided to try and fix it up for you. Took a lot of rubbing and polishing, but I think she cleaned up pretty darn good!"

Amanda flew into Jeremiah's arms and held to his neck with a vice-like hug. "Oh, thank you, Jeremiah. Thank you!" She sobbed onto his shoulder.

"Well, I was hoping it would make you happy," he said, rather confused as she cried in his arms.

"I am happy, Jeremiah. You made me very happy!"

"Then why are you cryin'?"

"Because I'm so happyyyyy," she sobbed even harder.

"I don't think I'll ever understand women."

January 21, 18 and 17
Vermillion Twp.

Dear Libby,

Bad weather and the winter snow has made it longer between mail rounds for Harmon. But just two days before Christmas here he come a-tootin. Bringing me your lovely letter. With all the goins on here I did not even get to read it till after the new year.

Harvey come home from his trading trip the week before Christmas. A few days later than expected, he was. And with a big barrel in the wagon. I could hardly believe it! He said it was a parcel from my sister Tabitha back in Penna. So she did not forget me after all. Found it at the dry goods store sent in his name. Must of been there two months or more. And when we opened that barrel, what do you think was in there? That new pair of shoes I asked her to send out to me. Way back last year! And not just shoes for me did she send. But a pair for each one in the whole family.

You been here too short a time to know that it is nigh on to impossible to get a sturdy pair of shoes in these parts. The pair I wore into this place from Penna finally wore clean out 2 winters ago. Nothing left to patch to. After going unshod for so long now, my feet have got right tough. I did work out a way to use skins and fleece to make passable foot ware for cold weather such as the Injuns make. Still not like a pair of real leather shoes. I wrote to Tabitha to send us new ones so long ago I figgered she never got my letter. Or else she was being pissy about sending the shoes. Knowing Tabitha she took pleasure in making me squirm a spell.

You see, Tabitha and me had a falling out when my first man and me left Penna back in '03. Tabitha and her husband Willard was to come to the Hio Country along with us. But at the last minute she got cold feet and talked him into staying behind. I do not believe she had to talk all that hard. Willard was not cut out for wilderness life. Being a judge he never did get used to any real work that draws a sweat.

138

I have to say that sister Tabby did a good job at guessing shoe sizes for everyone but me. Mine are at least 2 sizes too big. But they fit passable if I wear 3 pairs of socks. Harvey says they are lots warmer that way. I say she knew my size all along and sent this pair out to torment me. She never could do some thing nice without getting in a jab some way or other. Harvey says I am the one being pissy. I say she knew better as we always wore the same size. Even so I am thankful for a good pair of shoes to wear in this cold weather.

Tabby also sent a whole bolt of cotton cloth in a pretty pink calico print. Another bolt of light gray watered-silk. Said she thought with these girls coming to marrying age we should have proper goods for wedding clothes.

I never got the chance to have any real bride clothes my own self. Neither time I got hitched up. But with all this gray silk Tabby sent out we sure can make up some comely outfits for my girls. She sent along yards and yards of matching ribbon and lace for fancying up, too. Also a whole bolt of white muslin for petticoats and bedding and such. She even put in matching thread and new pins and needles.

I have to say that sending all these goods out to us was real nice of her. But she can afford the kindness. Being child less and married to a rich judge to boot. Everything in that barrel was wrapped up in lots of paper. So I smoothed it all out. Now I got me a real good supply of writing paper. That is how I have come to write such a long letter to you this time. I did not have the paper to tell so much before.

Tabby even sent small parcels for brother Jonathan and for Edie and her boys, too. That would be Harmon and Tom and young Willie. The last thing out of the barrel was a new pocket knife for Theodore and a big bag of candy. He shared candy all around with us on Christmas, which was real nice.

And if a barrel full of goodies was not a big enough surprise, Harvey traded all the produce he took to town for special foodstuffs for our Christmas dinner. Leave it to him to think of nothing but food. He got some real canned oysters. I made them into oyster stuffing for the big hen turkey he shot. And would you believe he brought a whole cone of sugar! And 25 pound of real white flour. Not the coarse brown kind we get at Kister mill. Also got me a cinnamon stick! So I made us up some fancy cinnamon buns for Christmas morning, I did. What a treat!

But I think the best things Harvey bought back was a brand spanking new coffee pot, a coffee grinder, and 10 pound of coffee beans! I have not had real coffee in over two years. That is when Harvey's old pot sprung a leak and we run out of beans. Never had me a real grinder, neither. Used to mash those beans in my hominy block. I took to smashing up dandy lion roots when the beans was all. Roasted roots make a fair drink. But it tastes nothing like real coffee. This coffee pot is something. Has a fancy basket inside to hold the ground-up coffee. No drinking dregs from the bottom of this pot. Harvey said he was so hungry for a good cup of coffee, he figured to part with some of that bounty money from those wolf scalps to get him one. On Christmas Eve we even put real sugar in our coffee!

So our Christmas turned out to be more excitement than a weasel in a hen house. And not just cuz of all the nice things Harvey brought home. Besides that barrel in the wagon, he had a some-one in the wagon, too.

And who do you suppose it was? Yep, my mother! She was on her way here to nurse my old coot of a Pa back to health. She left Penna soon as brother Jason told her what happened. Mother made the trip from Philadelfia back to Allegheny County with brother Jason. Then she came the rest of the way out here with Jonathan. He was sitting right up on top of that wagon with Harvey, too.

I did not tell you my little brother is a hog farmer. He does enjoy his work more than most folks would. He downright loves those pigs. I have gone visiting his place only to come across him singing and talking to his animals. If I did not know my ears was playing tricks on me, I would of thought they was answering.

Jonathan is past 30 now and says he is not ready to get hitched. Pa says he is the only smart one in the bunch. He surely is the most smelly one of the bunch. That pretty much says it all. He lives in a old shanty he found empty when he come to these parts. Left by some early squatter no doubt.

Besides his hogs he has Rip for company. Now I do agree that a dog can be worth its keep by warning of the approach of strangers. Or of a fox in the hen house. Edie still swears her old dog Jowler pulled Willie out of the river years ago. Saved his life when he was but a wee tot at his mama's skirts. She was pounding her washing on the rocks at the time.

But that Rip of Jonathan's has to be the most worthless animal I ever did see. Not just on account of his mangy, flea bit look. But because he is so dern lazy. I can not abide the way a body has to step over him when he has put down right underfoot. When Jonathan sees me start in to fret, why he picks the blame dog up and sets it somewheres else. Makes me fuss at him all the more. I do love my brother. But he is daft over his animals. I can see how no woman in her right mind could abide his ways.

You can imagine the commotion when they all got here? Pa was so happy to see Mother, he played up his broke hip for all it was worth. He was in fair spirits up to that time. But all of a sudden he acted like he was about to knock at death's door. Edie had even cleared him to walk around careful like on his crutch stick to keep his motion. But he will not get up off his beehind now that he has Mother to fetch and tote for him.

They been acting like a couple of love birds. Pa even put away his moonshine when she got here. I knew that could not last the winter. Sure enough, I went to change his bedding and hit my great toe on his jug. He had it stashed under the edge of his bed. That toe is so red and swelled up now that I cannot get my new shoes on. Even though they are 2 sizes too big. I still say Tabby knew it when she sent those clod hoppers out here.

So I have ended up with a whole cabin full of people for winter. In some ways it is nice to have the company. I was so glad to see my mother after all these years that on Christmas day I even wore that blasted hat she sent me just to make her happy. I am sure I looked the royal fool. Harvey had to remind me by busting out laughing whenever he looked at me.

I just held my head up high and acted like I was you. Used to wearing hats bigger than milk buckets. A real refined lady who had a new coffee pot and used real sugar. Pretty soon even Harvey stopped laughing. Do I dare tell the rest? Sure I do. The randy old goat tried to get me to put it back on after everyone bedded down for the night. But the walls in here have ears this winter. So I told him he could just sleep with that hat all alone till spring, if he got any of his funny idees, he could.

I have to say that after a month of all this togetherness, I am getting awful squirrelly being shut up in here with so many souls. Even the love birds have started to peck at each other. And Theodore has his nose way out of joint. He says my Pa has forgot about him and whittling all together. Now that Ma is here. So Theodore does his level best to pester his sisters. It is working just dandy. Nothing more shrill than a girl screaming the name of a pesky little brother at the top of her lungs.

We will all be glad to see spring come. But it is still a long ways off.

I hope you folks are getting on right good for your first winter way out here. I figure Harmon will try to make a break for it in the next few weeks to come up your way. He hates to let too many months go by without visiting round to all his sweet hearts. I aim to have this letter ready to go when the Febeeary thaw hits and maple sap begins to run. Maybe when Harmon comes back from making his rounds up north of Uniontown, he will bring me back a letter from you!

Your friend,

Ellie Mae

Dear E-M;

The days are lengthening at last. Winter is still with us, but hope for spring comes of the fact that we sup with the sun once more. I hope that you and yours fare well enough, but I know not when we shall next converse even from a distance. Still I would commit words to paper in the hope of feeling some audience other than that to which I have been confined over these last few months. We are feeling the restrictions of having none but each other's company, a situation not in our experience until now.

Zach hunts frequently, but I am on the verge of doing murder to these children of mine. Yesterday, as today, was not overly cold, so I ordered them out and bid them not to return of an afternoon. Before morning was out, however, Nate came back. I came full bore into a tirade about needing a bit of peace, when he managed to interrupt.

It seems that he and Simeon had lured Levi out onto the thin ice of the creek, and then when Levi proved too light to break through as they had hoped (you have seen that he is skinny as a rail), they each hopped on the ice, and then off again. They knew that the water was too shallow to prove fatal and thought it a lark. Levi, he said, was wetted to his armpits and came out fighting mad. Apparently, they had a little more fun with him yet before he ran off. They told him that he had better not go home and tattle, or I would probably skin him alive first and ask questions later.

The way I had sent them out, screaming like the banshees of which we heard tales in our childhood (one of Da's story themes, of course), it is no mystery that he took their warning to heart.

Later, Nate repented of his mischief and called out, but Levi was not to be found. Nate and his companion in crime conferred, and it was decided that, though the price might be dear, I should be called in. Simeon continued to search (or perhaps preferred to make himself scarce), while Nate was elected to speak to me. It did not take me long to find Levi. He came to my call as he would not to theirs, suspecting more pranks in store.

And after I heard his voice and started in that direction, I heard his teeth chattering before I actually saw him. He was chilled through to the bone. I sent the offenders to chop wood, though there was wood aplenty, telling them that their well-being would be in question if they did not give me wide berth. Finally, I issued the familiar promise that they could deal directly with their father upon his return.

Levi did not come warm that day, even with blankets piled on and a roaring fire beside him. But today he is recovered. I thought to keep him abed another day, but his chest sounds clear, and he slips out at every opportunity. Zach treated the incident lightly enough. He thinks that I made overmuch of it.

15 March, 1817

Ellie Mae,

The back of winter has broken at last, now that we have reached the Ides of March. Today I just received your lovely letters, both at once, one from late December last, and one from January this. Apparently they made the journey as far as the home of our nearest neighbor, Mr. Snow, where they sat until this latest thaw, when he came by to check on us, before making a trip south to Uniontown.

What an awful thing for the Harrisons to lose a baby that way! I cannot imagine how that poor girl must feel. And the father, too, of course. But I do agree with you that having another child right away will probably help to ease their pain.

I was sorry to hear about your father's mishap as well. But it sounds as though you had a merry holiday season in spite of his unfortunate circumstance. New shoes, fine cloth, family gathered together, and a magnificent feast! The description of the food captivated me completely.

We have been eating as poorly of late as we did upon our arrival. To hear of your turkey with oyster dressing. Oh my, I surely do miss the seafood of our Connecticutt! And sweet cinnamon buns and coffee with sugar. I believe I can almost smell them myself. We have long since exhausted our supply of dried apples and rose hips and coffee, and I sat many a winter evening cracking nuts until those were gone, as well. We even finished the remainder of our meal just last week. But can you believe it? This morning Mr. Snow brought over a large bag of cornmeal, newly ground. How wonderful of him!

Something fresh is wanted now. I think that I will try digging up some roots and experiment with them as soon as the ground softens enough. The worst I can do is to poison us, I suppose. Zach says that we are due for another cold spell and at least one more big snow before we should begin to think otherwise. I do not know where he gets this intelligence, but he speaks with such authority, it is enough for me.

I could almost see the scene you described, how your father would make the most of his infirmity, and your mother would cluck over him like a hen with a chick. I wonder if they are still with you and how the play unfolds. I understand your feeling "squirrelly," as I suffer the same malady.

I am grateful for the stacked beds that Zach made, the top one being anchored to the wall. It does make this cabin feel much more spacious. Lizzie gets the high bed to herself while Leesha and little Elijah share the bottom. The boys sleep low under the eaves up in the loft. We still have plenty of storage up there, as Zach and the boys designed shelves which they carried up the ladder and nailed in place near the edge of the loft and almost all the way across it, leaving just enough of an opening at the ladder for moving up and down. The boys like this, as it gives privacy to their quarters, yet it still allows warmth of the fire to reach them.

They also put up a section of shelves to separate our sleeping quarters from the living area. I have taken care to fill all shelves at the sight level, so Zach and I finally have a bit of privacy back. (Doing without space to ourselves has been a very hard thing!)

For Christmas this year, we satisfied ourselves with giving each other a Christmas wish rather than a gift. I think the worst one came from Levi, who wished that Leesha's "beaver teeth" would never kill anyone. She is at that age where new front teeth are all you can see to look at her. In truth, they seem out of place in her small head, so she covers her mouth whenever she smiles. Everyone had a laugh at her expense, but she seemed happy to be part of our merrymaking, and she smiled graciously for everyone to see the aforementioned teeth. It was a lovely day, with husband and children gathered round. We made do with a tasty venison stew for Christmas dinner.

Well, Zach and Mr. Snow have nearly exhausted their talk of spring thaws and seed corn and the success of this year's maple sugaring time, so haste needs that I bring this missive to a speedy finish, for I have asked Mr. Snow to carry this letter as far as the General Store in Uniontown. I am hoping that your Harmon will find it waiting when he next makes his rounds and will carry it the remainder of the distance down to you.

By the by, Mr. Snow says that ram you paid down on shows good promise, and he asked if Zach might be willing to deliver the animal when it reaches proper breeding size later this year. It is enough to give me hope of our further congress. Until then, I remain—

Your Friend, Lib

Chapter 9

Early Surprise
March 1817

She shivered and listened as the wind whistled through the cracks. Tugging at the quilts, Amanda tried to tuck the corners tighter around her chin. She shifted in the bed, searching for a more comfortable position. Jeremy snorted and turned over, pulling the blankets out of her grasp, as she yanked at the disappearing edges.

"How can he sleep when I'm so miserable?" she mumbled under her breath, giving him a slight kick.

"Hmmmm? What's wrong?"

"I'm cold. An' you have all the covers again," she said in her soft, drawl.

"Here, come closer. Let me warm you." Jeremy wrapped his arms around her.

It took great effort for Amanda to turn from her right side onto her left. As she shifted, a cold gust blew under the covers and sent a shiver through her.

"It's no good this way. I'm just too big," she said, trying to shift again. She finally came to lie with the curve of her back next to Jeremy's chest, and he wound his legs around hers, tucking the blanket in, over her shoulder.

She snuggled closer to absorb his warmth, and he rubbed her side, bringing his hand to rest on her swollen stomach. "Did you feel that?" he asked.

"Of course I felt it. What do you think." The strain of three sleepless nights in a row had begun to show on Amanda. Instinctively she held her sides in an effort to calm the squirming child.

A few minutes later, Jeremy's heavy, rhythmic snore next to her ear was almost more than she could stand. *"Well, at least I'm covered this way,"* she thought, closing her eyes. As she began to drift off, another sharp kick made her catch her breath. "Will this baby ever settle down so I can get some sleep?" she wondered out loud.

"Hmmm? You say something Mandy?" Jeremy roused and tried to ease her closer.

"Nothing." She tried pulling her knees to her chest, but curling up was nearly impossible. Every time she moved, the baby began a fresh round of jabs and kicks. She shifted yet again, rolling onto her other side to face Jeremiah, moving closer until her stomach pressed against his. *"If I can't sleep, he shouldn't be able to sleep, either,"* she thought, waiting for the baby to give another kick for his benefit. But now it lay still, as if in conspiracy against her. "It must be a boy."

She tried to smooth a lump out of the straw tick, struggling onto her back as she lay staring at the rafters. Her breath made little vapor clouds in the early-morning air.

"Oh, fiddlesticks! I give up." Amanda threw back the covers and rolled off the side of the high bed. Jeremy took a deep breath, pulled the blankets closer, and wrapped himself into a cocoon.

As soon as her feet hit the icy, puncheon floor, she scurried over to the fireplace and stirred up the coals remaining in the ashes of last night's banked logs. She added a few pieces of kindling, and within minutes she had a nice little fire blazing in the hearth. After piling on a few larger pieces of wood, she hurried to dress while letting the flames die down a bit. Although impatient for a cup of hot tea, Amanda had learned to wait until she could sit the pot over red-hot coals, rather than the sooty flames of a fresh fire.

It didn't take long for her water to begin bubbling. Amanda filled a crock with boiling water, added a small handful of dried chamomile leaves, and set it aside to steep. She poured the remaining hot water into the basin and twisted her long, auburn hair back in order to wash her face, hovering over the basin to absorb as much heat from the steaming water as she could.

Even though Amanda's middle had shown only a slight bulge in the early stages of this pregnancy, her rapid weight gain during the ensuing weeks after Christmas more than made up for her slow start. In three months' time, she'd "bloomed" to nearly twice the size she'd reached at Little Ben's birth. As nearly as she could figure, she still had at least another month and a half to go. *"I'll never get through six more weeks of this,"* she thought miserably.

All of Amanda's pot clanking had finally awakened Jeremy, and he strode over, tucking shirttail into breeches. "Trouble sleeping again, Mandy?" He came up behind her. As soon as he touched her shoulder, she burst into tears.

"Shhhhh," he whispered, patting her softly as he would a child. "Everything will be all right." He held her until the sobs began to ease. "Here, sit down and have some hot tea." He pulled one chair toward the fireplace, took a tin cup from its hook on the wall, and poured a cupful of the steaming brew from the crock where it had steeped.

She savored the cup's heat as it warmed her fingers, and she watched the burly man whose name she shared. Jeremy surprised her when he knelt beside her chair and put his ear against her belly.

"Hello in there. Do you hear me, you little Harrison baby? Your Mama's getting awful tired of so much tusslin' around in there." As if on cue, the baby kicked Jeremy in the ear, and Amanda chuckled. "Now that's better. At least we got your mama to smile."

Jeremy rose, pulled the other chair to the fire, and poured a cup of tea for himself. "Do you think maybe we should send for Ma Hawkins? You're sure looking ripe."

"It's not nearly time yet, Jeremiah. I still have over a month to go."

"Remember how you got right before Little Ben came? All restless and fidgety the way you've been these last few days? Maybe this tyke's just over-anxious to get here."

"I don't want to bother Mrs. Hawkins for no good reason. I can't imagine how it could possibly be ready to come yet," she said, rubbing her middle. "I have to admit I'm awfully tired of feeling this uncomfortable."

Amanda stared into the fire, watching blue flames lap at the edges of the logs. "I wish Grandmother could be here," she said. "She always knows how to take charge of everything... make everyone feel safe." She took the last swallow of her tea and struggled to get to her feet. Jeremy took her by the elbow and helped her to stand. "It's almost light, and you haven't started barn chores, yet, Jeremiah. I'd better start breakfast."

"Will you be all right?"

"Of course, I will. Go on, now," she snapped. "Bertha's waiting."

"I won't be long," he said, donning hat and coat.

He opened the door, and a gust of snow blew in, making a little drift on the floor at Amanda's feet. She shivered and grabbed for her shawl, wrapping it tightly around her shoulders. "I'll never get used to this climate," she grumbled. "Never!"

* * * * *

After finishing breakfast and cleaning up the dishes, Amanda spent the rest of the morning bustling about the cabin. Even though she'd gotten precious little sleep the night before, in a sudden burst of energy she swept the floor, stripped the bed and boiled all the bedding, while Jeremy spent most of the morning out in the barn oiling harness. When he came back in to eat the noon meal, he found sheets and blankets draped over the chairs and table, drying in front of the fireplace.

"What's all this?"

"I had a sudden urge to wash up all the bedding. So I did."

"Kind of unusual at this time of year, isn't it?"

"Oh, Jeremiah, I had to do it, is all."

"That's fine, Mandy. But where do we sit to eat?"

"Is it noon already? I lost all track of the time. I haven't even thought about food."

"I'd say that by the way my stomach's carrying on, it's long past noonin'. What do you have to eat in here?" he asked, nosing around in the pantry cupboard he'd made Mandy shortly after the fire. As he opened its door, a board folded down, held by leather strips, to make a small preparation area. He'd thought it a rather ingenious idea at the time he designed it.

"Oh, let me do that," she said, pushing him aside. In a few minutes she presented him a plateful of cold pancakes with the last of their blackberry jam rolled up inside each one. "Will this keep you till supper time?"

"I reckon it's better than eatin' worms," he teased, taking the plate from her. "Can I have something to drink?"

She went to the fireplace, poured a cup of hot water, and handed it to Jeremiah.

"Did you forget something?"

"Hmmm? What else do you want?"

"Something in this cup of water would be nice."

"Oh, I'm so sorry!" she gushed. "How could I be so forgetful?" She took a handful of comfrey leaves and tossed them into his cup, where they floated on top.

He gave her a funny look, as he stood there holding the plate of cold, pancake-roll-ups in one hand and the steaming cup in the other. "Where am I supposed to eat?"

"You could sit on the bed. Will that do?"

Jeremy walked over to the bed and sat down, balancing his plate on one knee while he began to munch on a pancake. Amanda bent over the fireplace to pick up the kettle, and when she straightened up, she let out a sharp scream.

Jeremy jumped up and ran to her side, letting his plate clatter to the floor. "What's wrong?"

"I... I think it's time," she said with an incredulous look, watching the water run down her limbs. "But it's too early,

Jeremiah! It's way too early." A pain gripped her immediately. "My God, this is happening too fast!"

"Let's get you over to the bed. I'll go fetch Ma quick as I can." He led her to the other side of the cabin and eased her up, onto the bed.

"Hurry, Jeremiah. Please hurry! Something must be wrong!"

"I'll be back in a flick of a donkey's tail." He raced out the door, letting it slam shut behind him.

* * * * *

Jeremy didn't take time to saddle Patsy but made a flying, barebacked trip to Luther and Netta Bailey's, the cabin nearest his own.

Netta heard Rufus announce a visitor with his insistent barking, and she stuck her head out the door to see who would come to visit on such a nasty day.

"Why, it's Jeremy Harrison. Hellooo-oo!" she hollered, waving the dishtowel she still held in her hand. "It's so nice to have some company at last!"

Jeremy reined in Patsy and slid off her lathered back. "Luther around, Netta?" He struggled for breath.

"I think so. That is, he's supposed to be, but you know Luther. Always wanderin' off without tellin' a soul an'–"

"Netta, I don't have time to stand and jaw," he broke in. "Mandy's in a bad way. I need Luther to go fetch Ma Hawkins *right now*. I can't leave Mandy alone so long to go that far myself."

"I'll find Luther right away! He told me he'd be out in the woodshed splittin' more firewood, but could be he's gone down to the sugar shack, to check on the maplin' pot by now. Oh my, where is that man when a body needs–"

"Don't waste time blatherin', Netta. *Hurry!*" Jeremy hopped onto Patsy and swung her around, spurring her back toward his own cabin. "Tell Luther to make it fast! Something's wrong. Mandy's having this baby way too soon." He galloped off with a rain of slushy snow flying up behind.

When he reached his own cabin, he hurriedly tied Patsy in the barn, not taking the time to brush her down after his hard ride. "Sorry, girl. You'll have to wait," he said, throwing a blanket over her to keep her from taking a chill. He raced toward the cabin, anxious at what he might find.

"I'm back!" Jeremy said, bursting through the door. "Luther's going to fetch Ma." He hurried over to the bed where Amanda lay in pain. "You doing all right?"

"I don't think this baby's going to wait," she said through clenched teeth. "You'll have to help me... I... can't... stop the...," she gave in to the next contraction, breathing hard to endure its tightening grip.

"I'll go wash." Jeremy jumped up, grabbed the kettle of warm water sitting by the hearth, and sloshed some into the basin. He lathered up quickly, rinsed off, then looked around for something dry to wipe his hands on.

Wet bedding lay spread all over the cabin, not a dry cloth in sight. At least he knew enough not to wipe his hands on his breeches. Jeremy waved his arms back and forth, as he strode back to the bed in the corner where Amanda lay on the bare, straw tick.

"We have to get your dress off, Mandy. Can you sit up?" He took her by the hands and tried to pull her into a sitting position at the edge of the bed.

"Noooo, Jeremiah, I can't! It's too late. Just push my skirts up an' catch this baby!"

Jeremy eased her down and did as instructed. Although he'd helped cows to calve and horses to foal, never before had he delivered a human baby. Oh, he'd remained with Mandy throughout the birth of Little Ben, much to Ma Hawkins' dismay, but Ma had tended to all the messy parts of that birthing. Jeremy did nothing more than hold Mandy's hand and help clean up the baby when it was all over.

As he pushed her skirts up past her stomach and pulled off her drawers, he saw a tiny, black-haired crown pushing its way between her legs. Involuntarily, she pushed with the next pain, and the baby made its grand entrance. Jeremy held the slippery body tightly under its arms and eased his own little daughter into the world.

"Well, hello you beautiful doll," he crooned, in surprise. "It's a tiny girl!"

She gulped in a big breath and then let out a big wail for such a tiny package. Jeremy held her upside down for a few moments to let the mucus drain from the baby's nose and mouth, as he'd seen Ma Hawkins do. Then he laid her across Amanda's stomach, while they waited for the afterbirth.

"You doing all right, Mandy?" With tears streaming down her cheeks, she couldn't say a word. Gingerly, she touched the baby's tiny hands and feet. Jeremiah found a clean handkerchief on the shelf beside the bed and wiped Mandy's face.

"How long till the sac comes? You remember?"

"I don't think... long," she said, lying there exhausted. In a few minutes, the contractions began again, but nothing happened immediately.

"Maybe I better cut this cord while we wait," Jeremy said, looking around for a piece of string or thread or something suitable to use to tie off the umbilical cord.

"In... sewing... box...," Amanda struggled to explain through the grip of another contraction.

Jeremy found the box and pulled out her sewing scissors and some thread. He tied a stout knot as close to the baby's stomach as he could, and another knot a few inches from the first. Then, nervously, he took the scissors and cut the soft flesh between knots. Not knowing what else to do, he took a large, dried comfrey leaf from the tea tin and pressed it onto the baby's wound.

With that procedure accomplished, he looked around for something to wrap her in, but he didn't see a dry blanket anywhere in the place.

"Did you wash every blanket we have?"

"Baby things... under bed... in box...," she struggled to tell him. He pulled out the box, opened it up, and took out a small blanket. As he wrapped the tiny body, he examined her closely for the first time. She looked perfect from head to toe, but so small! Hard to believe that for Mandy's huge size, the baby turned out no bigger than this. Why, he could fit her entire body in one of his big hands. He'd never seen a baby so tiny!

"Jeremiah?" Mandy struggled, "It's not... right, is it."

"She's perfect, Mandy. But she's so little! How can something this small be alive?"

"Is... is she... breathing?"

"She's breathing fine. Here, I'll tuck her in your arm while I clean you up some." He laid the bundle beside her, and she tried to look over the baby, but when another pain gripped her, she cried out at its sudden intensity.

"I can't hold her... you'll... have to...take..."

Jeremy picked the baby back up and tucked her into the crook of one arm, leaving the other hand free to help Amanda. He didn't think it had taken this long for the afterbirth when Little Ben made his entrance into the world. Mandy had been really bad off after such a long, hard labor with him. This time was so different—unbelievably quick by comparison. But why didn't the afterbirth come?

"Mandy, do you suppose I have to do something to help the sac along?"

"I don't remember," she panted. "Not the... same this time."

Amanda's contractions continued, but nothing appeared to be happening. Jeremy pulled out his pocket watch to check the time. An hour and 45 minutes had elapsed since he'd left the Bailey's. Surely Luther would get Ma back here soon.

"Jeremiah, I... think... something's... wrong. Too much... time... "

"The sac should be here by now, is that what you're tryin' to say?"

She nodded at him, sweat beads on her forehead slipping down into her eyes. Jeremy took the handkerchief from where he'd left it tucked under her pillow and wiped her face again. "You need a drink or anything?"

"Water... please."

He filled the dipper from the bucket and took it back to her. "Can you lean up on your elbows? I don't have another hand to help you," he said.

She leaned sideways on her elbow and took a sip of the cool liquid. "Thank you." She fell back down on the bed, giving in to another contraction.

Just then Jeremy heard the approach of horses. He ran to open the door, being careful to cover the tiny body in his arms with one side of the blanket before he did so. Luther had swung off his horse and was helping Ma down from hers. She grabbed a bundle from behind the saddle and made a beeline for the house.

"This little one couldn't wait, Ma," Jeremy said with a big grin on his face.

Ma took a quick peek under the blanket and headed to the basin to wash up, before turning her attention to the bed where Amanda lay, still panting hard. "How long's she been laborin' since the first one?"

"First one! You mean she's having more than one?" Jeremy asked in astonishment.

"Looks that-a-way," Ma said, matter-of-factly, after she'd taken in the small size of the babe cradled in Jeremy's arm and Amanda's continued laboring. Ma looked around for a towel. "Why's all the beddin' wet?"

"Mandy took a notion to wash up everything in the cabin this morning. Didn't make a lick of sense to me, but she did it just the same."

"Makes perfect sense to a woman about to give birth," she answered. "Bad timin' is all." She took a cloth from her bundle, wiped her hands dry, then went to check Amanda. "How you doin', girl?" She took a look below to size up the situation.

"As well as... I... can," she panted.

Ma straightened Amanda's skirts. "Luther, head home and tell Jeannette to get dry beddin' ready. Bring it right back over here." Luther still stood by the door with Jeremy. "Send for Ellie Mae. Tell her to get herself over here double quick. I'm gonna need her help."

"On my way, Ma," Luther said.

Jeremy strode back to the bed corner, crooning to the tiny sprite cradled in his arms. "I never saw such a tiny thing before, did you?"

"I did. But it takes a lot of care to keep early twins alive," she said. "They have a tough fight ahead. Good thing at least one's a girl. Gener'lly do better than boys."

Jeremy took in this information with a solemn look. "You mean she... they might not make it?"

"Hard tellin'. If they got spunk, they'll make it."

Amanda let out a loud groan, as another pain forced her to push once again. A second head appeared, and with a practiced hand, Edith Hawkins eased the second, tiny girl into the world. She let out a hearty wail before Ma even had the chance to clear her airways. "Reckon this one's smaller yet. But she's got spunk a-plenty."

Ma Hawkins made swift work of cutting the cord and binding the wound, then she wrapped the second baby in another blanket from the box, which still sat open beside the bed. "Can you hold on to the both of 'em while I clean Amanda up?" she asked Jeremy. She put the second baby into the crook of Jeremy's other arm.

He looked from one to the other, shaking his head in complete amazement. "Twins. Who wouldda thought?" He squatted beside the bed so Mandy could look at the tiny pair. "You did a bang-up job, my little yellow bird."

She smiled, breathed a heavy sigh, and closed her eyes.

* * * * *

Two hours later, Luther delivered Ellie Mae to the Harrison cabin to help her sister tend the early twins. Ellie lived a little over four miles further south of the Baileys. She'd brought along the bundle of extra bedding Netta had ready to send.

"I never saw such tiny babes, Edie," Ellie Mae said, cradling a baby in each arm. Jeremy had handed both babies over to the sisters, when evening chore time came around.

"We need to keep 'em mighty warm, or they ain't likely to make it through the night," Edith said, bending over the fire to stir the bubbling stew. After Ellie Mae arrived they'd gotten Amanda settled into a dry bed and managed to straighten up the cabin before supper. They hung all the wet bedding to dry on rope they'd strung from corner to corner between pegs. Now, with supper almost ready, Ma turned her attention to the tightly-wrapped bundles in Ellie's arms. "We'll have to find us some stones."

Ellie gave her a queer look. "Stones?"

"To warm up in the fire. Then we can put these little bodies right on top of those hot stones, so they keep nice and warm all night."

"Leave it to you to think up somethin' like that."

"Trick I learnt from old Gertie. When I lost my fifth baby, it was," Ma said, shuffling over to the freshly made bed to check on Amanda. She slept soundly. Edith went back to the fire and put the kettle in the coals to heat for tea.

Jeremy came through the door with a bucketful of fresh milk. "Got some warm milk here, if we need it," he said. "Mandy had so much trouble nursing Little Ben at first, figured I better bring in extra, just in case."

"She hasn't stirred since fallin' asleep an hour ago," Ma answered. "We'll give these little ones a chance to nurse after she wakes up... see how they do." She busied herself setting the table for supper. "Jeremy, you got any nice smooth stones around here we can heat up in the fire?"

"You better know I got stones. I bet I picked more stones out of these fields than I picked potatoes! Why do you want hot stones?"

"To lay those little babies on so they stay warm through the night," she said. "We need a box to put 'em in, too. I didn't see no cradle anywheres about."

"Figured I'd have at least another month to work on one of those. Looks like now I'll need to make two!"

"One box'll do for the both of 'em for a while. They'll stay warmer together."

"How about that wooden crate Mandy has full of baby clothes? They should fit about right in that."

"It'll do," she said, pulling the trammel away from the fire and taking down the stew pot. "Got supper all ready."

"Boy, am I starving! Never did eat dinner, what with all the excitement around here today." He hurried to wash, then scooted the cornmeal keg over to the table and sat down, motioning for Ellie and Edith to sit in the cabin's only two chairs. Ma pulled out a chair for Ellie, then took one of the babies from her and seated herself in the other.

"Reckon you want to pray again," Edith said, not asking, but stating a fact, as she bowed her head and screwed up her face in a grimace.

"Don't mind if I do." Jeremy bowed his head.

Ellie quickly put down the spoon she had hanging in mid-air above her stew bowl, shot a surprised glance in Edie's direction, then closed her eyes, too.

"Lord, I'm mighty grateful for two, fine, baby girls," Jeremy prayed, "and for these neighborly women to help us care for 'em right now. But I don't mind telling You, I'm more than a little fearful for these tykes. Please, Lord, give 'em the strength they need to make it through the night, and the spunk they'll need to grow up in this hard place. Please help my Mandy, too, Lord. She's gonna need extra strength with two babies to care for. Keep us all in your care this night. Oh, an' thanks for this fine food and the hands that made it. Amen." He picked up his spoon and dug hungrily into the stew before him.

Ellie Mae took up her spoon again and ate slowly, shooting a curious glance at her sister every now and again.

"Fine stew, Ma," Jeremy said between bites.

"Ellie got it started while I helped Amanda into clean clothes and a dry bed."

"We just took turns holdin' babies and a-stirrin'," Ellie said.

"Well, thank you for this fine stew, Ellie Mae."

"Much obliged," she answered, keeping her eyes on Edie the whole time. She'd never seen her sister treat a man with such respect. Most of them she ignored altogether.

Amanda woke after they'd finished their meal. Ma gave her a small bowl of stew. "I'm not very hungry," Amanda said, dabbing at the edges of the bowl with her spoon.

Ma put a little of the gravy in a mug, then added some hot water to it, along with a selection of herbs from the pouch in her birthing bundle. "See if you can get some of this down," she said, handing Amanda the mug. "You got to build up your strength fast now, with two babies to nurse." She took the bowl of stew away.

"What if I can't do it? Maybe I won't have enough milk for two."

"You have to drink a-plenty, girl, that's the trick. Don't matter what, neither. Just so's you drink all you can hold. I'll leave some herbs here to mix into teas and milk and such. They'll help your milk come in good and strong."

"But how am I going to nurse two babies at once? Isn't it hard?"

"You got two good spigots, ain't you? Lots of women do it with no trouble at-all."

Amanda didn't raise any more questions for the moment. She drank the rich liquid down quickly, making a face as she took the last swallow.

"'T'warn't that bad," Ma said, taking the empty mug from her and setting it on the table with the other dirty dishes. "I think maybe we ought to give these babes a chance to nurse. See if they got what it takes to survive."

"You mean they might not live?" Amanda suddenly looked terrified. "They're not right, are they. I just knew it! It all happened too soon!"

"Calm down, girl. These babies look real fine," said Ma, taking a baby from one of Ellie Mae's arms. "The next day or two might be nip-'n-tuck, is all. Never can tell about early twins. Long as they's breathin' good and you keep 'em plenty warm, why they stand a good chance of pullin' through," she said, laying one baby into Amanda's arms, "if they can eat, that is."

Amanda gave Ma a concerned look, then she unwrapped the blanket and looked over the smaller baby very carefully, touching the dainty fingers and minuscule toes. "She's so tiny." She quickly rewrapped the blanket around the mite of a body. "How can something so little be alive?"

At that question, the baby gave a hardy cry, obviously not happy at being disturbed. "My, she's got a big voice for such a little thing." Amanda unbuttoned her bodice and eased the babe up to a breast. The baby's instincts immediately took over, and she latched on to her mama, sucking strongly.

"Well, we got one a-workin'," said Ma. "Let's see how the other one does." She took the second baby from Ellie Mae and placed it in the crook of Amanda's other arm.

"I want to see her first," Amanda said. "But how am I going to unwrap her with both arms full?" she asked, looking from one baby to the other. "How am I ever going to handle two at once?" she whined, beginning to get excited again. The baby at her breast began to fuss; then Amanda began to cry. "It's too hard, I just can't to do it."

"Hush now, girl. You're gettin' all worked up for nothin.' And you're gettin' these babes upset for no good reason," Ma said sternly. "Take a deep breath now. Good. Now take another one," she said, watching Amanda respond to her firm leading.

Ma retrieved the second baby and unwrapped her so Amanda could take a good look for herself. "See, she's fine, too. A perfect little girl, just like the other one," said Ma, rewrapping the baby.

Amanda got the first one settled to nursing again. Then Ma laid the second baby back in Amanda's arm and pushed the other side of her bodice back. "Ease her up now, see if she'll suckle. If they can both eat good, they have a better chance."

Number two rooted around before latching on to Amanda, then she settled down to steady nursing. "Good," said Ma. "Real good. They're gonna make it, girl. You just watch and see if they don't."

At this early stage a baby didn't get much to eat, but Ma insisted all her babies take those "first juices" before a mother's milk came in strong. She believed it made a difference in surviving the first, critical hours of life.

While Edith helped Amanda set the babies to eating, Ellie Mae had busied herself cleaning up supper dishes. She stood smiling, as she sloshed dish water in the granite pan, and watched Amanda nurse the tiny twins. "Ain't that a pretty sight, Edie?" she said. "Two little tykes, and both of 'em downright perfect."

Jeremy returned with an armload of wood and stones, closing the door quickly, so as not to create a draft on the babies. He stacked the wood beside the fireplace and laid the stones on the hearth. Standing there, taking in the picture of Amanda with two babes in her arms, a tear slipped down his cheek; he didn't make any move to wipe it away. He walked over to the bed and knelt beside his wife and babies.

"Mandy, do you know how beautiful you are?" he whispered. She smiled uncertainly, then gave her full attention back to the suckling babes. He knelt for quite a time, before rising and walking back to the fireplace to stir up the coals and add more wood to the fire.

"You thought up any names yet?" asked Ellie.

Jeremy shook his head. "Haven't given it a single thought," he said. "How 'bout you, Mandy? What do you want to name these little beauties?"

"We never talked about a name, Jeremiah, let alone two," she said softly.

"Why don't you name 'em after both your mothers?" Ellie asked.

At the mention of her own mother, Amanda began to shake and cry softly. Jeremy returned to her side and put his arm around her. "We don't have to name 'em after anyone," he said, patting her. "We'll think up brand new names just for these two."

"Now look what you went and done," Ma scolded Ellie. "You got her cryin' again."

"I'm sorry. How was I s'pose to know talkin' about her mama would upset her?"

Jeremy calmed Amanda once more. "Here, blow," he said, holding a handkerchief up to her nose. She blew. "Good girl." He stuffed the kerchief back in his pocket. "Now, let's study on some names. What do you think of Alice and Abby?"

Amanda shook her head no.

"How about Ida and Ivy?"

She shook her head no again.

"Maybe Julie and Josie?"

Amanda made a face at him.

"I got a granddaughter Josie," said Ellie Mae, washing the last dish. "'Course her real name is Josephine, but we call her Josie for short." She picked up the drying cloth and began to dry and stack the clean dishes. "I sent Pa and Mother and Theodore over to Jason and Mary Sue's for a few nights while I'm here. So they'll get to see our little Josie. Pa's gettin' around right good now, Edie. You'd be proud."

Amanda's small voice piped up from the bed corner. "I like Lillian. That's my Grandmother Bently's middle name."

"Lillian, that's good," Jeremy said, nodding in agreement. "I like it. That takes care of one. Now, what should we name the other?"

"It would be nice to name her after your mother, Jeremiah. Her name was Camellia, was it not?"

"Camellia Irene," he said. "I'd like that, Mandy. I truly would." He stood in thought for a few moments. "How about we give them both your middle name... Jane?"

"Lillian Jane and Camellia Jane? Both the same?"

"Why not? They are twins. Sure do look alike, too," he said. "Which one we gonna name which?"

"Let's name the first after your mother, and the second after my grandmother."

"Sounds fine to me. But which one's which?"

She looked from one baby, to the other, then back again, a bit confused herself. "Why, I... I don't know which one's which! How in the world are we ever going to tell them apart?" she said, beginning to get upset all over again. At her agitation, the twins, who had both nursed quietly up to now, began to fuss, too.

"What am I gonna do with two cryin' babies?" Amanda asked, she, herself nearly in tears once more. "Jeremiah, take one of them, please!"

Before he could reach the bed, Ma Hawkins had scooped one twin, up and over her shoulder, freeing both of Amanda's hands to tend to the other. "Now you calm yourself down, girl," Ma scolded. "These babes are gonna do exactly what you do. You gotta be calm and strong so they will be. Understand?"

Amanda took a deep breath and nodded. "But how do we to tell them apart?"

"That's easy," said Ma. "Jeremy, hand me my poke, would you?"

He handed her the birthing bundle she took everywhere she went, and she handed him the baby she still held. From the bundle she pulled a spool of string. She unrolled a fairly long piece, then folded it in half, and in half again. After braiding the pieces firmly together, she tied the homemade bracelet onto one twin's ankle—tight enough to stay put, but not so tight as to cut off her circulation.

"See, this one's the first born. She's a mite heavier than the second, but she ain't likely to stay that way for long," said Ma. "She's Camellia." Edith placed the babe back in Amanda's free arm. "And that one's Lillian. If you look real close, you can see she has a mole back of this earlobe," Ma said, easing the other baby's ear back for Amanda to see.

"Just like my birthmark," Amanda said, touching her own ear.

"Far as I can tell, that's the only difference."

After both babies settled back to nursing, Ma moved over to the fire and began to stir it around, making room among the hottest coals to heat her stones. "You sure these ain't got no cracks? We don't want no rocks explodin' in here."

"Smooth as can be. I double checked them all," Jeremy answered.

She continued to fuss with the fire, until they heard the fast approach of a horse. "Hello the house!" called a man's gravelly voice as he pulled his horse up short.

Before Jeremy could reach the door, Harvey Thompson pushed it open and strode right in, stooping his tall frame to clear the doorway.

"'Lo, Jeremy. Misses," he nodded at Amanda, his eyes leering for a moment on the nursing mother. In acute embarrassment she dropped one baby to the bed, grabbing frantically for a blanket to cover herself. At her sudden movement, his expression changed, and he doffed his hat. "Beg your pardon."

In his hurry to close the door, Jeremy hadn't seen the exchange between Harvey and Amanda. But at a baby's cry, he rushed over to help her.

"I come to fetch Ellie Mae home," Harvey said, shooting a disgusted look at Ellie, who'd just put the stack of clean dishes on the shelf.

Edith Hawkins rose from where she squatted by the fire and moved to Ellie's side. "I'm gonna need Ellie's help keepin' these twins alive through the night," she said with a decided edge to her voice.

Harvey looked toward the bed where Amanda sat, now discreetly covered holding one twin, while Jeremy sat on the edge of the bed holding the other. "Looks like they're in good hands," said Harvey with an irritating smile. "You and Harrison and his misses can do a fine job without Ellie Mae." He motioned for Ellie to come. "She has a-plenty to do at home." He put his hat back on and took Ellie's wrap from the peg by the door. "Looks like you finished up your supper. Ellie and me'll just be goin' so she can tend to mine."

"You mean you didn't eat yet?" Ellie asked in surprise. "But I left a big pot of stew. An' I told Johanna and Katrina to see to your supper."

"I let 'em go off with Willie and a bunch of young folks. Some kind of doin's over to the Guthries," he said, wrapping the heavy cloak around Ellie's bony shoulders. "I worked me up a powerful hunger," he said in a tone that implied more than a hunger for food.

"Well you couldda et that stew without me or the girls to serve it up," Ellie said, obviously perturbed, but not bold enough to cross him.

"Stew burnt hard in the pot. Wasn't much left fit to eat," he said. "'Sides, nobody's home right now. First time all winter we ain't had your folks under foot," he added, obviously eager to get his wife home while they had the cabin all to themselves.

"You get Ellie right back here at first light, Harvey, you hear me?" Ma directed.

"I'll send Theodore up in a couple days when he gets back home... see if she's still needed," he answered in a tone that closed the subject.

Ellie turned to give her sister a hug and whispered something in her ear, to which Ma just shook her head. Out loud Ellie said, "I'll send food with Theodore." She made a hasty retreat out the door.

Ma scuttled outside to tell her something else, but Harvey had already boosted Ellie onto his horse. He climbed behind, pulled her close to himself with one arm across her bosom, then swung the horse around, his other hand firmly holding the reins.

Ma called to Ellie, "Tell my Willie to get his self right back home after he leaves them girls off at your place!"

Ellie waved in answer, and Harvey kicked the horse into a quick trot.

"Ain't hunger for food drivin' that mangy excuse for a man," she grumbled under her breath, but loud enough to be heard. She walked back into the cabin. "Chickenhearted cuss. Pushin' women around just so's he can feel all-mighty." She mumbled some more, but Jeremy and Amanda couldn't hear the rest.

Edith Hawkins went back to the fire and finished arranging the stones to heat among the coals. Once satisfied, she stood up, brushed off her hands, and said, "Welp, looks like it's up to the three of us to get these youngens through the night. Jeremy, I reckon you and me better take shifts to keep watch. Make sure these babes keep a-breathin'. Amanda, you sleep all you can between feedin's. We'll bring you the babes whenever they wake. They'll have to eat more often than full-term babes, you know."

* * * * *

Every four hours throughout the night, Edith and Jeremy spelled one another. They'd keep one set of stones heating in the fire, while the twins slept atop the other set in their box, covered over with a thick blanket to keep the makeshift-incubator toasty warm. Whenever the babies ate, they'd exchange cooler stones for the warm ones.

Most of the time, whenever one baby awoke, the other one did, as well. Amanda nursed them nearly every two hours, so she seldom slept more than an hour at a stretch herself, before needing to rouse and feed babies again.

By morning, none of the adults in the cabin had gotten much sleep, but the babies made it through their first, crucial night.

Ma huddled over the fire, heating water for morning tea, stirring up a pot of cornmeal mush for their breakfast. Jeremy had already headed to the barn to start morning chores, and Amanda sat on the bed nursing the tiny twins, her head jerking every now and again as she struggled against sleep while the babies ate.

"I don't know how I'll ever be able to tend these babies during the day, if I have to stay awake all night long," Amanda fussed. Ma took the babes from her and laid them back in their box, tucking a blanket firmly around the edges to keep in every bit of heat.

"You have to toughen yourself to the job, girl," Ma answered, giving her no sympathy. Edith had her doubts about Amanda's ability to cope with twins, but she didn't dare let a bit of her apprehension show. "You got to buck up for the long haul." Ma swung the trammel away from the fire and took down the pot of mush. She dished up a big bowlful and poured on a hearty serving of fresh cream and some of Luther's new maple syrup. "And you got to keep eatin' so those babies can keep eatin', too."

Amanda took the bowl and dutifully spooned into her breakfast, while Ma stood over her. Only when Edith satisfied herself that Amanda would continue to eat without complaint did she return to the fire to prepare a crock full of tea.

By the time it had steeped sufficiently, Jeremy had returned to the house, hungry. "Hope you made plenty, Ma. I'm starved."

She served up another big bowlful for him, then one for herself, pouring cups of tea for all three of them before sitting down to eat her own breakfast. They ate in silence for several minutes, but before any of them had finished, one of the babies began to fuss from its bed by the fire. Jeremy started to rise. Ma put a hand on his shoulder. "I'll tend her. You finish," she directed.

Not giving him a chance to argue, Ma scooped up the fussing babe and put it over her shoulder before it roused the other, who still slept soundly. She softly patted her back, dislodging the offending burp that had disturbed the baby's sleep. Ma laid her back in the warm box, easing her in, so as not to waken her twin, then she turned to check on Amanda. She'd fallen asleep and let her empty bowl and cup slip aside on the bed.

Ma retrieved the utensils and headed back to the table to sit with Jeremy. "While she's sleepin', I got somethin' to say to you." Ma stirred her mush around the bowl, trying to plan the words so they'd come out right. "You got any family you can send for... to come out here and help that girl with these twins? Between you, me and this hearthstone, I don't think she can handle two babies by herself."

"I can help her, Ma. You know that."

"I know you can manage babies just fine. That ain't the point. You got two of 'em here that need special tendin'... 'round the clock. And plantin' time's around the corner. What'll you do then? There ain't enough hours in the day to do all the farm work that needs done and still help Amanda with these babes."

Deep in thought, Jeremy pulled on the bushy beard he'd grown since Christmas to cover up his scars. He rose from the chair and walked to the fireplace, squatting at the hearth and stirring at the fire. He pushed the hottest coals to the center and eased the ashes over to the side.

Ma continued. "I can stay on to help for a while. I reckon Ellie can finagle a little time away from Harvey now and again to help out, too. But I don't know as anyone else in the township can spare much time to help with spring comin' on."

"I'll bring in more wood," Jeremy said, rising to head outdoors. He donned his hat and coat, but before he opened the door, he turned back to Ma. "I could send to Pennsylvania for Sadie. My sister's going on 15. She could be a big help to

Mandy." He went silent a few moments. "Sure have missed that pipsqueak these two years. I have my doubts Pa will let her come, though."

"Only one way to find out," Ma answered. "Yesterd'y Ellie told me brother Jonathan aims to make a trip east to take mother back home to Philadel'ia. Maybe he could stop by your pa's place and talk to him," she offered. "Send a letter along with him. Tell your pa what I think, if it'd help any."

"That's good of you, Ma," he answered. "I need to think on it, though. Bringing Sadie out here's a big step."

"Don't think too long. Unless I'm seein' it all wrong... an' I don't miss too often, mind you... I don't think your woman has the grit it's gonna take to keep up with two babies for the long haul."

"You convinced me. I'll start on a letter right away. I just hope Pa sees fit to let Sadie go."

March 8, 1817
Vermillion Twp.

Dear Lib,

It soon will be time to start seeds to get a early jump on the garden. We finished off the turnips last month. I am hungry for fresh greens. Maybe in another few weeks the nettles will be big enough to pick for nettle soup.

We were busy last month making maple syrup. Tastes mighty good all year long. We like to hard boil some eggs right in the sap while it cooks. Makes a good tasting egg. Kind of sweet.

I am lucky to have chickens laying again. I saved enough hens from the hawks last year to have a good chicken coop full. Some even kept laying all last winter! Between the hawks and the weasels year before, we lost all but 5 hens and 1 rooster. Then they up and quit laying till late March to boot. At least all them hens hatched out a good clutch of chicks last spring. Made up for the ones lost. We even ate a few roosters in the fall. Tasted mighty good. Harvey says that is my attitude. Chicken today, feathers tomorrow. But I am the one takes care of them. And I say there was plenty and enough to have my sister and her boys over for chicken dinner on a Sunday.

April 11

I picked the first flower of spring not long after I last wrote on this letter. A yellow daffydill. When I moved over here to live with Harvey, I planted a handful of bulbs from my other place. Those same bulbs started out with me from Penna over 14 years back. After all these years, they have doubled as many times by now. Sure is nice to see their pretty little yellow trumpets waving in the spring breeze. Listen to me, sounding like something out of a poem book!

I have been right busy of late, what with the heap of people round here. And Amanda Harrison being delivered of a set of twins girls. Day after I last wrote on this letter, it was. I been helping out with them as I can.

Then come St. Patrick's Day.

I do not know if youens celebrate that holiday or not. Your pa being Irish, I reckon you do. My pa had a good friend once who was Scotch-Irish, so now Pa says it is his bounden duty to honor the likes of a man as St. Patrick. One more excuse for him to get a snootful, more like. Which he did. I am sure it was a trial for him to stay sober so long with Mother here all winter. Well, Saint Patrick's Day was the last straw with her. They had a big too-rang. The shouting lasted into the next week. Mother had been talking about going back to the hills with Pa to look after him. Now he says that St. Patrick saved his life.

Once the weather broke, all the bodies in this cabin thinned out. And more than I ever thought they would. Harvey could take no more of the squabbling. He drove Pa over to Edie's place. Next thing was figuring a way to get Mother back home to Philadelfia. Jonathan said he would take her far as sister Tabby's in Allegheny County. Brother Jason could deliver her the rest of the way home to Philadelfia. But I did not count on her getting Katrina's ear about city life. Promising a proper coming out party to meet clever young gentlemen.

I cannot blame a girl her age for wanting to see more prospects than the mangy critters to be had in these parts. But it shore did hurt to tell her goodbye. Harvey was all for it. I could not stand in her way on account of my own selfish feelings. Mother will do it up proper for her. No doubt of that. Fancy dresses and parties and all that business. I sent the cloth from sister Tabby along with Katrina. We have no need of it here now as we have lost both Katrina and Johannah.

Far more startling than Katrina leaving was Johannah running off like she done. I knew that girl was chafing at the bit. But she was acting tetched altogether the day I picked them spring flowers. First she got out of bed. And without a word to a soul she walked out the door in her nightdress. I looked out and saw her turning in circles under a tree. Then I missed my little mirror. It was gone from over the wash basin. That mirror is about the nicest thing I own. I was ready to raise the roof when Katrina walked over and got it out from under Johannah's pillow. I asked what in blue blazes it was doing there?

I kept a eye on both them girls all morning. After nooning, they slipped out for a walk. We have not seen Johannah since. Katrina would not say a word till dark fell. Johannah made her promise not to. So we would not come after her. Seems the strange doings of this day was all about Johannah looking for signs of her true love. Katrina spilled it out all in a rush after dark. Thankful to have it off her mind.

She said Johannah commenced to counting 9 stars a night some 9 nights ago and kept it up every night since. Last evening with the mirror under her pillow, Johannah dreamed of her true love. A young man on a horse. Then this morning, turning 3 times under the cedar without having spoke a word, she heard music. Well, that says she'll be happy with this feller on a horse. To top it all off, on their walk a redbird flew right past them. Meaning that her love was coming to her. When the girls crested the hill and saw a horseman coming, that was the clincher.

He was a nice enough fella, Katrina says. And not hard to look at. When Johannah heard that he was on his way west, why she just hopped right up behind him and off they rode. Think of it! Riding off without so much as a backwards glance.

Harvey just said—Bout time. Myself, I sure do miss the girl. It is exciting. Riding off with a stranger into some new life. But it is the worrying if things go well with her that bothers me most. She did tell Katrina to give me a kiss and hug for a goodbye.

And then within a fortnight there goes Katrina flying the coup to boot! So here I am down to one chick. But that with no joy in it. And not the company of any of my girls. No son-in-laws to come to supper. No grandbabies next door. Listen to me snivel. It is such a switch all of a sudden. A whole cabin full. Then no one but Harvey and a pigheaded boy.

Jonathan plans to stop off in Fayette County, Penna. After he leaves off Mother and Katrina in the hands of brother Jason. He carries a letter to Jeremy Harrison's pa, asking if his sister Sadie might come on out here to help the Harrisons with their twins. No doubt he was there by now and on the road to home. With Sadie I am hoping. That Amanda sure does need help with those two little babes. Edie and me do all we can. But that Jeremy is going to drop soon if he does not get some releef.

Harmon just came from Uniontown with your nice long letter, Libby. I was so glad to hear from you and know you and yours are doing tollable well after a long winter.

I hope those children of yours soak up plenty of sunlight to help get over the winter peek-eds. Feels right nice to have sunshine bake the cold out of these bones again.

When you go to digging roots, try digging some sassyfrass to steep. Do you know sassyfrass? No doubt your Zack does. Him knowing so much about wood. The roots steeped up into a tea makes for a great spring tonic. Cleans out the blood. Right tasty too. Just make sure you clean them roots up good first. You can make tea out of the same roots 2 or 3 times. Tastes better with a little maple syrup in it. If you can find any over-wintered cranberries, they taste much better in spring. Winter takes the bitter out of them. Not much fun to pick, though. As they like swampy ground.

I will tell Harvey about the ram. It is good news.

I better get to cooking. Got some hominy and pork going. I spent a lot of the dark evenings shelling corn, I can tell you. Harvey went out to plow this forenoon and stayed out all day. He will be right hungry tonight. I think it too early to plow, but Harvey was itching to get ground fit for planting.

You all must come to the revival here in June. What church are you folks? Not that it matters for a revival. I hope that will be our next chance to meet up.

Your friend,

Ellie Mae

Chapter 10

Sadie
April 1817

"Jeremiah, come quick! Amanda screamed from the door. "This baby's not breathing!"

In the barn Jeremy dropped his pitchfork and headed for the cabin at a dead run. He rounded the porch and nearly collided with Amanda, who held one twin and pointed wildly toward the cradle inside, tears streaming down her face.

"She stopped breathing! What do I do?"

Jeremy raced inside, knelt by the cradle, and put his ear close to the baby's face. He felt the distinct tickle of a slight breath on his cheek, and he sighed in great relief. "She's breathing, Mandy. She's sound asleep and breathing just fine. See," He tickled the bottom of the baby's foot, and she pulled it back in an immediate, reflexive response.

"But she stopped breathing, I know she did," Amanda sobbed. "I touched her and she didn't move at all. I thought she was dead!" Amanda wailed and collapsed into a chair, still holding the other twin who'd also begun to cry at her mother's agitation. The past five weeks of sleepless nights and endless feedings had brought Amanda close to the end of her rope.

Sheer willpower alone kept Jeremy on his feet. He plowed all day to get his fields fit for planting, and every time Amanda hollered in alarm, he'd drop the reins, jump the furrows, and race to the cabin to deal with her crisis of the moment. She juggled constant feedings, fussy babies, and endless washing. By evening, she collapsed, completely spent.

After Jeremy finished his field work and tended to his usual evening chores, if they were to eat anything at all, it was he who usually fixed the supper. During the first three weeks after the twins' birth, Ma and Ellie Mae sent meals over to the Harrison's. But Ma had other mothers and babies to tend, and Harvey finally put his foot down to Ellie, so now Amanda and Jeremy fended for themselves and ate sporadically, at best.

Both babies awoke every three hours like clockwork, and since Amanda still had trouble dealing with two babies at one time when she nursed, Jeremy always rose to help her shuffle the twins at feeding times. If either of the Harrisons got two or three hours of solid sleep at a stretch, they felt lucky.

Amanda sat crying, so Jeremy, as always, tried to reassure his frazzled wife. "It's all right, Mandy. Camellia's fine." He took the squalling baby she held and jiggled her. "Shhhhh, hush, now, you little flower," he crooned to the howling Lillian. "You'll get your sister going if you keep this up. Then we'll be hours getting you both settled down again." At the sound of her daddy's deep voice Lillian began to quiet.

"I swear Camellia quit breathing," Amanda sniffled. "She lay so still. I thought–"

Jeremiah cut in, "Don't think so much, Mandy. You're too busy looking for trouble with these babies. You need to concentrate on making the best of things instead of looking for the worst to happen all the time."

"I'm stuck in here all day with crying babies, an' you don't seem to care whether they live or die!" she howled.

"Mandy, that's not true. You know it's not. I come in to help whenever you call."

"I take care of two starving, babies all by myself... all day long!" She began to wail.

Jeremy shrugged his shoulders in frustration. "Mandy, quit. That's enough of your hysterics over nothing." Jeremy continued to pat Lillian against his shoulder.

"Nothing! Nothing!!" Amanda's voice rose with each word. "You call it nothing when a baby stops breathing? You don't believe me, I know you don't!" She dissolved into a fresh gush of tears.

"Oh, Mandy, there's no need to get so upset." He tucked Lillian back into the cradle beside Camellia and gave it a push to set it rocking, then he went over to Mandy's chair, leaned down, and took her into his arms. "Shhhhh, hush now. Everything's all right. You're just exhausted. We both are," he said, patting her shoulder the same way he patted the babies. "That's why we're snapping at each other." She cried in his arms, and he held her until the sobs began to ease.

"Here," he said, pulling a handkerchief from his back pocket. "Blow." She blew. "Better?" She nodded her head in the affirmative. "Good. Looks like the babies might sleep a bit. So I want you to lie down and take a nap till they wake up to eat again. You'll feel better if you get a little sleep."

Jeremy turned her around by the shoulders, and she walked wooden-legged toward the bed in the corner. "I'll start supper when I finish up the west field," he said, easing her onto the noisy straw tick. He swung her legs up on the bed, removed her shoes, then pulled the coverlet up to her chin. Before he had it tucked around her shoulders, Amanda lay fast asleep. He leaned down and gave her a soft kiss on the forehead. "Sleep, my little yellow bird. We've still got a long haul ahead of us."

He trudged back outdoors, closing the cabin door quietly behind himself.

* * * * *

Later that evening, after hastily concocting a kettle of soup and mixing up some stick-to-the-ribs corn cakes, Jeremy and Amanda took turns eating and tending babies.

Between six and nine o'clock every night, both babes went through a fussy period without fail. Jeremy would pace the floor with a baby on either arm so Amanda could eat. But most evenings, Jeremy rocked one baby across his knees while he ate his supper, since holding two squalling babies at once still upset Amanda so.

Tonight they were lucky; by 8:30 p.m. the patter of rain had lulled Camellia to sleep and only Lillian continued to fuss. Jeremy sat, glassy-eyed, nearly falling asleep between bites, while Amanda paced the floor with her great-grandmother's namesake.

Suddenly the door burst open, bringing Jeremiah to instant attention.

"Jems!" gushed a slim, teen-aged girl who rushed into the cabin. She had light, chestnut hair pulled back into a single braid, and her bonnet dangled loosely around her neck. She flung herself into Jeremy's arms. Taken completely off guard, he hesitated a few moments, not knowing quite what to do.

"Well, what kind of a welcome is this for your only sister? Aren't you gonna hug me," demanded the brown-eyed imp.

"Sadie? Is that really you?" he asked, holding the comely, young woman at arm's length to get a good look at the baby sister he hadn't seen in nearly two years.

"It's me, in the flesh," she said, squirming free from his grip to pull off a too-big overcoat.

"How did you get here? I never heard any horse or wagon."

"Well, it's a wonder! We made enough noise to wake the dead, slogging around in all that mud," she joked. "Just look at me. My skirts are covered!"

"We?"

"Me and Jonathan. You sent him to fetch me, remember?"

Jonathan waved hello from the doorway where he stood, hat in hand, quietly waiting for an invitation to come inside.

"What are you standing there for? Come in and take a load off, friend," Jeremy said, motioning for Jonathan to join him at the table. "How'd you manage to get here so quick? I didn't look for you back for another two weeks, at least," Jeremy said, now wide awake and temporarily recharged at this unexpected turn of events.

Jonathan strode inside and sat in the chair Jeremy offered. "Didn't have to take Mother and Ellie's Katrina clear east after all. When we hit Pittsburgh, I checked at the stockyards to see if brother Jason might be in town. Turned out he was just fixin' to head Philadelphia way, so he agreed to take 'em both on home. Freed me up to drop straight down to your Pa's. Saved two week's travel, sure."

Amanda stood in a daze, looking from one face to another as if she didn't recognize a single one. Lillian, who still fussed in her arms, began to wail louder when her mother stopped pacing.

While Jeremy and Jonathan talked at the table, Sadie walked over to greet Amanda. "Hello, sister. Remember me?" she asked, gently easing the squalling baby from Amanda's arms. "Guess I look different than when I stood up with you and Jems at your wedding. Two years can change a person." Lillian began to quiet in the strange arms. "She's beautiful," Sadie whispered.

"How did you get her to stop crying so easily? I've been walking the floor for hours," Amanda exaggerated, frustrated by Sadie's immediate ease with the baby.

"Nothing special. I s'pose she was worn out and ready to stop, is all," Sadie answered, giving Amanda a warm smile. "What's her name?"

"Lillian."

"Lillian," crooned Sadie, softly tracing the baby's ear. "What a lovely name for such a beautiful little girl."

"We named her after my Grandmother Bently," said Amanda. "I'll put her in the cradle, now that she's settled."

"I can," said Sadie, already half way to the cradle near the hearth. She laid the baby gently inside, opposite her twin. "What did you name the other one?" she asked, turning her attention to the second baby.

"Camellia."

"That was my mother's name."

"I know. We named the firstborn twin for her."

"I never knew my mother," Sadie said, turning to look at her brother. "Jeremy's the closest thing to a mother I ever had. I never even knew what it was like to have a woman in the house till last year." She hurried back to the table where Jeremy and Jonathan sat talking. "Jems! Guess what? You'll never believe it—Paul married Melinda Hostetler last fall, and she moved in with us!"

"You mean after courting all these years he finally got around to asking her? I don't believe it!" Jeremy answered, shaking his head. "Whatever possessed him to finally tie the knot?"

"Guess he figured nothing stood in his way anymore, after Father died."

The color drained from Jeremy's face. "Father's dead?"

"You didn't know?"

Jeremy shook his head. Tears sprang to his eyes and slid down his cheeks. "He's really gone?"

She nodded yes.

"I can't believe it."

"But didn't you get my letter? I wrote in August right after it happened.

Words stuck in his throat. He shook his head.

"Oh, Jems, I'm so sorry to upset you like this. But I thought you knew."

"It's all right," he said, trying to compose himself. "You had no idea."

"Regular U.S. Mails ain't very dependable hereabouts," said Jonathan, obviously uncomfortable at the emotion unleashed in Jeremy. "That's why Harmon and a few other fellers started up their own letter service. But they can't carry out of state—not legally, no how."

Jeremy pulled out his handkerchief and blew his nose, beginning to get himself under control. "When did it happen? How?"

"Near the end of August. Father went to fetch the Fetter's Holstein bull, to put him with our heifers for breeding. He told us not to look for him back home till milking time."

"Who are the Fetters? I don't remember any neighbors by that name."

"They moved in right after you two left. Took over the Wilson place when ol' Horace died. Mr. Fetter brought along the biggest Holstein bull you ever saw. Stood *this* high!" she said, standing on tiptoe and holding her arm up as high as she could.

"Father wanted that new bloodline for our herd, so he and Mr. Fetter struck up a swap. Father could use the bull for a spell, and Mr. Fetter would get his pick of two heifers it sired by our cows. That old Wilson place is a goodly distance from ours, so when Father didn't come home by chore time we didn't get too worried," said Sadie. "Uuuu, I think I better sit down. I feel peek-ed all of a sudden."

"Well no wonder! You been traveling hard for weeks. Did you eat any supper yet?"

"It started to rain, so we didn't stop to make any. Just ate a few Johnny cakes awhile back," Sadie said, pulling loose hair away from her face and tucking it into the braid on the back of her neck. "I could stand something hot, though."

Jeremy poured two cups of hot tea from the pot sitting beside the hearth, then pulled the trammel away from the fire and dished up two bowls of soup. "It's not much to brag about, but at least it's hot," he said, setting bowls down in front of them.

Sadie took a big spoonful and smiled at Jeremy. "Mmmm, I've been thinking about your soup for the last three days. I never could make mine turn out to taste like yours." She ate several bites. Then she took a long sip of tea and heaved a big sigh, gathering the courage to continue her story.

"Father still wasn't back home by the time the boys finished milking and ate their supper. He never liked eating his supper so late. You know how stubborn he was about having everything run right on time." Jeremy nodded in agreement. "So Paul figured he better head out toward the Fetter's to see if something had gone wrong.

"When he got half way up the road to Uniontown, he found the bull. Had its lead chain all twisted up and wrapped tight around a tree. That bull snapped so many ropes, Mr. Fetter took to using a chain to fasten him with. Even put a chain halter on the beast, after it went and pulled a ring right out of its own nose." Sadie took a deep breath. "That bull had Father pinned fast against the tree. Paul shot it dead, right where it stood." Sadie stopped talking and ate her soup in silence.

"Father used to brag there wasn't an animal alive he couldn't handle," Jeremy said, by way of explanation to Jonathan.

"Paul gathered up what was left of him and brought his body home. Then he went right back to see Mr. Fetter and pay him for the bull."

"That'd be Paul," Jeremy said.

"Next day we buried Father. There was no way we could lay him out, the shape he was in," said Sadie. "Day after that, Paul went to Melinda Hostetler's father and asked permission to marry his daughter. Two weeks later we had the wedding. She moved right in and took over the house."

"It must have felt strange, having another woman around, after living your whole life with no one but men," Amanda said, now standing behind Jeremy and leaning against his powerful shoulder.

Sadie nodded at Amanda's apparent understanding. "Sure did feel funny for a while," she said. "She had some mighty strange ways about her, too. But I got to admit, it was kind of nice having help with all the work for a change." She stopped talking to finish the last few bites of soup. "Do you know what she did? First day she was there, she put lace curtains up in the windows! Can you imagine anything sillier? Lace curtains for a house full of men!"

"Maybe she wanted that house full of men to know she intended to make the place fit for a woman," Jeremy teased his sister. "Did you ever stop to think that maybe she thought you were the one doing things a mite strange? After all, you only had a bunch of men to teach you how to do 'women's work,' you know."

Sadie heaved a big sigh. "Oh, Jems!"

Jonathan pushed his chair away from the table.

"Got to be goin', folks. I better leave so's you all can rest whil'st those youngens sleep." He strode to the cabin door. "I'd bet it's been a good while since ary a soul checked on my hogs," he said, donning his hat. "Thank you kindly for the vittles." He reached for the door latch to let himself out.

"Wait, Jonathan, I want to give you something for bringing Sadie back here for us," Jeremy said.

"T'ain't necessary. I had to travel that-a-way anyhow."

"But you went out of your way to fetch Sadie," he said. "You had no cause to go clear down to Uniontown otherwise."

"Looked at some hogs along the way," Jonathan answered. "Made the trip more gainful, doncha know. Bought a breedin' pair o' Durocs from your brother. So, I'd best be gettin' 'em on home." He strode out the door and closed it behind himself.

"He brought hogs all the way out here?" Jeremy gave his sister an inquisitive look.

"Yup. Put them right up there in the wagon like a couple of prize-winners. Treated those hogs better than he did his own dog. He made Rip walk the whole way."

"That'd be Jonathan," Jeremy said with a smile. Amanda leaned hard against Jeremy's shoulder. He turned to see that she was falling asleep on her feet. "Come on, Mandy. Time we all went to bed." He turned and caught her arm, guiding her over to the bedstead in the corner. "All right with you to sleep up in the loft, Sadie?"

"That's my favorite spot. Always was," she said. "Lots closer to the stars up there."

"There's extra blankets in this chest here," he said, pointing to the wooden box sitting at the end of the bed. "If you can put up with the floor for tonight, I'll fix up a fresh tick for you tomorrow."

By the time Sadie had a sleeping mat laid out in the loft, Jeremy and Amanda both slept soundly. Sadie snuggled into the blankets and whispered a quick prayer. "Thanks for bringing me here safe, Lord. I sure have missed my Jems."

* * * * *

The next morning, Jeremy awoke to the scent of coffee bubbling over the fire. He hadn't tasted fresh coffee in months. He didn't want to wake Amanda before the babies cried to eat, so he carefully laid back the covers as he rose, then tucked them gently around her shoulders. She'd fallen asleep during the late-night feeding again, still propped up by pillows in a way they'd rigged up, so she could nurse both babies at once while lying in bed. After the twins had finished their nighttime meal, Jeremy changed both babies and laid them back in their cradle, hoping they 'd sleep through until dawn.

Outdoors, the world still slept, though streaks of pink had begun to tinge the eastern skyline. Jeremy pulled on pants, tucked in nightshirt and pulled up his suspenders, then headed toward the fireplace, where Sadie stooped by the fire, stirring something bubbling in a pot, sitting along-side the coffee.

"Mornin' Pipsqueak," he said, tugging her braid.

"Nobody called me that after you left home."

"Well, I guess you aren't much of a pipsqueak anymore," he teased. "You grew right up. And filled out real nice, too!"

She jumped up from her squatting position at the hearth to give her brother a big hug. "Thanks. I was afraid you wouldn't recognize me." She smiled her impish smile.

Jeremy suddenly felt self-conscious standing next to a grown-up Sadie. The young woman beside him held slight resemblance to the little girl he'd raised from a newborn.

"Sure smells good," Jeremy said, pointing to the coffee steaming away on the coals. "I haven't had any real coffee in months. How'd you come by beans?"

"I brought some from home. Jonathan seemed so excited to have coffee at our house, I figured it must be in short supply out here. Was I right?"

"Right as rain, Pipsqueak," he said with a smile, beginning to feel at ease with her once more. "We don't get fancy things out here. Just the basics," he instructed.

"I thought coffee *was* basic."

"You'll learn. Living out here in these woods is a lot different than life on a farm in Pennsylvania, where you have real civilization close by," he said, feeling on familiar ground with his sister at last. "We learn to make do."

"So, how far is it to the nearest town?"

"'Bout half-a-day's ride to Uniontown."

"Uniontown? You mean you have a Uniontown out here, too? Just like our Uniontown, back home?" she asked, pouring her brother a steaming cup from the pot.

"Quite the coincidence, huh? Talk is, they have to give this Uniontown a new name if they ever want to get a real U.S. Post Office, though. Some other Uniontown in Ohio already got one, so folks here have to come up with something else to call it."

"I never dreamed it could be such a popular name. Is your Uniontown anything like ours back home?"

Sadie was just as Jeremy remembered her—always full of questions. "This one's not as big. Just has a general store, a blacksmith, and a hotel, so far. A couple taverns, too. No churches yet." He took a long drink from his cup. "Boy, does this taste good."

"Is it hard to get dry goods way out here?"

"It's hard to get everything. Not because we can't get it hauled in. We can. But nobody has much in the way of hard cash to buy anything once it gets here. Real trouble is, merchants back East want their money up front, before they'll send goods out. We have a hard time coming up with enough cash to get many supplies brought out. Mostly, we just barter back and forth amongst ourselves for what provisions we do have."

"How come no one has any money? Don't you raise enough crops to sell?"

"We raise aplenty. But we have a devil of a time getting our corn or wheat or hogs to a market where buyers can pay in hard cash. We float what we can to ports downriver, but to get any real money to speak of, you have to take your goods all the way to New Orleans. That's a powerful long trip. Takes at least three months to get down and back—if you can travel fast and avoid any river bandits along the way."

"So once you get there, you sell your farm goods and bring back the money, right?"

"It's not quite that simple, little sis. If you do make it down there with your goods unspoiled, you usually find low prices, and a glutted market, 'cause everyone else is trying to sell their produce all at the same time. Most buyers won't even take a look at your goods unless you intend to spend the money right back buying new supplies from them. And I can tell you, it's no easy task bringing hard goods up-river. Much easier to haul em' in by wagon from the East. So, we have to settle for low prices in Southern markets, then turn around and buy supplies from Eastern merchants at highway-robbery prices. Doesn't come out too even that way, see?"

"But why can't you bring your supplies back up the river so you can get better prices down South?"

"Poling the whole way back up the Mississippi goes awful hard, Pipsqueak. With river bandits hiding behind every bend, it's a risky trip at best."

"I heard somebody built a new kind of steam-powered boat. They say it can go up a river as fast as it goes down a river. Is that true, Jems?"

"That's the talk we hear, too. Not many folks think it'll be practical. Takes so much wood to power the boilers, leaves little space on board for hauling cargo. Sure would be nice if they could make it work, though... if it wouldn't end up too costly."

Jeremy and Sadie focused so completely on their conversation they hadn't heard Amanda rise. When she appeared, rubbing her eyes, it startled them both.

"Do I smell coffee, or am I dreaming?"

"The real thing, Mandy. Little Sadie brought us quite a treat." He went to the hearth and poured a cup for her. "Here. Taste it."

She accepted the cup eagerly and drank down half of it before coming up for air. "I forgot how wonderful real coffee tasted," she said, flashing Jeremiah the first warm smile he'd seen from her in weeks. "Maybe it'll give me a little more stamina."

Sadie sat watching the pair, eyeing first Amanda and then Jeremy. When her oldest brother Paul brought his bride home, Sadie had the opportunity to watch a male-female relationship up close, for the first time in her life. The emotional "dance" between the sexes absolutely fascinated her. Brought up motherless among nine brothers, Sadie had no idea how a woman was supposed to behave around a man who wasn't related to her. Most women acted coy or shy—behavior that seemed completely foreign to her. Sadie possessed the straightforward frankness of a man, since that was all she'd ever experienced. She didn't know how to play the demure kind of courting games most men expected from women. She intended to watch this shy, southern sister-in-law of hers very closely.

"Well, gals, time's a-wasting. If last night's rain didn't make things too muddy, I need to hitch Patsy up and get to plowing."

"Aren't you gonna eat some breakfast first?" Sadie asked. "I fixed blueberry porridge special, just for you, Jems."

"Blueberry porridge? Where in the world did you find blueberries this time of year?" Jeremy asked his sister.

"I dried five sacks full last summer. I brought along half a sack of those, too. Thought you might welcome a little fruit after a long winter."

"I don't think I've tasted a blueberry in more than three years," said Amanda with an eager smile. "It's been ages since we've had any kind of fruit at all. I tried to dry wild cherries last summer, and we did get a few apples from the neighbors in the fall, but all our stores went up with the fire." Amanda said. It was the first time she'd spoken of the fire without bursting into tears.

"Fire?"

"We lost everything last fall when the cabin burned," Jeremy explained to his sister. "I never wrote you about it. Didn't see the need to trouble you all back home."

"You lost everything?"

"Just about." His eyes met Amanda's, and Sadie could see great pain displayed on both faces. Lack of communication had left the birth of Little Ben unknown back home, as well. Since Sadie was "just a kid" when she stood up with her brother and sister-in-law at their nuptials, she had not been privy to the unwanted pregnancy which had thrown these two people together in the first place.

"Thanks to the neighbors, we got a re-built cabin and enough basic supplies to see us through winter," Jeremy told his sister.

"They've been very kind to us," Amanda said.

Sadie was dying to ask more, but by the tone in both voices, she understood the subject to be closed—for the time-being, at least.

"Well, how about some of that porridge, Pipsqueak?"

Sadie bustled around, dishing up steaming bowls full for all three of them. As they sat down to eat, both babies began to stir in their cradle by the fire. Amanda put her spoon back down and started to rise from her chair.

"Sit and eat," Sadie instructed. "I'll tend the babies while you two eat. You'll prob'ly be finished by the time I get 'em both changed. Then I can eat while you nurse these two lovely little flowers," she said, already leaning over the cradle and cooing to the babies. "Good morning, Millie and Lilly! Aunt Sadie's here to take care of you two."

Amanda winced. "I would prefer you address them by their given names—Camellia and Lillian."

With raised eyebrows that asked the silent question, "Is she serious?" Sadie shot a curious glance toward her brother. Jeremy nodded with a look that told her she had better comply with Amanda's wishes.

Sadie shrugged her shoulders and returned her attention to the cradle. "Come here, Camellia and Lillian. Aunt Sadie's gonna love you little flowers to pieces!

Dear Ellie Mae,

I have received your long, newsy letter. My, we have had a very quiet spring compared to yours. I sympathize with your motherly feelings of loss at the departures of Johannah and Katrina, but the girls may both come back. We know not what the future holds.

And I was so excited to hear that Mrs. Harrison had twins! What a gift. While a child can never be replaced or forgotten, she will surely be too busy to turn morose over the one lost. I was very lucky to have my sister next door to me when Levi and Lizzie came along, as I also had three other children under the age of five at the time.

I cannot imagine now how I ever coped, even with Rose's help. I suppose that I was young and strong. It is good to have family nearby to help out, as with Mr. Harrison's sister coming. I wish that we did not live so far apart. I would like to help out myself, even though I do not know these people yet.

I am eager for the revival of which you spoke (we are Congregationalists, by the by), as it means we will meet again, and also that I may meet all the people about whom I have been reading in your letters. I feel I may even recognize some of them. Do you hear that, Ellie? We are coming to the revival! I am so anxious, I feel like a girl going to her very first party.

I have received a second letter from back East. Rose writes that Caitlin is with child. My sister says that though the girl has been moody of late, still her middle thickened with Rose none the wiser. It was not a town boy, and there was no proper ceremony, but they are trying to put things to rights. Rose says that the young man meant marriage, but my niece has gainsaid him at every juncture.

Caitlin puts no more than two words together, so Rose cannot take his measure. She writes that Garth has dispatched a man to Waterbury to fetch the fellow. Caitlin is a wild one with too much of our Da in her, and my sister hopes that the child will settle her (or Lord help it). Mayhap it would have been better had my sister named her firstborn Agnes, but no, Caitlin was she before the name took hold.

My sister is to be a grandmother (as would I be myself had my Lucy lived beyond the cradle). She wants me to tell her if this is wonderful or tragic. I wrote back that, as she has no choice in the matter, it may as well be wonderful.

The twins and Leesha came in all proud of themselves. "We know how you worry about snakes and warn us to watch out for them, Mama," they told me with big smiles on their faces. "So, today when we found a nest of baby rattlesnakes, we figured we should kill them now before they grow up and hurt somebody."

"We got sticks and killed every one, and I killed the most," Levi bragged. I thought myself that it did sound a good idea, until I saw Zach turn pale. It seems that he is the only one of us who knew that baby rattlers are even more deadly than the full grown.

But the children were safe and sound. He talked to them quietly for a moment about the danger they had put themselves in. When I handed him a hot cup of acorn coffee, I saw how his hands shook. This is a strange twist, friend, as I myself felt that there was no purpose to fret over what did not happen. We have learned another important lesson and are all still alive as proof of it.

Elijah turned 3 in April. That signifies Zach and I will be having our 20th wedding anniversary this July. Those dates are connected for me by the birth of Elijah nine months after our 16th anniversary. We had returned to the place where Zach proposed, just the two of us, gone to our old picnic spot on a beautiful summer day.

The meadow was filled with wild flowers. There was a barn across the road that had not been there heretofore, and another structure was partially constructed which would obviously become a dwelling. I felt a little sad that people were invading our "place," but Zach said that they undoubtedly had very good taste, as they would wake up each morning to one of the best views in the world.

We unpacked our basket and ate, whereupon Zach began raving about my quince jelly just as he had all those years before and pretending that we were once again those two young people. It was a lovely afternoon full of silliness and laughter.

At one point, Zach said that he would marry me all over again, and to prove it, made me stand beside him under a large elm tree while he jumped back and forth playing the part of both the groom and a Dutch justice with a very thick accent performing the service.

"You bromis to take te voman you holt py te hant to pe your vife, and tat you vill shtick to her through hell-fire and dunder?"

"I do, I do, I really do. Please, can I keep her? Can I? If I shtick to her."

"Vill te voman shtop vit te yuck-yuck? Den I bronouce you man and voman, by Cot." By this time, I was laughing so hard that tears were rolling down my cheeks.

And the groom kissed the bride. Then the justice kissed the bride. Then the groom again. Mayhap even the groom kissed the justice. All I know for certain is that everyone present was soundly kissed. It was at this point that it began to sprinkle. We hadn't noticed the clouds rolling in. I began hurriedly packing our picnic leftovers into the basket. Zach took it from me, grabbed up the quilt on which we sat while eating, and said, "Come on. This way."

He dropped the basket into the wagon, took my hand, and kept going. That's when I realized where we were headed, to the barn to seek shelter from the rain, which was no longer a sprinkle. We started to run toward it, as the rain grew heavier, Zach holding the quilt up over our heads. By the time we reached it, we were a sodden mess and breathless.

I pretended to pout, saying that our perfect day was ruined. But in all truth, our perfect day had a perfect ending. He saw fit to point out to me on the trip home that he surely had shtuck to me through dunder. Myself, I heard no dunder. Now that Elijah is talking quite a bit, Zach teases me that the child seems to have something of a Dutch accent.

So there is the promised story at last. Now I must go. I will be anxiously awaiting the revival and our social congress.

your friend,

Libby

Chapter 11

Revival
The Crossroads Meeting
June 1817

'"Ye shall keep the Sabbath therefore, for it is holy unto you,'" intoned the Reverend Harold P. Longbottom. '"Every one that defileth it, surrrrrellly shall be put to death,'" he said, adding emphasis to the word "death."

The Reverend paused a few moments to let that thought sink in to his congregation. Then he continued: '"For whosoever doeth any work therein, that soul shall be cut off from among his people.' So says the thirty-first chapter of Exodus, verse number fourteen, right here in this holiest of books." Reverend Longbottom waved his Bible in the air with one hand and thumped the pulpit with the other. Then he raised both hands above his head, motioning to the congregation, "And all the people said…"

"Amen!" chimed in the whole group of revival-goers sitting on rough-hewn benches in the large, center tent.

The Camp Meeting commenced on a Wednesday at Hayes Crossroads, led by three ministers who spelled one another at preaching duties in the main pulpit. Smaller tents, surrounding the center pavilion, served as gathering places for meals, group meetings, or shelters where mothers attended to the needs of countless babies and young children. Many folks who'd come from as far as 20 or 30 miles away set up campsites at the perimeter of the main camp, planning to stay for the entire four days of socializing and "preachments."

Harold P. Longbottom, the newest circuit preacher in these parts, and well known to the area's settlers, had led off the meetings with a stirring, fire-and-brimstone message.

The Reverend Olin Abernathy, Longbottom's superior from back in Allegheny County, Pennsylvania, followed with a sermon that upheld traditional, Methodist doctrine, although delivered with low-key emotion on his part. In contrast, the young Baptist preacher, Brother Woodrow Peterbaum, threw himself into a zealous spirit of renewal, moving several women to tears and bringing a few men to their feet with shouts of "Hallelujah brother, praise the Lord!"

Rev. Abernathy did such a splendid job of orchestrating the whole revival, with just enough understated teaching and ex-horttation, peppered in between all that hell-fire-damnation, that the emotional intensity of the four-day fest continued to build with each new sermon.

Now, in the final day of preaching, the camp's religious fervor had grown to such a fevered pitch that people kept "falling" in greater numbers at each altar call.

"Brothers and sisters," said Rev. Longbottom in his smooth, reassuring tones, "the Lord surely means for his children to be happy and healthy in this new land, but He expects you to obey His commandments if you are to prosper.

"In the book of Exodus, chapter thirty-four, beginning at verse number ten, the Lord tells us, 'Behold, I make a covenant: before all thy people I will do marvels, such as have not been done in all the earth, nor in any nation: and all the people among which thou art shall see the work of the Lord... '"

He paused again, then walked out around the pulpit, Bible still in hand, and strode toward the front row of benches. "Friends, I detect a strong impression that some afflicted person among us is in great need right now. I must be completely honest with you good folks, I do not normally stop in the middle of a sermon to act upon such an impulse as this. But the urgent sensation I perceive has descended with such a soul-shaking intensity, I have cause to believe that the Lord is trying to give us spectacular insight into the Word just given voice a moment ago."

Longbottom paused, took his handkerchief from his breast pocket, and wiped his brow. "Brothers and sisters, if someone in this congregation has need of a healing miracle, I ask that person to come forward and lay that need right here, at the foot of the Lord's altar this very minute. As you have heard with your own ears, the Almighty has made a covenant with man to perform fearful and wonderful miracles among His people."

A slight murmur arose in the vicinity of the back benches, and people in the front rows turned to see what had caused the stir at rear of the tent. An old, grizzled-looking woman hunched over a hickory cane struggled to her feet and began to inch her way forward with slow, painful steps.

"Ah ha! We have a child of God who desires a miracle," said Rev. Longbottom. "Come forward, mother, come forward."

The woman could not hurry, and the crowd's whispers increased as she shuffled her way toward the front. It took her what seemed an eternity to make her way to the foot of the rough-hewn altar, where the Reverend Longbottom stood waiting.

"Dear child of God," intoned the Reverend, laying his hand upon the stooped woman's head, "what manner of affliction do you lay before our Lord?"

"Reverend, sir, it's like this," the old woman began in a soft voice. "I had a acc-see-dent." Her severely stooped stance made her words fall weakly to the floor.

"Can you speak up? I can barely hear you with your head pointed downward so."

"I said, Reverend, I had a acc-see-dent," she said practically hollering this time. "Years ago, a tree fell right on top of me whilst my man was fellin' timber to build us a cabin. I been stooped ary after the busted bones healed up so crooked, like."

"How long ago did this transpire, mother?"

"Nine years back... goin' on ten, now... I been hunched over such."

"If you have lived with this affliction for so many years, why ask the Lord for a healing miracle now?" the Reverend asked.

"Past winter the rhumitiz set in these bones real bad, Rever'nd. I got so much pain now, I kin barely see to meals for my man. T'wouldn't be so bad if we had our daughter to help out. But after the youngen died of snake bite last fall when she was out a'huntin' ginsang to sell to the trader, there is just the two of us to fend alone," she said.

"My dear woman, you've lost your only child, as well as your health? Surely the Almighty will see fit to remove this heavy load of suffering. What is your name, mother?"

"Myrtle Jones, your honor."

"And your husband's name Mrs. Jones?"

"Mr. Jones."

The crowd chuckled.

"His Christian name, my good woman. His given, Christian name, if you please."

"Virgil. But most folks calls him Virg."

"Mrs. Jones, may I pray with you, and ask the Lord for a miracle on your behalf?"

"That's why I hiked clean up here, your honor. It's a power-ful long walk just to say 'Howdy,'" Myrtle said, as folks in the congregation tried to stifle their laughter.

"My good people," Reverend Longbottom addressed the whole congregation, waving his Bible in a huge arc to en-compass the entire tent, "let us go to the Lord in fervent prayer and ask for a miracle on behalf of this poor, stooped woman who has suffered so stoically these many long years. Let us kneel and bow our heads."

Myrtle Jones struggled to lower herself onto her knees, holding tight to her cane with one hand and to the arm of Rev. Longbottom with the other. A brief stir arose in the tent, as people stood, then knelt, women smoothing their dresses and men helping to shush the small children while all heads bowed in an attitude of prayer.

"Dear Father of us all, we humbly beseech Thee to hear our heartfelt prayers for this suffering saint of a soul," prayed the Reverend. "Mother Jones has not only endured crushing pain and disability these interminable years, but she has also relin-quished her only child into Your ever-loving care. Dear Lord, grant that Myrtle Jones may stand straight and tall in Your presence. Permit not only that her physical body be healed of this wretched debility, but also that her heart be healed of its overwhelming grief."

Reverend Longbottom paused, then continued with an intensity unmatched thus far. "Father of us all, make use of me, your humble servant, to be the vessel through which You send Your healing power to this wretched, suffering soul. Use me. Empower me with your Holy Spirit. Show this gathering what mighty works Your healing power can bestow." He paused again, breathing loudly and puffing with labored intensity.

"I feel it. I feel the power of Your Spirit upon me!" he shouted. "Lord, show this congregation the healing might of Your love, so they may surely be blessed by the wondrous works You shall employ among us."

The Reverend paused and laid his hands upon the woman's head and said, "Rise, Myrtle Jones. Stand straight and walk tall. Testify to the world what wonders the Lord of Hosts has done this day!"

Mrs. Jones leaned hard on her cane and struggled to rise, but she fell back down on both knees with a thud. Then Reverend Longbottom laid his Bible aside, walked behind the woman and put both his hands under her elbows. He heaved her up, and as her cane clattered to the ground, she let out such a loud screech, the whole congregation drew in a collective breath at the same moment. When he set the woman on her feet, she stood straight and tall, relying on the aid of her cane no more.

"It's a miracle!" she cried, tears streaming down her face. "It's a miracle sure as you're born! Oh, thank you, your honor! Praise the Lord, I can stand up straight!" She took a few, teetering steps like a freshly birthed calf, slowly trying out her ability to walk unaided. By the time she'd trucked half-way back down the aisle, the whole congregation had jumped to its feet, with folks jostling one another trying to crowd around her. People pumped her hand and clapped her on the shoulder, singing the hymn of praise that broke out the moment Opal Ann had gathered her wits sufficiently to start playing the pump organ. Opal Ann Newell worked both feet so fast on the pedals inflating the bellows of that little box-organ, she gave the hymn an entirely new dimension.

"Hallelujah, Thine the glory! Hallelujah, a-men! Hallelujah, Thine the glory! Revive us again!"

Many folks stood with tears streaming down their faces to match the tears Myrtle Jones also shed. Reverend Longbottom stood at the base of the altar clutching his Bible, seemingly stunned, and to all outward appearances, totally exhausted.

When people who had not attended this particular service heard shouts and strains of the greatly-accelerated hymn coming from inside, their curiosity got the better of them, and they gathered at the entrance of the great tent.

"What's the hubbub breakin' out in there?" asked Frank Putnam, who'd been helping a few other men gather firewood for the big, outdoor barbecue planned for this last evening's festivities.

"Nothin' in there but a old crow walkin' down the aisle," answered a toe-headed youngster at the front of the crowd, pushing his way out. "Shucks, I thought it might be somethin' good like ladies fallin' and gettin' their skirts all pushed up."

Frank shook his head at the wiry youngster running back to his buddies, who stood at the edge of the woods. "Just a old lady walking without her cane," Levi Howard reported to his teen-aged cohorts, each one charged up by surges of pubescent rebellion.

"Is that all?" said Theodore Thompson, spitting on the ground beside Levi's foot. "You took us away from a good crap game for some stupid old woman?"

"Shhhht! Keep that mouth of yours shut, Theodore! You want pa to hear and come box my ears?" The boys headed back into the woods, shoving and jostling one another in good-natured horseplay, disappearing under the hardwood canopy.

People began to pour out of the tent, men clapping one another on the shoulder and women dabbing at their eyes with damp hankies.

"What a stirring service! Can you imagine? I mean, really now, nothing like this ever happens right here, in Vermillion township, forheaven'ssakes," said Netta Bailey, babbling away, as she bounced her wiggling baby. "Did you see Myrtle Jones drop that cane and stand there so startled? Why, I never saw anything like it in all my born days. Who'da thought such a thing possible!" Netta continued to chatter at everyone within earshot, heading toward the large tables groaning with the noon-time meal.

Ellie Mae Thompson clung tightly to the arm of her cherished friend, Libby Howard, who'd traveled to this revival with her family all the way from Cranberry Corners north of Union-town. "Bet that woman sure felt strange... to be stooped over all them years, then all of a sudden like, stand right up straight. Ain't that somethin?"

"I must say, Ellie, I never have witnessed the like," Libby answered the friend she hadn't seen since her cabin raising the previous summer. "How long ago did you say she lost her daughter?"

"Why you askin' me, Lib? Never laid eyes on the woman before today. I thought she was from up you folks's way."

"Doesn't she live in this township?"

"No where's nearby I know of."

"Well, where did she come from, do you suppose?"

"Your guess is good as mine," Ellie Mae answered. "Folks come a powerful long piece for a camp meetin'. That's a fact."

By now a big part of the crowd had reached the lunch tables, where mothers fussed over food each one had added to the feast, and small children skittered back and forth playing tag, as they zigzagged around adults' legs. Some of the young boys tried to stick a finger in this pie or swipe a taste of that pudding, while grandmothers scolded and wagged their fingers in warning. Older girls tended babies, and grown men milled near the water pump, talking of crops and varmints and how the state legislature seemed to ignore the problem of no decent markets for struggling farmers.

Over the din, someone began to clang a spoon against an iron pot to get the crowd's attention. Reverend Abernathy climbed atop a bench to give himself better vantage from which to be heard. "My good people, let us give thanks for this day, and for this meal," said the Reverend in a small voice.

Seeing him standing there mouthing words, the crowd slowly began to quiet. Rev. Abernathy continued on in a louder voice, "In Proverbs three, and in verses five through ten, it says, 'Trust in the Lord with all thine heart, and lean not unto thine own understanding. In all thy ways acknowledge Him, and He shall direct thy paths.'"

He paused to draw a big breath. "'Be not wise in thine own eyes; Fear the Lord and depart from evil,'" he said, still louder. "'...Honour the Lord with thy substance, and with the first fruits of all thine increase, So shall thy barns be filled with plenty.... ' Come, let us all bow our heads in prayer," he said, pausing again until the men doffed their hats. "Dear Heavenly Father, we acknowledge Your blessings on this day, as the powerful miracle You have chosen to visit upon us can attest. We humbly ask Your blessing upon this food as we partake to refresh our bodies, just as You have already refreshed our spirits. Help us to be truly thankful for the feast we are about to receive, and bless the hands that have prepared it. In Jesus name, we pray. Amen."

"Amen!" joined in the crowd.

Men replaced hats, women passed plates to family members, and all took turns choosing vittles from the bounty laid out before them. Folks balanced their plates as they found places to sit down on blankets spread all over the ground. People looked forward to visiting with friends they hadn't seen in months, what with the seclusion of a long winter and the ensuing work of spring planting. Families stayed so busy on their respective homesteads, they had little time for the frivolities of social visits, so they made the most of any group gathering such as this. Nothing could beat a "dinner on the ground."

Most folks already sat around eating and visiting, but a few women and children still waited their turns to fill plates, as a group of noisy, teen-aged boys appeared at the edge of the crowd. The boys pushed their way to the head of the food line, and from their vociferous demeanor and the distinct odor they exuded, no one could doubt the source of their liquid appetizer.

"I got here first, Theodore. Let me by," said Levi Howard, giving him a push after Theodore butted ahead of Levi.

Not one to take a push lightly, Theodore retaliated in kind, which, in Levi's inebriated state, brought out the scrapper. Before anyone could step in to stop the fray, Theodore and Levi both landed squarely in the center of one food table, spilling dishes of pumpkin bisque, rabbit stew, and raspberry pies all over the ground.

"Theodore!!" shouted Ellie Mae, from where she sat on a blanket beside Libby. "What the devil's got into you?" Before either she or Libby could get to their feet, Zach Howard held each boy firmly by one ear and proceeded to drag them both away from the food mess.

"Oh, I'm so ashamed," Libby said to Ellie as Zach pulled the boys off into the nearby woods. Both women jumped up to salvage what they could of the remaining food.

Harvey Thompson overtook Zach as he stood ready to box two sets of ears. "No need for that now, Zach. The boys was just funnin'," he said, pulling Theodore to his feet and brushing the pie crust off his backside. "Don't you remember how it was when you'd just begun feelin' your oats? Let's just give the Devil his due, and let it pass."

"It's not right, ruining folks' dinner that way," said Zach.

"Ah, hell, there's still a-plenty left to eat. Come on, let the boys be."

"I'm not telling you how to fetch up your son, Harvey," Zach said, pulling Levi to his feet, "but I don't aim to let this misdeed pass without some recompense."

"Do what you have to, then," said Harvey, spitting a stream of tobacco juice over his shoulder. "I've had a belly full of preachin', myself. Come on, Theodore. We're headin' for home. We got corn that needs hoed.'"

Harvey and Theodore sauntered away, while Levi stood shoulder to shoulder with his father, glaring at him squarely in the eye.

No one in the noontime crowd seemed to notice that Reverend Harold P. Longbottom had not yet made his appearance at the food tables—a circumstance most out of character for one who never missed the opportunity for a free meal. If anyone did notice the Reverend's absence, no doubt he attributed that fact to the unusual service everyone still discussed.

Far from the eyes of those who sat savoring their venison stew and raspberry pie, Reverend Longbottom strolled along the camp's outer boundary. He came to a small opening in the woods, looked back over his shoulder, then disappeared into the shadowy canopy of new-summer's green.

When he reappeared some ten minutes later, he looked across the clearing and saw a small cart pulling up near the edge of the camp. Amanda Jane Harrison, holding two wrapped bundles, sat on the seat next to a comely young, girl driver, to whom he had not yet had the good fortune to be introduced. Not one to miss an opportunity to meet a pretty girl, Harold Longbottom hurried over to offer his assistance, as she pulled the horse to a stop and readied to hop down to tie it fast to the hitching post.

"My dear lady, allow me," he said, appearing at her side so suddenly it startled both women. Rev. Longbottom held his arm out to steady Sadie and help her down from the cart, but she side-stepped his advance, hopping neatly to the ground by herself.

"I take it you two lovely ladies are just arriving?" he said, tipping his hat to Amanda, still seated in the cart. "It's so good to see you, Amanda Jane. You are looking radiant, as always," he said in his smoothest, silvery tones. "By the way, I do not remember having made the acquaintance of your youthful companion," he said, gesturing toward Sadie Harrison, who busied herself fastening the reins to the hitching post. "Permit me to introduce myself. I am the Reverend Harold P. Longbottom, better known as Pastor Hal to most folks in this part of the state. I am at your service, lovely miss," he said with a bow and a flourish of his hat. "And who, pray tell, might you be?"

"I'm Sadie," she said, in her no-nonsense manner. She offered no more, letting her simple announcement stand as sufficient introduction.

"Sadie is my husband's sister," explained Amanda from her perch in the cart.

"And where might that strapping man of yours be, Amanda Jane? If I may be so bold as to ask."

"Jeremiah had to finish stacking the hay he cut this week," she explained. "He needs hot afternoon sun to dry it properly." She seemed rather embarrassed that her husband had not accompanied them to the revival. "He does plan to attend closing services this evening, Reverend. He'll be along later with Luther Bailey... after they get the last of the hay finished up," she said.

"No need to explain, my dear. No need. 'Make hay while the sun shines,' that's what I always say," he oozed, flashing his mesmerizing smile. "Here, allow me to assist you." He went around the cart and offered his hand to help Amanda step down.

"Excuse me, Reverend, but I think she'd better hand those babies down first," Sadie said, giving him an exasperated look.

"Did you say babies, in the plural sense?" he asked, reaching up to take one of the bundles, so firmly wrapped that not even a tiny nose protruded.

"Two of 'em," Sadie said, reaching up to take the other bundle.

"Twins, Amanda Jane! I must say, you certainly have taken me by complete surprise," said Harold Longbottom, holding his other arm up to help Amanda step down from the cart.

She smoothed skirts, adjusted bonnet, then took the second baby back from Sadie.

"Are they identical?" Rev. Longbottom asked, pushing aside the folded corner of the blanketed bundle he held to get a peek at the tiny babe inside.

"Both exactly the same," said Amanda, making a little cooing sound to the baby she held who'd begun to fuss.

"May I see that one, too?"

Amanda propped the baby up and pulled a corner of the blanket away to reveal a tiny face that duplicated the other.

"When did all this happen, my dear?"

"On March ninth. They decided to come early."

"I see. And what did you name them?"

"Camellia Jane and Lillian Jane... after Jeremiah's mother, and after my Grandmother Bently."

"And after you, too, no doubt," he said, bouncing the one he held and tickling her under the chin. "My, my. Lillian and Camellia, two absolutely lovely little flowers."

Sadie stood staring from Amanda to the Reverend in complete amazement, for Amanda usually got quite upset when anyone but Jeremy referred to her babies as "lovely little flowers." But there she stood, apparently enthralled by this smooth-talking parson.

"How do you ever tell them apart?"

"Well, if you look very closely, you'll see that Lillian has a small mole right behind her ear, there. See?" Amanda slightly tilted the baby she held, to reveal the spot.

"A mole. No doubt about it," he said. "But you say this one has no corresponding birthmark?" He tilted the baby he held to get a better look behind her ear, and as he did so, Camellia let out a burp that spewed regurgitated milk down the Reverend's vest.

"Oh, I am sorry," Amanda said, handing the Reverend a dry burp cloth. "I should have warned you that Camellia has a tendency to spit her milk quite often."

"Don't fret yourself about it, my dear," he said, dabbing at the clabbered smear. "It most certainly is not the first time I have been so baptized by an infant... and I'm quite confident it shall not be the last." He managed to clean up the spot, then he handed the cloth to Sadie, who rolled her eyes behind his back. "By the way, speaking of baptizing... I would be most honored to conduct a baptismal service to consecrate this lovely pair, Amanda Jane. Perhaps you had given some thought to such a possibility?"

"I was hoping you would do that, Rever–"

"Please, it's Pastor Hal, remember?"

"Pastor Hal," she said with a coy smile. "Jeremiah and I were hoping that you might include a small christening in tonight's closing services, if you don't mind," she said pushing the corner of the blanket back over Lillian's face. "I don't think I'd have risked bringing them out so quickly, had it not been for the fact they've not been baptized. I was not sure when you might be traveling back this way again."

"I'd be delighted to christen these lovely flowers, my dear. Tonight! Yes. New life! What a befitting conclusion to such a rousing revival!"

If you don't mind, would you please cover her back up, Reverend? Too much wind in their faces will give them the colic, you know," said Amanda.

"That's Pastor Hal, my dear. Or Harold to you," he said with a wink.

She blushed as she adjusted both babies' blankets, then glanced around to see if anyone else stood in the vicinity of the other horses tethered at the shady hitching post. "I don't see another soul about. Where is everyone?"

"I would suppose by this time they are all feasting on de-lectable dinnertime delights," answered Pastor Hal. At that moment he happened to glance over toward the woods and see Myrtle Jones stepping out from the same place where he, coin-cidentally, had emerged himself just a few moments before. In one fluid movement, he took Amanda's arm, turned her in the opposite direction, and headed her toward the meal tent. "If we don't make our way to join the others soon, we may not find a single morsel left to enjoy. I do think we should hurry before we miss out altogether on rhubarb pie!"

Left standing behind, Sadie straightened her bonnet strings and hoisted the baskets of baby things and foodstuffs out of the cart. She followed the pair disappearing into the massive revival encampment, shaking her head as she hurried to catch up.

Dear Libby,

Mighty nice seeing you again, Lib. And what a meeting we did have! More highfalutin preachment or sinners in one place would be right hard to imagine. If 10 people a day did not fall, I would eat my hat. Big as it is.

Why I can not pass a moment without seeing Frank Putnam down on his hands and knees barking like a dog. And Emma flopping around like a fish out of water. Or whale more like. Some folks do carry on so at any excuse. And speaking of carrying on. I expect there will be more births than a hound dog has fleas nine months hence. At least that is what Edie says. And she should know. One thing that still has me stumped. I have yet to find anyone who knows that Myrtle Jones.

I do have to apologize for my pa's behavior. Him calling you a city-fide female just like my ma. He had no right to talk to you that way. I am so sorry. A refined lady like you should not have to put up with the likes of his mouth. But when he pinched you on your beehind, well, that was just too much for any woman to abide. You handled it all so genteel-like. I would of flattened the old coot.

You see for yourself how cantankerous he can be. No wonder my ma high-tailed it back to Penna. I hope you can find it in your heart not to hold his bad manners against me.

Can you credit them boys, to commence drinking and gaming with the men that-a-way out behind the tents? That Theodore has got too big for his britches by half again. What is going to come of him is not to my knowing. But to go tripping around upsetting dishes of food and trodding on youngsters was way too much to bear.

I hope you do not feel the need to wait a seemly time before showing your face down here again. At this stage a boy's actions do not reflect on his up bringing near as much as they speak to his age. Still, I told Harvey that he should give Theodore the same treatment as Zack gave your Levi. The boy has been giving me the evil eye ever since.

One thing you folks did miss by heading off before first light. As the sun rose up, a god awful screeching and squawking made folks jump up right from their bedding. They thought to see the second coming they heard preached about all week. A man shape washed in sunlight and looking all gold and shimmery like stepped out of the woods. Then I heard some one shout something about a angel of the Lord amongst us. A long moment went by as the noise died out and the echo of that horrible sound faded. Then the light shifted, and I heard Sam Justice commence to laugh his fool head off.

Why that ain't no angel, says Sam. That there is old Zeke MacTavish, nekked as the day he was born, except for that dad-burned bagpipe he is blowin on, says he. Sure enough, that is what we saw. Not a pretty sight at that I have to say.

Such a shame Lucy and Henry Jarvis could not attend any services, what with Lucy just delivered. Edie says they have a fine little pup. Named for his daddy Henry, if you do not mind him. They call him baby Hank.

When Zach brings that ram down, I will send him home with a jug of maple syrup.

Sure hope you folks made it home safe and sound. And I hope you will write me again. Even though my father did treat you so poorly. I sure do like you myself.

your friend,

Ellie

July 1817

Dear Libby,

It has been so long since I heard from you. I hope that you and all those children have not had a bad turn of health. Nor nothing happened to put you on your way back to those Fire Lands.

I fear the reason you have not wrote back is that you are holding Pa's bad behavior agin me and my whole family. I feel terrible he was so crusty and down right rude to you at the revival. He can get awful testy. I do not think that a refined lady like yourself could ever get used to such ways. Even my ma could not tolerate him for too long at a stretch. But he is still my pa. I have to say in spite of him being so cantankerous, I do love the old coot.

I admit I was glad to see Jonathan take him back to his own home in the hills. Theodore will miss him. Those two were some pair. Pa wanted to take Theodore home to fetch and tote for him. Teach him to make corn juice. Harvey and I stood together on that one. The boy has enough idees in his head without adding that to boot. Pa's hip has healed up real good by now, but he will always have a limp.

He says he will get on right well, as God don't want him and the Devil won't have him. I expect there is some truth to that. So I do not worry about him over much. Enough about my pa. Again I have to say I am ashamed at his bad manners. I hope you can find it in your heart to forgive him. Even though he does not deserve it.

Ellie

Chapter 12

The Harrison's Happiness
July-August 1817

Summer came in hot that year, and for the first time since Amanda Jane had arrived in this northern clime, she finally began to feel truly warm. Now that the twins had reached their fourth month without life-threatening incident, she even began to allow herself the freedom to relax a bit in their day-to-day care. Both babies showed distinct weight gains and grew stronger and more alert with each passing week.

Amanda, too, grew stronger, not only recovering her health after the babies' births, but also gaining self-assurance and a growing confidence in her own ability to cope with twins. As a result of this new level of physical comfort and emotional composure, she felt a contentment she hadn't known since coming to this wilderness.

Having Sadie around to help out hadn't hurt, either. And Sadie, in her own, no-nonsense manner, managed to fit herself quite smoothly into the Harrisons' household routine. Although she saw to the bulk of the house chores, Sadie always sought Amanda's direction before undertaking any new task. Working alongside Paul's wife, Melinda, had taught Sadie that when another woman thought herself in charge of a household, that woman needed to feel in charge, whether that was the absolute reality of the situation or not.

"Would you like me to start washing diapers and baby clothes while you finish feeding those two little sweeties their breakfast?" Sadie asked her sister-in-law one Thursday morning as she finished up breakfast dishes.

"That would be a wonderful help. Thank you." Amanda shifted one baby over a bit when the other one kicked her twin as both babes lay nursing in Amanda's arms. She had finally learned how to sit in a chair and feed both at once, without getting all upset at their every kick or whimper. She also noticed that Lillian happened to be the one who did most of the kicking. Already their individual personalities had begun to emerge. True, they still looked absolutely identical, except for the fact that Camellia weighed just a tad more than her minutes-younger sister. But Amanda could tell that Lillian would be the feistier, more dominant of the two.

"Do you want me to strip the beds and wash bedding today, too?" Sadie asked. "Looks like a beautiful drying day outdoors."

"Don't you think we have enough to wash, with all these dirty baby things?"

"It's no trouble, really. I'd be glad to wash bedding while we have such a nice day... if you want me to, that is," she smiled. "Jems always taught me never to waste a good drying day. 'Course with all my brothers and so many beds, we always had a pile of washing to keep up with back home."

"Well, if you don't think it's too much extra work," Amanda acquiesced. She did appreciate how well Sadie managed most of the housework, which freed Amanda to care almost exclusively for the babies. Sadie went about all her chores so cheerfully. But honestly, sometimes all this courtesy could drive a body to the brink of madness. No matter how much her sister-in-law might rankle her at times, Amanda made up her mind that she would not allow anything to upset her newfound happiness—not even that ridiculous nickname for Jeremiah that Sadie insisted upon using—Jems. "I'm sure Jeremiah would appreciate sleeping on fresh sheets," Amanda answered politely, "even though it is not a bath night."

Now, when it came to running the household, Sadie usually managed to do just exactly as she wished. For she found that with a little calculated leading on her part, she could get Amanda to assign the very tasks she wished to accomplish in the first place—not quite as direct as handling her brothers, by any stretch of the imagination, but she was beginning to understand how to utilize these "womanly ways."

Besides, Sadie loved living here. She reveled in the glow of being near her favorite brother again. She'd do anything she could to please him. After Jeremy left Fayette County for the

Ohio country two years ago, she'd been miserable at home without him. None of her other brothers could even begin to understand her the way Jems did. Having the chance to live in the same house with him again fall right into her lap, she wasn't about to let anything stand in the way of making her Jems happy—not even his wife.

Sadie had come to like Amanda well enough, as a sister-in-law. But when it came to making decisions and getting on with the business of living, she didn't think too much of her namby-pamby ways. Unlike this genteel southern girl who'd been raised to quietly comply with any man's wishes, Sadie had a straightforward, impish honesty about her that did more to endear her to a man than any submissive, feminine foolishness.

Jeremy did seem quite taken with his little southern belle. Sadie hadn't failed to notice, that in addition to all his own field work and barn chores, how much more of the so-called "women's work" he had taken upon himself in order to make life easier for his "little yellow bird."

Sadie decided she'd do her best to lighten his load by taking over as many of the household responsibilities as she could manage. "While I have a fire going outside to heat wash water, maybe I'll just keep it going a little longer and surprise Jems with a nice, hot bath. I bet he'd like that after evening chores," Sadie said with enthusiasm.

"Do you think that's wise? Two baths in one week?" Amanda protested. "You do know that soaking in hot water too often can ruin a person's skin."

"Where did you ever hear a thing like that?"

"Why, every girl is taught that taking a daily bird-bath is more prudent than soaking too often in a warm tub," Amanda chided. "Don't they teach you northern girls such things?"

"Never heard that one before," Sadie answered. "Sounds like complete bunkum to me." She took the pan of dirty dishwater to the door and gave it a pitch. "Besides, Jems told me he likes to feel nice and clean before he jumps between fresh sheets."

"I am aware of his preferences, sister," Amanda said, beginning to get aggravated by the direction this conversation had taken. "Perhaps we should stick to washing baby things today and simply leave it at that."

"Whatever you say. I'll go out and get the wash fire started."

As Sadie headed outdoors, Jeremy walked onto the porch with a pail of frothy milk, fresh drawn from faithful, ol' Bertha. "Milk man's a-comin' with moo-juice straight from the cow!"

"Set it over there, Jems. I'll strain it soon as I start the wash fire," Sadie pointed toward the shady corner of the porch. "We got a mountain of dirty diapers to boil."

"You washing sheets, too? Be a shame to waste the great drying breeze we have goin' today."

"That's what I thought," Sadie answered, rolling her eyes and gesturing toward the cabin. "But Amanda thinks we should stick to baby things."

"I'll see what we can do about that," he said, giving her braid a tug, before he turned and headed toward the door. Jeremy poked his head inside. "How would you like fresh sheets tonight, Mandy?" he asked with a wink. "Hay's drying so well, I aim to finish stacking all the rest of it this afternoon. I'll need to take a good bath to wash off all that hay dust, so you won't have to sleep next to a smelly ol' dust ball tonight." He strode into the cabin and gave Amanda a peck on the cheek. "Sure would feel good to hop between squeaky-clean sheets after I get myself all scrubbed up. Whattd'ya say?"

He bent down and gave each of his little daughters a kiss, and at their Daddy's touch they both stopped their nursing and looked up at him with big smiles. "Darned if they don't know their Daddy already," he said, dropping to one knee and giving each a tickle under the chin.

"Here, Jeremiah, would you take one for a minute so I can put myself back together?" As he reached to take one baby, he leaned his head in closer and also took one of Mandy's breasts into his own mouth.

"Jeremiah! What are you doing!"

"You told me to take one."

"A baby! Hold on to a baby!" With her one free hand she fumbled with the hooks on her bodice. "Honestly, Jeremiah... what are you thinking?"

"Just checking to see if those milk jugs are giving quality nutriment for my lovely little flowers," he said, looking up with a wink. Before she could fasten her bodice, he latched on to the other breast for another quick suckle.

"Stop, now! Your sister could walk in!"

He let go, but gave her nipple a playful nip before he stood back up. Then he scooped the other baby from Amanda's lap and began to coo and make faces at his tiny daughters.

"You got me so flustered, I can't even get these hooks fastened," she mumbled under her breath.

"Want me to fasten you back up?"

"I do not! Stay right over there and keep both your hands busy holding babies, if you please," she said, finally managing to join each hook and eye to its proper mate.

"Now, if you would go lay Camellia and Lillian down on the big bed, I will see to changing them," she said, rising and adjusting her skirts. "I would like to get diapers washed before this morning is completely wasted."

"Anything you say, my little yellow bird." He strode over to the bed, laid each baby down gently, then pushed the bed pillows over to the edge so the girls couldn't roll onto the floor. Neither one had accomplished much rolling as of yet, but Lillian had managed to turn from her stomach onto her back three times already. He aimed to take no unnecessary chances with their safety.

"If you want to have clean sheets tonight, Jeremiah, then I shall see to it that you have clean sheets," she said, beginning to remove Camellia's milk-soaked sacque.

"Thanks." He leaned over to give her another kiss. "Maybe we can both enjoy having clean sheets tonight," he said with a wink and an ornery smile.

"You put those ideas right out of your head, sir. Do not forget that we have another person living under this roof , who happens to have very sensitive hearing, I might add."

"Sadie? You don't have to mind her. She can't hear a thing, sleeping way up there in the loft."

"Sound does carry upward, I believe, does it not?"

"All right, then. How about this idea... tomorrow let's you and me take a picnic over to the Honey Creek. We can get away from this cabin and have a little time all to ourselves. What do you say?"

"You expect me to drag these babies all the way over to Honey Creek, just so we can have a... a picnic?"

"Did I say anything about taking babies along?"

"But how do you expect me to leave–"

"We can leave them home with Sadie for a couple hours. They'll be just fine."

"But I have to feed them, Jeremiah. How can I leave those helpless–"

"We're only talking about a few hours at the most, Mandy. They sleep what, a good two, three hours when they go down for their afternoon naps, now? It couldn't hurt you to leave them for at least a couple hours for one day, now, could it?"

"But what if they wake up hungry and we're not back?"

"Then Sadie can feed them some sugar pap. That's what she grew up on, don't forget. She had no Mama to nurse her when she was a young pup, so I brewed up other rations to feed her."

"But I feel funny leaving–"

"Look, you've been cooped up with these two babies for nearly four months, Mandy... four months of double worry. Don't you think it's about time you got away for an hour or two at least?"

"But–"

"No more buts. Tomorrow we go on a picnic," Jeremy said in a manner that sealed the subject. "Besides, it's our second anniversary, Mandy. Did you forget?"

"Our anni... You mean it's July already?"

"July, 4... Anniversary. Tomorrow. Two years ago you became Mrs. Jeremiah Harrison? That day changed my life, Mandy."

"Mine, too." She stood quietly for a long moment.

"You don't regret becoming my wife, do you?"

"Oh, Jeremiah, whatever put such an idea into your head!"

"You forgot."

"I did not forget! I simply failed to realize we had come into July already."

"Then you'll go on a picnic with me? To celebrate our anniversary?"

"Of course I will go on a picnic with you... to celebrate our anniversary," she said, getting back to the baby-changing task at hand. "I believe I shall just let Sadie tend to the laundry chores herself. That way I can begin to make preparations for our anniversary meal."

"Then I better go get that hay field finished up, so we can go off and have us a grand celebration!" He gave a little hop-skip, then bounded toward the door. At that moment, Sadie pushed it open on her way back inside and collided with him head-on.

"Whoa there, Pipsqueak," Jeremy said, giving her hair a muss. "I didn't see you."

"Don't pay it any mind, Jems. You know I have a hard head. I had to, growing up with so many brothers!" Sadie took a moment to smooth the top of her hair back down and tuck loose hairs into her braid, then walked to the corner to retrieve the sack full of dirty diapers she'd come back inside to fetch.

Amanda, now nearly finished changing babies into clean day-sacques, cleared her throat and said, "Sadie, I have reconsidered the idea about washing sheets." She propped one baby up in the double cradle under the window, then sat the other one right beside her. "It is such a lovely day, I think we should strip the beds. It would be a wonderful time to air out all the blankets, too... with such a nice breeze an' all."

Sadie shot Jeremiah a curious look, and he gave her a reassuring wink. "We're getting ready to celebrate, Sadie. Tomorrow's our ann-i-ver-sa-ry, so we aim to clean up proper for such a big day!"

"Hey, why don't you two go on a picnic, Jems? I'd be glad to watch the babies."

"That's a wonderful idea, Pipsqueak! Thanks for the offer. Don't know why I didn't think of it myself."

"You can't fool me, Jems. I know you already did."

* * * * *

Amanda fussed with empty dishes and picnic leftovers while Jeremy lay back on the blanket, head in hands, taking great pleasure in watching his wife clean up their anniversary dinner.

"Chicken sure tasted good, Mandy."

"Thank you. I know we don't have that many hens to spare, but I wanted this to be a special meal. Chicken is your favorite."

"Did you kill that chicken all by yourself?"

"Yes, you rascal. I certainly did. And I cleaned it all by myself, too!"

"I can't help it, Mandy. You know I have to tease you about that first chicken," he said, laughing out loud.

"Will you never let me live that one down?" she asked in mock indignation.

"That chicken has got to go down in our family history, if for no other reason than to let our children's children know how far you've come, my little yellow bird."

"I have come a long way, haven't I?"

"We both have. In more ways than one."

"Thanks to you. If you hadn't taken the time to teach me so much and been so patient with me, Jeremiah, I don't know how I could manage."

"Has it been such a bad life, living out here with me?"

"Not a bad life at all. Just so different from anything I ever knew. You can't imagine how different." She grew quiet and seemed to draw far away.

Jeremiah sat and watched her for a few, peaceful moments. "Do you know how beautiful you are, Mandy?"

His voice roused her from her daydream. "Hmmm? Did you say something?"

"I said come here, you. Give me a big smooch." He took hold of her ankles and gave a gentle pull.

"Jeremiah! What are you planning to do?"

As he continued to pull, her skirts began to push up, revealing the skin of her lily-white legs. "I'm going to ravish my wife, that's what I plan to do," he said, stroking his hand slowly up her inner leg and coming to a stop just above her knee.

"Jeremiah, stop this instant! How can you even think of such a thing out in the open?"

"Look around, Mandy. Not a soul about for miles. Nobody's gonna see you with your drawers down, except me." At the mention of her drawers, he began a gentle tugging at those unmentionables.

"Jeremiah, I will not do this in broad daylight. You'll see everything!" She sat up and began tugging her under drawers back up.

"It's not like I haven't seen you out of 'em before, you know."

"But there's nothing here to cover myself with!" She pulled away, trying to readjust her drawers, as Jeremy reached around to unfasten the hooks of her bodice.

"Jeremiah, you shouldn't do that... you know I'm a nursing mother."

"And these are the two most beautiful milk jugs I ever did see," he said, freeing them both from the confines of their bindings. He leaned down, took one nipple into his mouth, and began a gentle rubbing of the other with a thumb and fore-finger.

When Mandy began to make little whimpering sounds, his free hand wended its way under her skirts and took up the job of rubbing other, more tender regions hiding under the cover of her petticoats.

"Jeremiah, we... I... "

"Shhhhh. I love you, Mandy. Give me a chance to show you how much."

* * * * *

"Hand up that sack full of nails, will you Pipsqueak?" Jeremy called down to his sister from atop the partially con-structed addition he was building onto the cabin.

"This one?"

"That's the one. Be careful climbin' up."

Holding the bag of nails in one hand, Sadie began to ascend the ladder leaning against the north side of the Harrison cabin. In late July Jeremy decided to expand their living area to provide a needed bit of privacy for Amanda and himself. He could hardly believe, after the prolonged and embarrassing start between them, given Amanda's first, painful, sexual experience, that she had finally come to let herself relax in their connubial unions, whenever they could manage a bit of privacy. Not one to discourage this newfound gratification, he told Amanda that he would build her a summer kitchen with new sleeping quar-ters for them above, in its loft.

"Better use both hands to climb, Pipsqueak. That ladder's none too stable," Jeremy warned Sadie from his perch on the rafters.

"How am I supposed to carry this bag and still keep both hands on the ladder?"

"You're smart. You'll figure it out," he said, sawing the end off another rafter to make it fit snugly into the ridgepole.

Sadie shrugged her shoulders, then put the bag's strings between her teeth and continued the climb.

When her head popped over the top, Jeremy took one look and let out a loud laugh. "You're priceless, Pipsqueak, you know that?"

"Well, I didn't have any pockets! What else could I do?"

"You always were the creative thinker of the bunch," Jeremy said, removing the bag from between her teeth and tying its strings to his belt.

"How long till you have this roof ready for shingles, Jems?"

"Should have the rafters all fit by tomorrow, I expect. Then I can start pounding down shakes."

"Can I help?"

"I don't know. It's awful dangerous work, this far off the ground."

"Oh, Jems, let me, please? I've never been afraid of heights. I like high places."

"We'll see tomorrow. Got to get all these rafters fitted first."

"I can hammer great, Jems. Honest. Paul always made me go out to fix holes in the roof back home."

"You mean to tell me that out of all those grown boys, they made a skinny girl like you climb onto the roof when it needed a patch?"

"Paul said I was the lightest one, so I wouldn't fall through. Besides, they were all too scared."

"Mandy won't like it, you know. She thinks this kind of thing's too dangerous for me, let alone a Pipsqueak like you."

"Then don't tell her. I won't if you won't."

"We'll see tomorrow," he said, taking one of the spikes out of the nail bag and hammering the rafter he'd just set into its place. "How about fetching me a drink of water? This is awful thirsty work."

"Sure thing. Coming right up." Sadie made a hasty retreat back down the ladder and hurried over to the pump, where she dipped up a gourd of water from the full bucket sitting there. She hurriedly shinnied back up the ladder with the water gourd in hand, before Jeremy could caution her again about climbing two-handed.

"Fresh water for my favorite brother," she said, handing him the jug.

He took a long pull, wiped his mouth, then handed the jug back to Sadie. "Thanks," he said. "I was parched."

"Did you notice how I well crawled back up here with one hand? See, I was born to climb!"

Jeremy mussed her hair, tweaked her cheek, then focused his attention back on the next rafter he was attempting to fit.

From down below they heard another voice. "Jeremiah! Youuuu Hooo! Jeremiah? Are you still safe up there?"

"I'm fine, Mandy. Only three more rafters to go."

"Oh, my lands, Sadie Harrison, what in the name of heaven are you doing up on that roof?"

"Jems wanted a drink of water, so I brought one up to him."

"You get yourself down from there this instant! A roof is definitely no place for a lady," she hollered in alarm. "My goodness, Jeremiah. Whatever possessed you to encourage your sister to climb to such dangerous heights?"

"You heard the boss, Pipsqueak. Back down to solid ground."

"Guess this means I can't hammer tomorrow," she said with a pout.

"We'll see," Jeremiah said. "We'll see."

Sadie made her way down the ladder, jumping the last two steps and bounding to the ground in one smooth motion, which nearly startled Amanda out of her skin.

"Sadie! How can you behave so? You are a lady, are you not?"

"Last time I looked," she smiled.

Above, Jeremy could barely stifle his laughter.

* * * * *

"How do you like it Mandy?" Jeremy asked with a sweep of his hand.

"It's lovely. Just lovely," she said, taking in the finished summer kitchen. "Can we put the table over here, across from the hearth? And perhaps a new shelf over there, by that window?"

"I'll put a shelf up anywhere you want, Mandy. Two shelves. You say the word, and it's done," he said, giving her hand a squeeze. "Now come over here," he said, pulling her to the far corner where he opened a door. "See, I put real steps up to the loft for you, too. No dangerous ladder to climb."

"Oh Jeremiah, real steps? For me?" She gave a little squeal and pecked him on the cheek. "Goodness, I didn't mean to get so carried away," she said, turning red and lowering her eyes.

"Go on up there and take a look. See how you like it."

She climbed up slowly, keeping her skirts tucked around her ankles as she ascended each step.

"Watch your head up at the top. Roof's a little low on the one side. You can stand straight up over in the middle of the room, though."

"Oh, my. There's a real bedstead up here!"

"You don't say!" he said, following her up to the loft.

"Jeremiah, when did you have time to make a bed?"

"Here and there. Now and then. I worked on it times you were busy with the twins. I wanted to surprise you."

"I am surprised. And impressed, too."

"Impressed enough to give me a big kiss?"

"Jeremiah. It's the middle of the day!"

"So, what's wrong with a little kissing in the middle of the day?" he asked, sidling up and giving her a little shove onto the bed.

She bounced down with a look of surprise. "It bounces, Jeremiah! It bounces!"

"Yup. I made it with rope woven across the bottom, so it has a little give to it. No more platform beds that put cricks in your back." He sat down on the edge of the bed and joined in with her bouncing. "Has a nice rhythm to it, don't ya' think?"

"Jeremiah! What are you thinking!"

"Well, Sadie's off hoeing that far piece of corn, and the twins just went down for their naps, so what do you think I'm thinkin'?"

Amanda sat silently a few moments, then she began to untie her apron. "Perhaps you should go down and close that nice, new door, Mr. Harrison. I feel a trifle warm with all these clothes on," she said, giving him a coy smile, as she pulled her apron over her head.

"Hot damn! I should have built us a new bed long ago!"

Dear Libby Howard,

I hope you are still up in them Fire Lands. After all this while, maybe you are surprised to hear from me. Well, it has been a good many months. But now that I have time to sit and write, I thought I must let you know how things go with me.

I am in jail.

I reckon that took you a mite by surprise. It is a long story. And as I have nothing but time on my hands now I will tell you the whole sad tale. If you wrote to me in care of Harvey, no doubt your letter went unanswered. Harvey still lives there far as I know. But I left after the accident.

Theodore is dead. I kilt him. Which is why I sit here in this jail cell.

I better start where it started. Last I saw you was at the revival. After that Jonathan took Pa back home. When Pa left Theodore missed his company so much he got to acting up something awful. Caused Harvey and me a pile of grief. Not so much Harvey directly. Mostly me. Theodore also reached that age when wild oats start kicking in. Inner urges beginning to drive him in a way no woman can rightly understand.

He made me the target of his devilment ever since the revival. And always when Harvey was not around to see it. So I had no one to back up my tales of woe about how bad the boy was getting to handle. Just the 3 of us living at the place now. Why he would even get into Pa's corn likker on occasion. You know what wildcat juice can do to a man. Let alone a boy what ain't used to it.

Theodore was bigger than me and outweighed me by half again. I might be scrawny, but I got a lot of strength left in me yet. Specially when provoked. I kept the upper hand with the boy, only as I could still scare him some. I knew it would not be long till he figgered out he could turn the tables. If push come to shove.

The boy finally turned the bend one day, while Harvey was away to Mt. Vernon. Had to go get a new ax head. Broke it clean in two on a piece of stone while clearing a new patch for planting next spring. Would you believe that tree had a rock buried in the trunk? Never heard such of a thing before. Saw it myself, sure as you're born.

Carried it right in the house, he did. Them two pieces of ax. Harvey, says I, get that thing out of my house this instant. You know better. It is bad luck to bring a broke ax right under this roof, I told him. Means someone is sure to die. He laughed and called me a harebrained old biddy.

Now, Harvey had no spare ax. And you know how much a man needs one out here. So he made up his mind to make a supply run. He needed gun powder and a few other things besides.

Theodore wanted to go with his pa. Natural for a boy. But Harvey made him stay to home. One cow was due to drop her calf. And there was a pile of hoeing to do in the corn. Harvey told the boy to take care of things while he was gone. Theodore kicked the dirt and told his pa he reckoned he could do that. After Harvey climbed up in the wagon and started off Theodore turned and gave me the meanest look I ever did see. Sent a chill up my spine it did. Turned my blood cold. I wished right then he went with his pa. Call it a woman's second sight. But I knew I was in for a fight before Harvey come back.

I tried to make light of it, but the boy stomped off to the barn and stayed out there till supper time. I had no say over him no more. With Harvey gone he would not do what I said. But I had work to get at, so I did not have time to stew about him for long. I spent the rest of the day tending my vegetable patch and washing bedding and hoeing corn rows.

When chore time come, I set a stew to cook for supper. Headed to the barn to see how much still needed done. I figgered Theodore at least started chores. But when I got to the barn, the cow already fresh was raising a big ruckus. The chickens was all stirred up, too. Boy nowhere in sight. I went about setting all to rights. As I sat there on the milk stool working up a pail full, the hair stood up on the back of my neck. I got the strangest feeling.

So I turned to see if the devil his self was standing behind me. There was Theodore with the wildest look in his eyes I ever did see. He was holding a big butcher knife in one hand and a jug of Pa's finest in the other. He just stood there staring. That look froze me to the stool. For the first time in all my days here, I got scared.

I made myself turn back to milking, trying to act natural-like. Theodore, says I in my normal mother voice, you better go slop them hogs, as I ain't made it out there yet. He just stood there not moving an inch. Xcept to flex his arm muscles. I was trying to think what to do if he come at me with that knife. Then I heard him stomp off toward the pig pen.

I told myself, Ellie you are making a mountain out of a mole hill. Scaring yourself silly for no good reason. This is a mixed up boy who needs a strong mother to guide him through this hard growing up time. That is all.

I finished the milking and commenced tending to the chickens. Went up in the hay mow to look for eggs. When I had a whole apron full of eggs, I heard Theodore come back in the barn. Theodore, says I from up in the mow, take that pail of milk to the cabin for me, would you? He said nothing. Just took a big pull from that jug and threw it down. Then he started to climb the ladder up to the mow. All the while still holding on to that knife.

When he got up there, he started walking toward me, kind of leaning to one side.

What in the name of God are you thinking, says I. Put that knife down!

You are not gonna tell me what to do no more, old woman, says he.

Theodore, is that any way to talk to your mother, says I.

You ain't my mother. My mother is dead.

Theodore, I got supper on in the house, I told him. Put down that knife and go eat. You got to be hungry. You never did come in for nooning. Go on now, like a good boy. So we can forget all this nonsense.

I kept up a babble. Hoping to distract him. But that corn juice already went to his head. Shut down the boy and brought out a monster in his place.

Shut up, woman, says he. I'm tired of hearing your voice. I'm tired of you telling me what to do. I'm tired of you!

He lunged at me with that knife.

I am still quick enough on my feet and I side stepped. He fell forward on the hay. I tried to get to the ladder. But he got up madder than mad. Jumped between me and that ladder. Knife still in his hand. What could I do standing there still holding my apron full of eggs? I threw some at him. Only handy thing I had to throw. If the whole thing was not so upsetting, it sure would look silly to someone who come in on the scene. A boy leaning to one side. Standing there with a butcher knife. And a scrawny woman pitching eggs at him.

Finally he sprung at me again. I did not move fast enough. He caught the hem of my dress and pulled me over. Held the knife to my throat. He pulled at my bodice and fumbled at my bosoms. I thrashed away with both hands, trying to get that knife away from him. But he was stronger. Lots stronger. For the first time he knew he had me.

But I was not about to let happen what he had in mind to happen. I gathered all the strength I had and heaved over. Rolled us both to the edge of the mow. He grabbed for the ladder with one hand and lost the knife over the edge. It fell to the barn floor along with lots of loose hay from my kicking feet.

I struggled to get up. He had one hand on the ladder and one trying to hold on to me. I gave a shove at him. He lost his balance and went over backwards. He landed on the barn floor with a thud. I figgered he would come up hollering like a banshee. But he laid there on his belly, stone still.

I was afeared to go down. Was he playing possum? Waiting for me to come see if he was alive?

But I could not stay up there. It was getting dark. Hard enough to see in the half-light. The thought of trying to walk by him in the dark, not able to see if he was reaching out to grab my ankle, got me moving down the ladder. I turned to look down at him after every step. Seen no movement.

When I reached the bottom, I seen the red puddle coming from under Theodore's chest. That is when I knew he would not get up ever again. Now I do not need tell what a feeling of sorrow come over me. All mixed up with relief, too. Strange to think I was glad this boy would not make trouble for me no more. But also sad cause I did love the boy. Hard as it was to love him most times.

Then it hit me. Harvey! My God! What would I tell Harvey? I saddled up the mule and rode right over to Edie's to fetch her back. I knew Theodore was beyond her doctoring. But I could not think what else to do. I told her that I kilt Theodore dead. She tried to get on behind. But the mule, Old Lucifer, sat right down. Took us some few minutes to hook up Edie's buckboard to her horse before we got on our way. I could only look straight ahead thinking what we was headed for.

We rolled the boy over and there was the knife sticking out of his chest. Handle had lodged in a hole of the floor, leaving the blade sticking straight up for him to land on. Edie tried to pull it out. The tip was lodged deep in bone from the force of the fall. I was scared to touch it. But I could not stand to see it sticking out of his body underneath that baby face of his. So we both put our backs into it till our hands got so slimy with blood they slipped off the handle every time we tried. I commenced to feel a strange heaviness that made moving harder and harder. My sister took notice and helped me into the house in front of the fire.

She heaped the pile of clean bedding I had brought in from the line so long ago on top of me in the rocker. Set about fixing me a hot toddy. I remember her bringing a pan of warm water.

She put it in my lap and washed the blood off my hands. I tried to tell her there was no help for it. He was crazed, was it. Just trying to save myself. Never meant for such a thing to happen. I am not real clear on the next part. One minute Edie was patting my shoulder and clucking like a hen. Next thing I recall, it was bright morning and Tom and Willie was carrying Theodore into the house.

They got him laid out. Edie washed him up. But no one could get that knife out. So Edie put a blanket over it. Then we waited for Harvey. Willie and Tom took care of the animals. Edie did some cooking. I could not do much of a thing but look at the unnatural way that blanket stuck out from the boy's chest. I was not looking forward to telling Harvey his son was dead. Same time, I wished he was there to hold me and take charge. Tell me it was not my fault. He knew the boy would come to this one day. Put his arms round me and forgive me.

But when he come home, he went plumb crazy with grief. Went on and on about how I kilt his only son. How he wished he never had set eyes on me. I was no good as a wife no how, says he, since I had birthed him no more sons. He said to pack up my duds and get out before he got the Justice to lock me up for murder.

He pulled the blanket off the boy. Grabbed that knife by the blade, just below the handle and started to pull. I tried to tell him how it was not my fault. But he did not hear a word of it. His boy would not go to his effin grave with a effin knife in his chest, says he. I saw the knife start to pull out. Harvey's blood running down through his fingers and onto the boy from where the knife was cutting into his palm. I thought it wise to make my exit right then. Wait till his grief run its course and he come back to his senses. So I left with only the clothes on my back and went home with Edie and her boys. Waited for Harvey to get to feeling better and come for me.

Sam Justice, the blacksmith, told me how when Harvey's first woman died of the consumption, he stayed likkered up for more than a month. Got it in his head that the doctor from Mount Vernon had caused her to die. He wandered around, shooting at trees and such, thinking that doctor was behind every one. Sam said Dr. Bradley had to vamoose from the territory till Harvey ran out of corn juice.

Sam took to hanging round Edie's place after I got there. Slept in the barn just in case of that for instance. Gave him a reason to be round Edie, too. Sam did go back to fetch some of my things and see whether Harvey was still in the drink. Dead to the world, he was, said Sam. I was mighty grateful to have my trunk, as Edie's clothes stretched to the sides where I need them to stretch up. Your letters was in there too, which I was right glad to have back.

Sam has been sweet on my sister from the time before her man Lloyd died. Sam's gun blew up in his face one day. Thought he was a goner. Went blind and deaf and dumb for a time. There he was down on the ground when his sight come back. First thing he set eyes on was Edie's face. Thought she was a angel. Saw her lips move but could not hear a thing. Instead of taking him to meet his maker, that angel tended powder burns on his face.

His hearing come back some days later. Partly, anyway. He seems to understand most people right well when they talk loud. But for Edie he some way turns around everything she says. Once he asked her to dance at a wedding, and she says, Go to the devil, Mister Samuel Justice. Next thing you know, he come back with a shovel, gets down on one knee, and says, Let's get hitched, Woman. I never saw my sister flustered and tongue tied before. With everyone watching and laughing. He says, you told me if I got you a shovel, you'd marry me in front of the Justice, didn't you?

When Harvey finally did come to find me, he was drunk as a skunk. Same fire in his eyes as Theodore had. Same devil let loose. Sam stood with his rifle, barring the door. Sent Harvey home in no uncertain terms. Sam can swear up some storm when he gets going. Come back inside and told me for the sake of my own neck I better lay low a spell.

I did not think it wise to stay on at Edie's much longer. So I up and took myself to Jason and Mary Sue's place. My old homestead. Stayed on with them about a month. Then I traveled back to Justice to ask after Harvey. Come to find out he went and took his self another woman! Now how do you like them beans? You think you know a man and he acts like a stranger complete. Got me so riled I rode out to his place to see with my own eyes.

Sure as rain, a woman come to the door. Wearing my spare apron, no less. Asked me what did I want. Can you imagine my feelings right then? I asked after Harvey. Went to get the Justice to track down his wife, says she. To lock her up for murder of his son. I took myself right off without letting on who I was. Headed back to Jason's to make a plan.

Well to make this already long story shorter, I settled into a little shanty down near Perrysville. On the Clearfork River where boatmen send farm stuffs down river to the Hio. On down to New Orleens. Made my way for a time cooking for those river men. Filled their bellies and mended up their duds. Figgered they are a hard fighting bunch to hide behind, if anybody should come looking for me.

But you know how it figgers. Not one of them rascals was near the day the Justice come for me. Which he did. Well if I had to go to jail, I would take some of my own things. I made them wait while I went back in the shanty and opened my trunk. Saw that big hat my mother give me sitting in there. Dammed if I did not take the notion to put it on my head and go to jail in style. Riding right up there on old Lucifer like a fancy lady.

So here I sit in the pokey over in Mansfield. Waiting for the circuit judge to come round. Jason come to see me this week. Brought me some writing things. I am grateful for that. So I can finally tell you about the fix I am in. Jason said that Tom come and got my mule. Soon as word got back to Justice. He knew the Constable aimed to charge me for boarding the beast. Jason also told me Mary Sue is in the family way again. I confess, my first thought was that the babe now has a jailbird for a grandmaw.

I do not worry over much about what will happen next. Could be most anything, I reckon. As it is I get fed three times a day. Not the best vittles. But filling at least. I have a pallet to sleep on that serves. And I got work for my hands. They got me mending for the county poor house. It is easy work and keeps me busy. So I am content as one can be in such a fix.

Now you know what become of me. How does life go for you Libby? You are so busy tending to others. Do you take any time just for you? Make sure you enjoy every minute. Never know when life will turn you upside down.

I will try to get the Constable to post this letter for me. God only knows when or if you will ever get it. I pray you are all well up in them Fire Lands. I think of you often as I sit here with my needle and thread. Sure wish you would write to tell me how it is with you. It would help to pass the time. Bet the leaves are changing about now. I always liked fall. Wish I could see the trees. Send me a letter in care of this here jail. And I will keep the faith that we may meet up again one day.

Always your friend (though it has been a while),

Ellie Mae

October 27, 1817

My dear friend Ellie Mae,

How relieved I am to have direct word from you! I have been trying to track you down these past few months with no success.

It started last summer, when Mr. Snow hired Zach to deliver that ram which Harvey had purchased. Zach came back with the news. You were gone. Theodore was no longer. He arrived to find no door of any kind on the cabin, animals wandering in and out at will, and Harvey lying on the floor in a drunken stupor. A female person was also there amongst the droppings and filth in a like condition. Zach said that there had not been a meal cooked nor a fire built in some time, as he observed a chicken nesting in your clay oven.

He made to rouse the man with some water, but this was successful only in part. Harvey began charging around the cabin screaming of murder and retribution, kicking a sheep that wandered in, and breaking the last standing chair. It took Zach some time to make any sense of it all, but he did learn that you apparently were safe. Zach stayed on a few days putting things to rights, with the animals out and a fire back in the hearth. Harvey never came completely back to his senses but worked alongside Zach, muttering to himself all the while.

Zach stopped at your sister's place to check on you and learned that you had gone to Jason and Mary Sue, but by the time my missive reached them, you were gone again.

I cannot imagine what you must have been through on that horrible day or since—the death of a boy you were raising as your own, waiting for Harvey with the news, fleeing your home, returning to find another woman in your place, making your way alone, and then to be incarcerated!

It is almost beyond bearing. Yet I am reassured to hear that you are tolerating the circumstances well enough and not fearing overmuch the future. The circuit judge must untangle the mess. If you are in need of a character witness, Zach assures me that he would accompany me on such a journey.

As to helping you to pass the time with news of us, I know not where to begin. I think here I will put in the pages of that letter which I sent with Zach to take to you along with the ram.

August 1, 1817

My friend Ellie Mae,

I am sorry to have caused you such concern with my silence. Of course we are still friends, and you must not doubt this. I found your father to be a very entertaining character and even charming in his rustic way. As for his venture into "greener pastures," I have endured far more uncouth advances in drawing rooms, and to this you should not give a second thought. Having thus assuaged your distress, I must with heavy heart recount the past many weeks and the reason for my prolonged silence.

When we returned home from the revival, all was as it should be. Zach unharnessed the oxen while Nate assured me that he had no difficulties and all at home was well. We had barely come inside, when he remembered the posts which had come in our absence. He handed me two letters: one from my brother-in-law, Garth, which I should have found strange had I taken a moment to ponder, but I assumed it was meant for Zach and gave it to him directly. I hurried to open the one which bore the hand of my sister, Abby.

What I read there made absolutely no sense. She spoke of a funeral and a journey, of needed stores and supplies. I checked to see if I had begun on the wrong page, because this one seemed started in the middle. A game? A riddle? I knew not what to make of it.

I started over from the beginning. It had been a beautiful service. I should not torment myself that I could not be there. The boys had held up like good little soldiers, so brave. Weather permitting, they would depart on the morrow. She hoped that she had thought of everything that would be necessary—enough food for the journey; extra pots, dishes, and linens; needles, thread, and fine cloth of layette quality;

even sweets to treat the children. It made no more sense on the third read.

A hand closed over mine. Zach's face told me that he could answer my question, but I could not form it to ask. My mind danced from the uncertainty, as now my pen does from the telling, as if to put it off would rob it of its power. Just say it quickly. My sister Rose is dead. There. It is no better however many times I say it. Under my breath, times without number, did I say the words on our journey east, and still they smote my heart yet again at this telling. Gone from this world, never to be seen by these eyes again in life. How so? I must act, must move. I must go to her. But the oxen required a rest, and Zach said that we should not begin until dawn.

I made Lizzie special guardian of Elijah with Nate over all, and through the night we readied to travel the road again, but in another direction. Zach did make me lie down before the light, held me down I might say. I kept Garth's letter in my hand, with its tale of my sister's struggle with pneumonia and her instructions when she realized that she would succumb, the message to me, "Take care of our girls, Olivia Rose," written in her own weak hand.

She had told Garth that the boys should stay with him, but that her wish was for him to bring Caitlin and Zan to me, that Zannah would be lost if she could find neither of her two, favorite "sissies," and that Cait, since she refused to marry, should leave the narrow society of Danbury to at least have the comfort of her aunt when her time to deliver came upon her. That's why speed was of the utmost importance. I could do nothing for my dear sister, for she was in the ground some time before the letters arrived. But Cait was making her way to us, and Zannah, brought by Garth.

He had sent the letters by the swiftest courier and asked that we meet him at a point in western Pennsylvania. He could not afford the time to await a reply from us, for the sake of Caitlin's own health and that of the child. Travel could be post-poned no longer in her condition without risk of complications. He would start out immediately, and if we could meet him, it would be that much sooner he could return to his boys, who remained with Abby meantimes, and to the mill. Our progress was tedious, and I would have pulled the wagon faster myself, but we finally arrived and then had a wait of two days before they made it thus far.

It wasn't until I saw Garth's face that I finally believed Rose was truly gone. Before we all parted, he told me that this mission had postponed his prostrating himself with grief, and once he completed this journey, he didn't know what further purpose he might find to keep himself from it. I hope that he will be able to take comfort in his sons. It did warm me to see Zannah's delight in finding one of her lost sissies. But Caitlin turned away and would not accept comfort. She barely speaks, and this cannot be good for the child.

The return home was like a time out of reality. I have no conception of its duration, but we arrived yesterday to find the cabin still standing, children solemn and uncomplaining. Oh, to be like Zannah. What joy she had at seeing all her little friends again.

Last night I woke to crying. It was Cait, sobbing as though her heart would break. I went to her makeshift bed, where she lay, clutching Zan and weeping into her hair. The poor thing. She said that she had made her mother's life miserable for all the years since she learned to speak and most especially of late, with her tempers and big belly. I held her and assured her that her mother loved her better than the moon and the stars, and that Rose had been happy and excited about her coming grandchild.

She told me that she overheard Aunt Abby saying her grief might mark her baby, and so she tried hard not to cry, because her mother had told her she would have a little girl, a beautiful girl, and as Rose sometimes knew those things, Cait didn't want to mar her daughter's face. I promised her that we should have a good cry and let out our grief, and it would not hurt her baby a bit, but do us all a world of good. So we did, and it did. Cait says that she would like to name the bairn after its grand-mother. I told her about your neighbor's Rosanna, but she in fact seems fixed on the name Rose Petal. Perhaps she will tire of this notion before it is too late, as young girls will.

Zach is already talking of the wing he will put on the north side of the cabin in the spring. He is also excited over the saw blade which Garth carried all the way to Pennsylvania to give him. Nights are spent once again talking of lumber.

I sometimes am not sure that my sister is not off visiting Hattie in Massachusetts. When I kissed her goodbye, I knew that I might never see her dear face again, but I thought that she would be in the same world with me still. I have no time to turn morose. The doctor had told Cait to expect her bundle in October, so I must teach her to handle a needle, with a layette to make ready. Zan will see to it that our garments are covered with flowers. Let us see if we cannot persuade Zan to make them roses.

Lizzie and Leesha are so glad of more female companions in residence. They are now no longer outnumbered. We have five males and five females under this roof, and if Rose was correct, soon the females will have the greater number.

I am sending this letter with Zach, as he readies himself to deliver that ram to you, as was arranged before our sudden departure. Please do not again doubt that I am and shall remain your friend.

Libby

(return to previous letter)

We have no baby as of yet, Ellie Mae, but Caitlin looks more ripe with each passing day. You will recall that I had hopes of her repenting the name Rose Petal? Well, she did. It seems that it was a child's fancy after all, so she told me, and that the proper name for her daughter came to her upon waking from a dream. She told me the infant should be called Rosebud. I did not laugh, friend, but it cost me dear, as I was in the process of drinking my morning tea. I took it down the wrong pipe and was saved the necessity of a reply by a ten-minute fit of coughing and sputtering. Cait hit me soundly on the back, the bruise in evidence for days, knocking out of me what wind I did have. Dear Cait. She had cheered so by then, you see. We still cry sometimes over our Rose, but we talk of her often and openly, and we laugh, too, in our remembering.

When she started to talk to me of her beau, it was like the opening of flood gates. She is crazy for that boy, but has never said as much to him or anyone. She now has the joy of speaking freely of him to another person, sharing all that she has kept locked up, and at times I would feign shut her up, did I not so well remember that morose alternative.

So I have listened time without number to how blue are his eyes, how his fairness to her dark coloring made them a most striking couple. She hopes that "Rosebud" will be fair and blue-eyed. Will, as she calls him, has what she names a "true man's heart." He talked to her at length of the travels he planned to make and the adventures he would have, before a time when he intimated that he would like to come back for her.

When she discovered her plight, she vowed to herself that she would not tell him of the coming child, knowing that he would do the honorable thing at cost to his dreams. She told me that having a wife and child thrust upon him would "bury his wild heart and snuff it out," and that was something she could not do. On this point, she was adamant, and also dewy-eyed. So when her mother discovered the state of affairs, and her father fetched the young man home, there ensued quite a scene with Cait acting the role of a very jaded young woman. She insisted that she cared for him not a whit, that he had been a mere dalliance in a string of the same.

Needless to say, her parents were aghast, as was the young fellow himself, and his departure was swift and final. The telling of her sufferings after that event rent my heart but seems to have unburdened hers. That her young man thinks so badly of her is a pain that she could bear, as long as she could place her hands on her middle and feel that part of him that she would keep. I tried to explain to her that a child is not a possession that we keep, but a charge entrusted to our care for but a few short years. She smiled and nodded and rubbed her belly as I talked so, but her eyes were glazed over, and I think she heard me naught. I believe that her mind was with Will Skillicorn in the past, or perhaps with her Rosebud in the future.

As for what the future holds, my dear friend, I wish you the very best in it. Only the good Lord Himself knows what shall come to any of us. Do not lose heart that all will come to rights in the end.

Your friend, Libby

Chapter 13

Downriver
Oct. 1817

"I tell you, it's the only way to beat glutted markets in the spring. We've got to try it now," said Jeremy to the small group of men gathered in Luther's barn cleaning their guns after a neighborly hunt. Although the men felt little need for the massive surround hunts of the past, the camaraderie of a fall hunt still brought many neighbors together.

"Rivers ain't dependable for travel this time of year," said Jonathan. "Water's too low. Won't draw much of a boat this far north of the 'Hio."

"But what if we could? Just think how much better our chances would be to bring back some real money," Jeremy continued. "You know how hard it is to get decent prices when everyone else is trying to sell the same thing in the spring. We've got to find a way to get some hard cash back in these parts to pay the taxes."

"Got to agree on that point," said Frank Putnam, swabbing the barrel of his gun with a cleaning rag. Though Frank could rarely hit anything farther than twenty paces, he did take immaculate care of his gun. "We sure could stand some hard cash here 'bouts. Too bad them tax collectors won't barter like everybody else."

"Won't earn near what we ourghtta, if we wait for spring floods to make the rivers fit for traffic," piped up Anson Guthrie. "That's a fact."

"I'm game to try hauling our goods to the Ohio now. If we can get that far, I know we could take 'em all the way down to New Orleans," said Jeremy. "We have to find a way, that's all there is to it."

"I reckon the waters far up as Caldersburg would float a small scow this time of year," offered Jonathan, caressing his Kentucky rifle with a polish cloth. "Three rivers link up there.

Makes the Muskingum a decent draw most any time for small craft."

"We could haul five or six wagons overland to Caldersburg, load our goods on a few scows, then transfer everything to a flat boat when we make Marietta," Jeremy said enthusiastically. "It'd work. I know it would!" He slapped his knee to punctuate his determination. "You been awful quiet, Luther. Got any thoughts?"

Luther sat chewing a wad of tobacco. "You give a mind to bandits?" he asked, aiming a stream of tobacco juice at a bucket sitting in the corner. "Got a better chance of slippin' past them rascals when there's more traffic."

"We'll need a couple crack shooters along for sure," Jeremy said. "Jonathan, you up for a little adventure?"

"Me?"

"You're the best shot in these parts."

"I'd be proud to go."

"How about you, Luther? We'll need a good lookout. No one can sniff out sign better. You could stand watch for pirates."

"Suits me," he said, giving a spit. "Who's gonna steer? You need a body who knows the Mississip better'n me."

"What about Zeke? Harmon says he knows that river like the back of his own eyeballs," Willie offered.

"You know how to contact him, Willie?"

"Harmon does. He hands off south-goin' mail to Zeke. Says he don't ask no questions about U.S. postal rights."

"Well, that makes four of us, then," Jeremy said.

"Four? I only get three by my count," answered Frank. "Jonathan, Luther an' Zeke."

"You better count me in," said Jeremy, "since I'm the one who thought up this harebrained scheme."

"What about that little wife of yourn," Jonathan asked. "Don't she have her hands full with those two babes?"

"Sadie sees to the household these days. And Mandy can handle the babies just fine, now. I reckon they'd fare all right if I left for a spell," he said, pulling on his beard. "Besides, with the harvest all in, that leaves only a few barn chores to speak of. Sadie can handle those."

"I'll help out," Willie jumped in. "See if your women folk could use an extra hand with chores, now and again. I'd be glad to check up on 'em, see they're doing all right," he hurried to say.

"You mean to see that *Sadie's* doin' all right, don'tcha?" teased Frank.

Willie reddened at Frank's jab.

"I'd be obliged, Willie," said Jeremy. "Thanks."

"Mebbe we should re-think this notion, before we let married men go traipsin' off down river," said Frank. "What about your wife, Luther? Don't she have a new one to do for now, too?"

"Netta's used to fendin' alone, now an again," Luther stated simply. All the neighbors familiar with Luther's solitary treks into the forest didn't question his assessment of the situation. "Way this new one screams, I'd be a damn sight better off out of earshot."

"I reckon I should go along, too," Frank offered. "Got just as many farm goods to move as any of you."

"They need straight-shooters on this trip," piped up Anson.

"I can shoot good as any man here," argued Frank.

"We ain't talkin' about your shootin'," replied Anson. "It's your hittin' we have trouble with."

"This new gun ain't sited in good, is all," defended Frank. "Takes a shot or two till I can hone in on a target."

"Pirates don't give you time to site in," said Jonathan.

"Well, if you won't let me go along, I'd be glad to keep a check on Jeannette for you, Luther."

"Much obliged."

"I reckon Winifred and Clara can hold down the fort. I'll tag along," said Anson.

"Hell, you're too old to make a trip like that," Frank poked back at him. "You'd just get seasick."

"What about Henry?" asked Jeremy. "He's a crack shot."

"Haven't you heard? He got his shoulder all stoved up when he borrowed Aunt Ellie's mule," Willie said. "Tom brought that blasted animal back home after the Constable hauled Aunt Ellie off to jail, and Henry asked if he could use ol' Lucifer to finish taking in his crops. His own animal just foaled, you know."

"Kind of late in the season for throwin' a foal, ain't it?" muttered Anson. "Why in blazes didn't he tell the rest of the neighbors? We shouldda been over there helpin' him, instead of out huntin'."

"Tom and I already did. Ma sent us to Henry's after she trussed up his arm an' shoulder," Willie explained. "Tom felt sort of responsible, since he didn't give Henry any warning before sendin' him out to harness up that mule." Willie finished swabbing his gun and propped it up against the grain barrel upon which he sat. "Tom's really the only one who can handle that crazy animal... 'sides Aunt Ellie, that is. She sure loves that stupid mule."

"Sorry to hear about your Aunt's calamity," offered Frank.

The other men muttered their condolences.

"I suppose that means Harvey won't be interested in helping with our river-running scheme," said Jeremy.

"He's been liquored up for weeks," said Anson. "Most apt he'll stay that way till his corn juice runs out."

"What about your brother, Tom?"

"He's not much of a one for traveling," said Willie. "Taking Ma to visit Aunt Ellie in the whooscow was 'bout as far as he ever has a mind to go."

"Mebbe he could check in on Winifred and Clara for me, whilst I'm gone with you boys," said Anson. "Clara's got her cap set for him, but he don't know that, yet."

"Who says you're goin'?" pushed Frank. "I'd lay a wager soon as you get out of Winifred's sight, you'll pop the jug and stayed cross-eyed till the boat docks down in New Orleens. Hell, you'd be useless for shootin' or polin' either one!"

"Now, don't you go gettin' me riled, Frank. I get awful mean when I get riled."

"Would Sam Justice be interested in going?" asked Jeremy.

"Don't reckon he can afford to take the time," said Anson. "He's got so many iron goods piled behind his place that folks need fixin', likely he'll pound steady at his forge till spring."

"Sure hope he gets my plowshare workable before fittin' time," said Frank.

"How many men do we really need, Luther?" Jeremy asked. "Four of us enough to handle a trip like this?"

"I reckon four oughtta do it," he said with a carefully aimed stream of tobacco juice. "One to steer, two to pole and one to stand lookout."

"Don't leave me out," said Anson. "I aim to see New Orleens at least once, whilst I still got a little zip left in my get-a-long. I got plenty of shot an' powder laid by. I can help stand guard and shoot river rats."

"Don't you boys let him guard that corn juice too close," said Frank. "If he breaks into the greased light'nin' he won't hit the broad side of a barn."

"That does it, Frank," Anson said, rising from his perch on the side of the feed bunker and raising his fists. "I ain't takin' no more slander from a one-eyed polecat like you. Put 'em up!"

"Now, don't go gettin' your tail feathers all tied in a knot," Frank soothed. "You know I don't mean nothin' hurtful," he said giving his friend a good-natured slap on the back. "Just testifyin' to the facts, pure and simple. You love your corn juice an' there ain't no gettin' round it."

Anson gave his old friend a contemptible look, then broke into a big grin. "Aww, hell, Frank. I couldn't stay provoked at you, no how."

With chore time drawing nigh, the other men began to rise and pack up gear in preparation to go their separate ways.

Before anyone left the barn, Jeremy said, "We better let the rest of the neighbors in on our scheme so they can get all their harvest goods packed up and ready to ship."

"Weather's fixin' to turn sour, once the moon changes," said Luther. "Ortta set out soon."

"Then we should head for Caldersburg by the first of next week," Jeremy said. "Does Monday morning suit?" Heads nodded assent all around. "Jonathan, could you pass the word? Maybe check with Sam, see how many barrels he has to spare?"

"Happy to."

"Let's line up all the wagons we can find and meet back here at Luther's. Soon as we get 'em all loaded, we head out," Jeremy said, picking up his gun and moving toward the barn door. "Willie, would you let Harmon know about our plan? See if he's willing to pass the word along to Zeke?"

"Sure thing! Harmon's due back home tomorrow."

"Tell him we'll see to the scows in Caldersburg and float our goods as far as Marietta. If Zeke could meet us there and have a flatboat lined up to carry us down the Ohio and the Mississip', we'll be all set."

"Sounds like a plan to me!"

* * * * *

"Toss that bow line an' jump on quick," Zeke hollered to Jeremiah in his thick, Scottish burr. "On the inside now, sct ycr pole ag'in' that rock. Give a harrrdy push."

Jonathan pushed, as Jeremy leapt for the bow.

"By Gott, I think you laddies 'rr fin'lly beginnin' t' understand river runnin'," said Zeke, giving the two a wink as he pushed the rudder hard to starboard to swing the bow around. "Ah'll make boatmen oo't of you landlubbers yet," he said, nosing the Kentucky flatboat back downriver.

"At least I didn't get dunked falling off the bank this time," Jeremy laughed, as he picked up the other pole and took his place on the deck opposite Jonathan.

The men watched Luther stride swiftly up the riverbank. "Bring back some good venison steaks," Anson hollered from his post atop the cabin in the flatboat's center. "I'll watch for pirates till you get back!" he hollered, leaning against a bale of deer hides. Luther gave a wave, then disappeared into the woods through a clearing in the underbrush.

"Zeke already told us we don't have to worry about bandits till we leave the Ohio," Jeremy said, setting his pole on the river bottom and walking the length of the boat, keeping pace with Jonathan on the other side, as they pushed the craft along.

"Aww hell, you're spoilin' all my fun," said Anson, aiming a long arc of tobacco juice out toward the river.

"If ye have a yearnin' to a toss back a drink or two up there, lad, today's the day t' do it," Zeke told Anson. "Do yerr drinkin' now, whilst we're still on the 'Hio. Once we hit the Mississip', we need our wits aboot us."

"That's the best news I heerd so far this whole trip!" Anson crawled down from his perch, rummaged around inside the cabin, then came out with a small jug and made himself comfortable back up on his deer hide settee.

"You laddies need not wear yerselves out polin'," Zeke told Jeremy. "We got good current here. Save yer arms for the tricky spots."

"Whatever you say," Jeremy said, setting his pole down on the deck and taking a seat near the stern, where he let his legs dangle over the side. Jonathan followed suit, lying back in a spot between pork barrels, butter crocks, and jugs of maple syrup. He propped his head in his hands.

"If you don't mind my asking," said Jeremy, "what's your last name, Zeke? Don't recall as I ever heard anyone mention it before."

"MacTavish, of the MacTavish Clan from Arrrgyll," Zeke said proudly. "Ma family comes from the highlands. Known as 'child'rren of the mist.'"

"Sounds like a story in there some'ers," Jonathan said, tipping his hat down over his face.

For the rest of the afternoon, Zeke regaled his novice crew with stories from ancient, Scottish lore while the flatboat drifted its way downriver toward the port of Cincinnati. By late afternoon Anson had nearly polished off his jug, and then he, one of the first settlers to locate in Vermillion township, began telling stories of his own.

"How much you boys want to wager ol' Luther comes back here with more 'an fresh meat for our table," he said, taking the last swig from the jug, wiping his mouth, then tapping the cork on tight.

"What else do you think he'd bring back here?" Jeremy wanted to know.

"Not a what-else. A who-else, I'm a-bettin'."

"I didn't think Luther hunted with just anyone," Jeremy said.

"Or-din-ar-ily, he don't."

"Then what in blazes are you jawin' on about?" Jonathan now sat cross-legged, cutting strips of buckskin to make new laces for his boots.

"I'm talkin' about that half-breed, son of his."

"What?"

"You got beans in your ears, boy? You heerd me straight. Luther has him a son. Reckon he'd be 12, mebbe 13 by now. Mostly full growed, I'd guess."

"I always took them stories about Luther keepin' a squaw to be a yarn."

"Well, think again. It's gospel, I'm a tellin' you."

"Does Netta know?" Jeremy asked.

"Reckon not. An' it's best if we all keep it that-a-way, if you know what I'm a-sayin'."

"Hold on, now," Jonathan said, "If Luther already had him a Injun wife, why in blue blazes did he go and marry Netta?"

"Well, now, that there's a long story," said Anson. "And I do believe afore I can tell it proper, I'm gonna need me another drink to grease my tongue a mite." He tried to stand up to go fetch another jug, but the motion of the boat, not to mention the effects of the first jug, caused him to pitch backward, lose his balance, and sit right back down where he'd started.

"I'll fetch ya' another," Jonathan said, moving to the cabin and handing up a second, smaller jug.

"Much obliged," said Anson, popping the cork and taking a long swallow. "Ahhhrrrg, that's prime corn juice, that is. Don't think Sam ever made better."

"You got your drink. Now tell us how Luther ended up with two wives," Jonathon insisted.

"Well, it's like this. When Luther come out here back in aught-three, he had him a partner, name of Ned Pritchard. Them two trapped and hunted this whole state, prac-tick-aly. Made 'em a pile of money, they did... tradin' with the Injuns... leadin' early settlers to prime spots."

"What does that have to do with Netta?"

"I'm a-gettin' to it. Give me a little time," Anson said, taking another swallow from the jug. "'Long about aught-five, Luther and ol' Ned took up with a couple of nice lookin' Injun gals. Never did know what tribe they come from. But I heerd tell some big chief made Ned and Luther a present of them gals, 'cuz they liked them two fellers so much.

"Squaws was happy livin' the wanderin' kind of life with Luther and Ned, too. Cooked for 'em, tanned buckskins for 'em, never complained a bit when those two got itchy feet to move on somewheres new.

"No doubt you all heerd of the Injun troubles what broke out back in 18 and 12. When that last war with the English come along, it was. We had us a passel of Delawares living down in Greentown, by the River there. All hell broke loose for a spell, afore the army moved 'em up north, above the Greenville line.

Had lots of killin's an massacrees. Injuns settin' fires, then the army comin' in and settin' bigger fires to burn all the Injuns out.

"'Long about that same time ol' Ned took a bullet tryin' to defend his squaw from a outfit of hell-raisin' soldiers out to kill every redskin they could find. Luther and his squaw was out huntin' for a good hidin' place so's all of 'em could hole up till the troubles blew over.

"Them soldiers kilt Ned's squaw. Left ol' Ned for dead, too.

"Now Pritchard had him a sister back in Virginnie, name of Jeannette. Lived with their grandmaw, she did. Ever since their parents took sick and died when the red fever got so bad back in '95. When Luther come back and found his pard'ner about to expire, Ned made Luther promise to take care of his sister, since he figgered their grandmaw warn't long for this world, neither. Course, Luther promised he would. Luther ain't one to walk out on a duty, nor turn his back on a body who needs him.

"So there he sits, havin' one woman already, be that she is Injun an' all. And her with a young'un to boot. But now he is stuck with another woman to look after. Well, he got that squaw and boy of his all hid in the secret spot they found. Then they set it out right there, till the troubles blowed over. Army finally moved most Injuns out from these parts... 'cept for the ones what stayed hid, of course. Luther, he would come and go as he pleased, but the squaw and that boy of his kept out of site.

"During times Luther left 'em alone, he was real busy workin' on that big cabin of his... gettin' it built an' ready for Netta. He sent word to Ned's grandmaw, tellin' how Ned had died, and what he promised him afore he drawed his last breath. So, 'long about 18 and 14, he went back to Virginnie, got hitched up with Netta all proper like, cuz her grandmaw would have it no other way. Then he fetched her back here where he could look after her an' his other women. So now, he has him one in the settlement, and another one, hid out in the woods."

"So that's where he disappears to, when he takes off for weeks at a time," Jeremy said. "He's not out hunting, he's with his other woman!"

"Sure's you're born," Anson said, taking one, last swig from the jug, then corking it up tight. "But I wouldn't say that he don't hunt… where'd you think all these skins come from? Tanned up real nice, too, ain't they?"

"Well, I'll be."

The sun settled near the western horizon, as Anson finished his story, and Zeke began to aim the flatboat for shore, toward the spot where he'd arranged to meet back up with Luther. "Get rrready t' jump wi' that bow line," he said to Jeremy. "Jonathan, set yer pole to guide us in. Good. Nice an' easy now."

As the boys beached the large craft, Luther emerged through the brush onto shore, carrying a little button-buck over his shoulders. Beside him stood a gangly looking, swarthy-faced lad.

November 6, 1817
Cranberry Corners

Dear Ellie,

Zach has read to us from the family bible on this cold, gray morn, that book which contains entries of births and deaths, into which we have entered a new name. I shall begin at the beginning of the event.

Cait complained to me of a gas pain that she had been having all morning. Upon being questioned, she said that it did come and go, but kept to the same position. Simeon was excited that his own birthday might coincide with the event, but Cait's little Bud did not see fit to share a special day with another, as through the night she labored, not intensely, but without progress. Though the labor seemed prolonged, the birth was simple enough and without complication.

I was becoming concerned in the afternoon of the second day. Things were not progressed to the point where I would put her to bed, and walking did seem to ease her "gas pain." The progress, when it came, was quite sudden, as nature deemed necessary. Cait stopped pacing in her tracks and called out for me. She screamed that she was bleeding, as she felt a wetness on her limbs. Now you and I know the state of matters, but this intelligence and the way it was imparted set off a chain of distress in our small cabin.

Zannah, to whom I had taken great pains in explaining the impending event gently and quietly, began to wail. Then Leesha started to cry, and so Elijah. I had long since banished the older boys, but the girls were helping me keep the fire going and water hot for when it would be needed, and the evening meal would still be expected, baby or no. I turned to Lizzie and motioned her over to calm the others, while I went to Cait, helping her to undress and to bed. I told her that these were the waters of childbirth rather than blood.

Lizzie grabbed her sister, giving her a shake, and Zan quieted abruptly to avoid like treatment. I heard Lizzie explain to them how babies amuse themselves before birth by swimming in a pool of water that is so pleasant that the babies would not want to come out of the fine pool and into the world, so the water must come out first, and then the baby will follow. This is why babies cry when they are born, she said, as they are angry at the loss of their recreation. Sister and auntie seemed enchanted by this explanation.

Calm was restored, but I knew it to be only momentary. Lizzie I could not spare, but the others I banished outdoors. I bade them dress warmly and go play until summoned, and a close eye they had better keep on the toddler, too. They went happily enough, hand-in-hand, being barely out of earshot when the pain gripped Caitlin in earnest.

The next few hours were hard on her, she trying to be so brave. Lizzie challenged that if Cait would refuse to scream, then Lizzie would do it for her, and a better job she could do of it, too, but Cait did join in, with all agreeing that she won, hands down.

The babe was eased into my arms once it crowned, as it was a tiny thing just over five pounds, I'd say. And that is a mercy, as Cait was not rent as was I with Elijah, who was born still in his "swimming pool," which was a tired thing by then, even had he not been over nine pounds.

Cait was on her feet in no time and thinks that women who lie abed are shamming. I did not tell her that childbed is a place from which some never rise, or rise but partially. Doubtless she will find herself there again and again in this life and know first-hand all its variances. I could barely credit that she did not seem to know the fate of her aunt, our Da's favorite sister whose namesake she be, but I was grateful enough that she did not. That girl having been in a similar situation and being one of those who had not risen.

There, and I didn't even tell you of the child's gender. When Cait felt her belly plop flat and heard the cry of the infant, she lay back whispering, "Rosebud," and closed her eyes. I knew that wave of satisfaction rolling over her (and never will again. I must say, I miss it greatly) and thought not to break it, but Lizzie giggled. Cait opened first one eye, then with effort both.

"You have a beautiful son," I told her.

"Rosebud?" This was a question.

"A lovely boy. Blue eyes, a fuzz of hair, and perfect of form and limb."

"Bud," she said, eyes closing again. Lizzie and I looked at each other, shrugging our shoulders, and I went to work with my sterile shears while Lizzie took up a warm sponge. Mother and son were soon clean, warm and dry as they slept by the fire. Cait slept hard for a few hours.

Lizzie went out with the news that all were allowed to return to warm themselves by the fire, but they must be still. Soon Mother (how strange to think of her thus, and still I am not accustomed to it) slept lightly, waking periodically to check on infant and reexamine flat middle. (This fascinated her, though her belly never was huge but just a small, low pot.) Soon infant awoke, and no one could sleep while mother had her first lesson in suckling her child. Ineffectual as the effort was, baby seemed satisfied with the exercise, and Mother gave the impression of being easy enough with it. By now, they both have become experts.

We have entered the babe in our family bible as William Robert, but all call him Buddy. My sister erred on the point of the child's gender. I only wish I could chide her for it. As it is, I have delivered her daughter of a healthy grandson, and she must be satisfied with that, as must we.

Here I confess to you that I have interfered with fate, knowing not if aught will come of it. After the birth, I dispatched a letter to Garth, telling him of the arrival of his grandson. I also enclosed a missive for the errant father and asked that Garth should try to track him to wherever his fancy had led him and forward the intelligence to those regions. I have some hopeful expectations of which I cannot rid myself, a wish to see them together and settled as a proper family, to straighten matters between them. It does sound of love when she speaks of him. I suppose hope is small, first to find him, then to achieve some communion and sway him.

And who can say with any certainty how Cait would receive him (but I see it in my mind so clearly—could she fail to show him his beautiful son and could nature fail to take its course?). I have done this without her knowledge, so that if it comes to naught, at least it will not add to her burden. She is so wrapped up in new motherhood that we all cease to exist for her at present, except as we are needed to help with Buddy.

Zannah is wonderful with the baby, gentle and loving. She takes care to keep Elijah from hurting the baby with his abrupt grabs. (My baby is quite jealous, I fear.) Our household revolves around this new inmate as we begin another winter of confinement. The Rev. Longbottom is to come by for services on his pass this way next week. We shall see if he would be willing to perform a christening for our Buddy at that time.

Zach has begun carving toys for Christmas. He has made some wonderful puzzles that fit together quite nicely and was pleased with his skills, until Nate made one so complex that it outshined his father's. Zach rallied and created a clever thing that moves. It is a bear that climbs up two strings as you move it back and forth. It will delight my little Elijah and has surely secured Zach's place as the master toymaker in afore-mentioned competition. He and Nate have now turned to making tops. This holiday promises to be much merrier than the last. Especially with many more stores laid by.

I hope that all goes well with you, my friend, and that your situation is being straightened out. Write if you are able.

Libby

Chapter 14

Husking Bee
Mid November, 1817

"I don't know how in the world I could have managed if you hadn't come along when you did, Reverend," Netta Bailey babbled happily, as she and Rev. Harold P. Longbottom bounced toward the Hawkins' place in her carryall buggy with the Reverend's horse tied on behind. "I mean, with two babies to bundle up, and pies and punch and all to tote along, why how in the world is one woman to manage all this by herself, now? I ask you?" She gasped a quick breath, not intending to give the Reverend the slightest chance to answer, but he took the opportunity to jump right in.

"It was indeed a fortuitous circumstance that I should have occasion to call, on the sojourn toward my next stop at the Putnams. Otherwise I might never have discovered the entire neighborhood gathering elsewhere for a communal endeavor."

"Huh?"

"I'm glad we'll find everyone at the Hawkins' place."

"Oh. Well, of course we will. No one in their right mind would miss a huskin' bee! I just love a doin's, don't you, Reverend? I know, what with these babes of mine, I shouldn't feel like I have to take bakery and such to a doin's. But how could I even think about showing my face if I didn't take along at least one of my pun'kin pies? I ask you, how could I? My Luther always says I grow the best pun'kins in the whole township, you know. And if anyone should know pun'kins, why it's my Luther. He knows so much about all kinds of plants and trees and such."

"No question about it, Mrs. Bailey, you do prepare the most delectable pumpkin delicacy I have ever had the distinct opportunity to sample," Rev. Longbottom purred, clicking Netta's horse into a smoother trot.

"And with all those lovely cranberries Luther brought home to me, why, how in the world could I even think of keeping them all to myself? I mean, you know how scarce fruit is way out here. I'm sure folks will be tickled to death with the cranberry punch I stirred up. I do hope the Hawkins boys have a nice fire going up close to the barn so's I can heat this punch up some. It's so much better served warm, you know. And it tastes just heavenly with a little cinnamon stirred into it. I have some, you know. Cinnamon.

"Did I tell you my Grandmother Rosanna gave me a big piece of a cinnamon stick to bring along with me when I came way out here to set up housekeepin'? Got it right here in my apron pocket. Sure don't want anything to happen to it. Spices are so dear in these parts," she said, giving her pocket a pat. "Lots of things are mighty hard to come by out here, but I got to admit, my Luther sees to it I have plenty of rations to keep house with."

"I'm sure that a capable woman such as yourself can fare quite handsomely with a few, basic provisions laid by, Mrs. Bailey," the Reverend said warmly. "By the way, would you mind if I called you by your given name? Jeannette, is it not?"

"Why heavenly days, of course you can. People here abouts just call me Netta, though. Luther says it fits me. I can't rightly say why he thinks that," she said, taking a quick breath. "Did I tell you Luther found them out in a bog? The cranberries. Why that man can bring home some of the most amazing things! I don't know how in the world he finds so many useful provisions out there in those woods."

"I take it that your husband makes excursions to the outer reaches quite often. Is that correct?"

"To where?"

"Trips into the woodlands."

"Oh my, yes," Netta gushed. "Why, I'm lucky if Luther stays home two whole weeks out of every month. Sometimes he stays away longer than that! But he does have to make a living for us... from all those things he gathers up out there, you know. Luther never did take much to farmin' ways."

Rev. Longbottom smiled, shook his head, and continued to listen to Netta's chatter.

"Did I tell you Luther's away right now? Oh, well of course, you already knew that, with me fixin' to drive over here by myself when you rode up. I reckon he'll be gone a lot longer than two weeks this time. He's headed down river to market. All the way to New Orleans! Can you believe it?"

"That's quite an ambitious undertaking for a solitary man, is it not?"

"Oh, he didn't go alone. Some of the neighbors joined up to take everybody's farm goods down there to sell this fall. Luther said they'd get better prices now. Before the spring floods. That's when most folks head down river, you know. In spring. This time of year all the rivers in these parts get mighty low. Makes traveling lots harder, Luther says. That's why they had to cart their goods clear down to Caldersburg. My goodness, the neighbors had such a pile spread out in our barnyard to pack up!

"I wish you could of laid eyes on the wagons they loaded down. Oats and wheat and cornmeal. You know if we had to keep all that meal till spring, a lot of it could go bad, after such a wet year. Or maybe go buggy. Course, my Grandma Rosanna taught me to put tansy leaves right in the barrel... that keeps the bugs away, you know. I told Winifred and Lucy about that, too."

Netta drew a big breath, but hurried on with her account. "Did I tell you Winifred sent a whole wagon full of butter and cheese? She makes the best cup cheese you ever tasted! Smells terrible, but it sure is a treat for the taster. Lucy, she sent a whole crate of soap to market. We heard those city folk don't make their own soap no more, so she's hoping it'll sell real good. Lucy's soap turns out so clear and mild. I can't figger how she does it. Mine never turns out that way. Did you know Jonathan takes all his pork back-fat over to Lucy whenever he butchers?"

"No, I did no—"

"He does. Course, he don't have anyone to home who can render lard for him. Jonathan always has lots of hogs on hand. Keeps everyone in the township supplied with fresh pork and smoked goods. Why, I don't know how many barrels of pork he had ready for market. All salted down and packed up real nice it was, too. Did I tell you my Luther sent maple syrup? And honey, and ginseng roots? I sent candles. I love making candles. Luther brings me lots of beeswax. That beeswax burns real nice, you know. My heavens, I can't remember what all else they had piled up out there. They had quite a wagon train headed for the river. No one can sell 'em in these parts. Their farm goods. At least not for what they're worth. That's what Luther told me."

"Might I be so bold as to inquire which other gentlemen from the vicinity accompanied your husband on his economic venture for the township?"

"Huh?"

"Who else went along?"

"Oh. Well let me see. There was Jonathan Johansen, and Anson Guthrie. Luther said they were supposed to meet Zeke-the-river-runner down in Marietta... so's he could steer the big boat out there on the Mississippi. Oh yes, there was Jeremy Harrison, and my Luther, of course. He's the best sho—"

"You mean Jeremiah left his little wife at home all alone?"

"Sadie's still there helpin' out. That's Jeremy's sister, you know."

"Tell me, my dear Jeannette, when do these men propose to conclude their enterprising mission? Do you have any idea?"

"What?"

"When do you expect them home?"

"Oh, not for weeks and weeks! Luther said they'd be lucky to get back before Christmas. They'll have to walk back, you know. Luther says it's nigh onto impossible to pole up-river all that way back home."

"That's an extremely long interval to leave you women fending for yourselves."

"Well, Winifred does have her Clara to help out. And I already told you, Sadie's still at Harrisons. Jonathan didn't leave anyone behind... 'cept for his hogs. But they're used to fendin' for their-selves. Did I tell you he's not married? He's not. That just leaves me. 'Course, I am in the habit of bein' alone a good bit of time. But I really can't say I'm alone any more, now, can I? What with my babies here and all. Did I tell you Frank Putnam's helpin' out with barn chores? He told Luther he'd look out for me. Now wasn't that nice? 'Course I don't have too much to worry about out there. Just one horse to feed and one cow to milk, is all. We don't do a lot of farmin' like other folks hereabouts. Luther makes a living for us from what he gathers up out there in the woods, you know. Trades for what we need."

"You did mention that, as I recall," Rev. Longbottom said, suppressing a chuckle.

"He doesn't tell me where he finds most things, though. Like ginseng and honey trees and cranberry bogs and such. Says I'd end up blabbin' it all over the township, then he wouldn't have any forest goods left for trade. 'Course he hunts, too. Brings home enough meat to keep us fed real nice. And buckskins? Why, you wouldn't believe how nice and soft Luther makes his buckskins. He took a big bale down to market. I asked him once how he does it... how he makes them so soft and all. But he told me it's such a long, odorous mess, he'd best keep that smelly business as far away from the house as he could. I didn't argue. Truth be known, I don't have a very strong stomach when it comes to rank smells," she said, pulling a handkerchief from her other pocket and dabbing at her nose.

"Just thinking about it makes me feel a mite queasy," she said, taking a few deep breaths. Before the Reverend could offer her any assistance, she already had her hankie re-folded and placed neatly back inside her pocket.

The buggy topped a slight rise, and in the gathering dusk, lights from the Hawkins' barn blinked into view. At the happy sight Netta jumped right back into her babble. "Oh, I can hardly wait to show off my Rachel to the neighbors. She's such a feisty little thing," she said, giving a little pat to the baby lying in the basket beside her. "Ma's the only one who's seen her so far. Sides Luther and me... and now you, o' course. Ma brought her into the world, so naturally she's seen her. But not one of the other neighbors has laid an eye on my little Rachel yet."

She caught a breath and continued on. "Did I tell you Luther calls her his little screamer? Says she's the most contrary thing he ever did see... or hear! I got to admit, when she gets herself all wound up, she can sure let out a mighty big screech for such a tiny thing." Netta adjusted the baby's coverlet, and Rachel began to fuss, as if on cue. "Oh, hush now, my sweetness. We're almost there."

With her sister's yell increasing in strength, Rosanna, Netta's one-year-old, who'd been asleep on a pile of blankets in the back of the buggy, sat up and also began to fuss. "Here you go, Rosanna," Netta said, handing the toddler a little piece of fabric that looked like a stuffed bunny. "Hold on to your Nannie. We have to stop the buggy before I can get you down, sweetheart."

Rev. Longbottom pulled the buggy up to a hitching post near the barn door and quickly hopped out to fasten the horse's reins. At the sound of buggy wheels, several neighbors had stepped out of the barn to give the newcomers a warm welcome and help with baskets full of goodies.

"Hellooo, Netta," Clara Guthrie called, rushing up to the buggy. "I can't wait to see that new little bundle," she gushed, holding out her hands to take the baby from Netta. "I didn't think you were coming, with this little thing so new and all."

"Why Clara! How could I ever miss a doin's?"

Ma Hawkins elbowed her way out through the crowd. "Jeannette Bailey, I thought I told you to keep that young'un indoors! What ever possessed you to bring a sucklin' babe out on a cold night like this? To a huskin' bee, of all things!"

"Now, don't go scolding me before you get a good look at Rachel. She's doing so fine, and I just couldn't stand to sit home alone for one more day, when I knew so many folks would be here at a doin's tonight. Why, not one of the neighbors has even seen her yet!"

Ma grumbled and grabbed the baby basket from Clara to take a good look at the child. Before she could pull the coverlet back for a peek, Rachel let out one of the loudest screams she had ever heard.

"Got good lungs, that's for sure."

"Let me take her inside, Mrs. Hawkins, please?" Clara held her empty arms toward Ma, begging for another chance with the new baby.

"Well, I expect since you're already here, it won't hurt to take her on into the barn," Ma conceded to Netta. "It's nice and warm in there." Ma handed the baby basket back to Clara, then took one of the food baskets, as someone passed it down from the buggy. "Hey, Jeannette, did you know this here pie on top's missing a piece?"

"That's all right. I gave the Reverend some pie before he brought me over here. Least I could do for all his trouble," Netta gushed. She shifted Rosanna in her arms, then hurried to catch up with Clara, the two happily gossiping away as folks ushered the newcomers into the barn.

A mountain of this year's corn stood heaped in the center of the barn floor. Men and boys sat all around the edges, husking ears and shelling corn kernels into their large baskets. Some of the men worked in teams, one man husking, another shelling. As each person finished with an ear, he'd quickly tackle another, while the pile of husks grew beside him, and a mountain of empty corn cobs kept pace behind.

Over to one side of the barn floor, women fussed with their contributions to the refreshment table brimming with foodstuffs. Young girls giggled and whispered among themselves, anticipating the prospect of getting a kiss from the first young man who discovered a red ear of corn.

"I do hope Tom finds a red one," Clara confided to Netta.

"Clara, I didn't know you was sweet on Tom!"

"Shhhhht, don't you say a word to Ma Hawkins, yet. That woman scares the bows right off my bonnet," Clara whispered. "'Course, if I aim to take up with Tom, I reckon I'll have to get used to her for a mother-in-law, though, won't I."

"Clara, you know perfectly well she's more bark than she is bite... least ways when it comes to womanly trials. I hate to think of the fix I'dda got myself into, if she wasn't such a good midwife," Netta said, giving her little Rachel a pat. "I hear tell she won't tolerate no shenanigans from her men folk, though."

"I just hope one of her men folk takes notice of me pretty soon, that's all I got to say," Clara said, giving Tom a big smile when he happened to glance her way. She stood there fussing with the braid coiled atop her head. "Do you know, in all the time he's been helpin' out while Pa's away, Tom hasn't said a single word to me? Not one! Only speaks to Ma when he has to. Acts like I'm no more than a stick of furniture," she said. "I even dipped into Mama's stash of dried fruit to bake him up some blueberry biscuits. Do you know what he did? Just grunted at me when he took one. No thanks, no smile. Nothin'! If he don't take the hint and come courtin' soon, I might have to do something rash to get his attention."

"Clara, you're so pretty, you don't need to do a thing to gain a man's eye. Why, I'm surprised ten men haven't proposed to you already."

"Two or three have come a-calling," she blushed. "Pa thinks I shouldda set up housekeeping with one of 'em long ago. But Mama, now, she don't seem all that eager for me to leave. I do have to allow as I got my heart set on Tom, pure and simple."

"Well then, there's nothing else for it."

"Pa said he'd bring me back a store-bought dress from New Orleans! I do hope it's a blue one. Tom'd have to notice me then. Sky-blue'd be best. To match my eyes."

Clara caught sight of Sadie Harrison, who'd just finished slicing two loaves of pumpkin bread she contributed to the table full of goodies, which would not be served until the men finished husking all the Hawkins' corn. Clara waved her over to the corner where she and Netta stood. "Sadie! I'm so glad you could come! Tell me if I'm wrong, but did I see you arrive with Willie a little while ago?"

"Sure did."

"I didn't know Willie had a buggy to go callin'."

"He doesn't. We rode Harmon's horse."

"You mean to tell me, he expected you to ride right up there with him?"

"Sure. I rode horses all the time with my brothers. Riding Harmon's horse is nothing new."

"I wouldn't even think of mounting a horse behind any man. Leastwise, not until he was my husband, I wouldn't," Clara said, with a sudden blush, just as the Reverend sidled up to the group of young women. "Oh, hello Reverend! What a surprise to see you here tonight!"

"Indeed. And what a pleasant surprise for me to find such a lovely bouquet of blossoming womanhood gathered right here in one place," he oozed. "I feel honored to behold such beauty." He made a deep, showy bow. "It is quite laudable to see you fitting into the neighborhood festivities, Miss Harrison," he said, taking Sadie's hand and giving it a few pats. "You don't mind if I use your Christian name, do you? Sadie, I believe it was?"

"Still is," she said, removing her hand from his and wiping it on her skirt.

"And where, might I inquire, may that lovely sister-in-law of yours be?" The Reverend scanned the crowd for Amanda's most proper, dainty figure.

"Home," Sadie said, offering no further commentary.

"All by herself?"

"'Course not. She has Millie and Lilly."

"We dare not forget those lovely little flowers," he said with an ingratiating smile.

Sadie rolled her eyes.

"Now, if you captivating ladies will excuse me, needs must that I take my leave."

"You mean you're goin' already, Reverend? But you just got here," Netta said in consternation.

"My dear lady, since I have spent the entire day atop my steed, I feel quite ill equipped to take part in the evening's merrymaking," he said, rubbing his backside. "In fact, after such arduous travel, I find it necessary to retire as soon as I reach my pre-appointed rendezvous at the Putnams. I believe it was they, at the completion of my last visit to Justice, who requested to provide for my comfort upon this present circuit."

He worked up a grave expression. "Frankly, I confess to be a bit astonished to find the Putnams attending this social gathering, inasmuch as they knew I should be making my preordained arrival at their abode this eventide." He leaned closer toward the group in a conspiratorial whisper. "You see, in order that I reach superlative, spiritual form for the morrow's scheduled ministrations, I require a minimum of eight hours' uninterrupted repose."

Clara leaned closer to whisper in Sadie's ear. "What did he say?"

"He said he needs plenty of sleep to wind him up for preachin'."

The Reverend smacked his sides and stood up straight. "Now, my lovely ladies, I shall make a speedy round to greet the entire company, ere I depart, during which time I shall most assuredly converse with Mrs. Putnam to confirm my accommodation in their byre, as was originally arranged."

"What did he say that time?" Clara whispered again.

"He's heading for the Putnams barn to bed down for the night."

"Oh."

"But, I thought you would see me back home, Reverend," Netta said with great disappointment.

"I'm sure, my dear Jeannette, that, should you inquire, one of the gallant chaps among this fellowship would gladly see you and your wee ones safely back to your abode. I doubt that anyone in the present company will make his departure for some hours yet, by which time I shall unquestionably have entered the reverie of dreams," he said, making a slight bow as he backed away. "Ladies, until the morrow!" The Reverend greeted several people, as he strode away from the group of befuddled women and headed for the refreshment table.

"I don't know why the Reverend can't stay on, least wise till we serve the eats," Netta said with a shrug.

"Didn't you see? He already ate a plateful right after he walked in here. Talked Winifred into serving him a big sample of everything," said Sadie. "And there he is, over there talking Emma into giving him more."

"Look, here comes Lucy," bubbled Clara, "and she has that sweet baby Hank with her. Lucy! Lucy, over here!"

Lucy made her way around the side of the barn floor, balancing six-month-old Hank on her hip with one hand, and holding the bail of a large jug in the other. Her husband Henry, with one arm firmly wrapped and resting in a sling, followed close behind. "Hello everyone. What a wonderful night for party." Lucy handed the baby into Clara's eager arms.

"Look at this sweet thing, would you? He looks just like a little man, already!"

"I'll take this cherry bounce over to Ma Hawkins while you girls keep Hank busy," Lucy said, moving toward the refreshment table. With his good arm, Henry tipped his hat to the women and made a hasty retreat toward the group of men working at the dwindling pile of corn.

Clara leaned to Sadie and whispered, "Hard to believe a big-boned woman like Lucy give birth to such a comely thing."

Sadie gave a curious grimace.

"I mean just look at her. How could anyone built like a big Friesian cow throw such a fine-boned child?"

"I thought they all started out small," said Sadie.

"Well of course they do," chimed in Netta. "But some of 'em stay pint-sized, no matter who throw'd em' nor how much they eat," she said, still bouncing Rachel to keep her from wailing. "Just look at my little Rosanna over there holdin' tight to Ma's skirts. I can't get that child to eat more than two bites before she pushes her food away. I'm at my wits end, lookin' to find ways to get that girl to take nutriment."

"Don't look like Lucy had that trouble," Clara sniggered, "nor Emma neither!"

"Lucy's not fat," Sadie defended. "She's a big woman, is all. Big-boned and tall enough to carry it well."

"All right, all right. I'll grant you that. But look over there at Emma. You can't say she ain't downright fat."

"Emma? She's just short for her size," Sadie smiled.

"She's short, all right. Nearly big around as she is tall. Look at her over there, standin' by Lucy. She has two feet on Emma if she has an inch," stated Clara. "Lucy has to stand a good six inches over Henry, too. When he has his boots on, no less!"

"They do make a unlikely lookin' pair, don't they?" Netta agreed.

"I'd like to know how those two got matched up in the first place," Sadie said.

"You don't know?"

"'Course she don't know, Netta. She only came here this year, remember?"

"Then I have *got* to tell you the whole story," Netta gushed. "You see, Lucy came out here as a mail order bride."

"No!"

"Yes. She did! Scandalized the whole township, too. Henry Jarvis came to these parts all by himself back in 18 and 10. That was before the war, you know. Got him a nice parcel and made improvements. Put up a barn and dug a well and all. Cleared off a new patch of land every year. But in 18 and 13, he decided it was high time he found himself a wife, so he finally started to put up a cabin."

"Where'd he live all that time, if he didn't have a cabin?" Sadie asked.

"Lived in the barn, bein's that it was just him. Set up a cozy little corner next to the horse stall. You shouldda seen it! 'Course, he knew no woman would ever want to live like that, so he commenced to buildin' a sturdy cabin for his new wife. Now we never did have a goodly amount of females in these parts, but back then, not a single marryin' gal could be had in this whole township. Nor in any neighborin' township, neither. So Henry writes him up an ad... to put in the papers back east?"

"You mean he advertised for a wife?"

"Sure did. 'Wanted,' it said, 'Hearty Woman for Matrimony in Ohio Country. Must be a good worker, not afeared of snakes.' Well, Henry sent that notice to three newspapers in upstate New York... fall of 18 and 13, Luther told me. Henry never did hear nothing back, though. By spring, he give up the notion of ever findin' him a wife. Commenced to work off his setback by clearin' off another patch for plantin'. But 'long about the end of July, in 18 and 14 it was, who do you think showed up but Lucy Peterman, holdin' on tight to that want ad! Ridin' right up there with Harmon, like the parcel of mail she was."

"No! She just showed up? Without writing to Henry or anything?"

"Sure did. Right on behind of Harmon. I know, 'cuz I was already here by then. Luther brought me out that spring. April of 18 and 14? We married up back in Charlottesville, in Virginia? Did it up proper like, so my Grandma Rosanna could see me wear my dear, departed Mama's weddin' dress. Made Luther a mite fidgety, though, havin' a proper church weddin' and all. But Grandma Rosanna wouldn't hear of lettin' me come out here any other way. 'Got to tie the knot right,' says she."

"What did Henry do when Lucy showed up?"

"What else could he do? He married her! Course, for a while there, the whole thing had Henry powerful bewildered. In case you haven't figgered it out by now, Henry's awful straight-laced. Won't drink mountain dew nor taste a thing with even a hint of spirits in it. So to Lucy, Henry says, 'I will not live in sin, Miss Peterman.' And she says back, 'I would hope not, Mr. Jarvis. My mother raised me a good girl, she did.' So until the old Reverend Blankenship came through on his circuit a month later, Lucy took up residence in the cabin, an' Henry went back to livin' in the barn right next to his horse. Wouldn't no Justice-o-the-Peace hitchin' do for Henry. No-sir-eee. Had to have him a real weddin' service done by a real preacher, he did. So he asked Jonathan to come over and bunk with him, till the preacher showed up... just so's folks wouldn't get any notions about unseemly shenanigans goin' on betwixt the house and the barn."

As Sadie stood there, taking in the whole of the story, a buzz began to rise from the direction of the men.

"Oh, look! I think Tom found a red ear of corn!" Clara could hardly contain her excitement, and the other girls pushed in closer to get a good look, as Lucy rejoined the talkative group.

"Can you see? Did he really get a red one?" Clara asked, dancing from one foot to the other.

But Tom pushed the ear underneath his shirt so quickly, no one got a good look. He huddled behind the mound of corn cobs with Willie and Harmon for a few moments while they whispered together. Then Willie emerged waving the red ear over his head, grinning from ear to ear.

"I got me a red one," he shouted, "and I'm bound to claim me a kiss!" He made his way across the barn floor to where Sadie stood. She wore a broad, knowing smile. "Come on, girl. We got business out behind the barn," he said, taking her hand.

"You mean you ain't gonna kiss her right here?" came a voice from among the men.

"Not with all of you skunks watchin' I ain't," Willie said, guiding Sadie toward the barn door.

Clara stood rooted to her spot, turning redder by the minute. She stomped her foot and flounced over to the refreshment table, as Willie led Sadie outside.

The assemblage surged toward the door. But Harmon interceded on Willie's behalf. "Looks like more'n two makes for too big a crowd out yonder," he said simply. "Whyn't we just get some fiddle music goin' in here and let them two love-birds be?"

"Won't be the same without Anson to fiddle," complained Sam Justice, shaking his head in chagrin. "Guess we'll just have to make do with you, Frank."

"I can fiddle just as good as Anson!"

"Maybe you can, and maybe you can't," said Harmon. "Leastwise, we'll have us some stompin' music to sashay to. Sam can keep time on his spoons there, and I'll get to twangin' on this here juice harp," he said, pulling the metal contraption from his pocket and waving it in the air.

The men began to clear away the corn-husking debris, women put finishing touches on their foodstuffs, and the make-shift band struck up something that sounded a bit like a Virginia reel.

"Emma, you see to it everybody gets one taste 'fore you let any of them fellers sneak back here for seconds," Ma instructed Emma Putnam.

Emma nodded in simple-minded assent. "I made a big bowl full of corn puddin'. There's a-plenty for everybody."

"Mind what I said. Them apples Harmon picked off the ground by Thompson's place only stretched for two plate fulls of dumplin's. You know how scarce the apples was again this year. Just make sure nobody hogs more than his share, you hear?"

"She already let the Reverend eat two dumplings before he left," tattled Clara, still obviously indignant.

Ma shook her head, mumbled something unintelligible under her breath, then stooped to pick up Netta's toddler. "Come here, Rosanna," she said, hiking the tot onto her hip. "Let's go get you a nice bowl of that tansy puddin' Winifred stirred up. That's just right for a young'un like you."

Winifred dished out a small bowlful for the child, and, with an all too rare grin, which was quite a departure from her usual prickly countenance, she handed the pudding over to Ma. Edith Hawkins found a place to sit down and started spooning the custard into Rosanna.

From across the room Netta watched in disbelief as her finicky child polished off the whole thing. Netta dodged her way across the dance floor. "How'd you do that," she demanded of Ma.

"Do what?"

"Get her to eat?"

"Why, I just spooned it down her. She did the eatin'."

"I haven't been able to get more than two bites down that child at a sitting. I simply must find out what Winifred put in her custard. Maybe I can finally fix something this girl will eat for a change. Winifred! Oh, Winifred, yooo hooo!" Netta began to make her way back to the food table, but before she could reach Winifred Guthrie, she noticed Tom Hawkins stirring at his cup of punch with something that looked suspiciously like her cinnamon stick.

"Tom Hawkins, is that my cinnamon stick you're stirrin' with? Why in the world did you go and fish that out of my punch? Don't you know my Grandma Rosanna gave me that cinnamon stick when I set up housekeepin'?" She hurried over to retrieve her treasured spice, before Tom should do something uncouth to contaminate it.

"Chicken-in-the-bread-pan, pickin'-out-dough," called Sam in his gravelly voice, as the makeshift band did the best it could to execute its rendition of dancing music. Four couples tried to dosey-doe and allemande-left at the proper times, while the rest of the assemblage milled around eating sweet treats, gossiping, and keeping time to the music—if music you could call it.

No one noticed Willie and Sadie reappear at the barn door— each one wearing a silly grin that stretched from ear to ear.

* * * * *

On the other side of Justice, Amanda Harrison tentatively opened the cabin door to an unexpected knock.

"My dear Amanda Jane, you look simply wonderful," Reverend Longbottom gushed, doffing his hat and making a ceremonial bow.

"Why, Reverend Longbottom, this is a surprise."

"Since you did not grace the Hawkins' festivities with your glowing presence this evening, I thought it prudent to stop by and pay my regards on my sojourn to my next scheduled layover at the Putnams," he glowed. "Since your cabin lay in such close proximity, I took this opportunity to pay a friendly call. Might I come in for a moment?"

"Well, you see, Reverend, with Sadie gone to the bee and all... I mean, do you think that's wise?"

"My dear woman, you needn't bother that beautiful head of yours over trifles. As an upstanding man of the cloth, I consider it a sacred duty to conduct myself in a seemly manner befitting my station," he said, brushing his hat and giving a tap to the crease in its crown. "Besides, I am dying to see how those lovely little flowers of yours have grown, Amanda Jane."

"I just put them down for the night, Reverend. But if you're very quiet, you may take a peek," she said, swinging the door wide enough to admit him. "They have grown since you last saw them on their christening day," she said in hushed tones.

Harold Longbottom made his way into the cabin, stopping momentarily to look around. "What have you done in here? I detect some changes in your abode. It feels much larger since I previously had occasion to call."

"Isn't it wonderful," she beamed. "Jeremiah added a whole new kitchen for me, and a real bedroom!" She motioned toward the new doorway beside the hearth. "It's so amazing what a little extra space can do. We moved the table and all my cooking things into the new kitchen after Jeremiah opened the fireplace up on the back side. I can do all my cooking over there, now. He added more beds in this part. For the twins."

At the sound of voices, the babies began to rouse, and Amanda gave a shush with a finger to her lips. "We best keep it down," she whispered. "It's too hard to get them both back to sleep if one of them wakes up."

"May I take a peek?"

At Amanda's nod Rev. Longbottom tip-toed over to the two, bent-twig cribs mounted in the corner nearest the fireplace. He looked down with true appreciation in his eyes, shaking his head as he looked from one, identical, cherubic face to the other. "Absolutely exquisite," he whispered.

Amanda motioned him toward the other room, and he followed her through the doorway into the warmth of her new kitchen. "Could I fix a cup of tea for you, Reverend? I just made one for myself. Water's already hot."

"Tea sounds absolutely delightful. The evening has taken on quite a chill," he said, placing his hat on the table. "I'm afraid these trail-weary bones do not embrace long hours in the saddle as well as they once did," he said, rubbing his backside. He took a chair from beside the table, pulled it to the hearth as close to the warm blaze as he dared, and eased his lanky form down. "By the way, I thought we had gotten past all this 'Reverend' business," he said, rubbing his hands and drinking in the fire's warmth. "If I am not mistaken, you agreed to call me Hal, remember?"

"As I *recall*, I agreed to address you by your given, Christian name," she said with a furtive smile, busying herself with the tea preparations. "So, tell me, Pastor Harold, do you bring any interesting news from your worship stops at the other settlements nearby?"

"Nothing of consequence. Unless you consider it newsworthy that this Ohio country suffers from extreme economic disparity brought on by a distinct lack of western markets."

"Why, that's exactly what Jeremiah says! You know he's on a trip all the way down to N'Orl'ins right now, to sell our farm goods?"

"So I gathered from neighbors at the corn fest."

"I do wish I could have gone with him."

"Somehow, Amanda Jane, I cannot picture your delicate person undertaking such a long and arduous journey," he said. "You do realize that the river-rodents navigating on the Mississippi have built a repugnant reputation for themselves... or so I'm told. Surely you could never suffer the indignities of such scurrilous company."

"Oh, it's not so much the trip I long for, as the destination," she sighed.

"How so, may I ask?"

"It's warm down in N'Orl'ins. And I do miss warm weather so."

"Have you heard anything from your people down in... where was it now, one of the Carolinas, I believe?"

"South Carolina. Charleston, South Carolina," she crooned. But she heaved a big sigh, and her countenance changed instantly. "No, Reverend, I have heard not a word from anyone back there," she said with obvious, controlled anger. She took a moment to compose herself, then added, "My family is here, now."

"So I see. And quite a wonderful family it is, too, now that you have those lovely little flowers to fill your arms after the unfortunate loss of your firstborn. So sad, that. It was just one year ago, now, that you lost him, was it not?"

Amanda turned away, swallowed hard with a shiver, then deliberately changed the subject. "Now, surely you have some good news to share from all your travels, Rev—I mean Pastor Harold, of weddings and births and the like?"

"Don't forget, to you it's Hal, lovely lady.

He gave her his most charming smile and a wink. "Of course I have had opportunity to welcome numerous infants, with their respective christenings, naturally. And there is the occasional demise, requiring my officiation at the funereal proceedings. However, I doubt that you have made the acquaint-tance of too many of those folks," he said, accepting the steaming mug Amanda handed him. "I do recall one unique situation that involved a rather hurried trip back East by a family up in the Fire Lands. After an unfortunate demise in Connecticut, I believe it was. They brought back a young maiden in the family way, along with a feebleminded lass of most unusual beauty." He took a long sip of the aromatic brew, savoring its scent and flavor. "My word, you used real English tea! How did you come by real tea out here?"

"It's the last Sadie brought us when she came from Pennsylvania in the spring. I'm afraid I used up all the real coffee she brought long ago."

"Coffee, indeed, is a rare treat in these parts. But I must admit, I have a decided preference for the luxury of real, British tea. Warms a body to the soul." He took another long sip, relishing its taste. "The warmth of a good fire and a fine cup of tea! What more can a man require for true happiness?" He grinned at Amanda with a rise of his eyebrows, which brought a sudden blush to her cheeks.

"I... ah, I think I had better go check on the babies, Reverend. Make sure they're covered. I can't rest a moment unless I know they're both sleeping soundly." Amanda hurried into the other room, taking quite a long time to calm herself before walking slowly back into the kitchen.

Harold Longbottom had removed his heavy frock-coat and hung it over the back of his chair. He now sat with his feet stretched toward the fire, sipping contentedly at his cup of tea. "Are you feeling better, Amanda Jane?"

"Whatever do you mean?"

"I perceived a distinct agitation in your manner, when you hurried to check on the babes," he said in an understanding tone. "Would you prefer that I leave?"

"No! Not at all. I mean... forgive me, Reverend. It's not you. It's just that... I–"

"It's quite all right, my dear," he said, rising. "You can tell me anything, you know. That's what I am here for."

"I'm just having such a hard time with Jeremiah gone, and all. I know he's doing what he has to, but I worry so about him. What if... what it he doesn't come back?"

"He is in the company of capable men, I'm told. Don't forget, he's quite resourceful himself," Longbottom said, rising and steering her toward his chair. "I see no reason why he should not return to you in due time."

"What will I ever do if I should lose him? I couldn't stand losing Jeremiah, too," she said, beginning to weep softly.

"You won't lose him, Mandy. I'm quite confident of that," Longbottom said, kneeling beside her and smoothly pulling a handkerchief from the pocket of his waistcoat. "Just because you lost Little Ben does not mean you'll lose Jeremiah, too."

At the mention of Little Ben, Amanda broke down in earnest.

"There, there. Let it all out, Mandy dear," Longbottom crooned in his most sympathetic tones. "You've harbored this festering pain inside much too long. It's time to let it out and be done with it," he said, patting her shoulder softly as he eased her head onto his own shoulder. "After all you've been through, if anyone deserves a good cry, my dear, it certainly is you."

"I... I never... never let... myself... cry like this before over... over," she hic-cupped. "Little Ben!" Her tiny frame shook with uncontrollable sobs. "I killed my own child, my own Little Ben!"

"It was a horrible accident, Mandy. These tragedies happen way out here where life is so difficult for all of us. You were not to blame for an accident, my dear. No one was to blame," he soothed. "Shhhhh. Let it go, now, Mandy dear. Let it all go."

The more she sobbed, the closer he held her, slowly easing her down onto the floor next to himself. Before she knew it, she sat in his lap, sobbing her heart out while he rocked her back and forth, as he would comfort a small child.

"He's gone, Mandy. Ben is gone," he said, kissing the top of her head softly and drawing her closer. "Give your grief to me, dear one. You've born this burden far too long. Let me carry away your pain." Harold Longbottom began to stroke Amanda's hair, then her arm, then her cheek. Pulling her closer he kissed the tears from each eye. "Shhhhh, my sweet. Everything will be fine. I promise it will."

Before she knew what was happening, Longbottom's hand wended its way down her arm, softly brushing a breast, as he took her by the waist and eased her gently onto the floor in one, swift move.

"Oh, I–"

"Shhhhh, my sweet," he said, pulling her into an embrace while lightly placing his hand over her mouth. "I know a way to help you forget all this pain. I can take it away and make you feel so much better," he crooned. "Let me help you forget every one and every thing of this world."

Amanda stifled an urge to scream, as she jolted to her senses, suddenly terrified. She struggled to free herself from the oppressive weight that bore down upon her, but outweighed by a good 100 pounds, her resistance came to naught. With mounting panic, horrifying phantoms from a long-buried memory deep in her past arose to saturate her present circumstance…

Charleston, Early February 1815

…A large hand held her down. She couldn't get away no matter how hard she struggled to escape.

"No, don't. Please!" The hand around her throat tightened to stifle her cries. Tears began to soak the blindfold tied around her head.

She fought harder, trying to strike out with fists, but two more hands pinned her wrists over her head. She kicked, trying to connect with anything, but more hands grabbed her ankles and pulled her legs wide apart. Another hand explored under her skirts, while yet another hand searched for the clasp that held it closed. He fumbled with the hook to no avail, then gave a hard yank, ripping open the side panel of the satin-lined frock.

The hand around her throat loosened for a moment and she cried out. "Noooo!" Immediately she croaked to silence, when the hand retightened its vise-like grip.

"You want to make noise, we can stop it permanent," said a raspy, faceless voice beside her. She ceased her struggle. "There, that's better."

"May as well enjoy it, girl. You gonna get it one way or other," said another voice overhead.

The hands continued their intense exploration, fondling, searching for an opening into her bodice. When the tiny buttons resisted clumsy fingers, a rough hand grabbed the top of her bodice and ripped it open, strewing buttons on the floor.

Small mounds of cream-colored flesh dotted with pink nipples stood exposed above the folds of her camisole. The hand twisted and squeezed while she writhed at the painful stimulation.

"Feel good, honey?"

"Give her more. She wants more."

"Go to it, boy." Several voices blurred around her, and a mouth closed over one breast, suckling, pulling, and biting mindlessly. He let go, then latched onto the other, doing the same thing all over again, this time with added gusto.

"Nothing like a little tit!"

"Nothing like a little ass, either."

A hand reached for her drawers and pulled them around her ankles. When the hands pinning her legs let go for a moment to pull off the drawers, she kicked for all she was worth, until hands grabbed her ankles and held her legs even tighter than before.

"She's still got some fight left in her, boys. We better see what we can do to take that right out."

Another hand reached between her legs, probing at her most private parts. She felt a hard jab, and another, then something big and stiff and hot rammed itself inside her. Ripping flesh sent bolts of pain, and she let out a sharp cry. Amanda wavered near the edge of semi-consciousness, bright lights flashing inside her head.

Water trickled across her face, and for a moment she didn't know where she was.

"You missin' all the fun, sweetheart. We just gettin' started here," said a voice to her left.

"Why don't you take that blindfold off, so she kin enjoy the show?"

"You so good, you want her to remember you, Pike?"

"Move over, you hog. My turn to ride."

Hands and bodies shuffled around her, and another, heavy weight landed on her stomach, as hands pulled her legs wider apart. More hot jabs. Then someone's hand slipped the blindfold over her head, and a dirty, sweating, shaggy face forced its mouth onto hers. When he thrust his furry tongue between her teeth, she gagged. As the tongue continued its sloppy penetration, she bit down—hard.

"Ahhhhrrrg! Goddamn bitch! You gonna pay for that." He yanked open his fly. "Move off. I'm gonna show this slut who's boss." He landed on top and thrust himself inside her with such force, it momentarily knocked the wind out of her. Through her tears, she saw another filthy man, dressed in a grimy red and black frock-coat, drop his pants in eager anticipation. She stared in horror at the appendage protruding from his hairy crotch.

"Hurry up, you bastard. It's my turn." He pushed his way close to her head and forced himself into her mouth. She gagged, trying desperately to twist her head away, then she bit down with all her might. A thunderous caterwauling filled her head before the iron-like fist struck, sending Amanda into oblivion.

* * * * *

With the first rays of sunrise peeking over the horizon, Sadie tip-toed her way into the cabin and tried to close the door without making a sound. She scampered across the floor, trying to avoid all the squeaky places. When she reached the platform bed in the corner that Jeremy and Amanda had used before moving to their bedroom up in the new addition, she quickly removed her dress and shoes. Snuggling into bed, she hugged herself under the thick, feather comforter and drifted off with a smile.

Less than an hour later, Sadie awoke to the sounds of crying. Groggily, she dragged herself from her warm cocoon and traipsed over to the other corner to tend to the waking babies, as she did every morning. When she peered into the cribs, she saw that Lillian and Camellia still slept soundly.

A trifle confused, she tried to shake herself fully awake. "I must be dreaming," she muttered. Still Sadie heard whimpering noises, apparently emanating from the other room. She stumbled her way to the kitchen doorway.

In front of the fire lay Amanda Jane, huddled in a tight, fetal ball. With hair tangled and clothes disheveled, and between hick-ups and heartrending sobs, over and over she repeated, "Papa... Papa... Papa...."

Chapter 15

Jeremy Returns
Mid December, 1817

"Well, boys," said Anson Guthrie, knocking his pipe against a shoe to empty the spent tobacco, "our last night on the road. I shore am hankerin' for a home-cooked meal. I can almost taste Winifred's pot-licker-stew, I can," he said, tucking the pipe into his vest pocket. "I got to allow I am mighty wearied of Johnny cakes and hard tack."

"Can't say that I don't long for something hot and home-cooked myself," Jeremy agreed, smoothing out the lumps under his bedroll. The travelers camped a few miles north of Mt. Vernon, within one, long day's hike of home.

"How about you, Jonathan... think them hogs of yours'll have a nice, hot supper waitin'?" Anson teased his other traveling companion.

"Don't you know hogs can find a meal when most any other critter'd starve?" Jonathan answered. "I'd take a hog any day, over the company of most women I know. Even if they can cook."

"Pshaw! You're pullin' my leg."

"You mean to tell me you never hankered after a woman?" Jeremy asked.

"Didn't say that."

"Who you got your eye set on, boy?"

"No one I'd tell you about."

"Let him be, Anson. Don't ruin our last night out tormenting Jonathan. We're almost home."

"You boys got them pouches buried good under your bed rolls?"

"Not to worry," Jeremy answered. "All secure."

"Shore don't want nothin' to happen this close to home," said Anson, getting settled into his own bedroll as close to the fire as he dared. "By gum these old bones shore won't miss hard ground," he grumbled. "Never thought I'd be so glad to see my own bed again."

"You mean to say you don't jump at the chance to bed down your own woman?" Jonathan needled him back.

"That ain't what I said, sow lover."

"Then what are you sayin'?"

"I'm-a-sayin' that what goes on betwixt the sheets of my marriage bed ain't none of your concern." Anson pulled the cover up to his chin and heaved a big sigh. "You boys just make sure you got all them accounts writ down straight so none of the neighbors can fuss that we cheated nobody."

"Everything's tallied up proper, you ol' buzzard," Jonathan goaded.

"Don't trust your brain to cipher up a thing."

"Not to worry, Anson," Jeremy reassured. "We've gone over all our figures so many times, we practically wore them right off the page."

"You just make sure them gold eagles don't go flyin' off no-wheres. That's all I got to say."

Jonathan built up the fire, then carefully emptied the contents of his pockets onto his blanket.

"What you got there, oinker breath?"

"Little somethin' for the womenfolk."

"I thought you didn't cotton none to females."

"Never said that."

"Then who you bringin' geegaws back for?"

"They ain't geegaws. They're buttons."

"Why in blazes are you bringin' buttons?"

"Cuz, you horny ol' goat, none of the women have any for sewin' on the shirts they make us, that's why."

"Winifred cuts the buttons off my old shirts. Uses them over and over."

"Well I'm tired of my sisters havin' to use crumbly old acorn caps for buttons. Time they had the real thing," Jonathan said, counting buttons into three, separate piles.

"I thought you only had two sisters in these parts. What's three piles for."

"None of your business, you horney-toad. Besides, if you was a thoughtful man instead of a heifer-lovin' ol' cheat, you'd have got some for Winifred, too."

"She'd find somethin' wrong with them, new or no," Anson said, heaving another sigh. "She'll give me hell for bringin' back what I did get."

"You mean that store-bought dress for Clara?" Jeremy chimed in.

"Naww. She's the one put me up to that foolishness. Can't see wastin' the hard cash, myself. If you ask me, no one but floozies and fancy women wear such kind of fandangles. But you can bet your britches Winifred'd be mad as a pie-eyed mule if I didn't bring her back somethin' just as nice."

"That shawl you got her is mighty fine," Jeremy agreed.

"Hell, she's honor bound to find somethin' wrong with it. Mark my word." Anson said, inching closer to the fire. "Sure could use a good snort to warm my blood."

"After the way you carried on down yonder, I'dda thought you had enough greased lightenin' to last clean into next year," Jonathan said, still sorting buttons.

"Why don't you take your damn buttons and go shove 'em where the sun don't shine, porker boy."

Jonathan scooped up his piles of buttons, deposited them back into his pockets, then grabbed his bedroll and stomped away from the fire in a huff.

"Now look what you went an' did," said Jeremy. "You got him all riled."

"Good riddance, I say."

"Ever since Luther left us a few days back, you been at each other's throats like a couple of randy he-goats. What gives with you two?"

"He's got too many hogs and not enough sense."

"I give up!" Jeremy rose from his bedroll, threw one of his blankets over the spot where Jonathan's bedroll had lain, to cover the freshly buried money pouch, and he hurried after Jonathan, who had already put a goodly amount of space between himself and Anson Guthrie. By the time Jeremy caught up with him, Jonathan was clearing off a new spot to bed down.

"Why don't you come on back by the fire. Anson didn't mean to be so contrary."

"I've had a stomach full of his odorous company," Jonathan said. "All his carryin's on was enough to make a grown man gag." He continued to fix a new nighttime nest. "So much tipplin' and friskin' with floozies. At his age it's downright re-volting. Serve him right if he caught a good case of the French pox, it would."

"Can't say as I approve of his behavior myself, Jonathan. But you got to admit, the man does have more than his share of trial with Winifred for a wife. It's no wonder he's taken to drink." Jeremy sat down beside Jonathan, picked up a stick and began to break it into small pieces. "There's something else eating at you, Jonathan. I can tell."

"Ain't nothin' you can fix."

"I can listen, if you want to talk about it."

After sitting in silence for several minutes, Jonathan asked his friend, "You ever have a woman get under your skin?"

"Sure enough have."

"Wish I could understand how they do it."

"Do what?"

"Take hold of a man's heart and squeeze it till it likes to bust wide open.

"Guess that's the singularity of the breed," Jeremy said, still breaking sticks. "Any particular woman squeezing at your heart?"

"Reckon so."

"Someone I might know?"

"Most likely. No one I got any right to notice."

"You want to unburden yourself, it won't go any farther than this tree trunk."

"It's Lucy Jarvis."

"Henry's Lucy?"

"The same. Been carryin' a torch for her ever since she come out here with that stupid newspaper ad stuck in her fist. Henry was such an ass."

"How so?"

"Didn't even have the honor to marry the gal right off. Had to keep her waitin' till a preacher come through."

"I'd heard that."

"Henry took so long chewin' the whole thing over, I made up my mind I was gonna marry the gal myself. Took a lot of spunk for a woman to come clear out here, all alone like that," Jonathan said. "She deserved better than Henry."

"No doubt."

They sat in silence for a few minutes, then Jeremy said, "You know we should head back to the fire. Leaving those money pouches will likely drive Anson crazy if we stay away too long," he said, boosting himself up. "Besides, it's downright bone-chilling way over here."

"Seems to me the ol' fool has turned the bend already," Jonathan said, beginning to roll his bedding back up. "Can't trust that reprobate to keep his own wick tucked inside his pants, let alone have sense enough to guard our hard-earned money."

"We only have to put up with him for one more night."

The two headed back to their original evening's encampment in amicable silence, as stray snowflakes fluttered their way earthward. Before glowing embers of the dying campfire glimmered through the shadows, they heard Anson Guthrie's rattling snores.

* * * * *

Nighttime descended early in December, and on this, the longest night of darkness, as on every other night for the past month, Sadie placed a candle in the cabin's south window. "Look, Sister. Look into the light," she said, kindling the wick with a flaming stick from the hearth. "Maybe tonight it'll bring our Jems back home to us." Sadie blew to extinguish the fiery brand, but under her breath she muttered, "If we're lucky he'll come home." She placed the blackened stick on the edge of the mantle to use again, then took Amanda by the hand and led her around to a chair by the kitchen fire. "Sit here where it's warm, Sister. I'll get the twins to bed."

Amanda sank onto the chair and sat, glassy-eyed, staring into the fire, as Sadie busied herself in the other room getting Camellia and Lillian into their night dresses.

"Hold still, Lilly." Sadie tried to pull the dress over the baby's head, but before she could complete the action, Lilly had twisted and escaped from Sadie's grasp. "You little imp. Come back here." She grabbed Lilly before she could tumble off the big bed. With one hand she held the baby tight, and with the other Sadie slipped the dress over Lilly's head in one, swift move. She tied the draw-string snugly around the baby's neck and tucked the ends of the double bow safely inside the nightdress.

"One down, one to go," she said, placing Lillian in her crib. "There, you're safe for the moment. Come here now, Millie. Your turn." Sadie scooped the second baby off the rug, where she sat in front of the warm hearthstone, quickly repeating the same bedtime task.

"I can always trust you to stay right where I put you, can't I, Millie," Sadie said, fastening the second nightdress securely in place. "But that sister of yours, now. Can't trust her out of my sight for a minute. There. You're done." She placed the second baby into her crib and tucked the covers in tightly.

Sadie glanced at the other crib, and there stood Lilly, shaking the side-rails for all she was worth. "Come on, Lilly. It's sleepy time." She lay the baby down once more and tucked the blankets all around. "I better make it a little harder for you to squirm out this time," she said, tying the ends of the top blanket securely to each corner of the bed. "That might hold you a little longer. I just hope it's long enough for you to get to sleep." Sadie leaned down to give Lillian a good-night kiss, and the cabin door burst open.

"Anybody awake in here?"

"JEMS! *You came back!*" Sadie bolted into his arms, causing him to drop the bedroll he held under one arm.

Sadie clung to him for dear life.

"Gee whiz, if I knew this kind of welcome was waiting for me, I'd have gone away more often... just so's I could come back!" The saddlebags he had slung over his shoulder dropped to the floor with a thud.

"Oh Jems, I thought you'd *never* get home! What *took* you so long?"

"We hiked as fast as we could, Pipsqueak. Got the calluses to prove it, too," he said, glancing toward the cribs. "How are all my girls," he asked, heading for the corner. By the time he reached the cribs, Lillian had already squirmed free from her cocoon and stood shaking the side-rails of the bed-prison with a big grin on her face. "Just look at how much you grew!" Jeremy swept the baby into his arms, and she giggled at his tickly beard when he gave her a big kiss.

"You're getting her all stirred up again, Jems. Now I'll never get her settled back down for sleep."

"Here, take her a minute. I've got to kiss my Millie, too." Camellia still lay exactly where Sadie had swaddled her under the covers, and the instant Jeremy picked her up, Millie let out a loud wail.

"Don't you remember your own Daddy?"

"She's been awful cranky lately, Jems. Cutting teeth, I think."

Jeremy bounced and patted the baby until her crying eased. Then she looked at him inquisitively, grabbed a handful of his beard, and gave it a hearty pull. "Hey, that's hooked on!" Jeremy lay the baby gently back into her crib and tucked the covers in tight. "Mandy upstairs? I thought she'd have come running the instant I opened the door. Guess she didn't hear me come in. Mandy! I'm home, Mandy!"

Heading for the stairway, Jeremy hurried around to the kitchen side of the fireplace, while Sadie tried to get Lillian settled back down in her crib. Before he reached the stairs, he spied Amanda, right where Sadie had left her, staring into the fire. He rushed to her side.

"Mandy!" Jeremy swept her up from the chair into a big, bear hug.

Startled by the activity, Amanda momentarily focused on Jeremy's face, and then she began to cry.

"You don't have to cry Mandy. I'm home, safe and sound."

Amanda continued to stare at him with huge tears streaming down her cheeks.

"Maybe you better sit back down," he said, easing her onto the chair and pulling a handkerchief from his pocket. "Here, my little yellow bird. Blow." He held the kerchief up to her nose, and at his command, she blew. He replaced the handkerchief in his pocket and knelt beside the chair, pulling her close. "Don't cry. Everything will be just fine now that I'm back," he said, hugging her tightly to himself. "I missed you so much." Jeremy began a gentle caress, but at his intimate touch Amanda's crying intensified. "Shhhhh, hush now," he said, removing his hand from her breast and simply patting her shoulder like a baby. "I'm never gonna leave you again, Mandy. I promise I'll stay right here by your side."

"So, Jems... how was your trip?" Sadie asked, reentering the kitchen after getting the babies settled again. "Did you sell the goods you took down to market?"

"Sold it all, Pipsqueak. Everything. And made a dandy profit, too. I can't wait to tell the neighbors just how much... give 'em all their share of the hard-earned cash." At that, he remembered the money bags lying on the floor, and he hurried back into the main room to retrieve them from the spot where he'd dropped them by the door. "Wait till I show you two what I brought back," he hollered.

"Shhhhh! Don't you get those babies all wound up again, Jems," Sadie warned in a loud whisper.

"Sorry," he said, reappearing in the doorway. "I'll have to get used to being around babies and females again. I can see that. Spent entirely too much time in the company of cantankerous men lately." He dug deep into one of the bags and pulled out a wrapped bundle. "Look, what I brought you, Mandy. A present!" He placed the package in Amanda's hand, then turned around as he fished another package out for Sadie. "Here, Pipsqueak. I hope you like it," he said, handing it to Sadie.

She unwrapped the tiny bundle while Jeremy continued to talk.

"We sold the whole boat full of goods to a Mr. Josiah Coggins, of the Coggins Mercantile Emporium down by the docks. At first he told us he wanted everything but our meal and oats. Said he didn't want to unload all those barrels and then find out he got stuck with moldy grain. No sir. But we convinced him there wasn't a moldy barrel in the lot, so he finally agreed to take the whole shebang. That is, after Anson told him we intended to spend a little of our earnings right back on a few fineries for our women folk back home. He was a lot more agreeable to dicker with us then," Jeremy said.

"Luther told us that might be the case. Said we'd have to scratch his back if we wanted him to scratch ours. We haggled a good while, but I think we struck a fair bargain in the end. Gave us 13 cents a pound for the butter and cheese, and 20 cents for each pound of Jonathan's smoked pork. Can you believe that? Twenty cents a pound! Why the most he ever got in any eastern market was 12 cents. And Luther got himself 30 cents a pound for ginseng roots. That's five cents better than anywhere else he ever sold it!"

Sadie studied the mysterious bone-like cylinder she held. "What is this thing?"

"Look here," he said, taking it from her. "You open up this little doohickey, see? Now look inside there."

"Hey, needles! It's a needle case! Pretty clever."

"It's made from horn. That Mr. Coggins had some real fancy things in his store, but I figured we best stick to useful things out here. Look what I got for my little flowers." He dug into his bag again and drew out two, disc-like lumps. "Look at this. Opens right up and makes into a little drinking cup," he said, pulling on the outer ring of one, which drew up concentric rings that fit tightly together. He gave it a tug to make them hold fast. "How 'bout that?"

"Never saw anything like it in my whole life, Jems. Does it leak?"

"Coggins poured one of these full of corn juice for Anson, and he drank it right down without losing a drop. Did I tell you we got 90 cents a gallon for the whiskey we took down? Coggins said he only pays 50 cents in the spring, what with the glutted markets then, so we got 40 whole cents more a jug by making this trip in the fall. Says he has a bigger demand for corn juice over the winter. Did I tell you these little cups were made out of horn, too. See?"

He turned to show Mandy. "Look, Mandy. Isn't this something?" Amanda sat glassy-eyed, still staring at the unopened package lying in her hand. "What are you waiting for? You didn't even unwrap your present yet."

She didn't move.

"Is something wrong?" Jeremy knelt down by Amanda, suddenly concerned at her prolonged silence. "Mandy?" He touched her cheek with a gentle caress. "Sadie, what's wrong with her?"

"She's been like that for weeks, Jems. Won't say a word to anyone."

The reality of the situation began to dawn on him, but Jeremy continued his homecoming chatter in an effort to deny the fist trying to punch through his stomach. "Look what I got for you, Mandy. Here, I'll help you," he said, taking the package from her and unfolding the brown paper. "It's a little mirror in a horn case. Opens just like this. See?" he said, demonstrating. "You can look right in there and see yourself."

Amanda stared at the mirror with a vacant gaze.

"Mandy. Look at me." He took her face between his hands and cocked her head toward his own. "It's me. Jeremiah. I'm home. I'm really back now, Mandy."

A tear slid down one cheek, punctuating her bewildered silence.

Jeremy dropped his hands to his sides, and Amanda let the mirror fall to her lap. "I never should have gone away," he said, rising and beginning to pace. "It's all my fault. I know it is. I thought she'd gained enough strength to handle it. But I can see now I was wrong. Oh, Sadie, how could I do this to her! After all she's been through?"

"Don't get yourself so worked up, Jems. We really don't know what set her off."

"We? Has Ma Hawkins come to see her?"

"Willie sent her over, right after I found Amanda all huddled up by the fire the morning after the husking bee."

"Husking bee?"

"We had a doin's over at the Hawkins' place, a little over a month after you left. About six weeks ago by now."

"Did Mandy go?"

"She didn't want to take the babies out on a cold night. But she told me to go on ahead with Willie and have a good time. Insisted she'd be just fine by herself for one night," Sadie said. "Next morning after the bee, I found her curled up on the floor in front of the fire. She wouldn't talk to me, Jems. Just kept crying and calling out to her Papa." Sadie went to her brother and put a hand on his shoulder. "Jems, it's not your fault," she said, shaking her head. "I think... well, I think it must be mine."

"What? How on earth could it be your fault?"

"I didn't come home until real late that night."

"How late?"

"Almost morning. I tip-toed back in, 'cause I didn't want her to hear me and start scolding me for staying out so late. So I didn't check on her, to see if she was all right? I just went straight to bed." Sadie dropped her hand to her side. "Crying woke me up, and I thought it was the babies. Took me a bit of time to realize they were both still sound asleep. It was Amanda I heard crying. I don't think she ever went to bed at all, Jems. Just stayed right there on the floor, curled up with her shawl by the fire. Probably out of her head all night long."

"What makes you say that?"

"Because nobody took care of the babies in the night, Jems. They woke up a soakin', crusty mess the next morning. The way their beds were all torn up, I could tell they must have cried and carried on a long time before they sobbed themselves back to sleep," she said, hanging her head in shame. "Poor little things. They had to be so scared when nobody came. I know it's all my fault, Jems. It has to be. I didn't check the babies or Amanda or anything when I came back home! I was thinking of nobody but myself."

"Don't fret over it, Sadie. This isn't the first time Mandy's been out of her head. I should have known something like this might happen while I was gone. But I really thought she was better. Thought she got past being, being... "

"Addled? I know. Willie's Ma told me how she was after that first baby died."

"What does she say? Does Ma think Mandy will snap out of it this time?"

"She doesn't say much. Calls it nervous collapse. She gave me three or four different potions and teas to give her, but so far nothing's helped much," Sadie said. "I have noticed Amanda seems a lot happier when she sits up close to the fire... 'specially when the Lucky cat's in her lap."

Jeremy and Sadie stood staring at each other in silence for a few moments.

"Does she ever say anything? Do anything?"

"Sits and stares, mostly. If I didn't lead her out to the privy once in a while, I don't think she'd ever move from that spot. She does cry sometimes, but that usually only happens when I take her upstairs to your bed. Lately, I just put her to bed right down here with me. She seems more peaceful that way. Makes it a whole lot easier to keep an eye on her and the babies with all of us sleeping in the same room."

"I'm so sorry, Sadie," he said, shaking his head. "You ended up carrying the whole load around here."

"It's not so bad, Jems. I've gotten pretty used to keeping house and tending the babies myself. Willie comes by every day to check on us... to help with the barn chores and such. Sometimes he brings his ma along, too. So, I haven't really been all alone."

"What would I ever do without you?" He took her into his arms and held her tight, not so much for her reassurance as for his own. "You're the one who left that light burning in the window for me, aren't you, Pipsqueak." Jeremy clung to her, feeling the warmth of her sigh against his chest, yearning for his own Amanda.

Suddenly he pushed Sadie to arm's length, then walked away from her, pacing once again. "How can I get through to her? What can I do?"

"Ma says it'll likely take time. Who knows, maybe she'll perk up when the moon changes."

"Well then," he said, "I expect I'll just have to be a patient man... and a prayin' one." Jeremy went back to Amanda and knelt beside her chair. "Mandy honey?" He placed his hand against her cheek; her head turned in response to his touch. "It's time to go up to bed now, my little yellow bird. Come on," he said, gently pulling her up from the chair. "Come with me, Mandy. Let's go upstairs."

Jeremy took Amanda's hand and led her to the stairway, then helped her up the first few steps, one at a time. "Night, Sadie," he said, pulling the stairway door closed behind himself and mounting the steps behind his puppet-like wife.

Amanda began to whimper in the darkened staircase. Then the door creaked open a crack, and a lighted candle appeared in the opening.

"Here, Jems. It goes lots easier for her with a light. She has a real hard time when it gets too dark... or too cold."

"Thank you," he said, taking the candlestick from his sister. "Sadie..., thanks for everything.

Dear Libby,

I get sprung from jail today. All has been set to rights. The judge did believe my story of the accident, even if Harvey did not. Harvey standing up in front of the bench and telling the judge what a blamed fool he was and carrying on so did him no good at all. Jason will pick me up. Mary Sue is having a bad time carrying this next little one. Much sickness of the stomach. Swollen ankles till she can hardly walk. So I aim to stay on with them and help out. I am right glad to be let out of this place, though they treated me passable. Will be a treat to have Christmas with my son and little Josie.

I have to say I was shore relieved to know you was not upset about my pa's manners. But I was most sad to hear about your sister Rose. I am so sorry, Lib. I know how hard it is to lose family. At least you have her Cait with you now. And your Zannah, too. And a new little Bud to fuss over. Bet the girls was disappointed at the women being out numbered again. At least Cait and Bud are both healthy and doing fine. It is always a releef to get a new mother through confinement safe and sound. You know that you are doing what your sister wanted. So you must have some comfort in that.

How does Zannah take to country life after living in the city? Hard for her to understand the changes, I bet. Can she help any? Or does it add to your load to do for her?

I am sorry to write such a paltry letter. I got to hurry before Jason gets here. So I can send this before we leave town. Do not worry about me. I will have a merry winter with my Josie.

Thanks for being such a good friend to me, Lib. Though I am a jailbird now. Your letters did help keep my spirits up. Made me feel still part of the world. I never had such a good friend as you. I will not forget it. When you take care of all those people up there in them Fire Lands do not forget about yourself.

See the new year in, and I will pray that we meet again in it.
Your grateful jailbird friend, just plain Ellie-Mae
(no more men's last names)

Chapter 16

Keeping The Home Fires Burning
Winter 1818

Jeremy awoke to the howling sound of blizzard-like winds and bone-chilling cold. He reached over to the other side of the bed, searching to pull Amanda closer for warmth, but his hand fell on empty covers where she should have lain. "Mandy? Where are you?"

He sat up, shivering, and in the half-light of dawn he saw a tiny figure huddled by the chimney's back where it extended through the bedroom floor, up through the roof—the same place he'd found her huddled every morning for the past two weeks.

"Come back to bed where it's warm." He threw the covers off and skittered over to her, pressed against the warm chimney stones. Taking her by the shoulders, he eased her onto her feet. "It's warmer under the covers, if you'll just let me hold you," he said, leading her back to their bed. "Come on, little yellow bird, let me warm you up." He tucked her back under the quilts, then hopped in beside her.

Amanda lay stiff and still beside him, in spite of his efforts to pull her closer to warm them both. "I'm not gonna hurt you, Mandy. Don't you know that by now?" He patted her gently, moving his hand down her arm and around her swelling belly, attempting once more to snuggle closer. "Sure wish you'd-a told me about this one on the way before I went gallivanting off downriver."

At his insistent tug, Amanda rolled onto her side, away from Jeremy, and curled into a fetal ball.

"All right, have it your way," he said, moving over and wrapping his body around her tiny frame, spoon fashion, from behind. He lay in silence, until he felt her begin to relax, hearing the slow, even rhythm of her breath as sleep reclaimed his befuddled wife. How long has she been this way now, he wondered, trying to sort it out. Three months? Four? "How long until you come back to me, my little yellow bird," he whispered into her ear. "I need you, Mandy," he said. "My God, how I need you." His body swelled in anticipation, despite his most conscious resolve to avoid it.

"Blast it all!" Jeremy erupted from his warm cocoon into the icy cold morning, leaving Amanda tucked warmly under the quilts. How he wished that sleep were the only oblivion claiming his wife. "Mandy," he whispered in agony. "God, please let her wake up and be herself again! I need her so much."

This morning, like every other morning since his return, God kept His silence.

Jeremy quickly dressed and hurried down the steps, tucking shirt into pants as he descended. Warm air greeted him when he opened the stairway door. "Mornin', Pipsqueak. Figured you had a fire goin'. Mandy knows as soon as the chimney warms."

"Was she hugging it again?"

"The heat comforts her," he said, pulling the gallowses over each shoulder. "But blazes, I wish she could find some comfort in my heat." His face suddenly reddened when he realized what he'd said, and to his sister of all people. "I mean she won't even let me hold her... to help warm her up."

"I know what you mean, Jems."

"Do you think she'll ever wake up and be herself again?"

"We'll just have to wait and see, big brother," Sadie said. "Hot tea's ready. Here." She poured a cup from the crock.

"Thanks." He took the cup she offered. "Guess I better spend the morning splitting more wood. Maybe that'll help me work off my... ah... my–"

"Breakfast?"

"Yeah. My breakfast." He drank down the tea in a few, quick gulps, then plunked the cup onto the table and proceeded to don coat, hat, and boots. "I'll see to the milking first. Bertha gets awful testy if I wait till after breakfast to tend her."

"I'll have mush and corn biscuits ready by the time you get back," Sadie said. "Don't worry about Amanda, Jems. I'll get her dressed and bring her down by the fire."

"Thanks." He pulled the coat collar up tightly around his face and ducked out the door. The wind sucked it shut with a bang, which immediately awoke both babies. They cried in fright and hunger till Sadie hurried to reassure each one. "Good morning, my little flowers," she crooned. "Welcome to another day in the mad house."

* * * * *

As nasty weather settled in for the winter, most of the neighbors stayed busy with the labors it took to keep their own home-fires burning. Only Willie and Ma Hawkins made an occasional call at the Harrisons, and every time Willie entered the cabin, Jeremy began to notice the way Sadie glowed.

On this particular afternoon, after dropping his ma at the cabin of some newcomers near Petersburg, whose family was about to expand with the help of Ma's expertise, Willie came on to the Harrison's alone. He brought along another potion his ma had concocted for Amanda.

"Ma says this one's the last remedy she has to try," Willie told Jeremy. "She got the recipe from that old Indian who used to live down by the falls where those funny, orange mushrooms grow. Took her a while to find any in these parts, so she could make this up." He handed the pouch to Jeremy. "Ma said to stir some of this powder up in a little whiskey to make it strong enough to do the job."

"Are you sure that's wise? Giving that poor thing hard liquor?"

"All I know is what Ma told me to tell you. She said if it works right, it ought to clear her head. If it don't, then at least it just might lift her spirits some."

"Well, I guess at this point, I'm willing to try anything," said Jeremy.

"You hungry?" Sadie asked Willie with a teasing gleam in her eye.

"I had dinner at noon. But I wouldn't mind a little something to tide me till supper time," he smiled. "Is that hot cornbread I smell?"

"Just took it out of the spider," Sadie smiled. "I'll go out to the barn and fetch some fresh milk to go with it," she said, reaching for her shawl and making a beeline for the door.

"I'll come help!" Willie hurried after her. They were careful to push the door shut softly, so as not to waken the babies napping in their cribs over in the corner.

"Young love," Jeremy smiled, shaking his head. "Sure is a welcome change in this cabin." He studied the pouch in his hand and headed to the trap door behind the stair steps to fetch his jug of medicinal whiskey. "I'll mix up a little bit of this stuff for you, Mandy," he said, talking to her the way he always did, as if she understood every word. "Ma says this should help you feel better."

He continued his idle talk while stirring up the potion. "I wonder how much of this powder I'm supposed to use in a cupful of spirits?" he questioned out loud. "Willie didn't say. I should probably go and ask, but I hate to bother the lovebirds out there in the barn. Oh well," he said, dipping a spoon into the pouch with a shrug of his shoulders, "I don't reckon it'll hurt to mix it up good and strong." He pulled the spoon back out and added a heaping measure to the cup of whiskey, stirring it thoroughly to mix the toddy well. He took a whiff of the stuff. "Hey, this doesn't smell half bad! Maybe I'll try a little myself... lift my spirits some, too."

He walked over to where Amanda sat rocking in the new chair he'd made her for Christmas. Though she didn't take much notice of things around her, she did seem to enjoy rocking in that chair. "Here, my little yellow bird. Drink this." Jeremy put the cup between her hands and guided it up to her mouth. When the cup touched her lips, she took a tiny sip, then stopped. Her eyes widened at the taste, and she tried to pull away.

"Ma said you need to drink this," he said, pushing the cup back to her lips. "Go on, drink it down. That's a good girl." She took several more swallows, then turned her head away.

She hadn't quite emptied the cup, and not one to waste anything, Jeremy drank down the last several swallows himself.

"Not bad," he said, as the potion began to warm the pit of his stomach. "How you doing, Mandy? Feeling any better yet?"

She didn't say a word, but her head turned toward him when he spoke, still giving him that silent, vacant stare. He knelt beside her, taking her into his arms, pulling her head onto his shoulder and holding her tight. "Oh Mandy, when are you coming back to me?"

Her hands went around his neck, and he stood up, pulling her from the chair into a standing position. He held her tighter. The heat in his middle began to mount. "I love you, Mandy. I need you back with me. I need my wife," he pleaded. "Won't you please come back, my little yellow bird?" He suddenly felt the tingle of gathering tears. "Don't you remember how it finally got between us, Mandy? How I tamed that skittish, little yellow bird to eat right out of my hand," he said, feeling her press tighter against him.

All at once the potion in his stomach seemed to move in a wave, straight to his head. "Jumping lizards, I wonder if this stuff is affecting you this same way," he said, looking down into Mandy's eyes. She appeared more red-faced than usual, and the eyes that had held a constant, glazed look of late, suddenly shone bright and clear. "Mandy? Can you hear me? Can you talk to me, girl?"

She didn't say a word, but she gave him a huge smile and snuggled deeper into his arms.

"Oh Mandy, are you really with me?" He hugged her ever tighter, kissing her head, then her cheek, and her neck, nuzzling her bosom and burying his face between her breasts.

She took his head in her hands and began to stroke his hair.

"Mandy, you remember now! You have to remember! It's so wonderful when we can fit together just so. It's been such a long, long time, my little yellow bird."

He stood upright, pulling her to him once more. "Lordy, I don't think I can wait until we bed down for the night to get a real taste of you. I'm so jo-fired now I can hardly stand it," he said, sweeping her up into his arms and heading for the steps to their bedroom above. "No one's gonna bother us for a spell," he said pulling the stairway door open. "I aim to sweep you right into paradise."

Jeremy mounted the steps two at a time, making a single bound between the last step and the bed. He sat Amanda on its edge, while he fumbled to unbutton his pants and at the same time undo her bodice and skirts. "Why in the world do you women insist on wearing so darn many clothes?" he said, finally pulling her chemise over her head and taking in the natural beauty of his delicate, little yellow bird.

"Papa? Is it time to get dressed for the party yet, Papa?"

Jeremy stopped dead in his tracks.

"I got a new party dress to wear, Papa. Wait till you see the beautiful, yellow dress Grandmother made for me!" Amanda giggled and rolled under the covers, curling up into her familiar, fetal ball.

The pain and confusion fighting inside Jeremy nearly doubled him over. With great effort he tried to re-button his trousers, getting the fly lined up all crooked, as his fingers fumbled to match buttons with buttonholes over his grossly distended private parts. He bounded down the steps, tears streaming and wetting his beard. He grabbed the jug of "medicinal whiskey" and made a beeline for the cabin door. The instant he pulled it open, Sadie fell inside, with Willie close on her heels—both brushing loose hay from their persons.

"Jems, what's wrong?" Sadie took in the whole of him in one glance. Red faced, tears streaming, with shirt tucked half in and half out and pants buttoned all askew, she couldn't help but notice the extreme bulge barely contained within his trousers, and her heart went out to him.

"I thought... I–"

"Willie, take that jug of milk on in, will you? I'll serve up your cornbread in a minute," Sadie said, stepping protectively in front of her brother to shield his vulnerable condition from view. Willie moved through the doorway into the kitchen.

"Are you all right, Jems?"

He swiped the back of his arm across his face, wiping away tears. "Let me out of here!" he said, pushing by her, trying to get out the door.

"Is it Amanda? What happened?" she asked, restraining him by the arm.

"Nothing! Just let me be!"

"Where is she?"

"Upstairs," he said, breaking free and heading toward the barn at a dead run.

All the clamor had awakened the twins from their naps, who now stood crying in their cribs. Sadie got them up and carried them around into the kitchen, where Willie sat waiting by the fire.

"Is he all right?" Willie asked with concern. "I forgot to tell him Ma said to only use a pinch of that powder stuff to mix up in a toddy."

"It's been awful hard on him... with Amanda addled so long, and all," she said by way of explanation. "Here, Willie, would you hold the babies a minute while I go check on her?"

"Nothin' I'd like better than holding two little beauties," he said, putting a baby on each knee, "unless it's holding you, Sadie," he said with a wink.

She hurried upstairs. Willie bounced and talked to the twins, setting them both to giggling by the time Sadie returned.

"She's sound asleep," Sadie said with a sigh of relief. "At least that's one less to worry about at the moment." She leaned down to retrieve one baby and headed for the other room. "How about bringing Lilly in here, Willie. You can help change her."

"Me? Change a baby? But I never–"

"Then it's high time you learned."

* * * * *

By the time Willie finally headed for home, the sun had set and the barn chores were finished. Sadie fed him and the babies supper before she sent Willie on his way, and after getting the twins settled down for the night and checking on Amanda, who still slept soundly, she headed out to the barn, quilt in hand, to look for Jeremy. If Willie had seen any sign of him while tending to evening chores, he hadn't mentioned a word.

She found Jeremy sprawled in the far corner of the hay mow, the jug lying to one side—empty. Since his basic nature bent toward that of a teetotaler, the corn whiskey hit him hard, especially on an empty stomach already stunned from the effects of a too-potent, medicinal toddy. He slept fitfully, sweat pouring from his flushed body in spite of the cold, while ghosts from the past plagued his rambling dreams...

...He and brother Paul knocked on the door of a bawdy house located in an alley behind the blacksmith shop back in Uniontown, Pa. There, three crimson-painted "ladies," wearing the most revealing garments he'd ever seen, invited them to step inside. Next thing he knew, Jeremy, a naïve and undefiled sixteen-year-old virgin, lay stripped and at the mercy of two, fleshy strumpets dead set on educating him into the joys of carnal delight. At their hands he thrashed and gyrated in agony—in turn both terrified and embarrassed, then impassioned and confused.

He floated forward to his marriage bed, trying to call out Amanda's name, but his tongue felt so thick and sluggish, only moans escaped his lips. She welcomed him, enveloped him, immersed him in her erotic warmth.

Then his dream took an unfamiliar twist, returning him to the bawdy house of the past, yet at the same time becoming strangely real. He felt himself fondled and manipulated, then taken into the warm, moist mouth of a chestnut-haired floozy. Jeremy knew himself for a drunken sinner, but if this was hell, he only regretted not visiting this place sooner, for it felt more like the rapture of heaven than the fires of the netherworld.

He tried to lift his hands to her head, wishing to feel her hair between his fingers, to smell the strangely familiar scent, to test the limits of this dream. But only one limb of his body responded, and that not to any command of his, but to her tongue only. He could hear the blood pounding at his temples, and perhaps another small, wet sound under that. If only he could stop spinning in circles he might know more.

The need to know anything for certain faded as he let sensations draw him more quickly around the circle rotating faster and faster. He moved toward something momentous—death, perhaps, or weightlessness. Then he burst forth into a place of light. As he arrived he heard a ragged shout issue from his own throat, then a familiar voice that said, "Sleep now, Jems."

Then nothing.

Jeremy next came to himself with awareness of a hum in his left ear and a sandpaper tongue against his cheek. Memories of the strange dream flooded his mind, bringing with it shame and dismay, yet also a satisfied tingle from his groin. He started to lift his head, but such a wave of nausea swept over him, he quickly lay back down and took inventory of himself. Sour mouth. Fuzzy tongue. There, one eye opened. Now the other.

"Ahh, so you're the one giving me strange dreams, Lucky cat." The humming near his ear grew louder as he spoke, and the cat jumped onto his chest. "Careful there, you. I don't know if I'm all here, yet," he said, testing his arms. He found them heavy, yet responsive, however the movement of his legs felt somewhat restricted. Looking down as far as he could without lifting his head, he realized that he'd been covered with a quilt from his own bed—the bed he shared with Mandy. Could she have actually come out here during the night? Had she known of his incredible need, even in her muddled state? No, it couldn't be. It had to be phantoms of a drunken imagination.

But the quilt was there. It was real. Sadie?

Sadie!

Had Sadie come out here and covered him?

"Did she see me in this disgusting state? What will she think of her big brother now," he asked the Lucky cat, shaking his head. "Owww, I can't do that." He lay still again. "How in the world can a man take to drink if he wakes up feeling like this?"

Making no answer, the cat continued her happy rumble, perched upon his chest.

The dream!

"Oh my God! What if she came out here while I was having that horrible, wonderful dream!" He could live with the embarrassment of his inebriation. But he wasn't sure he could show his face, if she even guessed he could conceive of such carnal desires.

As he lay there, eyes closed, trying to muster the strength to sit up, he heard soft footfalls upon the hay.

"Jems? You awake yet?" she whispered.

"Uh hum. I don't feel so hot, though."

"Here," she said, kneeling beside him. "I brought something to help you feel better."

"I don't think anything could make this head feel like it belonged to me again."

"Drink this. It'll help."

He eased onto his elbows, then with great difficulty pushed himself up into a sitting position. "How can you even stand to look at me, after what I've done?"

"What? Get a little tipsy?"

"More than a little, I'd say," he said, holding his head.

"I'm surprised you waited so long to do it."

"What?"

"You heard me. Takes some kind of a man to put up with all you have for so long and not go 'round the bend a mite yourself," she said, handing him the cup. "Here. Drink it."

He took the cup and thirstily drank down the warm brew. "This tastes pretty good. What is it?"

"A secret recipe I concocted for Michael to clear his head after a night of tippling in town with the twins."

"You mean Michael hit the jug?"

"Not just now and then, either. Father would've had his head, if he'd known. So I made it my business to make sure he never found out."

"How did you get to be so wise?"

"I had a good teacher."

"Is Mandy all right? Did that toddy do anything to help her?"

"Hard to tell. She's been sleeping ever since you came out here yesterday."

"Yesterday?"

"It's the dawn of a brand new day, Jems."

"Then, I reckon I'd better get to chores," he said, trying to rise to his feet. "Woo! I don't know if these legs will even hold me. They feel like spindly saplings."

"Take it slow. The sun's just now peeking up," she said, taking the cup and heading for the ladder. "The babies are still sound asleep. I'll go and get a start on the milking... till you get yourself back together," she said with a nod toward his drawers.

"Oh," he said, embarrassed at his state of undress. He began to button up his trousers. "Thanks, Sadie."

"Anytime, Jems," she said with a knowing smile. "Anytime."

* * * * *

After lying for more than 12 hours in a coma-like sleep brought on by Jeremy's too-powerful toddy, Amanda thrashed beneath the quilts as she rose through multiple layers of unconsciousness to a place of fitful slumber. After he'd mixed so much tranquilizing powder into one analgesic concoction, Jeremy would never know how dangerously close his wife had come to a permanent sleep. The fact that he had drunk a goodly portion of it himself probably saved her life.

Now, as the effects of that drink began to wear off, Amanda's benumbed mind struggled to break through the mental fog still holding her hostage. For the first time in weeks, she began to dream...

...She drifted down the Edisto River south of Charleston in a bright yellow casket, surrounded by thousands of floating peach blossoms. Decked out in her yellow wedding gown, and sitting upright in the funerary box, she waved farewell to all the neighbors lining the docks at every plantation she passed by. Curiously, the people she saw at those landings were not the southern friends and relations she had left behind once before, but rather the frontier neighbors in her present realm, transported now to her bygone world.

Had she not felt so apprehensive about something, she should have enjoyed this leisurely, river voyage immensely. But she watched with growing alarm as the floating coffin-vessel drew ever closer to a huge bend in the river.

What perils lay ahead? What heartbreak? Could she bear to live through one more loss, one more misfortune—one more painful disaster?

Suddenly the water began to churn over hidden rocks and shoals, and the casket bobbed precariously, pitching her first one direction, then another. The coffin bashed against the rocks on its death run down the rapids until it broke apart, throwing her headlong into the rushing torrent.

She felt the swirling waters close around her, welcoming her, drawing her into their watery depths. But before she could release her hold on the last, tenacious strand of life—let go her final breath—she felt a hand lifting, lifting, lifting her high above the swirling waters onto a soft place of safety, high above the furthermost shore.

"Amanda Jane, we must talk."

"Grandmother Bently? Is that you?"

"What's the meaning of all this dying business, pray tell? Don't you know you have Bently blood coursing through your veins? Bentlys never give up without a fight."

"But it's been so hard Grandmother! So many terrible things have happened. I can't go on... I just can't!"

"Nonsense. You underestimate yourself, my girl. You can survive, and you shall, Amanda Jane. You simply must, you see. It's in the blood."

"But how will I ever manage, after... after–"

"Do you think you alone have suffered that greatest of insults at the hands of men?"

"How can you ever know what it was like?" she began to whimper.

"I know, because I lived through the very same anguish, my dear."

"You?"

"Yes, me."

"Who?"

"Suffice it to say that Chickasaw blood still imparts a great strength to the blend of your life's vital flow."

"Redskins?"

"A chieftain's son, himself a great leader. Bent Leaf," she said with a regretful smile. "Our first meeting may have been far from an agreeable one, but I did come to bear him great respect... as well as a son."

"You?"

"Me."

"But how did you endure the disgrace?"

"With dignity, and with fortitude," she said. "And so shall you."

"But how *can* I, Grandmother? How can I go on?"

"Take a deep breath, put one foot in front of the other, and keep yourself moving forward," she said. "And Amanda Jane..."

"Yes, Grandmother?"

"Never, *never* look back."

"Yes, Grandmother."

"If ever you should come to doubt yourself again, just remember the brooch—this one. The one I gave you before," she said, placing the treasured heirloom in Amanda's hand. "Remember?"

"I remember, Grandmother."

"Pin it on, right over your heart, close to that which pumps your life force. It will remind you whose strength drives your spirit."

"I will, Grandmother," she said, holding the brooch tight.

"The blood runs weak in your father—my grandson, Amanda Jane. The wife my son took for himself brought a regrettable failing that defiles the lineage yet. And with the taint of your mother's pompous mediocrity, those feather-brained sisters of yours don't stand a chance.

"But in you, Amanda—in you, and in your daughters, and in the boy you now carry—Bent Leaf's noble strength still flows, strong and true." She took her great-granddaughter by the chin and raised her head high, tilting it slightly to reveal the small birth mark hidden behind her right ear. "Remember this, Amanda Jane: nothing can stand in the way that you, or they, cannot surmount. Do you believe me?"

"Yes, Grandmother. I believe you."

"Then rise from your bed and go look after your daughters like the noble, Bently woman you are. You must teach them whom they, also, someday shall become. Listen to me now, Amanda. You must be careful for your son. Heed my words, for I cannot come to you again. Up, now. To the day!"

"Yes, Grandmother. I know you are right, Grandmother. I'll always remember," she said, clutching the brooch. "I promise, I shall forever keep it over my heart." Amanda's voice echoed in her own ears, as she squeezed the brooch tighter. She jumped with a start, when its pin pricked the palm of her hand.

Amanda looked around, and saw that she sat on the edge of her bed, gripping Grandmother Bently's brooch. She had on not a stitch of clothing. "My lands, I'll catch my death!" She jumped up and quickly pulled on her chemise and house dress, making sure to pin the treasured heirloom securely over her heart. She hurried downstairs as fast as she could to build up the fire of a brand new day.

* * * * *

After finishing the morning chores, Jeremy and Sadie walked back to the cabin arm-in-arm, as much to steady Jeremy as to enjoy one another's company. Still a little woozy, but beginning to feel hungry, Jeremy opened the door to be greeted by the pleasant aroma of baking griddle cakes and steaming tea.

"When did you start breakfast?" Jeremy asked his sister.

"I didn't."

Then who?" As quickly as his throbbing head would allow, he hurried into the kitchen, with Sadie fast on his heels. They both stood in astonishment, watching Amanda, stooped over the fire, turning flap jacks and piling them onto a plate warming by the hearth. "I thought you two would never get back in here," she said, flipping another cake. "Breakfast is all ready. The twins already ate theirs," she said, pointing to the babies sitting securely strapped into their double chair. "My lands, I swear those two grow faster every night."

"Am I seeing things? Is that really you?"

"Who else would it be fixing your breakfast, Jeremiah?" she said with a smile. "Be sure you wash up, after being out there with that cow," she said, stooping to dip more batter onto the griddle. She rose with a hand to her back to ease the ache of pregnancy's changing posture. "And how many times do I have to ask you to leave those filthy boots over by the door? I do try to keep a clean house, you know."

"Right away, Mandy. I forgot, is all."

"Thank you for tending the babies and letting me sleep through for a change, Sadie," said Amanda. "A whole night's sleep did me a world of good."

"You're welcome."

"It's left me feeling like a brand new woman."

"It sure enough has," Sadie said, tapping Jeremy on the back and shrugging her shoulders in a silent question. He answered her with a look of equal bewilderment.

"I do hope you two are hungry. I made a double batch."

"Can I help with anything?" Sadie asked.

"Don't be silly, sister. I'm perfectly capable." Amanda brought hotcakes to the table. "Jeremiah does say I make the best flapjacks in the whole township, you know."

"In the whole damn state!" Jeremy said, hurrying to his wife by the table.

"Sit yourselves down, now, both of you," she said, taking her usual place at the foot of the table. "I woke up with a tremendous hunger today, myself." She piled three hot-cakes onto her plate. "I do need to eat for two now, you know."

She gave Jeremy the biggest smile he'd ever seen. "He's going to be a strong one, this baby," she said, patting her middle. "A boy who will be noble, and hardy, and true." She patted the over-sized brooch pinned near her heart. "And I have that on the best of authority."

The End of Book I

Hearthstones II: *Let The Sparks Fly!*

Excerpt Chapter 1

The Kicking Bee
Justice Settlement, Vermillion Township
Mid April, 1818

"You pound that board down good and tight on the end of that wool, now," Emma directed her near-sighted husband, Frank Putnam, as he anchored the last woolen strip fast to the floor of Netta Bailey's cabin. "Sure don't want that cloth workin' loose once we get her all sudsed down."

Frank pounded at the last nail, missing it two blows out of every three. "Dad-blasted hammer! Never could whack a blamed thing with it," he complained.

"If you ask me, it ain't the hammer's fault, you keep a-missin' that tack," Anson Guthrie teased his best friend. "You didn't ask me, but I'm-a-tellin' you just the same."

Frank squinted his one, good eye to get a better focus on the tack. "I could hit just fine, if I didn't have to put up with so much of your botheration, you red-nosed souse."

"Forget about Anson and finish tackin' them yard goods down," Emma snapped in an obvious huff. "Netta's got three, big wash-tubs full of hot water, all ready for stirrin' in soap suds."

The strain of responsibility for organizing this work party was beginning to show on Emma Putnam. Even though a good many other township women surpassed Emma when it came to God-given intelligence, she was doing her best to oversee this neighborhood Kicking Bee, since she's the one who'd woven all the woolen goods ready for felting.

In spite of her obvious shortcomings, Emma did know how to weave. Once she got past her initial bafflement at stringing up her loom, Emma turned out the best yard goods in the township. Of course, she had the only loom within a 30-mile radius, so everyone expected her unquestioned involvement in this day's festivities.

And festive, it was. After spending a long, lonely winter holed-up in their respective cabins, neighbors from the Justice settlement on the western side of Vermillion Township gathered at the largest, centralized cabin for their work party, and came bearing all manner of foodstuffs for the big party sure to follow. After all, who could waste such a nice clean floor after all that sudsy kicking? It certainly called for a dance, at the very least— and at most, an all-night frolic to celebrate a new-born spring.

"Haven't you got those yard goods fastened down yet, Frank?" Netta Bailey asked, hurrying to the far corner of the cabin where Frank sat sucking on a bleeding thumb with wife Emma scowling down at him. "Oh my lands, you hurt yourself! Let me see that thumb." Netta grabbed his hand to examine the bleeding appendage before he could say a single word. "We got to go soak that thing in cold water right away, 'fore it swells up more than it already has!"

By the time Netta had finished bandaging Frank's smashed thumb, Edith Hawkins arrived and had taken charge of organizing the incoming foodstuffs. Being one of the oldest women in the territory, "Ma" Hawkins was used to giving orders and having them obeyed, no matter what the occasion.

"Clara, you see nobody touches these pies till after all them yard goods gets taken up, you hear?"

"You can count on me," eighteen-year-old Clara Guthrie said, smoothing wrinkles from her crisp, blue dress.

"Mind me, now, girl. If that Reverend Longbottom shows up, you better be double careful he don't sweet-talk you into givin' him a piece or two."

"I promise, I won't let no one touch a single pie," she said, moving this way and that, to set her skirt to swaying.

Edith Hawkins looked her up and down. "I don't s'pose you had brains enough to bring along an apron to cover yourself up

2

with," she said shaking her head. "What in blue blazes possessed you to wear such a fancy frock for a work-doin's, gal?"

"Pa bought it for me... on his trip down to market! I just had to wear it, see?"

"Vanity ain't no excuse for poor sense," said Ma, taking Netta's every-day apron down from its peg. "Here, cover that thing up with this extra smock of Jeannette's."

"But Mrs. Hawkins—"

"No buts. Put it on. Can't see compoundin' poor judgment with downright waste by ruinin' that fancy thing," she said, shaking her head.

Clara's eyes began to swim. Dutifully she took the stained apron from Edith Hawkins and tied it over her pretty, store-bought dress, all the while trying valiantly not to cry under the scrutiny of that crusty woman. Thankfully the Harrisons' arrival diverted Ma's attention. She hurried over to check on the Harrison twins and a very pregnant Amanda Jane.

One of the twins wiggled and fussed, despite Jeremiah Harrison's best efforts to quiet his daughter. "Sadie," he said to his sister standing nearby, "take this little wiggler would you? She sure don't want her Daddy right now."

"Come to Aunt Sadie, you little dickens," she said, leaning in to take the squirming Lillian from her older brother. "I got somethin' that'll keep you busy for a while." Sadie reached into her apron pocket and pulled out a lump of maple-sugar candy. "Look what I found out on that food table... some of Miss Netta's maple candy." She set Lillian down, handed her the candy, and guided the toddler over toward her mama, Amanda Jane Harrison, who still held the hand of Lillian's twin sister, Camellia. When Camellia saw Lillian sucking on something she didn't have, she started to fuss for a piece of her own.

"Here, Millie, Aunt Sadie has some for you, too," she said, leaning down and handing a second piece of candy to the mirror image of the tot she shepherded.

"How many times do I have to remind you to call them by their given names?" Amanda scolded her sister-in-law. "I don't know why you can't seem to remember such a simple request," she said in obvious disgust. The more aggravated Amanda Jane became, the more pronounced turned her southern accent.

"Just got a short memory, I guess," Sadie shot back.

Amanda looked down at the twins. "Oh my goodness, what in the world have you given them now?"

Camellia and Lillian, obviously enjoying their sweet treats, had already managed to get their hands and faces covered with the sticky stuff.

"They've ruined their new dresses already. Just look what you've done! Sticky sugar all down their fronts!" Amanda struggled to bend down to remove the sugary lumps from her daughters' hands, but before her bulging middle allowed her to do so, the twins took off running right across the stretched-out yard goods, toward Willie Hawkins, whom they'd just spied on the other side of the room. "Those little scamps know I can't run after them in my present condition," said an exasperated Amanda. "Giving toddlers sticky candy–"

"Let 'em be," Ma Hawkins piped in. "They can run all they want in here today and it won't hurt a thing. A sweet treat now and again won't hurt em' a bit, neither… long as they's eatin' proper." She took a scrutinizing look at Sadie. "Looks like you been eatin' good," she said to Sadie. "You're gainin' a mite in the middle, ain't you?"

"I, ah, think I'd better go look after the babies… make sure they don't get sticky sugar on anybody," Sadie said, making a hasty retreat around the cloth-tacked floor.

"I should hope you would," Amanda called to her retreating sister-in-law following after the twins. They'd reached Willie and begun to pull on his pant legs. "See that they get cleaned up properly, too!"

The two women left standing behind could not see the big smile that lighted Sadie's face as she neared the red-headed Willie Hawkins.

"You take any notice of her plumpin' up some?" Ma asked Amanda.

"I haven't given it much thought. Now that you mention it, she does look a little heavier."

"She been actin' funny like to you?"

"Funny? What do you mean by funny."

"A might queasy or sick on her stomach?"

"Not that I'm aware of," Amanda said, rubbing the side of her own distended stomach. "Ooo, this one sure wants to stretch out in there. I swear he must be two feet long already."

"What makes you think it's a he?" asked Ma, gently touching Amanda's belly to gauge the strength of the baby's kick.

"Ouch. It's kind of sore right there," Amanda said, rubbing her left side after Ma had removed her hand. "I just know, is all. It's a boy." Amanda stood quietly for a moment, seemingly lost in thought.

"You know, now that I think about it, I do recall Sadie seeming out of sorts a couple months back. Wasn't a bit like her, either. I wanted Jeremiah to come for some of your stomach powders, but Sadie wouldn't hear of it. Said it wasn't worth bothering you for just a touch of the pips."

Amanda stretched and rubbed her lower back. "I can tell you one thing, she hasn't been much help at all with the twins lately. She's always running off with Willie to go fishing or mushroom hunting or some other such nonsense."

"The nonsense part's more my guess," said Ma with indignation. "I guarantee they ain't done much fishin'!" She shook her head in dismay. "I better go have a talk with that son of mine right now," she said, heading toward the other side of the room.

Sadie saw Willie's Ma coming with fire in her eyes, so she quickly guided Willie out the back door toward the water pump with both twins in tow. Before Ma could corral her youngest son, Netta Bailey waylaid Edith Hawkins half way around the kicking floor.

"Guess what? Henry said, that Harmon said, that he heard the Reverend might be comin' this way today. Do you reckon we should wait to start kickin' up suds till he gets here? I mean for him to say a prayer or somethin' before we get started?"

"What good's it gonna do to pray over cloth goods?"

"Well, you never know. I mean, anything could happen. Besides, it's just not proper to go startin' up a doin's if we know the Reverend might come, now is it? I mean, we are almost ready to pour out the suds. But do you think we should wait to call the men in here, till he shows up?"

"No one knows nothin' for sure about that smooth-talkin' preacher. So you just round up them kickers and get this shindig started, Jeannette. I got no time for nonsense, you hear? I got to go turn a reckless boy into an honest man," she said, brushing Netta aside and continuing toward the back door.

Out at the pump Willie and Sadie each washed a set of sticky fingers, while both twins whined for another helping of the maple candy.

"Do you *have* to tend these babies all day?" Willie asked with longing in his voice.

Sadie dried Lilly's hands with the drying cloth. "I most likely will," she said, giving the child a drink of water from the dipping gourd beside the water bucket.

"Why don't you send these babies back in to their mama so you and me can go do a little *fishin'*," Willie said with an ornery smile, raising one eyebrow and swatting Sadie on her behind.

"There ain't gonna BE no *fishin'* today," said Ma Hawkins, coming up behind them, "nor any other shenanigans, neither." She gave Sadie another hard look up and down. Sadie held her head erect and met Ma's gaze, not cowering in the least to the older woman's penetrating stare.

Edith Hawkins turned her attention toward Willie. "William Lloyd, I got somethin' to say to you." She stomped off toward the barn. Willie shrugged his shoulders to Sadie, then hurried after his mother.

"Come on, you pretty, little flowers." Sadie knelt to wipe Millie's hands dry and give her a drink from the same gourd. "Let's go back inside and see what your papa's up to." She stood upright, and hesitated for a moment to rub the small of her back.

She shot a concerned look toward the barn, then turned to guide both toddlers back into the cabin.

Inside, kicking festivities had gotten underway without benefit of a formal blessing, since no traveling preacher had yet made an appearance. Chattering and laughing females lined the perimeter of the tacked-down yard goods, while bare-footed men and boys kicked and stomped in the center of the floor, as they sloshed warm soap-suds over the newly woven wool.

"Can't you get them feet of yours movin' any faster?" Emma chided her husband Frank, who was doing a half-hearted shuffle over in the corner next to Anson Guthrie. "You two quit your jawin' and get to kickin'."

"You better be careful over there," warned Netta. "We don't want nobody fallin' on their bee-hinds in here today," she said, bouncing her seven-month-old daughter, Rachel, who'd begun to fuss. Netta's toddler, Rosanna, clung to her mama's skirts in fright, for the day's unusual activity had her quite confused. "All I need is someone fallin' down and breakin' their hucklebone."

"Who's that?" Clara pointed toward the cabin door, where several strangers entered, one among them a beautiful, young woman. "Who is that girl?"

"Why, I don't have a clue," Netta answered. "Never saw them before in my life." She tried to walk over to greet the newcomers, but Rosanna kept tugging her back.

"I sure hope Tom don't see that girl. She's so comely! Just look at that blond hair, would you! How can anyone in the world have hair that color?" Clara fussed at her dress, fluffing her skirts and smoothing the bodice over her tiny waist, while looking to see if Tom had noticed the strangers. " I knew it. I just knew it! He's lookin' at her," she whined. "Now he's never gonna take notice of me!"

"Stop your fussing, Clara, and let's go meet the new folks," Netta said, walking toward the strangers. "I don't recall seein' youens 'round about before. You must be new to these parts." Netta took a quick breath and continued on before the new-comers could get a word in to answer. "I heard someone moved into that deserted homestead outside Petersburg, down below Jonathan's place. A cooper, I think he said. Might you be them folks?"

"I'm Rebecca Simpson, and this is my oldest daughter Lo-vinia," said the plain-looking woman, turning to pull the lovely girl forward. Lovinia ushered the rest of the brood inside the cabin. "And these are my other children, Sol, Dora, Jessie, Albert, Paulie and Snooks," she said, pulling each one to her in turn. She mussed the five-year-old's hair. Nine-year-old Albert and eight-year-old Paulie began to push and shove at one an-other, so their mother smacked them both firmly on their heads. "Straighten up, you two. Act like company."

"They're all right," Netta said, patting each one affecttion-ately. "Why don't you boys take off your shoes and socks and go join the fellas out there kickin' up suds? That ought to work off some of them orneries."

They looked to their mother for permission. At her nod, they tore over to the corner piled high with shoes and socks and be-gan to strip off their own.

"Your husband? Did he come along with you?"

"He's out seein' to the horse," Rebecca said, looking around the room. "So, where do you want us to put these vittles?" she asked, pointing to her girls, each holding a basket full of food.

"We have a table all set up back in the lean-to," Netta said, taking a basket from the youngest girl. "Here, I'll show you. Just follow me around to the back door over there," she said, thread-ing her way through the crowd. Netta kept up her jabber as the line of newcomers followed her to the food table.

By now quite a suds covered the entire floor, and young boys began to slip and slide around, trying to see who could knock down whom, between the legs of the older men. Several of the women, lining the perimeter of the cabin, held brooms, which they periodically used to sweep escaping suds back onto the yard goods.

Amanda, over to one side, using her broom more as a leaning post than a tool, watched the boys with an amused smile. "Won't be long till you're out there with all those boys, Joseph," she said, giving her middle a knowing pat.

"You're dead certain it's a boy?" Sadie asked with a raised eyebrow.

"Quite," Amanda said. "Grandmother Bently told me so."

Sadie rolled her eyes when Amanda alluded to the dream about her dearly departed grandmother, who had returned from beyond the grave to predict that Amanda carried a son. But Sadie's attention quickly returned to her charge, as she hurried to recapture the rebellious Lillian, trying to make an escape onto the suds-covered floor.

Amanda lovingly patted the obedient Camellia, until Sadie returned the recalcitrant twin to her side. "You little rascal," Amanda said, leaning down to give the child a befitting swat on the seat. When she straightened up, a sudden movement drew her eyes toward the front door, and her hand flew to her mouth when she saw a lanky man remove a black, broad-brimmed hat.

Amanda's face turned a deathly shade of white.

"What's wrong?" Sadie held tight to both twins.

A speechless Amanda could do no more than point a shaky finger toward the black-garbed figure standing with his back to the kicking floor, greeting folks gathered around him as if they were long, lost friends.

"Amanda? *Amanda!*" Sadie tried to get her sister-in-law's attention without letting go of either twin. "Amanda, what's wrong with you?"

Amanda suddenly dropped her broom, picked up her skirts, and, as well as she could in her gravid condition, began to run across the suds-covered floor toward the back door. She got no more than half-way across when Albert and Paulie came sliding toward her, clipped her from behind, and sent her sprawling to the floor. She landed heavily on her right side, hitting her head so hard as she went down, that it knocked the pregnant woman out cold.

"Oh, my Lord! Amanda!" Lucy Jarvis, holding 11-month-old baby Hank, was the first one to reach her side, Jeremiah following close behind. "Where's Ma Hawkins? Has anybody seen Ma?" Lucy called.

"Out to the barn," answered Sadie, holding the twins even tighter.

"Somebody go and bring her back here *quick*," Jeremy said, kneeling beside his wife, lying prone in the suds. He cradled Amanda's head and gently patted her cheek. "Mandy? Speak to me!" He eased Amanda up, into his arms, then carefully rose to his feet as Netta burst through the back door.

"What's goin' on? What happened? I heard someone holler."

"She fell down," Clara whispered, still holding Rachel tight. "I don't know how it happened, but all of a sudden, there she was, feet flyin' every which-of-a-way, and they went right out from underneath of her. She went down hard, too."

"Oh, my lands. I just knew if we didn't say a startin' prayer, something like this was bound to happen," Netta babbled. "Where's Ma? Has anyone gone for Ma?"

"A fall like that will put her into labor for sure," said Anson Guthrie's somber wife, Winifred, with her usual doom-and-gloom conviction.

"I need a place to lay her down," Jeremy said, walking toward Netta.

"Upstairs. Put her in my bed upstairs." She moved swiftly toward the door that opened into a steep set of steps leading to the loft bedroom above.

"Ohmylands, why did this have to happen today?" said Netta, turning to Lucy, who followed close on Jeremy's heels. "Where is Ma? Did anybody go to fetch Ma?"

Lucy turned to Netta before following Jeremy up the stairs. "You better keep things goin' down here, Netta. And make sure Ma comes up the minute somebody finds her." She handed baby Hank to Netta. "Would you keep an eye on him for me, please? Don't let anyone else up here, just Ma." She closed the stairway door behind her, and her long legs took the steps two at a time.

"All right, all right, people," said Netta, attempting to gain the milling group's attention. "Let's keep them kickers workin' up more suds over there. We've got a lot more cloth to put down after this batch gets all kicked and rinsed. And we sure can't put out dinner till all that cloth gets kicked up." She shifted the chubby Hank onto her other hip and attempted to keep Rosanna from tangling her skirts. "And forheavensakes, don't nobody else fall down!"

In the flurry of activity that followed, no one noticed the lanky, black-garbed Ephriam Alonzo Simpson—who bore a striking resemblance to the circuit preacher, Reverend Harold P. Longbottom—take his two, high-spirited sons firmly by the ears and pull them outside the cabin.

* * * * *

**Hearthstones II: *Let the Sparks Fly!*
Due out in 2011.**

About the Authors

Sheryl Drake Lawrence   MaryLee Marilee

MaryLee Marilee, published humor columnist (15 years in The Holmes County Bargain Hunter), former editor & feature writer (Graphic Publications), motivational speaker, and most recently bed and breakfast owner, currently devotes her time to writing while traveling the country between visits to children and grandchildren.

Sheryl Lawrence, office finance-coordinator, former English teacher, and short-story author, has published stories in "Girls To The Rescue" series, printed by Meadowbrook Press. Sheryl lives with her husband of 25 years, stays current with their children and grandchildren, and keeps multiple offices organized and humming.

"We met in a creative-writing class nearly 30 years ago and haven't stopped talking since! We encourage and motivate one another at a time in history just as challenging, in its own way, as that of our frontier sisters."

www.Hearthstones.net

MaryLee@hearthstones.net   Sheryl@hearthstones.net

www.ingramcontent.com/pod-product-compliance
Lightning Source LLC
Chambersburg PA
CBHW070210260626
47160CB00002B/505